Jo Beverley's Romances Are

"FANTASTICALLY ENTERTAINING."
—Night Owl Reviews

"QUIETLY POWERFUL."—*Booklist*

"DELIGHTFUL, DEFTLY PLOTTED,
[AND]…CHARMING."
—*Publishers Weekly*

**Raves for the Novels
of Jo Beverley**

"Ms. Beverley's opulent descriptions of the glittering ton with their witty dialogues and lively dalliances set against a dark background of intrigue continue to elevate this series beyond the normal historical romance."

—Smexy Books

"A fabulous, intelligent tale."

—Genre Go Round Reviews

"Extraordinary storyteller Beverley mixes witty repartee, danger, and simmering sensuality with her strong and engaging characters, including a fetching Papillon, in this delightful, delicious gem of a book."

—*Romantic Times* (top pick)

"With wit and humor, Jo Beverley provides a wonderful eighteenth-century romance starring two amiable lead characters whose first encounter is one of the best in recent memory. The tale is filled with nonstop action."

—The Best Reviews

"[E]nchanting . . . a delightful blend of wit, intrigue, and emotional victories."   —*The State* (Columbia, SC)

"[Readers] will be engrossed by this emotionally packed story of great love, tremendous courage, and the return of those attractive and dangerous men known as the Rogues."   —Joan Hammond

"[Beverley] can be counted on to come up with clever and creative ways of mixing passion and intrigue to create a beguiling love story."   —*Booklist*

continued . . .

REGENCY
THE ROGUE'S WORLD
Lady Beware
To Rescue a Rogue
The Rogue's Return
Skylark
St. Raven
Hazard
"The Demon's Mistress" in *In Praise of Younger Men*
The Devil's Heiress
The Dragon's Bride
Three Heroes (Omnibus Edition)

THE MALLOREN WORLD
Seduction in Silk
An Unlikely Countess
The Secret Duke
The Secret Wedding
A Lady's Secret
A Most Unsuitable Man
Winter Fire
Devilish
Secrets of the Night
Something Wicked
My Lady Notorious

MEDIEVAL ROMANCES
Lord of Midnight
Dark Champion
Lord of My Heart

OTHER
Forbidden Magic
Lovers and Ladies (Omnibus Edition)
Lord Wraybourne's Betrothed
The Stanforth Secrets
The Stolen Bride
Emily and the Dark Angel

ANTHOLOGIES
"The Raven and the Rose" in
Chalice of Roses
"The Dragon and the Virgin Princess" in *Dragon Lovers*
"The Trouble with Heroes" in
Irresistible Forces

A Shocking Delight

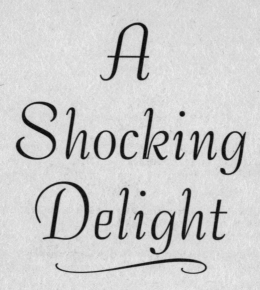

Jo Beverley

A SIGNET SELECT BOOK

SIGNET SELECT
Published by the Penguin Group
Penguin Group (USA) LLC, 375 Hudson Street,
New York, New York 10014

USA | Canada | UK | Ireland | Australia | New Zealand | India | South Africa | China
penguin.com
A Penguin Random House Company

First published by Signet Select, an imprint of New American Library,
a division of Penguin Group (USA) LLC

First Printing, April 2014

ISBN 978-0-451-46801-7

Printed in the United States of America
10 9 8 7 6 5 4 3 2 1

A
Shocking
Delight

Chapter 1

London
May 13, 1817

Lucy Potter sat in the library of her home hoping that this was the day when everything would change. Or rather, that on this day, her life would return to the way it used to be—without her beloved mother, alas, but with her father once more a part of her life.

One year ago Alice Potter, only forty years old, had died from influenza. Lucy's father had covered her mother's portrait here in the library with black crepe. Six months ago, he'd drawn the cloth back so it only framed the painting in black. Surely today he would remove the dark shroud entirely, and Lucy hoped that would signal another change.

That he would cease avoiding her.

She knew why he did it. When she looked in a mirror, she saw a face almost identical to the pretty one in the portrait hanging above the fireplace. Blond hair, full lips, and big blue eyes, though Lucy's own no longer showed such unbridled expectation of joy and delights.

The Honorable Alice Stanley had been eighteen when the portrait was done, and newly launched into the beau monde. Lucy was now twenty-one, but she looked as young as her mother had been in the portrait, making her appearance a challenge, even before the resemblance had caused her to be cut off from her father.

Her mother had never expressed annoyance at having the sort of looks that made people think her empty-headed, but Lucy would have welcomed having her father's blunter features. When she went out with him about the City of London—when she had used to do so—even sober gowns and a cap beneath a plain bonnet hadn't overcome her pretty face.

She was far from empty-headed, however, and fascinated by business, so she had persisted. In time her father had been able to let her conduct some small pieces of business herself, choosing cargos at auction and finding good markets for them and also identifying unmet needs and seeking sources of goods, sometimes from distant lands.

She'd loved it, and planned her life around it. But her involvement in the exciting City world had died with her mother.

Her father had soon returned to his businesses, working all hours as he tried to drown his grief, but he'd never again invited her to go with him or discussed business with her. He'd spoken to her only out of necessity, and if he dined at home, it was always with guests present.

Now Lucy tried to concentrate on the latest issue of *The Gentlemen's Magazine*, but she was listening for his footstep. Surely he must come.

She'd marked the day by putting aside the grays and violets of half mourning, with no regret. She didn't like to think she was vain, but such colors didn't suit her. She'd chosen a favorite gown that was more than two years old. The cerulean blue was bright, but the cut was simple. Not too shocking a transition, she hoped. She might have worn a pale gown, but her mother was dressed in white in the portrait, so that wouldn't do.

The library clock struck two.

She had a pale sprigged gown ready to wear tonight, when she would mark the end of her official mourning by attending an assembly ball at the Crown with friends. She intended to dance every dance. She had hoped her father would escort her there, but he still hadn't come.

Lucy looked at the portrait, wondering whether it would be a sin to pray to it, as some did to saints. Surely her mother must be a saint. Surely she must want her husband and only child to regain happiness. She had risked all to achieve her own.

Alice Stanley, second daughter of Viscount Blount, had been presented at court and was about to take her place in society and find a good husband. With beauty, fine birth, and a dowry of nine thousand pounds, her path must have seemed smooth.

Instead, she'd set eyes on lowborn Daniel Potter in an inn yard—at that moment in his shirtsleeves and loading boxes into a cart—and instantly lost her sanity. Within days they had been meeting in secret and within weeks they'd been off to Gretna Green.

Lord Blount could well have cast his daughter off and even destroyed the portrait, but he'd given it to her along with her dowry. He had not, however, seen or communicated with her again. That had been a sadness, but it hadn't overwhelmed Lucy's mother's happiness here on Nailer Street in the City of London.

Until last year.

Lucy pulled a handkerchief out of her pocket to blow her nose. If her father came, he mustn't find her weeping! But she'd often thought she'd been orphaned on that cruel day. What was she to do if this was the new pattern of her life? What if things *didn't* change today?

When the door opened she looked up, afraid to hope.

It was him!

She straightened, smiling but trying not to let her flaring hope show.

"Good day, Papa."

"Good day, pet." He walked forward, looking surprisingly at ease. He glanced once at the portrait, his expression somber but not agonized, then back at her. "I've had an enquiry for your hand."

The words were so unexpected that they made no sense. But he was here, coming to sit in his big leather chair that faced hers across the fireplace, looking—yes, truly—as if the darkness had passed.

He wasn't a big man, for he'd been raised in a foundling home where skimpy food didn't build height and bulk, but these days dressed in the finest clothes, and his wiry frame was elegant. Beneath the elegance he was physically strong, but, more important, he had strength of mind, cleverness, and wisdom. He'd built his vast fortune from nothing and she admired him above anyone in the world.

She pulled her wits together enough to say, "A marriage proposal, Papa? And made through you? From whom?"

"An unknown party represented by a lawyer called Polyphant."

She chuckled. "How ridiculous."

Wonder of wonders, he shared her smile. "Isn't it, pet? But intriguing. Polyphant represents a titled gentleman."

"That's even more ridiculous!"

"Some fool of a lordling," he agreed, "broke through folly and seeking a rich dowry. All the same, there are many men of business who'd pay to see a daughter married into the nobility, to have noble grandchildren."

"Not you, Papa."

"You don't think it'd be a feather in a foundling's cap to have a grandson inherit a title?"

His eyes twinkled with the joke.

How long was it since she'd seen that twinkle?

"You'll have to make do with nephews," she teased

back. "The Honorable Jeremy Fytch, who will one day be Lord Caldross, or Percival Stanley, due to be Viscount Blount."

He didn't seem amused. "Plenty of City daughters would be happy to exchange a handsome dowry for a coronet, pet."

"I suppose that's true."

"You have a very handsome dowry."

"Too handsome! You'd no need to increase it."

"No reason not to with business prospering as it did during the war, and you helping me from time to time."

"Then I thank you again, especially as the thirty thousand is mine now that I'm twenty-one."

"I was probably rash to make it so, but you've always been a sensible girl."

Still, he seemed uneasy, and she didn't know why. Did his grief in some way play a part?

"Tell me more about this odd proposal, Papa."

"There's nothing more to it. The solicitor assures me that Lord Penniless is of good character and health and will treat you with loving consideration."

"I'm sure I should be moved to tears of gratitude. But instead I wonder: How could a stranger even know the size of my dowry?"

"He could assume that my only child would be generously dowered, but there are lists for sale."

"Lists! Like auction catalogues? How shabby. But how do the list makers know?"

"It needs only one person to spread the word."

"Leland spread the word?" she asked, unable to believe their solicitor would do such a thing. Daniel Potter could hide his thoughts and feelings from most people, but not from her. "Papa! Surely you didn't?"

His raised chin was acknowledgment. "No reason to keep it secret, pet. I'd like to see you in your rightful sphere."

"My *rightful sphere*?"

"The nobility. Your mother wanted to see you in her world. She'd have wanted you to take up your aunt Caldross's invitation to enjoy a Mayfair season now that your mourning's over."

Lucy wanted to protest that—forcefully. Her mother had never said anything to indicate that she wanted her daughter in the nobility, and though she'd kept in contact with her sister, they'd never been close.

But the loss of his wife had put some odd ideas in her father's head. He'd blamed himself, as if influenza couldn't have afflicted his wife if she'd married as she ought to have. He'd fretted that he could have done more to make her life perfect in all ways. That wasn't true. He'd always done everything possible to compensate for all she'd given up for him.

The wood burning in the hearth here was testament to his efforts. Most people in London used coal, but her mother had loved the wood fires of her childhood home in Gloucestershire, so when Lucy's father had renovated and expanded this London house he'd had suitable fireplaces installed. Throughout the colder months cartloads of prime wood arrived from the country and were stocked in a shed at the end of the garden.

"*This* was her world, Papa," Lucy said gently, "and this is my rightful sphere. This house, this street, the City. I'm perfectly content with my life."

"Sitting alone, reading a dry magazine?"

"I was out all day yesterday with friends and this evening we go to the assembly at the Crown. This issue of *The Gentlemen's Magazine* is juicy with information."

He gestured that away. "It's time you were wed, pet. Your mother wouldn't have wanted you to end up an ape-leader, but you're well on your way. You've had plenty of suitors but dismissed all of them."

Lucy felt under attack, an attack she'd never expected.

It had to be another aspect of grief, but how to deal with it?

She kept her manner light and used an argument he would have to respect. "Remember, Papa, that Mama wanted me to love as she loved. I've not yet met a man who appeals to me in that particular way."

"Which worries me. By now you should have fallen into a dozen foolish adorations."

"You're disappointed that I've not run silly over delivery boys and carters?"

He didn't laugh. "It'd only be natural. Look at your friend Betty acting the idiot over that groom at Blackley's."

"That was years ago. She was fifteen!"

"But at fifteen, you did nothing like that."

"And you reproach me for it?"

"Not reproach." He was looking harried, but that was how she felt. "I'd have made sure you didn't do anything foolish. But I've taken up too much of your time with my affairs. I blame myself."

"I love being involved with your affairs."

"And that's not natural. I want your happiness."

"I *am* happy," she protested, beginning to feel frightened. "I have my friends, my interests, and my reading. There's a most interesting piece here about merchant stations in Jakarta. Let's talk of that."

Of business and opportunities, and exotic products from distant lands.

"Not now, pet. I have something else to tell you."

Some other blow hovered. What could it be?

"I'm going to marry again."

The words hung there, unbelievable. *"What?"* Lucy managed at last.

"Don't be like that, pet. It's a year since your mother died."

"But *why*?"

He rolled his eyes. "I'm forty-five years old, Lucy. Am I to be celibate all my life? Now there, see. I shouldn't have said that to you. I've been used to thinking of you as a man."

Lucy was blushing, but she thought like a man. She wanted to ask why whores wouldn't do.

"But you aren't a man," he said. "I need a son."

It was as if something dropped out of Lucy, leaving her painfully hollow and mute.

"It was always a sadness to your mother and me that we didn't have more children, but it was God's will and our many joys compensated, but now . . ."

"Are you saying you're glad mother's dead?"

"Damnation, Lucy!"

She covered her face with her hand. "I'm sorry, I'm sorry. I know that's not true. But I never thought you'd find anyone to replace her."

"And I never will. Charlotte knows that."

"Charlotte?"

"Charlotte Johnson. She's accepted my offer."

I'm sure she has, Lucy thought bitterly. It would be a grand match for the widow of a doctor. But her father had made a typically suitable choice. The only time he'd acted irrationally in his life had been when he'd eloped with a viscount's daughter.

Mrs. Johnson was a neighbor, a sensible woman of about thirty. More important she was mother to two healthy young children. Girls, but there was every chance of boys in time.

Charlotte Johnson wasn't a substitute for her mother, but Charlotte's firstborn son would be a substitute for herself. Lucy had always assumed that she was her father's heir and would gradually take on more and more tasks in the business, but perhaps her father had never seen it that way. Or if he had, all was now different with the possibility of more children. Charlotte Johnson's son would steal her place.

"I'm sorry you don't like it, pet, but Charlotte will be a kind mother to you."

A new mother?

Ruling in her true mother's place?

Lucy instinctively hid the extent of her shock and pain. But inside, her thoughts were seething. She'd find a way around this. She'd make everything right again. Somehow. For now, she must say nothing she'd regret, burn no bridges.

"It was just such a surprise, Papa. As you say, you deserve a wife, and Mrs. Johnson will be a good one. I wish you well."

He smiled his relief. "That's my girl. And you'll enjoy having little sisters and a woman to advise you. Charlotte might be able to help you on the way to marriage yourself."

Lucy smiled, but wondered if it could look natural. She felt ready to explode.

Her father didn't seem to see anything amiss. *That's my girl,* he'd said. His *girl*, and thus eternally excluded from his world? Women did run businesses. Daughters did inherit them. Rarely, but it happened.

Was it her appearance? Prettiness didn't mean a feeble mind. He above all men should know that.

He rose and came to kiss the top of her head. "You are my precious daughter, Lucy, and I love you dearly. You know that, don't you? It's my dearest wish to see you happy."

She melted a little. "I know."

"And restored to your rightful sphere."

It was an effort to keep calm until he'd left the room. Even then she didn't move.

Rightful sphere.

In his eyes she didn't even belong here, in her home, in her world.

In a quarter hour she'd been turned upside down and shaken hollow and she didn't know how to fill the void.

She leapt to her feet, staring at her mother's portrait as if it could help her, but it was only in fantastical novels that the dead returned to help or torment the living. She turned away, tears blurring her vision. She couldn't be exiled from all she loved!

Her life-long friend Betty Hanway lived across the road. She hurried over without even a bonnet.

"Your father and Mrs. Johnson?" Betty said, once they were alone in Betty's bedroom. "A stepmother?"

Lucy seized on that excuse. "Unbearable, isn't it?"

"Completely!" Betty declared, hugging her.

Betty was slim and brown haired, with fine brown eyes and plenty of common sense. "Mrs. Johnson is a pleasant woman," she said, "but she'll be mistress of the house."

"I know. It's horrible. I can't remain there." As soon as Lucy said it, she knew it was true.

"How can you not? Lucy, don't do anything rash."

"Rash?"

"Such as grabbing any suitor who's to hand."

Lucy laughed. "That's the last thing I'd do! But I must find somewhere else to live. For a while at least. As I grow accustomed. As I think . . ."

Of a way to overcome this. There has to be a way.

"You can't leave your home now," Betty protested. "It might look as if you object, as if you can't bear the future Mrs. Potter."

"I *can't* bear *any* future Mrs. Potter."

"Your father's a young man. He was bound to marry again."

Lucy let out a breath. "Why was I so blind to that? I

thought their great love . . . I'm losing faith in my rational abilities. Another reason I need time to adjust myself,
which I can't do at home."

Betty drew her to sit on the sofa. "Let's try to find a
way. What about relatives? Are there any you could reasonably visit for a week or two?"

"With my father a foundling and my mother a scandal
to her family?" Lucy scoffed, but then she paused. "My
mother's sister, Lady Caldross, invited me to join her for
the season once my mourning was over. Cousin Clara is
making her curtsy. I declined, but . . ."

"Move to *Mayfair*?"

"It's not darkest Africa! And it would seem reasonable to take up such an opportunity. What's more, I could
escape to there within days. The fashionable frolic is already underway."

"But you'd know no one."

"I know my aunt and cousin."

"Oh, yes. You have sometimes visited."

"Once Aunt Mary married, she could invite mother to
visit, and when I was older, I went with her. The visits were
rare, however. My aunt and her family are in London only
in the spring and she and my mother were never close."

"Haven't you said that your aunt is dull and disapproving?"

"True."

"What of your cousin?"

"Clara's three years younger than I, but as best I remember, she doesn't have two sensible thoughts to rub
together."

"Lucy, you'd hate such company."

"Betty, I have no choice!"

"That's what Isabella said in *The Curse of Montene-
gro* before she ran off to an Italian nunnery."

"This is *not* a novel! I don't know how anyone as sensible as you can bear the things."

"Sometimes it's fun not to be sensible, but I was teasing, dearest. I do fear you'll be jumping out of the boiling pot into the fire. You know how the so-called beau monde refer to people like us—as Cits."

"I'm only half a Cit."

"You're fully the product of a great scandal, which your appearance there will revive."

Lucy had overlooked that. "Why do you always see things so clearly?"

"You normally do."

"Normally, my life isn't turned upside down in a moment. Given the scandal, it's a wonder Aunt Mary has invited me at all. She probably sees me as a duty and a sacrifice."

"Then you can't go."

Lucy rose to pace the room. "I have to get away for a while, I have to, and a few weeks with Aunt Mary is the only acceptable means I can imagine. Everyone will understand my seizing such an opportunity. I can even pretend to most that it's been planned for some time."

"But you'll be miserable. All your friends are here, and there's your involvement in your father's businesses."

Lucy had never told Betty that he'd cut himself off from her. She was surprised her friend hadn't guessed, but Betty had probably thought Lucy busy with her father when she'd been in the library reading books, magazines, and newspapers to keep informed.

"He'll have to manage without me for a month. The more I think on this plan, the more it appeals. Perhaps I have been too sensible. Observing 'the great' at ridiculous play should amuse."

"Just don't laugh aloud."

"My manners will be perfect. And I might enjoy some parts of it. I've been to many assemblies and private dance parties, but never to a ball in a grand house. There'll be Venetian breakfasts and musical evenings featuring the finest performers, not to mention rubbing shoulders with dukes and dandies."

Betty didn't look convinced. "Might it not be better to marry? Arthur Stamford is probably still interested."

Lucy shuddered. Arthur Stamford had offered for her only two weeks ago. She'd rejected him, just as she'd rejected a string of other suitors. Men in the City of London didn't need a published list to tell them which was the largest golden apple on the tree.

"If you don't care for Arthur, there are others. Charlie Carson has never given up hope and Peter Frome . . ."

"I'm not going to marry!" Lucy snapped, then quickly added, "Not until I fall in love. You're in love, Betty. You'd deny me the same?"

Betty smiled in the way she always did at any reference to her beloved James Greenlow and their upcoming wedding, but she didn't lose the thread.

"I long for you to fall in love, Lucy, but what if you fall in love with a lord? An arrogant, wastrel gambler who gets staggering drunk every night of the week?"

That made Lucy laugh. "Can you imagine my doing anything so idiotic?"

"No, but you'll be going to a world as different as Africa. Who can tell?"

Lucy sat to hug her friend. "When you become idiotic, I know you're upset. There's no need, I promise."

"But you'll be so far away."

Ah, now Lucy understood, and it was another blow she hadn't thought of. How dense she was being.

"It's only three miles."

"We've lived on the same street all our lives, and if you marry a lord, even a decent one . . ."

"What?" Lucy prompted, bewildered by the pause.

"Who knows where you'll end up? Your mother's family comes from Gloucestershire. You could end up anywhere. In Scotland, even! I couldn't bear that."

Lucy raised her right hand. "I hereby make a solemn vow that I will not marry a Scottish lord. And speaking of marriage, have you any news of when you can expect your father?"

That distracted Betty. All was settled for her friend's wedding except the date, which must wait until her father returned from a business journey to Philadelphia. Never had a father's return been so fiercely longed for.

Lucy listened to new details of the changes being made to some rooms in the Greenlow house, where James and Betty would live at first, and perhaps forever. James was the oldest son and would take over the family's building business in time. Even now, at only twenty-three, he was running everything in his father's absence.

The situation Lucy had hoped to be in one day.

Betty's excited chatter over her wedding made Lucy think of how the preparations for her father's would go. It was a marriage of older people, but there'd be the same talk of clothes, the wedding breakfast, and—she suddenly realized—changes to her home.

Her home!

She found a way to take her leave and hurried back across the road as if she could protect the house against attack, already searching for signs of change.

She paused outside, letting out a breath. It was still the same—large, handsome, and elegant. Her parents had started married life on this street in rooms over a small warehouse. Later they'd turned the building into a house; then ten years ago her father had bought an adjacent home and joined them to create the largest house on the street.

Many of the richer City men were moving out to live in more rural surroundings, "aping the gentry" as her father put it. He preferred to be in the middle of things. In particular he had wanted to be close to his family, not traveling into the City in the morning and returning home late in the day.

Lucy was of one mind with him on that. The City of

London was vibrant with life, the hub of the economic empire, with excitement on every corner. Who needed vistas and trees?

Who needed an intruder, a usurper? But here she came, walking down the street with her younger daughter in her arms and the older one alongside.

Mrs. Johnson was a sturdy, dark-haired woman with a rather homely face improved by a warm smile. Lucy had never paid much attention to her, but she would have described her as pleasant.

The smile was in place now. "Good morning, Miss Potter."

Lucy had no choice. She smiled and dipped a curtsy. "Good morning, Mrs. Johnson. Father told me the news. I'm delighted, of course." *But if you're on your way now to invade my home and begin repainting walls, there'll be bloody war.*

"So kind of you. I know this will be difficult for you, to see me in your mother's place, but I hope we will be friends."

Pleasant and sensible. Too sensible to suggest that she'd be a new mother.

Mrs. Johnson looked down at her older daughter. "Jane, make a curtsy to Miss Potter. She will soon be your big sister."

The little girl, who strongly resembled her mother, looked as if she shared all of Lucy's misgivings, but she made a creditable curtsy. Lucy returned the honor, which made the little girl smile, but then she tucked herself into her mother's skirts.

Lucy would not feel a kindred spirit with the mite.

"I must hurry home," she said. "I just went to share the good news with my friend."

"Miss Hanway. I understand she is to marry as soon as Mr. Hanway is safe home. Our weddings could take place in close succession."

"An abundance of joy," Lucy said brightly and went into her house, praying to all the powers that Charlotte Johnson not follow her in.

She didn't, but Lucy wondered if Mrs. Johnson had been on her way here but had been perceptive enough to see that it would be a bad time. Unreasonable to find the woman's virtues intolerable, but she didn't feel reasonable about any of this.

She had her escape, however, and it would give her time to think, time to find a way. After all, even if her father had a son, it would be decades before the lad could play a meaningful part in the business, so perhaps he'd come to see that he still needed her.

Would that be enough?

It would be a start, and she did have her thirty thousand pounds. She could begin her own business with that, carve her own place in the City. She certainly had no intention of handing it over to a wastrel lord.

The first step was to compose herself and find a way to tell her father of the plan to visit her aunt without revealing the reason for it.

She went to him in his office, attempting as lighthearted a manner as possible.

"Lord Penniless has made me think I should take up Aunt Mary's offer. It will be interesting to see the nobility at play, and I suppose it's possible that I might lose my heart to a lord."

She feared he understood all too well, but he approved. "An excellent idea, pet. You've always enjoyed parties and dancing, and a wider knowledge of the world never comes amiss."

"Just for a few weeks, of course," Lucy said. "I'll be back for your wedding."

"And with interesting stories to tell. Perhaps you'll identify Lord Penniless and find he's more worthy than he seems."

Lucy returned to her room fighting tears again. Her father had clearly been relieved. He probably hoped she'd marry Lord Penniless and never return home at all.

She almost hoped she did identify that idiot, for then at least she'd have someone upon whom to vent her frustrations.

Chapter 2

The south Devon coast
May 13, 1817

David Kerslake-Somerford, the reluctant seventh
Earl of Wyvern, was relaxing over ale with a friend.
They were in the earldom's seat, Crag Wyvern, in the
room he chose, tongue in cheek, to call his lair.

He'd been born and raised in nearby Kerslake Manor
as foster son of his aunt and uncle, and when he'd
claimed the earldom, and thus been obliged to take up
residence in this mock-medieval monstrosity, he'd done
his best to create something as normal here. He'd had
the earl's bedchamber and adjoining parlor stripped and
scoured—necessary, when his predecessor had been known
as the Mad Earl—then remade.

The walls of the parlor were now paneled and painted,
the ceiling plastered, the floor carpeted. He'd econo-
mized by buying most things secondhand, but he'd indulged in one way—he'd had a window knocked into the
outer walls here and in his bedroom.

Crag Wyvern had been built two hundred years ago
to look like a stark medieval keep, and had only arrow
slits in the outer walls. The rooms did have windows, but
they all looked inward to a courtyard, not out to open
vistas. Now his private rooms had windows that looked

out to sea, which was pleasant but also practical. He needed to see what went on out there, because in addition to being the earl, he was also deeply involved in the Freetrade. In smuggling.

He was a strapping young man with broad shoulders and long legs, but a lifetime on the hills and cliffs of this coast had made him lean. His jaw was square, his careless hair a blond that was close to brown, and his eyes a changeable gray-blue.

His friend was also fair haired, rather more so, and of lighter build, but he, too, looked as if he could climb cliffs if he needed to. His name was Nicholas Delaney, and he rode over frequently from his Somerset estate to help and advise.

Until last year, David had been employed as the Earl of Wyvern's estate manager, which was as good a position as could be hoped for when he was known to be the bastard son of Miss Isabelle Kerslake and a tavern keeper. He and his sister, Susan, could have been raised in a tavern if his mother hadn't abandoned her children to her brother and sister-in-law. Coming from Kerslake Manor had given Susan and him a tenuous place in the gentry.

He'd been happy enough with his job, but then his life had been turned upside down.

Proof had been discovered that his mother had been married to the Earl of Wyvern when she'd borne her children. Despite the fact that she'd already fled the marriage and was living with another man, that made her children legitimately her husband's, and David the legal heir.

David hadn't leapt at the chance. He had many reasons not to want to be earl.

A major one was that he wasn't the son of the previous earl, no matter what the legal situation. In addition, he much preferred a simpler station and home like the manor. And what sane man would want the responsibility of a bankrupt and neglected estate?

But above all, it would tangle badly with his position as Captain Drake, leader of the local smuggling gang, the Dragon's Horde, which he'd inherited from his true father, Melchisadeck Clyst.

Eighteen months ago Mel Clyst had been caught and transported to the Australian penal colony Botany Bay. John Clyst, a nephew and his designated heir, had been killed in the same disaster. David had been the only person the remains of the Horde would accept as the new Captain Drake. Juggling his legal and illegal responsibilities was likely to turn him into another Mad Earl of Wyvern and he'd always known it.

In the end, however, he'd agreed to assert his claim for the sake of others.

The man everyone had believed to be heir to the earldom, Lord Amleigh, had a fine home of his own and wanted no part of the title or Crag Wyvern. That might not have swayed David if his sister, Susan, hadn't been in love with Amleigh and wanted what she wanted. In addition, if David accepted that he was the earl's legitimate son, it would follow that his elder sister was also legitimate, and Susan had wanted to begin her married life free of the stain of bastardy.

So he'd taken on the burden and was doing the best he could.

Including by marrying money.

"So you've settled on Miss Potter?" Nicholas said.

"Largest dowry," David said, "plus her being an only child. She could inherit the lot, and though they live quite simply, her father's notoriously rich."

"With very lowly origins."

"I took that into account. A man like that will be giddy with triumph at his daughter being a countess, so he won't blink at my oddities. I've instructed my solicitor to write to Potter on the matter."

Nicholas paused in the act of drinking. "Isn't that a trifle old-fashioned?"

"You think I should go up to London to woo her? I prefer an honest, businesslike approach, and I can't leave the Horde unshackled for weeks."

"You need to find a replacement for Captain Drake."

"Applying?"

Nicholas raised a hand. "I thank God I live too far away. But is it so difficult?"

"A few generations ago it required only toughness, brains, and organizational ability. . . ."

"Only? Would that our ministers had such qualities."

David ignored that. "Mel's father turned it into an orderly business, and Mel improved on that with records, ledgers, and complex accounting. Worked so well he absorbed some nearby groups, but now the leadership demands are more complicated. The new Captain Drake will have to be able to cope with the paperwork, plan and supervise runs, and rule the Horde, by force if necessary."

"You've managed."

"I spent as much time as I could get away with hanging around Mel and the Horde, and taking part in runs. He'd growl and tell me I must become a gentleman, but he never tried to stop me, and he shared some of the Horde's ways with me. But my main authority comes from being his son."

"Inheritance, just as with the earldom. But you do have a natural ability to command."

David shrugged. "I'm big and strong."

After the briefest knock, the door opened. "Trouble, cap'n," said Maisie, one of the maids.

The "cap'n" revealed all. The trouble must concern not the earl but Captain Drake.

"Lloyd?" David asked, rising.

Lieutenant Lloyd was the new riding officer in these

parts, a battle-hardened, ambitious Welshman who was determined to advance his career by crushing the Free-trade in his territory. He wanted to put an end to Captain Drake and his organization, once and for all.

"No, cap'n." Maisie looked uneasily at Nicholas.

"Don't worry about him."

"It's some of the men, zur. They're off to Bradhole Cove to get the goods, zur, the moon being overcast and a sea mist coming up. Aaron's in the side room."

"Damn and blast them!" David flung open the curtains and saw, indeed, a dense mist that didn't even show the cliff's edge.

"Goods?" Nicholas asked.

"A short while ago we landed a rich load, but a naval ship interrupted, so we stashed the contraband in a cave in an inaccessible cove. I've been waiting for a safe time to move it."

"And they've run out of patience."

"Which could land them in jail or worse." He headed for the door, but paused. "Are you coming?"

"Wouldn't miss the excitement for the world," Nicholas said, rising with easy grace.

"Pray God there's no excitement to it."

They entered one of the narrow corridors that ran between the Crag's rooms and its outer walls, except where the two new windows had been cut through.

"They know how chancy a sea mist is," David muttered. "It might hide them now, but it could shred away in a moment. Damn the fools."

David ran down one of the circular staircases that sat in each corner of the Crag. On the ground floor he walked swiftly to a small room that could be entered directly from the outside. The door was never locked. It would be a foolhardy thief indeed who tried to steal from Crag Wyvern.

Aaron Bartlett stood there, a man in his forties, stocky

and disgruntled. "Overwhelmed me, cap'n. I was order-
ing them to have sense, but they were all fired up. And
drunk."

"Who fired them up?"

"Saul."

"No surprise there. What exactly are they planning?"

"They're already off, zur. In the boats, to get the goods
and bring 'em into the village to stash. All the easier to
move 'em on, see. And get their share."

"Greed."

"Well, zur, some's need. Times is hard, and having a
rich cargo stuck in a cave for nigh on a fortnight . . ."

"No one's in that much need." David glanced at Nicholas. "I'm going to ride along the cliffs to Bradhole to
oversee and keep them safe. I'd like you to stay here, in
case."

"Not trying to protect me from danger, are you?"

"No." It was flat and absolute.

"Then aye, aye, sir."

Maisie came running in. "Zur! Lieutenant Lloyd and
his men are here, zur. Asking for you! What should I
say?"

David let out a string of oaths. "They must have been
keeping watch. They'll have set up a trap." He thought
quickly. "Get a few of the remaining men," he said to
Aaron. "Ones that can run. We'll need crab pots and climbing ropes. Come on," he said to Nicholas and strode out.

With an amused smile, Nicholas followed.

David led the way back up the circular staircase, then
along a corridor to where the only normal stairs in the
place ran down to the cavernous great hall. The stone
walls of the hall were hung with weaponry, the furniture
was all of uncomfortable dark oak, and the room was
perpetually cold. The Crag never had welcomed visitors.
The lieutenant and his men certainly looked uncomfortable as they stood there waiting for him.

As he descended the stairs, David said, "A strange time to call, Lloyd."

The long-faced Welshman scowled. David guessed he was disappointed to find him at home. "My apologies, my lord. I thought I should inform you that some people from Dragon's Cove are up to no good."

"Thieving or wenching?"

Lloyd's lip curled. "Smuggling, sir."

"With the moon half-full?"

"And the clouds heavy, not to mention the mist."

"I'm surprised you risked riding here in such weather."

"It's clear a bit inland, my lord, and we were careful."

"Glad to hear it. However, I was about to retire. What do you want?" It wasn't in his nature to be discourteous, but here he must play the arrogant earl.

"Only to inform you, my lord, as a courtesy. If the men from Dragon's Cove return with laden boats, we'll arrest them."

"As is your duty."

"Precisely, my lord."

After a moment, David said, "Be about it, then," as if he couldn't imagine why the Preventive officer was lingering.

Lloyd's lips tightened, but he bowed and stalked out, his men trailing.

"Don't you feel some compassion for him?" Nicholas asked.

"No. He has a job to do, but he would dearly like to see us all hang, especially Captain Drake. He suspects that's me, but isn't sure. If he catches me red-handed, my being the earl would not deter him."

"Nor should it."

"Turning republican? There has to be some advantage to my having the title. But we'll debate that later. For now, I'm off. If I do end up in jail, I hope your ingenuity can get me out."

"So do I."

David went to his bedroom and took out the dark shirt and pantaloons he wore over his clothes for these ventures. They were made of cotton and dyed in a mottled way that would help him hide in shadows, but of thin cloth so he could bundle them small and hide them. He rubbed soot from the chimney over his face, then pulled on dark leather gloves and a dark cap over his hair.

He didn't take a pistol. If it came to that the game was up, and he wanted no deaths. He did carry a sharp knife in a sheath. You never knew when that might be needed.

He left the Crag by the small room, meeting the four fleet-footed men Aaron had chosen. Each carried a load of wicker-and-rope crab pots, with a long climbing rope coiled around them. David didn't take any, for he needed to make the most speed. Most of the men could escape up the cliffs by rope, but the boats needed explanation. Putting down crab pots would provide that.

They set off to run the three miles through the misty dark along cliff tops to Bradhole Cove, which was inaccessible without climbing aids since a landslip had wiped out the path leading down to the water. That and a cave had made it a good place to hide the brandy, tea, and gin brought in from France at the dark time of the moon. The cove would become a trap, however, if the wind blew the mist away and a prowling navy vessel spotted them.

But for now, the quiet and the mist told David the sea was calm. Sails would be useless, but it would be easy rowing for the Dragon's Horde men. They could be there already.

He had to arrive before disaster happened.

Even shrouded in mist, the sea and coastline held no mysteries for the men of Dragon's Cove; they were all fishermen in their honest hours. The smugglers had quickly reached the small cove, with its sandy beach and its cave, which was set high enough to stay dry in all but the worst high-tide storms.

Their plan was to slip in, slip out, and carry the contraband back to Dragon's Cove, where it would disappear into secret basement and attic sections and holes in the ground. As soon as Lloyd was busy elsewhere, they'd move it inland to make a fine profit for the Horde.

Of course, Captain Drake had forbidden them to act without his word, but he was young, the new captain, and too cautious. Came of being raised as gentry by his mother's family.

They dragged the boats up the sand and then left one man with each vessel. The rest of the gang scurried like ants up the rocky slope to the gaping cave, then slipped and slid back down with loads on their backs.

Before too long, the lookout yipped a warning. All the men looked around. Some swore. A light breeze had sprung up and was tearing holes in the misty veil. The moon was still covered by cloud, but some light escaped to touch silver ripples on the black water.

And out in the channel the keen-eyed ones could see a damned navy ship.

"They can't see us," growled Saul Applin. "Carry on."

"Perhaps we should take off with what we've got," Bill Carter said nervously. "We can come back."

"One more load each and we're done. Get moving!"

They moved. Saul Applin was a big man with big fists, so no one complained, but some were beginning to regret agreeing to this. Captain Drake had said to wait, that the right time would come. His second-in-command, Aaron Bartlett, had tried to stop them. Saul had knocked him out.

Times were hard. They all needed money.

But perhaps they should have obeyed Captain Drake. In fact, now that time and labor had sobered them, most worried about what the captain would have to say. Especially if they got caught and lost the whole cargo.

They hurried. One man slipped, tumbling down the slope, a keg of gin smashing to seep into the sand, the smell sharp on the air. The men in the boats squinted at the ship, trying to detect any sign that they'd been seen.

But then there was another sound.

Someone above?

The men carried on with the loading, but some looked up. Was Lloyd up there, too? Not too bad if he was. By sea, they could outpace him back to Dragon's Cove.

But now someone was coming down the cliff by rope, hand over hand, nimbly kicking off the chalk. His clothes were dark, his face smudged with soot, but they knew him.

The captain was here.

Every man hunched, as if he could make himself smaller, even shrink away.

They expected a tongue-lashing, but the crisp voice said, "Lloyd's in the village, waiting for you. Now the mist's cleared, he'll signal the navy ship to come in closer."

"Sorry, cap'n," someone muttered.

The apology was ignored. "Get the goods back in the cave. Crab pots are coming down. Some of you will go out to put them down, about your honest business. The rest come back up the cliff with me. More ropes are dropping."

"It's all loaded," Saul protested. "We can—"

The captain's gloved fist slammed into Saul's jaw.

Saul staggered, but rallied to swing for the captain's gut. He managed a glancing blow but the captain used the movement to duck and turn, then land a two-fisted blow to Saul's back that made him grunt.

"Get to it!" he snapped to the watching men, before kicking Saul's knee so he went down. Grabbing Saul's shirt, the captain said, "Still think you can lead the Horde, Saul?"

Saul spat blood. "Mel would've—"

The raised fist silenced him. "Mel got caught and took good men to Botany Bay with him. You're coming up the cliff with me."

"I can't," the man whined, eyes going wide. He was known to be afraid of heights.

"Then you'll stay in the cave until someone has time to collect you by sea."

David stood, rubbing his knuckles, watching his men haul the contraband back up to the cave. More ropes had slithered down, with crab pots tied to the end.

He glanced down at Saul. "What are you lying about for? Get the crab pots and take them to the boats."

Saul pushed to his feet, swaying slightly, fingering his face, glowering. He obeyed, however.

Soon the goods were back in the cave and the crab pots were stowed. The boats were shoved off, two men in each. No one could be arrested for taking crab pots out at night.

Four ropes were dangling down the cliff, and the nimbler men had stayed behind. Plus Saul. David would dearly love to get rid of the troublemaker, but he was a Dragon's Cove man and his family went back further than David's. He was Captain Drake's to take care of, and the Earl of Wyvern's, too.

He looked around once more to be sure he'd not overlooked anything. "Smooth the sand," he told Saul, then grabbed the remaining rope to climb up.

They made a sport of this in Dragon's Cove. David was too big a man to win at it, but it was easy work for him. Saul was too beefy by far, and had his fear as well.

Aaron wasn't a good runner, but he'd arrived at the cliff top to take command there. He'd already sent the other men off, to slip in ones and twos back to their homes. Lloyd was watching for the returning boats, not for men on land.

He gave David a hand to haul him up onto the grassy top. "All right?"

"As right as it can be."

"Saul's a menace."

"What do you want me to do? Hang him for insubordination?"

"Nay, but perhaps a storm'll come up and drown him."

"Leaving a widow and four fatherless children."

"You can't save 'em all, Davy."

Aaron was a cousin on David's Clyst side and was entitled to use the fond name when they were alone together.

"I can try. I can do no other. Especially not now."

"Now you're the earl."

"Now I'm the earl. Off with you. We'll hold a meeting tomorrow."

"And many'll not sleep well at the thought of it. Go carefully, lad."

"And you. I can't afford to lose you."

Aaron was the most experienced of all the Dragon's Horde's council and a trustworthy man, but he struggled with numbers. He couldn't run the business side of the Horde.

They clasped hands, and Aaron walked away, soon to be out of sight. David took a moment to sense the air again, seeking anything out of the ordinary that could be trouble.

All was quiet, and the fickle mist was drifting back. He was glad it had cleared for a while. If this rebellious enterprise had gone well, the Horde would have become even more difficult to control. Though he'd spent time with his father and taken part in smuggling runs for the thrill of it, he'd not been raised to be Captain Drake. Mel had wanted him to be as much of a gentleman as was possible.

He was lucky to have the build to impress most men, but in the past eighteen months he'd had to learn to command, by words if possible, but by violence if necessary. Sometimes he worried about what he was becoming. But he had no choice.

If he didn't run the Horde, people like Saul Applin would bully their way in and carry everyone in the area into disaster.

He stripped off the black overclothes and stashed them beneath a scrubby bush, weighed down by a stone. He took an oilcloth bag out of his pocket and used the wet cloth it contained to clean his face. He took off his gloves, which were stained with Saul's blood, and put them with the clothes. His knuckles were sore and bruised, but they'd show no damage to a casual eye. Gloves kept his hands and nails in a suitable state for an earl.

A reluctant earl, and a reluctant Captain Drake.

Once, he'd been a free and happy man.

Not much more than a year ago.

He set off to walk back to the Crag. No real danger in that. An earl could go for a walk on a misty night if he wanted to. If he needed an explanation for eccentric behavior, the blood of the mad earls of Wyvern ran in his veins.

In theory at least.

He returned to the Crag undetected, and found Nicholas waiting in the lair.

"All safe?"

"No thanks to those idiots. As Aaron said, though, some were driven by need. Smuggling's gone on here for generations, but the decades of war saw it flourish, so other work's been neglected. The Mad Earl did nothing to build up agriculture, fishing, and trades, and in my time as estate manager I could achieve little when he was draining every penny possible for his mad schemes. I'm working on improving things now, but I need money in the meantime. Let's hope Papa Potter approves my businesslike approach."

"What of Miss Potter? Doesn't she get her say?"

"Favoring the rights of women again? Judging by my experiences, she'll trip over her feet in the rush to agree. My necessary visits to London have been hair-raising. I appreciate how a fox must feel during a hunt."

"She's a City woman, however, not a tonnish one."

"According to Polyphant, they're even worse, all dreaming of becoming my lady. He found ways to observe the most promising highly dowered candidates and Miss Potter showed no interest in worthy occupations. She was seen shopping, and strolling about with friends, doubtless flirting with men. She was seen in a bookshop with said friends, but they only perused the shelves of gothic novels."

"Perhaps she'll find Crag Wyvern romantic."

"Then I hope it distracts her so she won't wonder why her husband is often absent on moonless nights."

"You hope to marry a fool?"

"With all my heart."

Chapter 3

Lucy allowed herself only a week to prepare for her adventure, and a week seemed too long. Mrs. Johnson was already invading daily and even asking Lucy's opinion on the changes to be made. Perhaps she thought that a kindness, but it was torture.

The wedding was set for one month hence and Mrs. Johnson also tried to involve Lucy in those plans. All Lucy could do was be busy elsewhere as much as possible, and preparing for her fashionable adventure provided an excuse.

The day after her father's devastating news she traveled to the west end of London to talk to her aunt about the plan. On the journey she studied the women strolling down fashionable streets and saw that the styles of their dresses were different, even from the newest ones in the City.

She owned plenty of fine gowns, but all dated from before her mother's death and some were older than that. She wasn't so foolish as to discard favorites before their time, but she realized they would make her dowdy here. That would never do.

Hems were heavily ornamented, often with feet of flounces, lace, or fringing. She thought it inelegant, but it was clearly the fashion. Bonnets were tall, but often the extra height was achieved with flowers or feathers, so some of hers would need only retrimming. She had the money for new bonnets, but not the time. For that reason she hoped some of her gowns could also be made to suit the style.

When she arrived at her aunt's residence, she was relieved to find that Aunt Mary seemed pleased at the prospect of her visit, even though she expressed it with an endless stream of advice. Cousin Clara was fervently delighted and chattered in counterpoint. Lucy remembered the old saying "Sticks and stones may break my bones but words will never hurt me." Not true in so many ways, but she assured herself that she could tolerate chatter when she had to.

Aunt Mary was taller and thinner than Lucy's mother had been. Her hair was concealed by a stiff cap with lappets, but in some gesture to fashion she had corkscrew curls around her face that had to be the work of a curling iron. Clara had her father's sturdy build and thick brown hair, so her corkscrew curls were a thicket.

No curling irons for herself, Lucy resolved. Fashion be damned.

"You must be here by the twenty-third, dear," Aunt Mary said, consulting some sort of record book. "That is the night of the Countess of Charrington's ball. Her first, for they haven't been much in Town since marrying, which was nearly two years ago now, so an excellent debut for you. She is the Angel Bride, you know."

Lucy didn't and looked for clarification.

"You must know *My Angel Bride*!" Clara exclaimed. "Sebastian Rossiter!"

"No, I'm sorry. He's the earl?"

Both the others laughed. "The earl is a Knollis," Aunt Mary said, as if everyone should know that. She wandered off into the Knollis genealogy, but Clara dragged her back.

"Mama, Lucinda wants to know about Sebastian Rossiter."

Her aunt and cousin were using her full name and Lucy decided to let them. Lucy Potter had no place in this world. Perhaps Lucinda Potter would fit better.

"He was Lady Charrington's first husband," Clara explained. "A poet—you truly haven't heard of him? How odd!—and much of his poetry was written about her and their children. Such beautiful sentiments! *My Angel Bride* was his most famous work. Everyone knows of it."

"I'm afraid I haven't read it."

"You must," Aunt Mary stated. "We will read some of the poems together when you're here."

"We have all his work," Clara added, "and in the finest, leather-bound editions. It will be so exciting to meet her! The Angel Bride, I mean."

"I tell Clara she might be disappointed," Aunt Mary said. "I hear she is quite an ordinary woman. But then, that is the poetic genius, to see wonders where we mere mortals see only clay."

Lucy felt sorry for the poor widow, destined to disappoint everywhere she went.

"You mustn't come *on* the twenty-third," her aunt said, frowning at her book. "You will need time to settle, and must attend some smaller events first. Perhaps Tuesday or Wednesday? Of course Wednesday is Almack's. . . ."

Lucy understood that hesitation. "I don't expect to gain admittance there, Aunt."

Her aunt bridled. "You are my sister's daughter. I'm sure I can achieve it once you are seen to be a perfect lady."

Was that a statement or a pious hope?

"I intend to be a perfect lady, Aunt."

"Of course you do, dear. But you are perhaps a little direct in your manner."

"Direct?" Lucy was genuinely confused. Clara was hardly a shrinking violet.

"A suggestion of cleverness, dear, and perhaps even decisiveness. All perfectly natural, I'm sure, given your upbringing, and not completely out of place in a wife. In some circumstances. But in a young lady, one not already known . . ."

One being scrutinized and judged, in other words.

"I understand, Aunt. I'll attempt to be as brainless as a bird and as decisive as a pudding."

Clara giggled, but Aunt Mary didn't seem to see the joke. "Do your best, dear. Do your best. You could come sooner than Tuesday, but you will have preparations to make."

Was that a hint about her outfit? She was wearing a sea green gown and matching spencer trimmed with braid, all new not long before her mother's death. It had two frills around the hem, but clearly that was not nearly enough, and it completely lacked pointed Vandyke lace. That seemed to be the very latest thing. Clara had some around her neckline and Aunt Mary dripped with it.

"Tuesday, then," Lucy said, rising. "You're most kind, Aunt, and I very much look forward to my visit here."

On the way back, traveling down busy Piccadilly, she saw a bookshop and halted the carriage. She went into Hatchard's and asked for ladies' periodicals. An eager minion took her to a selection.

She flipped through *The Ladies' Repository*, *La Belle Assemblée*, and *The Lady's Magazine*. *The Lady's Magazine* made her think wryly of *The Gentlemen's Magazine*, especially when she read the full title. *A Companion for the Fair Sex, Appropriated Solely to Their Use and Amusement*. She doubted that included anything about politics, international affairs, or business.

She purchased it, however, and all the ones with illustrations and descriptions of the latest modes. Thus armed, she returned home and summoned Betty. Together they went over the fashions.

"So much trimming," Betty said. "I wonder if fine ladies actually wear such styles."

"They do. I've seen it. The fringing on Clara's hem must have been a foot, and that was for a day gown. I confess, I did like the way the fringe moved. It must be particularly pretty in a dance. Plenty of tonnish ladies are in more moderate dress, of course, but I intend to be the epitome of style."

"Of course you do," Betty said with a grin, "and you'll certainly have the finest materials."

"Having access to the best warehouses, and discounts to boot."

"Which you share with me. For which I am extremely grateful."

"What else are friendships for?" Lucy said. "Sharing, and advice. Do you see how wide the shoulders are for evening? That gown looks likely to slide right off at any moment."

"Which doubtless attracts all the men's attention."

Lucy wondered if she wanted that, but she had no intention of being dowdy.

"Then I must have the style."

"Altering shoulders will be difficult," Betty said.

"I'm sure it can be done."

"What about the corset straps?"

"They must be making them without."

"Which has to mean stiffer boning, but perhaps you'll have to suffer to be à la mode."

"So it would seem, but there are aspects to the mode that I like. Look at those bright green half boots, and here's a pair in red and white."

"Perhaps a little much?"

"But fun, and I can have shoes and boots made to fit, so no torture." Lucy picked up the magazines. "To market, to market, to buy a fine ensemble."

Betty chuckled. "You're no poet."

"Thank heavens. Have you heard of one called Rossiter?"

Betty wrinkled her brow. "Perhaps. Yes. A few years ago everyone was talking about him. I remember his verses as rather syrupy. Not a patch on Byron. Why?"

"My aunt mentioned him. Apparently his widow is now the Countess of Charrington and I'm to make my grand debut at her ball."

"My, my! And only think—she can't have been very grand. I never had the impression Rossiter was rich or titled."

"I'll look that up. Come on, we have work to do."

Betty followed, but saying, "How are you going to get so much alteration done in a week?"

"Money," Lucy said, and so it was.

Money secured the complete attention of three local seamstresses, her corset maker, bonnet maker, and shoemaker. A few items would have to follow, but she would be ready to face the ton in record time.

Chapter 4

The George and Dragon tavern hunched beneath the Crag Wyvern headland, in the fishing village of Dragon's Cove. A hanging sign would fare ill in a storm, so the name was painted on a board nailed to the stone wall with a crude painting of a fire-breathing dragon alongside.

Travelers who ventured that far liked the primitive look of the place and the simple taproom furnished with wooden tables and benches and a few casks of ale and cider. A true smugglers' haunt, they'd think to themselves and buy rounds of drink in order to listen to local tales.

They would have been astonished if they'd been allowed to venture into the back regions where the innkeeper lived, for Mel Clyst had fitted it up for his Lady Belle with carpets, paintings, and gentry furniture.

The new tavern keeper, Rachel Clyst, lived there now, using all the rooms except for the Captain's Parlor. Though small, this paneled room could almost be a gentleman's study. It contained a sofa and two upholstered chairs near the fireplace, but a gleaming table took up half the room. It was occasionally used for dining, but mostly for gatherings of the Dragon's Horde council. Captain Drake would sit in the large chair at the head, his six lieutenants in the chairs on either side.

The most recent meeting was over. David remained seated as the men filed out, each bearing a share of the proceeds from the Bradhole Cave contraband to distribute to those under their command. Because the sea was watched so closely, they'd hauled the goods up the cliff and carried them away westward when Lloyd had been patrolling to the east. It had still been risky, but the Horde had been restless and some of the local people were truly feeling the lack of income.

Even with money to share out, it hadn't been an easy meeting. Some were in sympathy with Saul Applin and resented the cautious way David was running affairs. But Saul had served as a lesson. David had physically defeated him and also thrown him off the council. That would keep them in line for a while.

Rachel Clyst, round as a ball but brisk with it, came in to clear away the tankards. "All right, love?"

She was another Clyst cousin. David could have been a Clyst himself if his mother and Mel had married. Everyone had always wondered why they hadn't. Of course it had been because of that secret marriage to the Mad Earl. Even Mel and Lady Belle had balked at bigamy.

"They don't like change," he said.

"Few do."

"Fair enough. I wish I were still the earl's estate steward."

"You were always up to more than that, Davy. You and your sister, both."

"Susan's happy to be Viscountess Amleigh, but I'd rather not be Earl of Wyvern, and that's the flat truth. I'd rather not be Captain Drake, either."

David heard his own tone and despised it. He'd accepted both roles of his own free will. He'd been compelled by necessity and the needs of others, but he'd accepted them. No whining allowed.

"Let me know if there's trouble brewing."

"Play spy for the earl?" she asked. It was a tease, but she added, "They're right to worry, lad. It's a tangle for the mind the way things are. The earl's supposed to be on the side of the law, and the captain's supposed to run rings around it."

"I'll find a way to untangle it, but for now they can't be let off the leash." He gathered up papers. "Mel wrote to me." He'd never told anyone but his sister, but he'd be interested in Rachel's reaction. "Before going aboard for Australia. He told me to look after the Horde."

"There was no one else who could, lad, and he'd no notion then of you becoming the earl."

"He knows by now and he's sent no other orders."

"Likely he can't think what to do, either. You'll do what's right, lad, as you always have. And we pray for you."

"Do you?"

"Course we do. You hold us all in the palm of your hand."

She bustled away, leaving David staring. Her words echoed in his mind, all too like a description of God.

"Hell and damnation," he muttered and left by the back door that opened into a lane, turning left toward the path up to Crag Wyvern. It was steep enough to deter invaders, but he made easy work of it. At the top, where sheep cropped the grass that surrounded the stark stone walls of the keep, he paused to savor the crisp sea air and the view he loved.

Chalk cliffs ran eastward to his left and south for a while on his right, down to a headland that curved around into Irish Cove, Bradhole Cove, and on toward Sidmouth, Exmouth, and finally toward Cornwall.

This was the smuggling coast, slowly being closed down by the army on land and navy by sea. He saw no navy ship today, but they cruised by frequently, gun ports open, cannons poking out, threatening British people. . . .

"Consider me the mountain, coming to Mahomet. Or hill, perhaps."

David turned to his secretary, Fred Chumley, who was a head shorter than he. "Something urgent?"

Fred had letters in his hand.

"Probably not, but I appreciate a bit of fresh air as much as you."

Fred was a stocky young man with strong features and dark hair that was already thinning at twenty-four. David was grateful that his own was still thick at the same age. Fred sighed for the days of wigs. David was deeply grateful those days had passed.

Fred was the son of a local farm laborer, but he'd shown early promise and been sent to school by David's uncle, Sir Nathaniel Kerslake. He'd done so well there, he'd been sent to Oxford. He'd finished his studies just as David had taken on the earldom.

He'd been the answer to a prayer. As earl David needed a secretary, but he hadn't wanted to bring a stranger into this mess. Fred understood perfectly why the Earl of Wyvern was never around when a smuggling run was taking place, and also why the earldom's horses were tired the day after. He didn't question activity in the Crag's cavernous under chambers and had occasionally lent a hand at tricky moments. He acted as accountant as well, neatly blending illegal income with legal so that it would take a detailed investigation to sort them out.

Fred was also content with doing things the way David wanted. A nobleman's secretary should open all correspondence and take to his employer only the papers needing his particular attention. David preferred to open letters himself, just as he preferred dressing himself—simply. The valet he'd hired on becoming earl had left in disgust, so now he was happily making do with William, his only footman, who wasn't a particularly good footman or valet, but was good enough.

David took the pile of sealed letters and flipped through them. "Ah," he said, passing the rest back and breaking a seal. "At last. Polyphant. Wish me well." He scanned the neat script. "Damnation."

"Not well?"

"Not at all well. Miss Potter's father says she will make her own choice now she's twenty-one."

"Not unreasonable."

"Perhaps, but Polyphant took it on himself to keep my name out of it. He's patting himself on the back, but a countess's coronet might have done the trick."

"He might have mentioned your rank without the title."

"He should have followed my orders," David snapped.

"He doesn't know you have the power of life and death."

David gave him a look. "There's worse."

"She's already betrothed?"

"No, but she's off to Mayfair to dangle her thirty thousand before the cream of the aristocratic fortune hunters. As Polyphant puts it, I'm going to have to contest for her hand against all comers."

"That's a shame."

David turned to him. "You think I can't do it?"

"No, no," said Fred, raising a hand. "Merely that you won't like it."

"That's true enough. I had to go to London twice to speak at hearings about the title. Dirty, noisy, crowded. A million people live there. A million!"

"Spread over a large area, and broken into parts. The old City of London is separate from the west end, and the political area of Westminster and St. James is apart from the new residential area of Mayfair."

"I forget you must have visited there from Oxford."

"Frequently. There's everything in London. Pleasure, learning, exhibitions."

"I'd take you as guide, but I need to leave someone I trust in charge here."

"You're going, then?"

"Thirty thousand pounds," David reminded him, "and I need every penny."

"Didn't Polyphant present you with the names of four well-dowered ladies?"

"The only one approaching Miss Potter for riches is Lady Maud Emberley, and she's empty in the attic. The other two, Miss Rackman and Miss Tapler, have only twenty and fifteen thousand. What's more, they both have brothers and sisters. Miss Potter's an only child. She could end up with the lot."

Fred whistled. "A twenty-four-carat golden prize. Perhaps she's ugly."

David grimaced. "Pretty, according to Polyphant, and there's more."

"More horrors?" Fred asked.

"You're an impudent wretch. Polyphant's initial enquiries failed to uncover that Miss Potter's mother, the simply named Alice Stanley, was from a noble family of Stanleys. My thirty thousand will be going into the beau monde under the aegis of her aristocratic aunt, Lady Caldross."

"Settle for one of the others," Fred said.

"If you're trying to taunt me, it's not necessary. I've accepted all the tortures of my inheritances thus far. Why balk at another? I can kill another bird while in London and take my seat in Parliament."

"And be presented at court," Fred reminded him.

"Damn you. Do you know I'll have to wear a powdered wig, as if it were the last century?"

Fred wisely kept his silence.

David glared out at the sea. By any justice it should be gray and stormy to mirror his mood, but instead it presented its pretty face. The water reflected the bright

blue of the sky and the waves merely rippled onto the
pebbly shore, whispering sweet promises.

We've always been here.

We'll still be here when you return.

"How soon can I go?" he asked.

"You have engagements, but the only important one
is the Lord Lieutenant's dinner in five weeks' time."

"I'll be back by then. Cancel the rest."

"It might take longer to woo and win."

"It can't. I won't leave the Horde unmastered for longer than a month. If at all possible, I'll be back before the
next moonless night."

Fred gave him a dubious look, but he walked away,
back toward the monstrous house.

A keep. It could mean "keep safe," but to David it
said "keep imprisoned." Tall gray stone walls were sur-
mounted with battlements and broken only by narrow
arrow slits. There were even snarling gargoyles at the
corners and an army of them around the huge main
doorway. The massive wooden doors bound in iron could
admit a coach and horses, but as best he knew that had
never been attempted. How would such a vehicle climb
the hill?

For normal use a small door was set into the large
one, and the spiked portcullis hanging above was completely ornamental.

He couldn't live there all his life, but he didn't see the
way out. Even if he owned a home like Kerslake Manor,
an earl couldn't live in such a place. And without money
this earl couldn't change anything.

Thirty thousand pounds. Perhaps his pursuit of that
would provide an excuse to avoid the Lord Lieutenant's
dinner. When his claim to the title had finally been
stamped and sealed six weeks ago, the dinner had been
arranged as his formal introduction to the highest ranks
of Devonshire society. He didn't know how much the

Lord Lieutenant had had to grit his teeth to get it done, but his own jaw clenched at the thought of it.

Plenty of the nobility still saw him as the Mad Earl of Wyvern's bastard-born estate steward, son of a smuggler and a wanton. Many also doubted his claim to the title, court rulings be damned. Those who did believe him the Mad Earl's legitimate son would be on the watch for insanity.

With such tangled origins, did he have any chance at all with Miss Potter?

If she was plunging into the tonnish season, however, she must be looking to trade her dowry for a title, the higher the better. He was certainly willing to be bought.

Chapter 5

On the morning of her departure Lucy went for a walk to take farewell of her familiar world. She knew it was extreme to think that way, but it was as if everything was changing around her. Perhaps it was Charlotte Johnson in and out of her home, not yet changing anything, but obviously with plans in mind.

Or it could be the morn-till-night involvement in altering her clothes, often in ways she didn't truly like. Certainly every time she assessed finery in a mirror, she saw a changed person. Lucinda, not Lucy.

For this last walk, she was Miss Potter, who'd gone with her father to these same wharves and warehouses, spoken freely, and struck bargains. She wore a Miss Potter outfit of dark brown dress and spencer and close-fitting black bonnet. Some people greeted her, and no one thought her being here on her own unusual.

Soon she'd have to return home and put on the pink walking dress she'd chosen to wear to enter the beau monde. There she'd never be able to go out alone without being thought scandalous.

She paused to look at the busy river, trying to guess at a distance what goods the incoming vessels might carry: tea or timber, oil or oranges, cotton or coffee. No business of hers at the moment and clocks were striking ten. At eleven her father's coach would carry her into the beau monde.

She hurried back, but a display in the window of Winsom's Stationers and Booksellers caught her eye. She was generally most interested in the reading material, but today a pile of prettily bound books was stacked on view, one open to show plain pages.

Lucy had such a notebook and carried it with her nearly everywhere, along with a pencil and a knife to sharpen that, but it was bound in brown leather and scuffed. She'd promised Betty details of life in Mayfair and a pretty journal seemed just the thing for Silly Lucinda.

She went in, setting the bell over the door jingling, and greeted wizened Mr. Winsom. He must be seventy if he was a day, but he was still sprightly despite seeming to live eternally inside his premises.

"My fortune is made!" he declared. "Miss Potter comes a-purchasing."

"I do indeed, Mr. Winsom. I'm interested in one of the new journals."

"A gift?" he said. "Perhaps for Miss Hanway?"

"For myself. I'm off to the west end."

"Ah, yes, I heard." He indicated a nearby shelf where more were displayed face forward. She could see why. They were bound not just in color, but in figured silk.

"Very fine," she said, drawn despite herself to a pink one with a design of butterflies. She took it down. It opened well, and the paper was of excellent quality. Just the thing for a journal of life in the ton.

She noticed that Winsom had cleverly set the display alongside the section of the bookstore most popular with the ladies—the novels. Yesterday evening, when Betty had come over to take farewell, she'd suggested that Lucy might want to take some novels to Mayfair to support her persona as Silly Lucinda.

The conversation had begun with Lucy worrying about where she'd live when her father was married.

"I can't possibly live here with them as newlyweds."

"I don't suppose they'll mind."

"I'll mind! I'll need more time. Perhaps I should travel. The Lakes, the Peak District. Dramatic landscapes suited to a tragic heart."

"Lucy."

"A joke. But I can't return here so soon. But nor can I travel alone."

"Rachel or Jenny?" Betty suggested, naming two of their unmarried friends.

"Jenny's become so bitter, but I suppose Rachel would be an amiable travel companion. Will a few more weeks be enough, though?"

"You could always take ship for Canada, like Laura Montreville in *Self Control.*"

"First a convent, now paddling a canoe down a river, fleeing fierce Indians."

"You read it?" Betty asked in surprise.

"Of course not, but I oblige my dearest friend by listening to her relate the stories."

"You'll get your reward when Silly Lucinda can join in discussions."

That was when Lucy had realized the horrible truth. Her cousin and aunt were in ecstasies over a silly poet, so they were probably addicted to novels, too. They'd want to talk about them morning, noon, and night. She'd prepared herself to endure, but when in Rome one was supposed to do as the Romans do. She should buy some novels.

She put her chosen journal on the desk and walked to the shelves of slim volumes with gilt lettering.

The bell tinkled again. She glanced to see who'd entered and her attention was caught. She realized why. The tall young man was dressed in country style. Leather breeches and top boots were not the norm around here.

He asked Winsom if he carried books about agriculture and was directed down one of the narrow passageways between the shelves. He walked there with a little more vigor than she was used to seeing in the neighborhood. He was also quite handsome. . . .

Lucy turned firmly away to concentrate on a different sort of folly. She'd long known that to marry would undermine her ambitions to become a merchant and she was armored against good looks and even charm.

The Spectre Bride. Betty had enjoyed that one and shared the story. Lucy felt no desire to revisit the idiotic plot.

Midnight Nuptials.

Forbidden Affections.

Were all novels about love and marriage?

The Animated Skeleton. That sounded amusing, but her eye was caught by the title *Self Control.* That was the one about Laura Montreville, canoes, and Canada. Anything further from self-control was hard to imagine.

She moved on, but then turned back. She could remember quite a bit of the story, which meant she might be able to get away with only pretending to read it. She took the two volumes and looked for another novel.

Love and Horror. Now there was a combination that promised good sense. Was it about the horrible fates that lurked behind love? Even though her parents had been happy together, she'd long been aware that her mother had been demented by love to act as she had, and that it could easily have led to horror.

She took down the slim volume, flipped past a preface, and came to the opening.

The storm was beating tempestuously and the lightning glaring around the playhouse . . .

She smiled, imagining animated lightning angrily glaring at the audience. But then it seemed Mr. Thomas Bailey was only just entering the playhouse. He took his seat, where he fell to sighing and weeping at the play, grieving for a lost wife.

That was too real a horror for Lucy. She was about to close the book when she saw a line. She read the words again. He'd lost his beloved two hundred years ago? How could that be . . . ?

Blast it! She'd read the entire first chapter, gobbled it down without thought.

She shoved the dangerous book back on the shelf, but then took it off again. She might have to truly read novels now and then, so she might as well have ones that went down easily. She added the two volumes of *The Animated Skeleton* for good measure.

Five volumes was more than enough and the clock was ticking away the minutes, but she couldn't resist turning to the section containing books on trade. She could at least look at the shelf where Winsom kept the new books.

The country gentleman was there, but further down, so no need for alarm.

No need for alarm in any case.

Clearly even a brief exposure to novels deranged the mind.

Observations on the Use of Machinery in the Manufactories of Great Britain. She knew all the arguments against machinery, but progress could not be halted.

A Treatise on the Abuses of the Coal Trade tempted simply because she knew little about it, but it formed no part of her father's businesses.

An Introduction to Trade and Business. She certainly didn't need that.

On the top shelf she read, *The Evils of the Freetrade.*

There had recently been parliamentary debates about how smuggled goods harmed legal trade by undercutting prices. The so-called Freetrade was also damaging agriculture because men who could make money through crime didn't want to work the land. She couldn't take such a book to Mayfair, but she could buy it for later. Also, her father might be interested in it.

She went on tiptoe to reach it.

"Allow me, ma'am."

She froze. The country gentleman was almost touching her as he reached easily for the book.

He looked at the title. "You're interested in smuggling, ma'am?"

Lucy wanted to tartly ask why not, but she murmured, "For my father," as she took the book. She was going to have to act a part for weeks, so she might as well start now.

"If there are any other volumes on the higher shelves I could assist you with . . ."

He had a pleasant voice, and was only attempting to be kind. She didn't like being rude, so as she said, "No, thank you," she glanced up and gave him a slight smile.

She was caught by blue-gray eyes, all the brighter for being surrounded by skin that confirmed him to be a stranger in her world. No City man was exposed to the elements enough to tan like that.

Handsome as she'd thought.

Square jaw.

Fine lips . . .

A warm smile. An interested smile.

She quickly moved away, pretending to look for another book as her heart slowed its pace. She didn't know why she'd been so overset by a smile.

Calm again, she turned to go to Winsom's desk, make her purchases, and leave, but she realized she'd made a mistake. She'd moved away from the front of the shop, so the country gentleman now stood in her way. He wasn't doing it deliberately, for he was once more looking over the shelves, but the passageway was narrow and he was large. She'd have to push by him to get out.

Leave, she silently urged him, aware of time passing, but he took down another book and opened it.

Winsom's clock chimed the half hour.

Lucy walked away from him to go around the shelves, but then came to a halt. This was one of the cul-de-sac sections that ended only with a window.

Oh, what was the matter with her? Was a brief reading of a novel enough to turn her into an overwrought idiot? She'd be running away to a French convent, next, or taking ship for Canada.

She adjusted the six books in her arm and walked forward.

Alerted, he glanced round, and then pressed back against the shelves to give her more room. She nodded and passed, squeezing away from him as much as she could, pulling in her elbows.

One volume slid free to slam to the wooden floor with a sound like a pistol shot. She stared at it, mind empty of what to say or do.

He bent and picked it up. "*Love and Horror,*" he read from the spine. "Lighter reading than smuggling, but an odd combination of words."

She snatched it. "Or a natural match? As in *Romeo and Juliet*?"

"Or *Othello,*" he agreed. "I grant you your point, though it's a pity to see love used as a vehicle for tragedy."

"Or a pity that love addles its victims. All would have been well if Juliet had made a sensible choice and Othello had been less persuadable."

"You don't believe in overpowering passions?"

"Definitely not."

"Yet there are all too many cases of jealous men murdering women."

"That's different," Lucy said, annoyed by his good point, and by having completely lost Silly Lucinda at first attempt. "Consider *Romeo and Juliet*. I don't know of a single occasion of young lovers dying together through a misunderstanding."

His lips twitched. "There, I grant you your point."

Twitching lips should not have such a powerful effect.

The clock chimed the three quarters. "Your pardon, sir, but I must be on my way."

She turned toward the front, but he said, "May I help with your load?"

One book was slipping again, so she saw no way to protest as he added hers to the two he'd selected. His hands were a great deal bigger than hers.

"This is an excellent shop behind its shabby appearance," he said as she led the way to the front.

"It is."

"It's a regular haunt of yours?"

She came alert. Was he a fortune hunter, armed with a list and prowling around her home area? Had he seen her leave her house and followed her here? He certainly looked in need of a fortune. His leather breeches were repaired in one place, his boots well-worn, and his hair in need of a barber.

"Very regular," she said, enjoying the prospect of him lurking in Winsom's to no purpose, for she wouldn't return here for weeks.

He showed no reaction, but then, he was looking at the spines of all her books. "An *Animated Skeleton* goes oddly with a book on the evils of the Freetrade, but why do I suspect that both are for you?"

"I have no idea."

"I wouldn't have thought the Freetrade of interest to anyone in the City."

"There, sir, you are wrong. Those wretches bring in foreign goods to compete with British-made ones, and they avoid taxes that honest traders must pay. In addition, I understand their practices are vile."

"The Hawkhurst Gang," he said with a sigh.

"Precisely! Vicious, evil men."

"I agree, but a century ago."

"You defend them?"

"The Hawkhursts? No, but I'm sure not every smuggler is evil and nor are all the people who benefit from the trade. Are you entirely sure that everything you eat, drink, and use has paid full tax?"

"Yes, of course."

"It can be hard to tell, except by price. Most people don't look too closely at a bargain."

Lucy remembered the cheap silks and wondered about her mother's tea and her father's brandy. She suspected he'd not be overly scrupulous about its origins.

"If you're not careful, sir, I'll suspect you of being a Freetrader."

He smiled. It really was a very nice smile. "I'm merely a simple country gentleman, ma'am, struggling to make ends meet in hard times."

They walked over to the desk where Winsom was waiting to take their selections. Lucy knew she should be glad to have done with the man and yet she felt a tiny pang of loss.

Perhaps it was because he'd talked with her as an equal, in an easy and direct way. She'd had too little of that recently. She was tempted to linger, but he glanced at the clock and she suspected he was in as much of a hurry as she was. Her urgency wasn't acute. If the carriage had to wait ten minutes, so be it.

"Please, sir, pay for your purchases first. I'm thinking what else I might wish to buy."

He thanked her and gave his books to Winsom.

As he'd read the spines of her books, she did the same with his. *A New System of Drainage* and *An Introduction to Trade and Business*. She couldn't imagine a fortune hunter making those selections. Clearly he truly was a simple country gentleman trying to survive in hard times.

He paid Winsom and took his books, now neatly wrapped in brown paper tied with string.

He inclined his head. "I wish you good day, ma'am, and eternal freedom from the horrors of love."

There was a hint of humor in that which could beguile. Lucy smiled as she dipped a curtsy and said, "Good day, sir," with a true touch of regret.

It seemed as if he might say more, but he turned and took his leave.

She wished she knew what had brought such a man deep into the City.

She wished she knew his name.

She wished they might meet again.

Winsom cleared his throat.

Lucy turned, blushing. "I'm sorry."

Winsom seemed to be concealing amusement, but he asked, "For how long will you want the novels, Miss Potter?"

"For how long?"

"Miss Hanway generally takes any one for a fortnight."

Oh, yes. The novels were part of Winsom's lending library. "I'm removing today to my aunt's house in Mayfair. I shall probably be gone for a month."

"That presents no difficulty. I shall make the lending period that long." He wrote the price for that, the cost of *The Evils of the Freetrade*, and the pink journal, then gave her the total. She took a pound note out of her reticule and received back change.

He probably often wondered why she didn't buy on account and have her bill settled monthly by her father, but for a long time now she'd not wanted her father to know what books she bought for fear he would disapprove. With hindsight that should have told her something. How easy it was to hide from an unwelcome truth—in her case, that her father had never really seen her as a possible heir.

As he wrapped the parcel, Winsom said, "I'll miss your visits here, Miss Potter, but I predict mayhem amidst the gentlemen of the ton." He tied the string and snipped off the ends. "You certainly had an effect on that gentleman."

"Nonsense," Lucy said, though inside her something purred.

That was truly alarming, and already she was late. She took her parcel and left the shop, wondering if he might be hovering.

He wasn't, and she was aware of a twinge of regret. That meant she'd had a lucky escape. She hurried home and found the coach already waiting outside the house. She apologized to the coachman, and then to her father, who opened the door, asking where she'd been and why she wasn't dressed. She ran upstairs to change, trying to wipe the incident from her mind.

She rang for Hannah, dumped her package on the bed, and began to undress. She could get out of these clothes by herself.

That purr of satisfaction when Winsom said she'd had an effect on him.

Her enjoyment of that man's conversation.

How she'd not wanted it to end.

How she'd wished she knew more about him.

Hannah ran in, also exclaiming over how late she was, where had she been. . . .

"Don't fuss," Lucy said, quickly washing with cooling water. "Pack that package."

At least her stays and petticoat were suitable for the fine gown, so it didn't take long to put it on. Her stockings weren't soiled, so they would do, even though they were an everyday pair. She put on her new pink leather half boots and sat so Hannah could brush out her hair.

Thank heavens it didn't require elaborate dressing. She wanted to arrive at Aunt Mary's in prime twig. That was the important matter, but the country gentleman wouldn't leave her mind.

She always tried to be honest with herself, so she accepted that she wished they might meet again.

Even if he was a fortune hunter.

If he was a fortune hunter, she had a fortune. . . .

"No, no, no!"

"Beg pardon, miss?" said Hannah, startled.

"Not you, Hannah. Only that time's flying. That'll do. Where's my bonnet?"

Lucy tied the ribbons on the tall confection, wondering whether this was how her mother had felt on the day her life had been turned upside down.

If she'd brushed against the idiocy of love at first sight, she'd escaped before it could take root, and she thanked the heavens for it.

Chapter 6

David hurried in search of a hackney stand. What had possessed him to linger in that bookshop when he was already late?

He knew what—or rather, who.

What he'd first taken for a plain Jane had turned out to have the biggest, clearest blue eyes he could remember seeing. Those eyes, that heart-shaped face, those pretty lips, all together with intelligence and a fine ability to debate.

A shame she had strong opinions on smuggling.

What did her opinions matter? He was here in London to win the hand and fortune of Miss Lucinda Potter. That was what had brought him into the City of London this morning. He'd thought he might learn something from her home and area. Now he was shamefully late for an appointment. He found a hackney stand and ordered the driver to make all speed to Bond Street.

He'd arrived in London last night to stay with his sister, Susan, and her husband, Viscount Amleigh. He'd claimed the earldom largely for Susan's and Con's sakes, but there'd been another reason, gently argued by his uncle Nathaniel and aunt Miriam, the people who'd raised him and whom he regarded as his true parents. Though Con would do his duty, his first love would always be Somerford Court. If the domain of the Mad Earl was to be healed and restored, it needed a resident earl who cared only about it.

So he'd accepted his fate, but with the need to come to London and win Miss Potter's money, he'd written to Con and Susan, pointing out that the least they could do was support him through the ordeal. They'd replied that they were already in London for the season, and that the Company of Rogues were in Town en masse, ready to help, including Nicholas Delaney, leader of the Rogues.

Nicholas had formed the group at Harrow School for protection from bullies, be they senior boys or masters. The bond held, and they stood ready to help one another by fair means or foul. Now, they would help David, for a Rogue's sake. For Con's.

All very well, but David was wary of the Rogues, even Nicholas.

He'd accepted the earldom of his own accord, but he wasn't sure what would have happened if he'd refused. Would Con's need have overruled his own? The school-boy group had become a coterie of formidable men from all ranks, with a range of expertise and influence and a cavalier attitude to convention and the law.

Nicholas had visited Con's house the previous evening to plan how to smooth David's way into society and help him capture Miss Potter. He'd brought two other Rogues, ones David didn't know. Sir Stephen Ball was a skilled lawyer and politician, and the Earl of Charrington was known for his diplomatic skills. Lord Vandeimen hadn't been there, but he'd been promised for this tailoring expedition. He, at least, wasn't a Rogue. He was simply a friend of Con's known for dressing in the latest style.

David had been given his say and his opinions had been listened to, but he'd still felt like a deftly manipulated puppet. Susan had assured him everyone had his best interests at heart. Perhaps, but he'd keep up his guard.

Being still used to country ways he'd woken early. Rather than twiddling his thumbs he'd set out to clear his head with a walk. After a stroll around the orderly streets of Mayfair he'd headed east toward the City of London to scout out the Potters' world.

He'd not breakfasted, so he'd corrected that at a tavern alongside laborers of all kinds. He'd learned much from their conversation, in particular about the great needs of the metropolis. Goods poured in and money flowed out to those who provided them. Fish was particularly appreciated. Fresh was best, and in shortest supply, but smoked and dried would do. He was sure his coastal area could produce more smoked fish if people turned their energies to it instead of smuggling.

He'd found Nailer Street and been surprised by the simplicity and dignity of Daniel Potter's house. He'd expected such a self-made man to blazon his wealth, probably in a tasteless way. Potter's house was the finest on the street, but not ostentatious. It was double-fronted and had probably once been two properties, but they'd been blended well. Everything about it was of the best and maintained excellently. David didn't know what it said about Miss Potter, but it made him uneasy.

A quietly elegant house didn't mean the daughter would be quietly, elegantly perceptive, but he'd decided to observe her before making a final decision.

The hackney came to a stop, pulling him back to the present. He was about to open the door, but he realized he wasn't at his destination. Instead, they were tangled in a press of vehicles, most of them carts and wagons.

All very well for Fred to say that the million people in London were spread out. The fashionable part was appallingly crowded, even in the morning when most of the ton was asleep. That was when goods were delivered and this jam came from such wagons and carts. The shouts and curses almost drowned out the street vendors crying their wares. Could anyone be sleeping through this?

The jam broke up and his carriage could progress again. He called to the driver to make haste. The man obeyed so that David was rattling over cobblestones at a speed likely to loosen his teeth. *Grit and bear it.* Vandeimen would be waiting for him at the premises of Messrs. Storn and Watkins.

The hackney rocked to a halt and David jumped out and paid the driver. In moments he was inside the elegant establishment and ushered into the parlor, where Lord Vandeimen awaited. He was certainly the epitome of a beau, with his stylishly cut blond hair, brown jacket, and cream-and-gold-striped waistcoat, not to mention the elaborately knotted white cravat stuck in place with a golden pin. He was also wearing pantaloons.

David had purchased many new garments to fit his role as earl, including two pairs of pantaloons, but he much preferred breeches and boots.

"I was beginning to think you'd turned tail," Vandeimen said.

"Why would I have done that?"

"Because you're dressed appallingly?" his advisor asked, looking him over.

David reminded himself that Vandeimen had been a cavalry officer from the age of sixteen and carried a jagged scar on his cheek as evidence of action. If he could bear to dress like a damned dandy, David could tolerate it, too.

"I was ordered to send all my better clothing here to be assessed and updated. In any case, I've been exploring London in the early hours where ton style would not have been appropriate."

"Did you discover wonders?"

A heart-shaped face and big blue eyes . . .

"Gossip in a tavern and a book on drainage. Shouldn't we get to business?"

"Mr. Watkins stands waiting," Vandeimen said, indicating a tall, thin man who'd stood so still David hadn't seen him.

He decided an earl wouldn't apologize and went with the tailor and Vandeimen into another room, where his clothing was laid out.

"Evening clothes first, Watkins," Vandeimen said. "Lord Wyvern is to attend the Countess of Charrington's ball four days from now."

David shot him a look that said, "I am?" but saw no point in fighting that battle. One ball was as good as another as long as Lucinda Potter was there.

Watkins picked up David's dark evening wear, made by his tailor in Honiton only six months ago.

"Not intolerable work, my lord," Watkins said, "but we would like to attempt some small improvements. If you will consent to undress—a tiresome business, I know, my lord—and put on the coat?"

Vandeimen sat with elegant ease in an upholstered chair and a minion appeared to assist David in undressing and then re-dressing. There was nothing wrong with his coat. He'd worn it to an assembly attended by some of the best in Devon and no one had turned pale with horror.

"This is well made for provincial work, my lord," Watkins said, smoothing the shoulder, "but the fashion now is for a greater rise in the collar. With your permission, we can devise that. And there is a slight creasing at the waist. That will never do. Pins!"

David surrendered to being a clotheshorse.

After two hours, he escaped and Vandeimen carried him off to his town house for refreshments. As they settled with coffee in a comfortable, manly parlor, Vandeimen smiled. "Feeling hard done-by?"

"Lady Charrington's ball? I have no say in what entertainments I attend?"

"In unknown seas be guided by skillful pilots. Best to make your first formal appearance at a Rogue event, and Miss Potter will be there."

David nodded. "Until then I'm a free man?"

"Until then your time is planned to the minute, but all manly events where fashion doesn't matter. There's a select gathering tomorrow at the Duke of St. Raven's country haunt, Nuns' Chase."

"'Select' hardly sounds like the appropriate word."

Vandeimen's lips twitched. "You've missed the best days, but so did I, alas. Cyprians and shocking wildness. Now St. Raven's married, it's to be hard drinking and virile contests. Riding, fencing, shooting, even quarterstaff."

"Pity there's no cliff climbing on a dark night."

"Wrong sort of terrain. It doesn't matter how you perform. The purpose is to show the guests you're a good 'un and on warm terms with men of good repute. They'll report back to their women, and the women rule this world." Perhaps David didn't look convinced, for Van added, "The Rogues en masse are very effective."

"I know it. They had a hand in my becoming the legitimate son of the Mad Earl."

"Being an earl brings advantages."

"Name them."

Vandeimen seemed truly surprised.

"The earldom is almost bankrupt," David said. "What remains—the title, the seat in Parliament, and Crag Wyvern—hold no value for me. I wasn't raised to be noble. It's only by the kindness of my uncle and aunt that Susan and I weren't raised in a tavern."

"But you were raised in a manor house, firmly in the gentry."

"As known bastards. When I attend elegant events it's

obvious that in the eyes of most I'm still a well-raised bastard suitable at best for employment as an estate manager."

"They'll come around. The British nobility are surprisingly pragmatic. There are quite a few cuckoos in the nest, some of whom have inherited titles, and some of them bear an inconvenient likeness to their true fathers. It's simply not mentioned, for what would be the point? To tamper with the rules, to allow fathers to pick and choose, or declare grown sons not their own, would create chaos."

David drank more of the excellent coffee. "Nicholas thought that some who suspected the truth would be glad that the Mad Earl's blood wasn't being passed on."

"He's right. Insane peers are bad for business, especially with unrest because of hard times. The French Revolution is a close memory."

"I'm surprised my supposed father didn't set up a guillotine somewhere about the place. He installed a torture chamber among other monstrosities."

"So I heard. And raped his way around the county."

"There, you're wrong. The women came to him willingly, because if they didn't conceive, he sent them off with enough money to make a nice dowry. If any did, she'd become his countess."

"And yet he was married to your mother."

"Secretly, and he meant it to stay that way so he could marry if he wanted to."

"Pardon my confusion . . ." Vandeimen said.

"Oh, I do. The Mad Earl's ways confuse everyone."

". . . but why not hold to the marriage with your mother and establish you as his heir?"

"He knew I wasn't his. I was born too long after she fled him. As it was, he seems to have lived in terror of her producing the proof of the marriage and foisting me off on him. He'd have dearly loved to kill her and Mel, but in the Crag Wyvern area Mel had more power than he did. Mel could have gone into the Crag and thrown the earl over the battlements and there'd have been plenty to say they saw him jump."

"'Struth. Is this our civilized nation you speak of?"

"I'm sure there are pockets of Sussex with their arcane ways."

Vandeimen grimaced, but didn't deny it. "So the earl desperately wanted a legal son of his own get, and she was willing to keep their marriage secret for her own convenience."

"So he had no legal hold over her, yes. And all was well for more than twenty years, except that all his attempts to get a child failed, which added to his insanity." David considered his words and then added, "She probably killed him."

"Your mother killed the Mad Earl?"

"You don't think a woman capable of it? Despite the earl's acrimony, there was some sort of pact between him and Mel by which the earl protected the Horde in return for money for his mad projects and his concoctions—the ones to increase his fertility and find the secret to eternal life. But when Mel and his men were captured the earl did nothing and Lady Belle was like one of the furies. When she resolved to follow Mel to Botany Bay, she gathered all the wealth she could, including going up to the Crag to filch anything portable. A few days later the earl quaffed his latest concoction and died of it. Odds are she put something lethal into one of his pots and left in the pleasant conviction that she'd be avenged sooner or later."

"Quite a woman."

"I have to confess to some admiration, but her ruthless pursuit of her own desires has sown a great deal of trouble, not least by beggaring the Horde and the earldom before leaving."

"It sounds as if the Mad Earl did most of the work."

"True enough. What he spent on books and ingredients! We sold his collection of dried penises from many species for a thousand guineas, and made five times that for his library, but couldn't recoup a fraction of his outlays."

"Hence your predicament."

David was annoyed with himself for complaining. "This fortune hunt would be more endurable if my situation hadn't become so notorious. Originally we thought that with no one else claiming the title it would slide through, but there seem to be flocks of crows in the offices and courts of London who love nothing more than to peck a claim for rotten spots. It all cost a shocking amount of money. I took on an impoverished earldom, but lawyers have moved me from pauper to debtor and left me a walking scandal to boot. The court hearings into my mother's marriage were packed with spectators. The papers dubbed it 'The Mad Earl Affair.'"

"Broadsheets and ballads, too," Van agreed, sympathetic at last. "There's even a play in the making. How the innocent maiden was coaxed into a secret marriage, but when ravished by her husband the wicked earl, fled into the arms of a local smuggler."

"Hades! I hoped it'd fade from notice now it's settled."

"In time it will. For one thing they'll not use real names, so in a few years the play will merely be about the Earl of Dragonham, or Wormwood, or some such."

"I doubt any rational lady will be willing to marry me."

"You might as well say that no gentleman will marry a fortune if it comes with a whiff of scandal."

"A sordid business, isn't it?"

"Only if you make it so. Maria and I began with only a convenient association."

"And now you're in love?"

"Madly."

"Doesn't it bother you to be insane?"

Vandeimen laughed. "Not when it's such delicious lunacy. I wish it for you."

"Don't." It came out more sharply than he'd meant.

Van poured more coffee, but his look requested an explanation.

"My mother fell into the earl's clutches out of greed and ambition, but insane love pushed her into Mel Clyst's arms. Miss Isabelle Kerslake of Kerslake Manor, living at the George and Dragon with the tavern keeper?"

"It can't have been easy growing up as the consequence of such a scandal."

David didn't welcome such perceptive sympathy. "My aunt and uncle accepted Susan and me and so the local gentry followed suit for their sakes. If Lady Belle had raised us in the tavern, it might have been different."

"Perhaps that's why she didn't."

"Are you seeking nobility in her? Mel might have thought that way, and she'd do what Mel wanted, but she had no motherly feelings at all. Trust me on that."

"She certainly was devoted to him, to follow him to Australia when he was transported and she took the trouble to write to you, telling you the details of her secret marriage, which gave you a claim on the earldom. Why?"

David put down his cup, considering. "I assume she saw another way to strike back at the Mad Earl, even though he was dead. Or it could simply have been to claim the title Countess of Wyvern. Did you hear that she's using the title in Sydney at the same time as running a tavern called the Wyvern Arms? With, of course, the arms on the sign."

Van laughed aloud. "A magnificent woman! I wonder how she'll take to becoming the dowager."

After a moment, David shared the laughter. "I wish I could see her face. Suddenly, marriage has some appeal."

Chapter 7

"The Earl of Wyvern is in Town!" Aunt Mary declared.

Lucy looked up from her needlework, because clearly she was expected to. In her three days in Lanchester Street, she'd learned how to fulfill expectations.

Her cousin Clara exclaimed, "At last!"

Lucy had no idea why the earl's arrival was so exciting, but she soon would. Aunt Mary never left a thought unspoken, and rarely read a word in silence. She'd known her aunt and cousin were chatterers, but not that they never stopped, nor that she'd be expected to be with them all the time.

Most of her time in the house was spent in this elegantly appointed drawing room, which was overly perfumed by potpourri. The windows were never opened. Aunt Mary did not approve of open windows.

She also hadn't realized that her aunt held many firm beliefs that would prove inconvenient. Aunt Mary did not approve of ladies reading newspapers or the more serious magazines. Hence, Lucy was starving for information. Her aunt did not approve of ladies wearing their hair short, for which she cited the Bible as her authority.

She couldn't make Lucy's shoulder-length hair grow, but she tutted at it and urged her to wear it up so that the sin was less apparent. She refused any request from

Clara that she have her hair cropped. Given her cousin's frizzy mass, that was unfortunate.

Aunt Mary did not approve of young, unmarried ladies sleeping alone. That meant Lucy was sharing not just a bedroom but a bed with Clara, when she'd never shared a bed in her life. It made it hard to sleep well, and also meant that even going to bed gave no relief from chatter.

She had no privacy anywhere, for if she went apart for any length of time, one or the other came in search of her. It wasn't badly intended. They seemed to seriously fear that she might be weeping her sorrows or overtaken by some dread disease. Lucy hadn't realized how much she enjoyed solitude and silence until now.

She hadn't dared open her journal. Though she'd experienced interesting things in the past days, she hadn't recorded them, for Clara would be nearby and demand to know every word. Neither Clara nor Aunt Mary had any concept of privacy. They shared every moment, every thought, and expected others to do the same. Lucy suspected that they found her worryingly taciturn.

Three days already felt like three weeks.

If it were possible to run home, she might.

When the footman had entered the drawing room to present a newspaper, Lucy had been astonished, but had hoped that the flow of words might have some substance.

Instead, it had soon become clear that the *Weekly Social Enquirer* contained nothing but the comings and goings of royalty and aristocracy, and information about upcoming social events.

"Wyvern's residing on Millicent Row with his sister, Lady Amleigh," Aunt Mary said. "I'm surprised Amleigh welcomes him when he snatched the earldom from him."

"Lady Amleigh *is* Wyvern's sister, Mama," Clara reminded.

"But from the same dubious origins. Most deplorable."

Lucy was intrigued by the story. "Lord Wyvern snatched the earldom from his brother-in-law? That must make the family situation awkward."

"Not just awkward, dear, but scandalous. You probably haven't heard the story."

Lucy dutifully admitted that she hadn't, allowing her aunt to relate the whole.

"The earls of Wyvern have always been odd, but everyone agrees that the sixth earl was entirely deranged. He never married, or so it was thought, and died without legal issue, so the title passed to a distant Somerford line in Sussex. That is, to Viscount Amleigh, a most excellent young man, much commended in the war. However, later a letter was received from a woman claiming to have been secretly married to the earl, which made her children, a son and a daughter, legitimate."

"Lady Belle!" Clara exclaimed with delight.

"She was titled?" Lucy asked.

Aunt Mary smirked. "Only in her own mind, dear. In the world's eyes she was, I regret the word, a trollop. Despite having been born into respectable circumstances, she lived most of her life in an unsanctified relationship with a tavern keeper called Melchisadeck Clyst."

"What a fascinating name," Lucy said, beginning to enjoy this story.

"I do not approve of such names."

"Isn't it from the Bible, Aunt?"

"This one was not," her aunt said, with sublime neglect of logic. "Not only was he a tavern keeper, but he was eventually exposed as a smuggler. Yes, it's true! He was caught and transported more than a year ago, and the shameless hussy followed him."

"She was transported, too? Are you teasing me, Aunt? This sounds all too like a play."

"There's to be a play!" Clara exclaimed. "I can't wait

to see it. A wicked lord, a dashing smuggler, and a fair lady much abused."

"Much abused, indeed," said Aunt Mary with a sniff. "She brought all her problems upon herself, including her removal to Botany Bay. It is apparently possible for people to pay their way to the penal colony, but her wishing to do so says everything about her."

"That she was driven by the truest, deepest love!" Lucy declared, much in Clara's manner, enjoying herself.

"To return to the earldom," Aunt Mary said firmly, "upon receipt of her claim, which I gather was backed with details of the marriage—"

"A clandestine one," Clara interrupted. "On Guernsey. I didn't know people could elope to the Channel Islands as well as Scotland, but it would have been much more convenient from Devon, so the earl wasn't completely insane."

"I do not approve of clandestine marriages," Aunt Mary stated. "But, alas, they are legal for the purpose of a title. Viscount Amleigh nobly stepped aside in favor of the earl's estate steward."

Clara clasped her hands in delight. "It's like Cinderella, isn't it?"

Lucy could think of many ways in which it wasn't, but didn't argue. "And now the dubious earl has come to London? Raised in a tavern? He must be sadly ill at ease in society."

"I fear so," Aunt Mary said. "He will be seeking a rich bride, of course. One with impeccable breeding to counteract his own."

"And we will see him at last," Clara said, sounding too much like a huntsman after a deer. "We were sadly out of Town when he appeared to give testimony about the situation last August."

"Everyone is out of Town in August," Aunt Mary said,

as if feeling the need to defend against a fault. She turned a page, ending that subject. "Mrs. Colchester has a son. She must be greatly relieved after four girls. And Mrs. Storbury, also, though I do believe the marriage was in December."

Clearly Aunt Mary did not approve. What a remarkable talent, Lucy thought, to be able to remember the dates of marriages so as to detect sin.

Lucy set another stitch while reviewing the story of the poor Earl of Wyvern. She pitied him, but his arrival might eclipse the scandal that surrounded her own story. At events over the past few days her resemblance to her mother had been noted by some of the older ladies. That had stirred memories of the scandal that had been attached to her own character. People were now seeking both the taint of the City in her and signs of inherited folly.

She'd even overheard a few upsetting remarks about "poor Alice Stanley" as if her mother had ended up in a workhouse. It had been a struggle not to point out that her mother had been happy all her days and had ended up richer than the lot of them rolled into one. She'd managed to keep to Silly Lucinda.

She was trying her hardest to make a success of this exploration of the ton. She hadn't expected it to be so hard.

Her first night had been a quiet one at home, during which her aunt had instructed her on the particular etiquette of the beau monde. That had been interesting, but the subsequent recitations from the poetry of Sebastian Rossiter had been less so. At least if anyone mentioned him, she'd know what they were talking about.

On the next night, the Wednesday, her aunt had taken her to a musical evening while Clara had gone with a party of friends to Almack's. Lucy definitely wanted to attend the holy of holies at least once, so that was added incentive to appear a mindless epitome of propriety.

Last night they had attended two routs and a choral evening hosted by Lady Cholmondely in her grand mansion. It had definitely been glittering. Lucy had enjoyed herself until she'd been pestered by an idiotic gentleman who thought he was a poet and had declaimed some clumsy lines in her honor.

Lord Stevenhope had been only one of a number of suitors, so the word was out about her dowry. She'd also been the victim of unctuous kindness from some ladies clearly wishing to secure her for an improvident brother or son. She'd managed to retain both feather-wittedness and bland sweetness, but she was surprised not to have chipped her teeth from clenching them.

Tonight was the Countess of Charrington's ball. Lucy had high hopes of her first grand ball, but there'd be even more bothersome gentlemen there and she didn't know how to deal with them without being blunt.

Aunt Mary put aside the newssheet. "Nothing else of interest. Let's consider the new invitations, Clara."

Clara eagerly went for them and she and her mother sat side by side on the sofa, absorbed in weighing the appeal of balls, dance parties, musical evenings, lectures, Venetian breakfasts and charitable benefits. Aunt Mary recorded their choices in her book, which made Lucy think of her pink journal, as yet without a word in it.

This business of the invitations was a daily ritual and she thought she now had the measure of it. She rose and excused herself, and received only a murmur in response. With any luck, they might not notice her absence for as much as a half hour. She went quickly upstairs to her bedroom and soon inhaled the tranquility of solitude.

Truly, if returning home was a bearable possibility, she would admit defeat. Her aunt and cousin could drive her mad inside the house, and her suitors were spoiling her pleasure when she went out. She had always detested insincere flattery, and she felt sure most were inspired only by her wealth, but sincere admiration was even worse when she had no plans to wed.

She'd already had to reject one offer of marriage. Sir Mallory Outram was only a little older than herself, and both sensitive and overblown. She'd met him on Wednesday, and on Thursday he'd declared his love. She thought he believed it at that moment. When she'd gently said they would not suit he'd claimed she'd broken his heart.

She'd protested, as sweetly as she could, that no one's heart was endangered in a day. He'd cited her parents' marriage, the wretch, and insisted she must share their natures. He'd even offered to elope, if that was to her taste.

Oh, she'd wanted to shake him!

She still did.

Then she remembered her journal. She finally had the opportunity to record some of the idiocies and irritations.

She opened the door and listened. Her aunt and cousin were still happily assessing one event against another. She closed the door again, took a key from her trinket box, and unlocked her small desk. She took out the pink book and a pencil, sat, and opened it to the first page.

She recorded her arrival and her surprise at having to share a room. How much she disliked it. How absurd were her aunt's edicts. She wrote of drinking tea in fine company where people rarely had anything sensible to say, and of a drive in the park where the beau monde thronged to see and to be seen. She recorded the folly of the gentlemen she'd encountered thus far, such as Outram and Stevenhope.

She turned the page.

Could she recall any of Stevenhope's lines?

Plump cherries set in marble skin
With pearly teeth lodged shyly deep within . . .

"Are you all right, Lucinda?"

Lucy started and covered the page with a hand. "Yes, of course!"

"What's that? A journal? How interesting." But then Clara stared. "Lucy, is that *poetry*?"

She'd not covered Stevenhope's lines quickly enough. What could she say? How to explain writing them down?

"Never say you're a poetess, cousin?"

Clearly it was appalling, but better to confess that than to recording the folly of others. "I admit it. But a very bad one. Please don't ask me to share any of it yet."

It seemed a babble of nonsense to her, but Clara said, "Of course not! Mama and I understand the requirements of the muse."

"You do?"

"Sebastian Rossiter," Clara reminded her.

"Ah, yes," said Lucy, mystified.

"He lived not far from us in Surrey. He lived quietly with his beloved family, but occasionally he would attend a social event and honor those present with a reading. He often said how important tranquility was for his muse."

Lucy circled this, seeking a trap, but didn't find one. Frightened of shattering the precious opportunity, she plaintively said, "It is, it is. . . ."

Clara backed away, whispering, "I will leave you in tranquility, cousin. . . ."

A moment later Lucy heard her running along the corridor crying, "Mama! Mama! Lucinda is a poetess!"

Lucy sank her head in her hands, shaking with laughter. What had she done now?

When she'd overcome hilarity and wiped her eyes, she began to hope. As a poetess, would she be allowed time alone rather than being invaded by people concerned that she was at death's door?

She opened the book again, but then realized that the merest glance at the first page would see prose. How was she going to keep up the pretense when she could be interrupted at any moment?

Could she write her observations and thoughts in the appearance of verse? That merely meant in shorter lines.

As an experiment she transcribed some of what she'd written onto a new page.

> *There is a spare bedroom here,*
> *So it's most unfair.*
> *I can't imagine what evil might arise*
> *From solitary sleeping,*
> *But if there is any, Cousin Jeremy is exposed to it.*

It was working!

> *Cousin Jeremy is as much a chatterer*
> *As Aunt Mary and Clara, but less often home,*
> *Being out in a striped waistcoat*
> *And monstrous cravat, doing foolish things.*
> *Aunt Mary enjoys scandals,*
> *Perhaps because they allow her to show superiority*
> *Through disapproval, and that's because*
> *Lord Caldross is not quite as he should be.*
> *What a lot one learns*
> *When living under the same roof as others.*

Now, could she write original thoughts in the form?

> *I do believe that I have found the way*
> *To enjoy some sweet tranquility every day.*

She frowned at the rhyme. There was no need to go to extremes, but the plan was working.

She used her small knife to carefully cut out the first page. She folded it and hid it in her desk. Her book would be entirely in poetic form.

"Thank you, Sebastian Rossiter. May you be truly with the angels now."

After a tentative tap on the door, Clara came in. "I apologize for interrupting you, Lucinda, but it's time we prepared for our morning visits."

Lucy could smile in true good humor. "Of course it is, and the muse has done with me for now."

She locked the book away in her desk, but put the key in her pocket. She'd find a secure hiding place, for despite her relatives' reverence for poets, she'd lay no money on them being able to resist trying to get a glimpse of her inspired verses.

That evening Lucy had another period of privacy.

They were all preparing for the Charrington ball, and a hairdresser had come to attend them. Lucy's hair had needed little, for he'd only had to gather it into a knot and secure the Grecian tiara she was to wear. Clara's hair was a mightier work requiring pomade and curling irons. As that was taking place in Aunt Mary's room Lucy took out her journal to record some more tidbits and thoughts.

> *Aunt Mary normally holds a rout*
> *To fulfill her social obligations.*
> *This year, of course, Clara must have a ball*
> *So assembly rooms have been booked.*
> *Not Almack's, though they are for hire*
> *Except on sacred Wednesdays.*
> *Will I achieve the entrée soon on a Wednesday*
> *If I maintain Silly Lucinda at all times?*
> *Perhaps not, being a Cit.*
> *I have heard that word used,*
> *Despite my mother's birth*
> *And my aunt's sponsorship.*
> *A Cit, with the T spat as it is spoken.*

Her lead broke, and she realized she was angry. She wouldn't give them the satisfaction. She sharpened the pencil, then locked everything away, choosing happier thoughts.

She was going to a ton ball, one hosted by a countess, no less, and a countess who had been a poet's inspiration. She anticipated opulence beyond reason, extravagance without restraint, and expanses of fabulous jewelry.

For her true social debut she'd chosen a gown in a silky opalescent material, which was now ornamented with golden beads and fringing and cut wide on the shoulders.

She had some fine jewels inherited from her mother, but her parents had never flaunted their wealth, and she suspected that the ton would be watching for some vulgar display. So she'd chosen a parure of delicate gold set with topaz and diamond chips, which wasn't costly but glittered delightfully under candlelight. Instead of the matching bandeau for her hair she was wearing a golden Grecian headband that had been a favorite of her mother's. She touched it, for luck, and to be sure it was secure.

Clara rushed back and stared at Lucy. "You look magnificent!"

"You look lovely, too," Lucy said, and it was true.

Clara's tightly dressed hair improved her, and she sparkled with excitement. She was soon dressed in a moss green gown overlaid with spider gauze that suited her coloring, and then she added pearls.

Lucy wondered if she should wear pearls for her ton debut. She had a magnificent string. Too magnificent, she realized, and she was hardly a miss in her first season. She took stock in the long mirror, fluttering her golden lace fan.

"Perhaps that gown is just a little too low?" Clara said hesitantly.

A good portion of Lucy's upper breasts showed. She

pushed away misgivings. "This isn't my social debut, Clara. I'm twenty-one years old."

"That's true. The gentlemen will positively swarm you, I'm sure."

Lucy smiled, but the word "swarmed" made her think of changing into something more demure. No, because the true appeal was her money. Even one of her plain gowns wouldn't deter the fortune hunters.

Her mind slid back to Winsom's. Had her country gentleman returned to his boggy acres? Despite all her willpower, she hadn't been able to avoid looking for him when traveling through crowded streets, and even at social events, where he'd never be. Of course she hadn't seen him, and she refused to be disappointed by that.

She turned her mind to the delights to come and took a few dancing steps in front of the long mirror. Her golden slippers, jewels, and Grecian headband glittered in the candlelight and all her golden fringing swayed.

She was ready to sparkle at her first ton ball!

Three streets away, Susan came to inspect David.

"I wish it were possible to capture you instantly in a portrait. Aunt Miriam would be in alt to see you so elegant."

He smiled at her. "I could say the same to you."

"She's grown accustomed to me playing the fine lady."

For most of their lives Susan had been careless about fashion, but now she did her best to live up to her station as a viscountess. Tonight she was wearing a fine bronze striped gown with half a yard of flouncing around the hem and shoulders that seemed ready to slide off, which seemed to be the latest device to drive men mad.

Her brown hair was almost entirely concealed by an ivory turban cockaded with a sprig of bronze flowers set with glittering stones. He knew they were paste and not diamonds only because Con couldn't afford jewels of that size. The Viscountcy of Amleigh was only comfortably prosperous, even if it was far more prosperous than his earldom. If there had ever been family jewels, they'd disappeared, entail and legalities be damned.

"You do look very handsome, David. Miss Potter won't be able to resist."

"I pray you're right, for then I won't have to do this for long." He turned to the mirror. "I feel like a shopkeeper playing tricks to fool customers into buying inferior goods. This isn't me."

The operation to remove the creasing at the waist of his jacket had pinched it in. It was the latest style, but he thought it looked ridiculous. He was wearing the essential black pantaloons, but had been allowed to retain his old dancing shoes, even if he hardly recognized them with such a high shine. His hair had been severely cropped by a master in what was called a Caesar.

"That hairstyle makes you look formidable," she said. "You should keep it. It will help you cow the Horde—especially when you glower like that."

That made him laugh. "I assure you, I won't dress like this back home, not even to rule the world. This cravat seems likely to strangle me."

"Other men survive," she said unsympathetically. "And by fashionable standards, it's quite modest."

"Only because I fought off all comers."

She came over to adjust the pearl-headed pin that fixed the starched folds in place. "Your twenty-first birthday present. Uncle Nathaniel and Aunt Miriam could never have imagined you'd end up an earl."

And I wish their imaginings had been true. But he managed not to say it. "At least the fashion is for limited ornament for the male. I can get away with just the signet ring."

She looked at the red coral engraved with a dragon.

"Con never wore that. He was as reluctant as you." She kissed his cheek. "Thank you."

Of course she understood.

"Let's get to it," he said, picking up his cloak, hat, and gloves. "What if Miss Potter doesn't admire the latest style? Perhaps a City lady prefers something simpler."

"Unlikely." Susan linked arms as they left the room. "I met her at Mrs. Gilbert's yesterday afternoon and she was dressed in very fine style. A large pendant pearl, smart green half boots, and two rows of Vandyke lace around her hem that must have cost a fortune."

"She's going to beggar me through haberdashery?"

"You could see it as bringing a rich dowry of trimmings."

"I'd rather spend her money on trimming hedges. Is she as featherbrained as reported?"

"She's certainly no bluestocking," she said as they went downstairs. "Because I know your requirements, I tested her a little. I dangled the topic of parliamentary reform and she responded as if she scarcely knew what Parliament was. She became more animated when the talk turned to bonnets, but when some ladies compared the cost of feathers with the cost of silk flowers it was as if they spoke Greek." At the bottom of the stairs she frowned at him. "Are you sure you could bear that, my dear?"

"She sounds perfect."

To a depressing degree.

As David went with Susan and Con out to the carriage, his mind slid back to the lady of the bookshop. He shouldn't allow that brief encounter into his mind, but he seemed to have no barriers against it. He'd even found himself en route to Winsom's yesterday and only just managed to turn back.

He knew his duty, and that his tastes played little

part in it. He wouldn't marry a woman he disliked for he'd not be able to disguise that, which would be misery for both of them. But if Miss Potter was tolerable, he'd win her and her money, and then be the best husband he could.

Chapter 8

The Amleigh carriage joined the line in front of Lady Charrington's house, where he'd have to face the beau monde en masse for the first time. Many would doubt his right to be there, and some might even be hostile. Even though his mother truly had married the Mad Earl, David represented flagrant, unrepentant immorality by one born high enough to know better.

They joined the queue to go upstairs and were soon warmly greeted by Charrington and his wife, whose simple, good-natured smile seemed a contrast to her husband's polished style. David took it as evidence that couples didn't have to be alike to be happy.

Music was playing, but not yet for dancing, and so he strolled around with Con and Susan, exchanging greetings with those he knew and being introduced to others, especially ladies. He tried to sense the atmosphere as he would the winds. He'd have to be dead not to feel the attention focused on him, but he didn't detect outrage. He was entertainment for a jaded world and could only hope the interest would fade.

"Do you see Miss Potter?" he asked Susan.

"No. But there's Maria Vandeimen. I don't think you met her niece on one of your visits to our area. Her first husband's niece. Natalie's as well-dowered as Miss Potter, but don't try your luck there unless you can honestly profess love. Van and Maria would have your guts."

David recognized a warning. When he was introduced, he understood why. Miss Florence wasn't at all beautiful, being short and plump with nondescript hair, but she was pure delight. Despite still being young, she sparkled with joie de vivre and confidence and seemed well disposed to all. She deserved complete adoration.

After a few minutes of conversation, Susan nudged him. "Miss Potter has arrived."

David turned, to see a cluster of men encircling two women. Miss Potter must be the shorter one, for the taller was brown haired, but all he could see of his thirty thousand pounds were some blond curls and a golden headdress.

"As you'll note, you have competition," Susan said. "Come, I'll introduce you."

David turned away. "I don't think so. She'll not be impressed by another panting hound."

"Then how do you plan to meet her? I doubt her hounds will leave her alone."

"I must retreat to plan a strategy."

Despite her protests, he went in search of privacy and found it in the room put aside for men who wished to smoke a pipe. This early in the night, no one was using it.

At the tailor's Vandeimen had suspected he would turn tail and run, and here already the accusation could prove true. It was one thing to devise a coolheaded plan to marry a stranger for her money. It was quite another to carry it through when faced with a real person.

Miss Lucinda Potter was here in the flesh, but as her father had pointed out, she would expect to be wooed. David wasn't sure he could make convincing advances to a woman about whom he cared so little.

Or if an honorable man should.

*   *   *

Clara had been right—Lucy was being swarmed. As a consequence, she was close to losing her temper.

The clustering was ridiculous and she feared it was making her ridiculous, especially when the men began to vie with one another. Lord Launceston claimed she outshone every lady present, which was hardly likely to make her popular. Outram admired her tiara in gushing terms and declared her a goddess. Stevenhope then crowned her the Gilded Aphrodite and attempted a stanza on the theme.

She wanted to snap at all of them, but to keep to her persona, she could only be flustered. When Outram and Stevenhope began to quarrel over who had first claimed her to be a goddess, she dismissed both for distressing her.

Two down, eight to go.

In an attempt to disperse the rest, she chose a partner for the first set. Sir Harry Winter seemed a sensible man, but the tactic failed. Most hovered on, demanding the second.

Lord Northcliff asked Clara for the first dance, which improved Lucy's opinion of him, but that was doubtless why he did it. All the other young ladies must be wishing her in Hades, which is where she wished the men. For every one that left, a new one arrived.

When her cousin Jeremy whispered, "Lucinda—a word with you," she stepped aside with relief, though she couldn't imagine what he wanted.

Jeremy was of an age with her, but much younger in every other way. He looked ridiculous in his wasp-waisted jacket, which required a corset, worn with an enormous cravat of blue-and-yellow-striped satin. His hair was dressed to stand on end, so with his wide, panicked eyes, he looked as if he'd had a fright.

"What's amiss?" she asked. "Is it Aunt Mary?"

"No, no. It's Stevenhope and Outram. They've gone mad."

"What are those idiots doing now? Truly, I'm ready to *shoot* one of them!"

"They're going to save you the trouble. They plan to shoot each other."

"A *duel*? Over me? You can't be serious!"

"Am. Were naming seconds when I came to find you."

"I'll have their guts for garters. Where are they?"

"Down that corridor over there." Jeremy seized her arm. "You can't interfere."

"Then why come to tell me?"

"Perhaps mother—"

"Would have a fit of the vapors and your father's not here."

Lucy tried to think of some other gentleman to help her but found none. She'd not involve any of her unwanted suitors in this.

"Take me there—and stop looking like a rabbit heading for the pot."

She needed to hurry, but made sure she and Jeremy moved around the room at a pace in harmony with the glittering crowd, waving away any suitor who came close. She tried to look as if she hadn't a care in the world, but she was seething. A duel could ruin her.

Jeremy led the way into a quiet corridor. "They've gone," he said with relief.

But Lucy could hear a raised voice from a room and went that way. Jeremy grabbed her again. "That's the gentlemen's smoking room!"

"I won't choke on the fumes." She pushed through the half-open door snapping, "Gentlemen, stop this madness!"

But then she realized three men were present, not just two, and that it was the third who was speaking.

Who was . . .

Could it really be?

The man from the bookshop? There was nothing of the country about him now. He'd glanced at her once, but not interrupted his reprimand.

". . . can only bring a lady's reputation into question, as well as risking both life and liberty for the most foolish of reasons. Be grateful this has gone no further."

The two rivals took the implied dismissal like schoolboys. Sir Mallory slipped out of the room sheepishly, even murmuring an apology to Lucy as he passed. Stevenhope stalked out, trying to pin her with one of his fierce, Byronic looks. But he went.

Lucy was tempted to scurry after them, but her pride wouldn't permit it—and she was transfixed by it being *him*.

The honey-brown hair was now impeccably barbered, and his dark evening clothes were in the latest style, but she recognized those blue-gray eyes in that tanned face, even though they were now fixed on her coldly.

"The Gilded Aphrodite, I believe," he said.

She flicked open her fan in defense. "Please, sir, if I must be a goddess, let it at least be a golden one."

"Appropriate, Miss Potter, given the size of your dowry."

"Which you know because you consulted a list of the largest dowries available and then lurked near my home. A despicable hunt, wouldn't you say?"

"Gold endures whilst other attributes crumble." She was about to let loose another cutting comment when he looked her over. "Quite a transformation, ma'am."

The wretch! She looked him over in exactly the same way. "Are you in any position to complain of it, sir? You were dressed simply in Winsom's."

"I had a reason. Had you?"

"Yes!" She took a steadying breath. "Given that you're after my fortune, sir, I'd have expected at least an attempt at courtesy."

"I assure you, Miss Potter, I have no designs on your thirty thousand pounds."

"When you know the exact sum?" Beneath her sneer, she was hurt. She didn't want to marry him, but hadn't expected to be dismissed like a leaf stuck to his shoe. "I can't imagine why you're being so unpleasant, sir, but I'll take my leave." She paused at the door and turned back. "In courtesy, I suppose I must thank you for preventing an embarrassment."

"You see men risking death over you as merely embarrassing?"

Lucy's cheeks were flaming and she hated it. The heat was fury, but he might see it as shame. "Dueling is ridiculous. Such madness should have died with the periwig."

"Or ladies should resist dressing in a way designed to drive men mad."

"By that argument gentlemen should wear smocks and gaiters. As I suppose you do, when tramping your boggy acres!"

His lips twitched, and a dangerous brightness flickered in his eyes.

She fled.

Jeremy was hovering outside, open-mouthed. She grabbed his sleeve and steered him back toward the ballroom. "Why didn't you tell me someone else was involved?"

"I didn't. . . . He wasn't. . . . Who was he?"

"I don't know."

"Sounded as if you knew him."

"Nonsense, and you're not to speak of this, Jeremy. Mind my words."

"Don't know why my mother and sister think you're such a sweet little thing," he muttered.

Oh, Lord.

She'd smashed Silly Lucinda to smithereens. She could only hope Jeremy would put her lapse down to temporary insanity.

*   *   *

David watched Miss Lucinda Potter leave, banners flying, taking his hopes and plans with her.

He'd intervened because those idiots were about to make a scandal of the lady he already considered his. When someone had burst in he'd registered only glittering gold. When he'd finally seen that it was the lady from the bookshop, he'd been shocked into anger.

She accused *him* of deception? Why had she been in that bookshop dressed like an impoverished dowd? Why was she now trying to convince the world she was a feather-witted chit? She was bold, clever, and apparently devious to the bone.

Nicholas Delaney walked in. David noted crossly that he was allowed to wear evening clothes that were comfortably years out of date.

"I heard there was a contretemps," Nicholas said.

"Is the story burning through the place already?"

"Only some wisps of smoke, already being smothered. Miss Potter?"

"Two young idiots coming to pistols over her."

"I doubt Outram and Stevenhope are any younger than you."

"They acted it."

"Did your intervention help or harm your cause?"

"Killed it. It won't do."

"Why not?"

"She's sharp as a thorn and blunt as a cudgel."

"Brings to mind a spiked mace. How are your hopes dead?"

"Would you marry a spiked mace?"

Nicholas's lips twitched. "Eleanor wouldn't like the description, but quite possibly. There's nothing amiss with a forceful wife."

"Is there not? You know my requirements. Miss Potter wouldn't miss an ant on the floor, never mind a husband oddly missing on moonless nights. And once she knew, she'd wield that cudgel."

"Rather extreme for an ant. I keep telling Eleanor that she should create a Society of Lady Viragos. Miss Potter sounds like a prime candidate."

"It's no laughing matter. She's an ardent opponent of smuggling."

"You discussed that?" David could see all kinds of speculation on his friend's face. When he didn't respond, Nicholas said, "Back to the ballroom with you. You need to scotch any rumors and pursue other honey pots. Lady Maud Emberley is present and doubtless available to dance."

David had already seen poor Lady Maud, seated beside her grim mother, looking as if her mind was completely vacant. He felt a strong desire to punch Nicholas Delaney in the nose.

When Lucy approached the ballroom, Outram pounced.

"I am most terribly sorry, Miss Potter. Got carried away by my ardent devotion."

Remember Silly Lucinda.

"You distressed me most terribly, Sir Mallory. I have rejected your offer and must beg you to respect my decision."

"You must marry someone, Miss Potter. Why not me?"

"You know we would not suit." When Outram looked ready to persist, she held up a hand and murmured, "Please," in a manner worthy of the most distressed heroine. "There are many young ladies here who are more worthy than I. Ladies who'd walk on air if you asked them to dance."

"But it's you I love!" he declared, grabbing her hand.

"It cannot be!" she exclaimed, snatching it free and escaping, aware of people nearby sniggering.

"Outram's not too bad a fellow," Jeremy said.

She unclenched her hands before she ruined her fan. "I don't love him. It wouldn't be fair."

"He wouldn't mind. Needs to marry money. Pockets to let."

She was saved by Lord Stevenhope stepping into her path, if "saved" was the right word.

He took his poetic stance.

My Aphrodite, here I stand to make my plea.
If you desire I will do so on my knee.
If I transgressed, 'twas only from my heart,
Compelled to blood by my desperate lover's part.

Lucy heard someone choke on a laugh.

When Stevenhope reached for her hand she stepped out of reach. "Please, my lord, your behavior distressed me greatly. I fear I was to blame."

Instead of protesting, he nodded. "There is perhaps a flightiness in you, Miss Potter. I'll say no more for now except, be mine!"

Lucy would have loved to vent every angry thought in her mind on him, but instead she turned her head away, letting it droop a little on her neck—an action she'd noted in other young ladies and which seemed to signal admired spinelessness. Hesitant breathiness worked, too.

"I must ask you to desist, my lord. . . . Perhaps in time . . ." She went all the way and put a hand to her head. "But you must not press me now. . . ."

It worked. He spoke in a hushed tone. "I understand you, my goddess. Your frailty becomes you. I will compose a sonnet in its honor."

He bowed, retreating as he did so, as if she were royalty. Lucy struggled with giggles, bringing up her fan as concealment, but the amusement of others killed any urge to laugh. Her suitors' behavior would be on everyone's lips, but some of the sniggering would spread to her.

Worse, their apologies would have everyone wondering about the offense. That could lead to gossip about the duel, and like the Winsom man, the ton would decide it was all her fault.

For being pretty.

For having a rich father.

For sporting a low bodice.

For breathing!

A convent in Italy was beginning to appeal. The wilderness of Canada might be even better. She couldn't endure the speculating eyes and hurried in search of the ladies' room. There must be one somewhere and she could hide.

Clara caught up with her. "You can't run away, Lucinda. Will they be out at dawn?"

"Is Jeremy blabbing it all over?"

"He only told me. But I think Outram said something. You look upset."

"Of course I'm upset! How can everything become tangled so quickly?"

"Perhaps a fairy's taken a hand, like Puck in *A Midsummer Night's Dream*."

"I certainly feel like poor Helena, bewildered recipient of unwelcome devotion."

"Jeremy said you marched in on the duelers like a battleship."

Lucy wanted to protest the scrambled metaphors, but she was more concerned with what Clara made of her scrambled personality.

"I get overly bold when angry."

Clara giggled, not apparently making much of anything. "I wish I'd seen it! But all the devotion can't be unwelcome when you seek a husband."

"I'm waiting for true love," Lucy declared grimly.

"Of course, but how will you find it if you don't allow men to pay court?"

It was a surprisingly good point. "I only wish they'd court me in smaller numbers."

"You could grant vouchers to the select few as the patronesses of Almack's do."

That made Lucy laugh. "What a tempting notion. How many should I allow at a time? Three?"

"Too few. Five at least."

"No more than that, however."

"The more the merrier as far as I'm concerned. The disappointed gentlemen turn to me."

Lucy heard no edge to the comment. "Then I shall welcome them en masse. But remember, they're all fortune hunters."

"No, they're not. All of them would like to marry a rich dowry, for what man wouldn't, but only some are desperate for funds. Stevenhope's well-to-do, as are Northcliff and Sir Harry."

"Never say there are lists showing gentlemen's fortunes."

Clara frowned in puzzlement. "Lists? One just knows such things."

No, one didn't.

"Come," Clara said, linking arms. "You must return to the dancing or people will wonder." As she steered Lucy back toward the music she asked, "Who was the man who tore a strip off your warring suitors? Jeremy said you spoke as if you knew him."

Damn Jeremy. "We met once. For mere moments. He seemed to be a country gentleman. I don't know how he comes to be here."

"Most of the men here are country gentlemen in season."

Another thing Lucy had forgotten.

She'd expected the ton to be a different world, but she'd not realized how different. People in the City lived most of the year in one home. Some of the wealthiest had villas on the river for the hottest months, or visited a sea resort for a while. They might take a tour of scenic wonders such as the Peak District, or even the distant Lake District, but not for long. City men needed to pay attention to their businesses, and commerce took no holidays.

The beau monde, however, flitted from country estates to Town elegance and in-between times to seaside resorts, Shire hunting boxes, and Scottish moors. Such a wandering life.

"Perhaps your champion won a lottery," Clara said as they approached the ballroom. "Do you remember that corn trader who won one and purchased an estate? His antics were the talk of the Town."

Lucy didn't know anything of the man, but clearly he'd been another outsider and thus a figure of fun. Had he run back to his own world as she would like to do? She'd never liked the idea of everyone "knowing their place," but perhaps there was a point to the saying. It wasn't pleasant to be out of place.

"In we go," Clara said. "Any talk will pass, especially as the Earl of Wyvern is here."

"As long as he doesn't pester me."

"He probably will, being in need of a fortune. But the main point is that his notorious presence will wipe your adventures from everyone's mind."

"Then hail the arriving earl!" Lucy said, stepping back into the nest of vipers.

Chapter 9

If there was talk, it hadn't deterred her suitors. Five converged. She was happy to be able to remind them that the first dance was promised to Sir Harry, and even happier to see him coming to claim it, allowing her to escape.

"You look a little distressed, Miss Potter," he said as they walked onto the dancing floor. "Anything I can do to help?"

"You heard about the duel," she said with a sigh. "It's all smoothed away."

"Good. Nonsense like that should be a thing of the past."

"My thoughts entirely, sir."

Here was another admirable man, and he was handsome enough in a stolid way. Potential husbands weren't in short supply in the ton, but she didn't want to marry anyone. Was it so unreasonable to want to enjoy the social delights and dance until dawn without unpleasant repercussions?

What was needed was a signal. If a lady wore a flower behind her right ear, she was open to proposals. A flower behind the left ear would warn suitors away. That whimsy melted her irritation and she smiled as they took their places.

But then she saw the Winsom man joining the line

dance, partnering a handsome brunette wearing magnificent rubies. He should have looked out of place at her side, but he didn't.

"Who's the lady with the rubies?" she asked Sir Harry.

He glanced down the line. "Lady Arden. Arden's the heir to Belcraven."

That clearly meant a great deal, but to Lucy it simply reinforced his deceptiveness. He'd said he was a simple country gentleman, but as such he should be far from the orbit of dukedoms. He smiled at something Lady Arden said as if they were on easy terms. Lucy wanted to ask Sir Harry who he was, but resisted. She didn't know what to make of him in this new incarnation, but he was definitely to be avoided like the plague.

The musicians keyed that the dance was about to start. Sir Harry bowed as she curtsied, and she could escape thoughts in the dance, among opulence beyond reason, extravagance without restraint, and expanses of fabulous jewelry.

Sir Harry proved to be a good dancer, and the ladies and gentlemen she intertwined with all seemed amiable. Lucy relaxed into enjoyment—until she realized a problem. In a longways dance she would dance with all the men at some point.

She would have to take a turn with him.

She prepared herself, and when the time came, acted exactly as she had with other men, briefly meeting his eyes, smiling, stepping, joining hands.

Suppressing a shiver when his hand briefly touched her waist.

How could such a connection be fierce as fire?

She couldn't help but stare at him.

Did he look as startled?

Thank heavens the dance sent her safely on her way. Safe until they would meet again as the dance progressed through its cycle, sending each couple up and down the line.

Avoid him like the plague. She certainly felt feverish. It wasn't a physical disease, however. It was a return of the effect she'd felt before—the affliction that had engulfed her parents.

If it had been like this, she could begin to understand why they had acted as they had. This was no force to be calmly reasoned away. It truly was a fever that would build with every encounter, and now she couldn't take comfort in never seeing him again.

But she could avoid and resist.

With every scrap of strength she possessed she would resist such a disastrous form of love.

David watched Miss Potter dance on, furious that he was still susceptible to her, even when he knew her true colors.

At a glance she was simply pretty, though she was doing her best to drive men mad with that low-cut gown that threatened to slide off her at any moment. He wouldn't have guessed that she'd have such a lush figure.

Her fatal attraction, however, came from something else, from the attributes that made her impossible—her intelligence, spirit, and quick wit.

Yes, she was a virago, but a magnificent one.

He had no doubt that if he'd not been there to stop those fools, she'd have ripped into them and sent them off with their tails between their legs.

Most men would see that as a fault, but he admired strong women. Susan was redoubtable, and his aunt Miriam, though a conventional lady, was rock solid when it came to anything that mattered. His mother was so far removed from feminine frailty as to fall off the edge, but he had to confess a part of him had always admired the way she'd faced up to a scandalized world and enjoyed life to the full.

As he progressed through the dance, he couldn't resist stealing glances at Miss Potter. Light on her feet, blond curls bouncing, sparkling gold from her slippers to her Grecian tiara. She was right. Those two had been dolts to call her gilded. She was a twenty-four carat goddess.

But not for him. He couldn't risk marrying a woman who could dazzle him so easily, and practice deception with such skill. A useful skill, perhaps, if she was in league with him, but disastrous if, as was more likely, she was horrified by his role as Captain Drake.

By the time the dance ended Lucy could understand the word "possessed." She could no longer resist.

Casually waving her fan, she asked Sir Harry, "The man dancing with Lady Arden. That isn't Lord Arden, is it?"

"Not at all. That's the new Earl of Wyvern."

Lucy needed a moment to understand his words. "Truly?"

"You think it unbelievable?"

"Only that some expected a clodhopper."

And he'd called her deceptive! In Winsom's he'd claimed to be a simple country gentleman—those exact words—and he'd looked the part. Yet here he was, an earl, dressed in fine style, at ease with a marchioness.

"Quite a surprise," Sir Harry was agreeing, "but not for me. I was introduced to him the other day at a shooting gallery. A decent shot, but not a patch on Middlethorpe, Austrey, and a few of the others he was with."

At ease with the great! Lords Marchampton, Launceston, and Worseley came jostling to beg for the next dance. Lucy fended them off—until she realized that she was waiting for the upstart earl to join them. He needed to marry a fortune after all, and she would relish turning him down.

He made no move, and she remembered him stating rudely that he had no interest in her. Now she could see why. It looked as if he was already partnered with a dumpy, frizz-haired chit.

Thoroughly out of temper, she chose Worseley, looking forward to meeting the deceitful Earl of Wyvern in the dance and showing by chilly distance that in her eyes he was a slug.

The dance, however, was an eight. Three circles of eight were forming in the long set of rooms and the slug was leading his partner into the set farthest away.

Lucy concentrated on Worseley, putting Lord Wyvern out of her mind. Too late she realized that Worseley was now convinced he was her choice! He even asked her for the next dance. Two dances in a row would be as good as a public announcement, so she gave him icy disapproval and chose Marchampton for the next, but she blamed the Earl of Wyvern for all her problems.

He'd returned his partner to an elegant lady. One Lucy recognized. Maria Celestin! She was a highborn lady who'd married a merchant, so she and Lucy's mother had been friends. That presented an excuse to go over and join the group.

Lucy firmly turned away. This was a crowded ball attended by hundreds. She could and would avoid the wretched man.

The next dance was the supper dance, and she chose Lord Northcliff. According to Clara, he wasn't a fortune hunter, and he had graciously danced with her cousin. After the dance, they went to the rooms set out for supper. There they joined Clara and her partner and Jeremy and his, a pretty young brunette called Clarabel Ponting. Lucy relaxed, but she didn't escape Wyvern entirely.

When the gentlemen went to get food for them, Miss Ponting gasped, "So handsome!"

Lucy didn't think she'd been able to gasp a word, even

at seventeen. She thought Jeremy a surprising cause for gasping admiration, but then learned her mistake.

Clara said, "Lord Wyvern," her eyes as bright. "He's delicious, isn't he? I wouldn't have expected it."

"An estate steward can't be handsome?" Lucy asked, irritated by the unfairness.

"Ruggedly handsome, perhaps," Clara said. "Not in such a polished way."

Miss Ponting leaned across the table, endangering the arrangement of flowers in the center. "Mama wants me to attract him," she hissed, "but I'd be too afraid. They called his father the Mad Earl!"

She could also exclaim in a whisper. What a lot of interesting skills the girl had.

"He doesn't seem to be deranged," Clara said, but uncertainly. She was looking beyond Lucy's shoulder, which told her where Wyvern had ended up. The enemy was at her back. The *deranged* enemy. If Lucy needed any more reasons to avoid Lord Wyvern, there was one. Blood will out, especially insanity.

The gentlemen returned with food. Lucy hoped for a change of topic, if only to horses or hunting, but they, too, were fascinated by the newest earl.

As Sir Harry had indicated, he'd been all around the gentlemen's part of Town, and even at a house party where noble gentlemen had enjoyed contests in shooting, riding, and fencing.

"Gentlemen still fence?" Lucy asked.

"For exercise only, Miss Potter," Northcliff said.

"Does Lord Wyvern fence?" Clara asked.

"Not that I know, Miss Fytch, but I saw him show himself very well at the quarterstaff."

"Isn't that a rather *lowly* weapon?" Lucy asked, spearing a piece of pickled herring with her fork.

"Say rather that it is an ancient one, Miss Potter, and thus to be admired. Like the bow and arrow."

"I'm very good with a bow and arrow." Miss Ponting fluttered her lashes at Jeremy. He would be a viscount one day. That must be the explanation.

Everyone began to discuss the possibility of an archery contest here in Town, which was a pleasant change of subject but made Lucy feel even more an outsider. She indulged in no arcane exercises, and nor did anyone she knew. She assumed some City men practiced with a pistol as many would carry one when traveling. Her father did. Quarterstaff, though? That was the long pole carried by medieval peasants who couldn't afford, or perhaps weren't allowed, something more lethal. Yet here, in this modern age, lords and dukes wielded it.

The beau monde should be the *monde fou*.

They were about to rise from the supper table when Stevenhope walked into the room, paper in hand.

"To Miss Potter!" he declaimed. "A sonnet in praise of the admirable frailty of a goddess!"

The whole room fell silent, and Lucy felt pinned in place like a butterfly in a collector's box.

The poem was worse than usual, packed with delicacy, sighing, and even fainting. She'd never fainted in her life!

He ended with:

Thus Aphrodite is a wilting bloom
To flourish soon as goddess of my drawing room.

He couldn't even get the rhythm right.

Lacking any alternative, Lucy said, "That was very touching, my lord."

"But will you marry me?"

She assumed a wilting pose. "You must not press me, my lord. I am quite overwhelmed."

"I will protect you!"

Lucy was aware of smirks all around—was he not?

"Please, my lord . . ."

He took what she assumed to be a tragic-lover stance. "I shall compose an epic, Miss Potter, on the subject of broken hearts."

He stalked out of the room and laughter and chatter broke free. Lucy had turned to watch his departure and her eyes clashed with Lord Wyvern's. He might as well have said it: *See how you drive men into making fools of themselves, you wicked woman.*

She turned away, seething, but made herself dally a while, smiling and talking to show she was unaffected by Stevenhope's idiocy. As soon as possible she murmured to Clara that she needed the ladies' room and they both left. Alas, Miss Ponting came with them, going on about how stupid Stevenhope was, but somehow implying that Lucy was, too.

The retiring room was busy, so there was no opportunity for private conversation, and indeed, what did she want to say? Her thoughts and observations were for her journal alone.

In poetic lines.

Heaven help her.

She survived the next few hours by concentrating fiercely on the dancing and not allowing herself to notice the Earl of Wyvern at all. However, as she rattled home just before dawn with her aunt, Clara, and Jeremy, the talk turned to Wyvern like a compass needle to north.

Her silence might be obvious, so eventually she said, "He seemed to favor a very ordinary young lady."

"Miss Florence," Aunt Mary said with a disapproving twitch of her nose. "Lady Vandeimen's niece, or to be precise, the niece of her late husband, Celestin. A merchant and, worse, a foreign one."

Lucy remembered now that Celestin had died. So Maria had married a lord, returning to her true world, as Lucy's father would put it. Had Maria's second marriage bolstered her father's obsession?

"The girl's fortunate that Maria Dunpott-Ffyfe made a more suitable marriage the second time around," her aunt went on. "If a marriage can be suitable when the husband is nearly ten years the wife's junior."

"My goodness!" Lucy said, genuinely startled.

"Quite," Aunt Mary said. "Be sure you do nothing so foolish."

Marry a lad of eleven? Lucy managed not to say it.

"A wild young man to boot. Lost his whole fortune at cards."

"I would have thought Maria too sensible for that." When her aunt showed surprise, Lucy had to explain that she knew Maria.

"Alice and she must have appreciated congenial company, situated as they were. Note, girls, that a lady takes the station of her husband, and folly can carry her into very uncongenial company."

Lucy couldn't resist a contradiction. "The Celestins lived in Mayfair, did they not? I assume they mingled with the ton?"

Aunt Mary's nose pinched even more. "She was a Dunpott-Ffyfe, and thus related to all our best families. Also, Celestin had already made his fortune when they wed."

Unlike my father, who was living in rooms over a warehouse.

A disturbing thought stirred. "Celestin was very rich. His niece is probably well dowered."

"Almost as well as you, dear," Aunt Mary said, not seeming to see any significance in it.

Lucy told herself there was none. She wasn't on the hunt for a husband, so she couldn't consider Natalie Florence a rival. And if she were on the hunt for a husband, the despicable Earl of Wyvern would be the last man she'd choose.

Maria Celestin had always seemed so composed and

mature, sleekly perfect in appearance and far above folly. Why on earth had she given herself and her fortune to a young wastrel in her second marriage? It had to be that madness called love.

Perhaps insane love had plunged Maria into her first marriage as well, for even a rich merchant had been a misalliance.

Maria was yet more proof that succumbing to irrational passions could lead to disaster.

Chapter 10

A long night's dancing had tired Lucy out, so she should have fallen asleep easily, but she lay as if on a bed of thistles, plagued by *him*.

The Earl of Wyvern.

A wyvern was a type of dragon, and there was something predatory about him.

He should indeed have been a clodhopper, or at least ill at ease, but instead he was every inch a ton beau comfortable with the great. She'd learned that the "heir to Belcraven" meant that the Marquess of Arden would one day be a duke, and his ruby-wearing wife had been Wyvern's first partner.

What had such a man been doing in Winsom's, disguised as a simple country gentleman?

Up to no good, that was sure, but apparently not after her dowry.

Why not? Everyone acknowledged that he was here to hunt a fortune.

Was he playing a deep game and pretending lack of interest in order to trick her in some way, like a merchant turning away from goods he wanted in order to make the other party more eager to bargain? That must be it. But was he expecting her to pursue him? He'd catch cold at that! But he was a very dangerous man. Dangerous in the way he'd dealt with Outram and Stevenhope. Dangerous in his ease in the highest reaches of the beau monde. Dangerous in the effect he could have on her.

No, she was secure because marriage, especially to a nobleman, would end any hope of involvement in trade. She would never risk it. The Countess of Wyvern, accepted by the men in the City. Laughable!

She woke heavy-eyed to hear various clocks striking the full twelve of noon. Finally, she was sleeping like a fashionable lady. Clara was still fast asleep, so Lucy slipped out of bed, put on her dressing gown, and went to her desk.

She would record her first grand ball for Betty in a letter. It was time to let her friend know how things were. She chose not to relate the shortcomings of her life here. Instead she offered a detailed description of the Earl of Charrington's fine house, including the rooms opened up for dancing and the decorations of plinths, urns, and flowers. She wished Betty were across the road so she could go to her and express all her confused irritation over the Earl of Wyvern. But perhaps that would be too revealing even for a friend. Some things were better not put into words at all.

She did share Clara's whimsy about giving suitors vouchers.

She's cleverer than she seems, and perhaps we were as silly at seventeen. When she steadies with age she'll probably be a sensible woman, and kinder-hearted than her mother. . . .

"What are you writing, Lucy? About the ball?"

Lucy twitched with embarrassment, as if Clara could read what she'd written. "A letter to a friend," she said, folding it. "Shall I ring for our maids?"

Not knowing she'd be sharing a room, she'd brought Hannah, which was proving to be awkward, though not when everyone was preparing for a significant event such as a ball. Aunt Mary had hinted that Lucy should send Hannah home, but she'd ignored that. Hannah would be enjoying being part of a ton house and why shouldn't she have some fun?

Clara's maid, Ann, responded to the bell, but then both returned. Ann had the washing water and Hannah carried the breakfast tray containing chocolate and sweet rolls. Perhaps they were sensibly combining their duties.

When she and Clara sat to their breakfast, Lucy asked, "What do we do today?"

"Morning visits and the theater, I think. Some routs before, of course. And company to dine. Associates of Father's. Dull company."

Dull was better than dangerous. A Wyvern-free day.

In that, she wasn't quite right. Everywhere they went people speculated about him.

He was surprisingly handsome.

He was surprisingly well-mannered.

He was surprisingly at ease with eminent friends.

Again, Lucy couldn't help but feel some sympathy for him. Probably some of these ladies had expected her, too, to be like the unfortunate corn merchant, completely out of place.

Then the speculations became odder.

"He was like a prince in waiting," Lady Christina Fanborough said to Clara and Lucy over tea at Mrs. Fox-Langley's. "Because the Mad Earl murdered any heir, he was concealed as a peasant until the day came for him to announce himself."

"Wasn't he the earl's estate manager?" Lucy asked.

Lady Christina gave her a reproachful look. "Concealed all the same. Or the earl would have murdered him, wouldn't he?"

Lady Christina flounced off, and Lucy looked to Clara in bewilderment.

"*The Peasant Earl*," Clara explained. "A novel. That's the exact plot."

"How does it end?"

"With him marrying his one true love, a shepherdess called Iphigenia."

"A shepherdess with a name like that? Surely not."

"She is, of course, the lost daughter of the king."

Clara's lips were twitching, and Lucy burst into laughter. She smothered it as an attack of coughing, but she wished she could share that story with . . .

Drat the man!

She was wishing she could share it with the simple country gentleman of Winsom's with whom she'd bantered so enjoyably, but that hadn't been the true man. He'd been an earl masquerading as a peasant. She was fully aware of the silliness of the thought, but she liked it. The Peasant Earl indeed.

That evening they went to the theater. This wasn't a novelty for Lucy as she had attended performances at various theaters all her life and her father had always rented a box. Then, however, she'd been anonymous. Now as soon as they took their seats she was aware of attention.

"I wish people wouldn't stare and comment," she said to Clara.

"It's what one does before a performance. Look, there's Lady Christina attended by Lord Wareham. Might it be a match? He must be more than ten years her senior."

To play her part, Lucy said, "I see Maria Vandeimen and Miss Florence, but without Lord Wyvern in attendance. Instead, Miss Florence has a dashing blond beau."

Clara giggled. "That's not her beau, Lucinda. It's Lord Vandeimen."

"Maria Celestin's husband?" Lucy couldn't keep the astonishment out of her voice. She'd gathered that Maria had married a young rake, but she'd not expected him to be quite so dashing and handsome. No wonder she'd been tempted.

But, she quickly reminded herself, how very, very foolish Maria had been to succumb.

The next day was Sunday, which by Aunt Mary's edict must be quiet and thoughtful. Lucy only wished that were the case. On the way to church and on the way home talk flowed like the Thames. Lucy wondered whether her hook-nosed uncle, slumped in his corner of the coach, had learned to be deaf to it.

At least the chatter wasn't all about Wyvern. After church they'd learned that there had been a scandalous masquerade on Friday during which two noblemen had fallen to fisticuffs over a doxy.

"I do not approve of masquerades," Aunt Mary said.

They had also heard that Lord Marchampton had lost ten thousand at hazard.

"Gaming is the work of the devil," Aunt Mary declared.

Lucy was in agreement with her there. If it ever came to marriage, Marchampton would be off her list.

Lord Howton was said to be bringing a crim con case against a Mr. Thrayne.

"I hope he wins enough to destroy the man," Aunt Mary said. "Of all things, I abhor a scoundrel seducing a lady from her duty."

If she were feeling foolhardy, Lucy would have asked if it could not have been the lady seducing the gentleman. Even in the Bible Delilah and Salome came to mind. Whichever the case, it was yet more evidence of the destructive power of love.

"A shame Miss Potter didn't attend our church," Susan said to David as they walked home, Con on her other side. "As she wasn't at Lady Wraybourne's last night, you've left the field clear for your rivals."

"Need better intelligence," Con said. "Spies in the household."

"This is not a laughing matter!" Susan protested. "Thirty thousand pounds."

"With a person attached," David said. "I'm not going to marry her."

Susan stopped. "Why not?"

"Because she's quick and clever—"

"Miss Potter?" she interrupted, astonished.

"And thus, deceitful."

As they walked on, he told them about the way she'd reacted to the duel, and also about the encounter in the bookshop.

"It's not a sin to dress plainly for a visit to a shop," Susan said. "I like her spirit."

"So might I if she were honest with it, but she'd still not be a suitable bride. She's active, forceful, and holds strong opinions on the Freetrade. I could hope she'd be too clever to betray a husband, but when she's so skilled at deception, I'd never be able to trust her."

"It does seem a shame," Susan said. "She could dupe a Preventive officer with ease. I think you should learn more about her before giving up hope."

David didn't attempt to express his deep sense of vulnerability where Lucinda Potter was concerned. "I can't afford to waste time on her. I need to settle this quickly, so I'll look more closely at Miss Tapler and Miss Rackman."

"There have to be any number of well-dowered ladies whirling around the ton. Not thirty thousand or even twenty, but well enough. Cast your net wider."

"Turning your nose up at merchants' daughters? What then of Miss Potter?"

"Don't be irritating. In her case I want you to take more time. Thirty thousand, David. I know you could use every penny."

"I don't know why Con hasn't strangled you by now."

She chuckled. "Because I'm always right!"

David looked at Con, but the besotted man showed no offense.

That should turn him scathing about the follies of love, but he knew it for the gift it was and envied those allowed it.

"Please, David," Susan said, manipulating now. "Give it a week at least. A week in which you pay serious court to Miss Potter. You might find that all will be well."

He knew her insistence came from caring, but also from guilt. If he led an unhappy life because he'd accepted the earldom, she'd feel the burden of it. When he agreed, it was because he wanted to try to make Susan happy.

But also from a weak hope that Miss Potter would prove honest and true, and safe for him to wed.

Chapter 11

Everyone retired early on Sunday night, but that meant that on Monday Lucy was awake early. She normally woke feeling freshly ready for the day, but today she felt sluggish. The tedious Sunday spent mostly sitting meant she hadn't fallen asleep easily, and she'd woken in the dead hours of the night remembering a dream of a church abuzz as a hive with scandal. Scandal about her mother and herself.

Buzz, buzz. Wicked folly.

Sting! She'll be like her mother.

Sting! She'd run off with a rascal. . . .

She'd lain awake in the dark fighting to dispel the nonsense, knowing it grew in some way from the wretched earl. She'd met Lord Wyvern twice. Three times if the two occasions at Lady Charrington's ball were counted separately. No one could tumble into perilous insanity in such a brief time.

That's what her mother had done, though. *Sting!*

Marriage, any marriage, would shatter her hopes. But it was what her father wanted for her. Marry her off. Get her out of his new home. His and Charlotte's home.

Buzz, buzz. Sting! Sting!

The house on Nailer Street would be more of a home to Charlotte's two daughters than to her. It would be entirely the home of Charlotte's future children, especially the eldest boy.

Who would in time inherit it.

And there was nothing she could do to stop that.

Nothing.

Nothing.

Nothing.

Now, in the morning light, the tormenting thoughts were only memories. That didn't mean they weren't true, however.

Monday. It had to be better than Sunday.

Surely they would flit about Town all day and dance until dawn and she wouldn't have to think about anything. Especially if she had the good fortune not to meet Wyvern.

Exasperated, she climbed out of bed and went to look out through a gap in the curtains. The window gave only a view of other houses, but the sky said it was a beautiful morning. That was what she needed. Fresh air and sunshine to drive away the dismals.

A glance at the clock told her it was only just ten. That would have been late at home, but here Clara could sleep on for hours. At home, she would go out into the garden to enjoy such a morning, but this house had only a yard at the back that ended with a high wall that separated it from a lane, then the backyards of a similar row of houses on the next street. The people who lived in these fashionable terraces seemed to feel no need for a garden. She supposed they had ample greenery on their country estates, and if they pined here, they visited one of the nearby parks.

The parks.

Lucy rang the bell, but she waited at the door to tell Hannah to be quiet about bringing the washing water so as not to wake Clara.

"I'll wear the mouse-brown traveling dress," she whispered as she washed as quietly as she could. "It's easy to get into. And the small bonnet."

"A bonnet, Miss Lucy?"

"We're going for a walk."

Once the corset was laced, she said, "I'll finish dressing. You get your things and meet me in the hall."

The maid went and Lucinda put on the gown, which fastened at the front. She added a short spencer and the simple bonnet that went with it. She'd brought the traveling outfit because she'd brought nearly everything, but she'd not expected to wear it.

She left the room and went downstairs, enjoying the quiet of the house.

In the hall she eyed the door to the library. She opened it and looked in. Deserted. And as she'd hoped, three newspapers were spread on the table. Aunt Mary certainly Would Not Approve, but she went over to read the *Times*, turning past the advertisements on the front page, hungry for news.

She scanned a summary of last week's parliamentary business. The first part was on international affairs. She normally tried to keep abreast of that, but she sped on to national matters. An item on climbing boys was interesting. The practice of using young boys to clean chimneys certainly should be banned. There were other ways.

She saw a small article about an exhibition of new inventions for the home. It didn't seem likely to appeal to her aunt and cousin, but she'd like to go. Inventions were always intriguing, often useful, and sometimes excellent investments.

Then came a slightly longer account of a parliamentary debate on the detrimental effects of smuggling on industry. One speaker from Sussex complained that the Freetrade in his area meant there was none of the trading enterprise that was making the midlands and north so prosperous. It was Parliament's duty, he said, to crush the iniquitous trade lest Britain's ancient parts crumble whilst northern upstarts rise in glory.

"Miss Lucy?"

Lucy started, but it was only Hannah. She reluctantly closed and smoothed the newspaper, then pulled on her gloves and left the house, wondering which side Wyvern would be on. Was his land in the north, midlands, or south? His mother's lover had been a smuggler, so surely on the south coast somewhere. He was interested in agriculture, however, for he'd purchased that book. As smuggling damaged agriculture, he must be opposed to the vile trade.

His views would be interesting. But she had no desire to discuss the matter with him. Really, she didn't.

The street was abustle with servants on errands, street vendors pushing carts and calling their wares, and cows and goats being led along to dispense milk on demand. There were no fine carriages and no sauntering dandies to trouble her, for the ton slept.

The air felt fresher, however, and Lucy resolved to come out in the morning more often.

She was soon in Hyde Park, and found the nearer part the domain of children and nursemaids. She watched a young girl running along, trying to get a kite to fly. It reminded Lucy of the times her father would help her to fly a kite or sail a boat on a pond. He'd always been busy, but he'd found time to spend with her, even when she was too young for business matters. Her mother had sometimes complained that he encouraged her in boyish games, but he'd always laughed and said it would do no harm.

She recognized that he'd longed for a son. If Charlotte Johnson gave him a son, he would find even more time to play boyish games with him. Then later, he'd introduce him fully into the manly world, and the manly world would accept him warmly.

She sniffed back tears as she turned away from the kite.

There, only yards away, stood the Earl of Wyvern, watching her.

He walked forward. "Tears, Miss Potter?"

Hannah stepped forward as if to protect her, but Lucy waved her back. "Hay fever," she said.

"I see no hay."

Lucy pulled her handkerchief from her pocket to wipe her eyes and blow her nose, making good work of it to support her excuse. "As I'm sure you know, my lord, it can be caused by new-mown grass. You will allow there to be plenty of grass?"

He smiled. "And newly mown."

That smile shouldn't be allowed, nor should he be allowed to wear the country clothes in which she'd first seen him.

"Pretending to be a simple country gentleman again, my lord?"

"There's no pretense."

"The Peasant Earl in truth?"

She walked on, but he kept pace with her. "What does that mean?"

Hannah had dropped back discreetly. Lucy knew she should avoid a private discussion with Lord Wyvern, but what could be the harm here in a park?

"Your latest designation from the gossips. From a novel about a hidden heir raised in a hovel. In the end, you marry a shepherdess called Iphigenia."

"A most unlikely shepherdess."

"She's revealed to be the daughter of the king."

He laughed. Such a laugh shouldn't be allowed, but Lucy couldn't help but smile.

"So you truly are addicted to novels," he said. "How goes *Love and Horror*?"

"Flourishingly, all around Town. And more horror than love."

"As bad as that?"

"If that duel had actually happened, yes."

"Miss Potter, on that occasion, I fear I spoke to you discourteously. I apologize."

Lucy glanced at him and saw sincerity. That must mean he was after her fortune after all, but she couldn't be cold in return. Not here, and not with him being the Winsom's man.

"I was a little intemperate myself, my lord. Do you come often to the park?"

"Especially in the morning, though it can't compare to the Devon coast."

As she'd thought.

"So far away," she said, reminding herself that distance was another bulwark against insanity. Devon wasn't as far from London as Scotland, but it was too many miles for her. "You must be interested in the parliamentary debate on the Freetrade, my lord."

"Not at all."

She stared at him. "How can that be?"

"Nothing will stop smuggling except lowering excise. The government won't do that because it needs every penny of tax to pay the debts from the long wars."

"You can't *condone* illegality."

"I can't stop it, either."

"You're an earl!"

"Earls don't have armies anymore, Miss Potter. Even an army would be hard-pressed to guard the whole coastline of Britain on a moonless night."

"You could forbid your tenants to take part."

"As Canute forbade the sea to roll in? There's a law that says that anyone loitering within five miles of the coast is liable to arrest. Like too many laws, it's nonsense.

Much of my land lies within five miles of the coast, including farms, villages, and a fishing fleet. Some of the men and women are fond of idleness, but are they loitering if the area is their home? Are their friends and family, when visiting?"

"It can't be hopeless. Smugglers are breaking the law."

"Did you check where your tea comes from?"

Lucy marched on, irritated by his question but warm with the enjoyment of rational conversation.

He continued to walk with her. "That means you didn't because you know."

"That means I didn't because I didn't have time. Will you speak in Parliament on the issue?"

"Are you going to berate me for that, too?"

His question made her realize she was being alarmingly impertinent. She looked at him to apologize, but saw that twinkle in his eye. "*I* would."

"Speak in Parliament? About what?"

"About legitimate trade. I agree with you on tax reform. We're overburdened with taxes that are strangling enterprise."

"You truly are a City woman, aren't you?"

"Born and bred."

"And I'm a country gentleman. You see everything in terms of trade. I see things in terms of land and sea. You long for grass-free streets, and I for the wild openness of the grassy coast. But we're kindred spirits all the same."

She felt that, but also all the impossibilities he'd expressed, and he didn't know the whole of it. "Hardly," she said, as coolly as she could.

"Everyone outside a fairy circle has more in common than they have in difference."

"You have an odd way of putting things, my lord. Fairy circle?"

"Didn't Lady Charrington's ball feel that way to you? Magical but unreal?"

"It seemed all too real."

"You mean those fools? They won't repeat that."

"I know. I'm sorry. It was only that I wanted to enjoy the ball and they spoiled it."

Especially by causing you to be so harsh to me.

His expression became unreadable, perhaps even frozen. He bowed. "I wish you happier events in future, Miss Potter. Fare thee well."

Lucy watched him go, feeling as if something had been snatched away.

Fare thee well? An odd, archaic phrase, but one that translated to farewell, which was a rather absolute goodbye. True, they had established how different their lives were, but discussing that had created something. At least for her.

He mustn't have been paying full attention to his surroundings, for the girl with the kite careened backward into him. He steadied her and grabbed her string spool before the kite carried it away. But the kite was failing, fluttering down, until he ran backward with it, his hat tumbling off disregarded, until it soared. Once it was high and flying well, he gave the spool back to the child, who beamed up at him before looking up in wonder at her high-flying kite.

He smiled at the girl for a moment, a surprisingly tender smile, then picked up his hat and hurried on his way.

Lucy avoided Hannah's speculative eyes and returned to Lanchester Street in a daze of disturbing thoughts. She found Clara up and breakfasting in Aunt Mary's bedroom, so she could take out her journal and try to record the morning. All that came out was disjointed phrases.

The Peasant Earl.
I know the darkly masterful man is real.
And dangerous.
Especially if he's skillfully after my fortune.

Yet the country gentleman seemed real, too.
Like a lad with a kite,
Hat flying as he made it soar.
Tender smile to make my heart soar
If I were so foolish
As to loose its string.

She stared at the last lines, wishing she could obliterate them, but it wouldn't obliterate the truth.

With a sigh she added,

Happy Iphigenia.

Chapter 12

That night David attended the Duchess of St. Raven's ball, aware that Susan expected him to court Miss Potter. Susan didn't know about the park. That interlude had been disastrous. They'd fallen into such easy conversation. Too easy by far for virtual strangers. They'd also touched on their differences.

It wasn't only a matter of trust anymore. Miss Potter loved London and he disliked it. He loved the countryside, and especially the Devon coast, and she wept at new-mown grass! The daughters of the aristocracy were at ease in the countryside, but she'd been born and raised in the City. How could he transplant her to the Devon countryside and hope that she could thrive?

He couldn't do that. Perhaps he'd take Susan's other suggestion and look around for a country-bred heiress who was either stupid or trustworthy.

"Miss Potter looks particularly charming," Nicholas said, coming to his side, his wife on his arm.

"She does," David agreed. Stupid to say anything else.

She'd just arrived, and was wearing white tonight—some filmy, floaty material embroidered with sprigs of flowers. There were more flowers in her golden hair. What goddess was that? He should know, but gazing upon her, he found his mind was empty of anything but her.

"Those pearls don't tempt you? She's wearing a small fortune around her neck." When David didn't respond, Nicholas said, "I never suspected this martyrish tendency," and strolled off.

"You mustn't glare at him."

David turned to Nicholas's wife. "You seem far too rational to be linked to him."

"Oh, it was force majeure," Eleanor said, "but we rub along."

As they were clearly devoted he sensed a hidden joke, which annoyed him even more.

"I'm sorry," she said. "We are irritating to those unaccustomed to us. But Nicholas believes, and I agree, that love truly does conquer all, as long as it's true love. Not lust, nor the desire to possess, but love that respects, cherishes, nurtures, and above all compromises."

"A remarkable testament, but can there be compromise when it comes to matters of law?"

To his surprise she chuckled. "We'd be beyond hope if not! At another time, remind me to tell you about housebreaking, and perhaps, if I think you can stand it, more serious matters. Will you dance the first set with me?"

"You're an unconventional woman."

"A prerequisite for a Rogue. I am, you know. Not just a Rogue's wife. I might explain that to you one day as well, if it suits me."

Bemused, he led her onto the dance floor, but caught sight of Nicholas walking toward Miss Potter and her coterie.

"What the devil is he doing?"

Eleanor glanced over. "Inviting her to dance, I suspect."

"He'll never get through."

She just smiled.

Lucy was already weary of her suitors and she'd been in the house for only a quarter of an hour. She was very

tempted to state that she wasn't dancing, but if she did
that, she'd have to hold to it all night, and she enjoyed
dancing.

She'd glimpsed Wyvern at the far side of the room and
thought that perhaps, after their time in the park, he might
ask her to dance. But he'd made no move to approach,
which made her want to growl. Clearly he was a gentleman who felt a lady of firm opinions was to be avoided.
She was going to have to choose a partner for the first set,
so she sought one least likely to become a pest.

Then beyond the wall of suitors, a blond man smiled
at her. He was more tanned and more blond than
Wyvern, which created an interesting impression that he
was made of gold. He smiled, and somehow, by a look in
his eye, suggested that he was a means of escape. She had
no idea who he was, but she smiled back and walked
toward him. Men stepped back, allowing her through.
She put her hand in his and he led her away.

"Thank you," she said.

"I thought you needed relief from the siege."

"That's exactly the word." She took the bold approach. "I'm Lucinda Potter."

"And I'm Nicholas Delaney, a friend of Lord Wyvern."

Her heart pattered, but she wondered how he could
have been friends with an estate steward. Despite his
casual demeanor he was very much part of this world.

"Only a recent acquaintance of the current one." He
went on. "But my friendship with the previous Earl of
Wyvern is long."

"The Mad Earl?" she asked, surprised.

"The temporary one, now Lord Amleigh. We were at
school together."

Lord Amleigh was Lord Wyvern's brother-in-law. A
tenuous thread of connection, but it thrilled her foolish
heart.

Lucy would happily have talked more about all things

Wyvern with this man, but they were on the dance floor and must take their places. She should be grateful to be protected from her own folly. When she'd first spied Wyvern across the room, fully the earl again in dark elegance, her heart had truly skipped a beat.

As they settled to the longways dance, however, she saw Wyvern join it with an auburn-haired woman. They would meet in the dance. She couldn't help but smile.

David had been impressed by the ease with which Nicholas had snatched Miss Potter. It was easy to underestimate Nicholas, but he was heir assumptive to his brother, the Earl of Stainbridge. More impressive was Nicholas's position as unquestioned leader of the Rogues. For the most part, they were men of quality, rank, and expertise, and he was a commoner who chose to live a rural life. Even so, he ruled.

David wasn't a Rogue, however, and had no mind to be steered by Nicholas Delaney's iron whim. All very well to speak of the wondrous powers of love, but what of Romeo and Juliet, and Othello?

Susan was also dancing, and as they turned together at one point she said, "You promised not to avoid Miss Potter."

"I'll meet her in the dance."

She gave him an older-sister look and he sighed. "I'll ask her for a dance."

The effect of meeting her in the dance was so powerful, however, that he lost his nerve. He'd never understand his mother's rash behavior, but he was beginning to see how this kind of obsession could ride roughshod over common sense and will. He couldn't dance with her. It wouldn't be safe.

At the end of the dance, Lucy couldn't resist asking Mr. Delaney a question. "Was Wyvern truly an estate manager?"

"Yes, and he'd rather still be that than here, an earl buffed to a shine."

"I met him in the park yesterday morning in country clothes. He seemed more comfortable."

"Are you suggesting that he should wear such clothes here?"

"That would be folly, but it seems a shame that anyone be uncomfortable."

"Hush! Such an outrageous notion might start a revolution. Cravats and collars would become soft, corsets would be thrown off by men and women, and hair would be allowed to take its natural form."

She chuckled. "What an astonishing world that would be."

"You would like to be part of it?"

"I never wear anything uncomfortable as it is. Nor, I suspect, do you, sir."

He smiled. "You're right, but we are both blessed with a pleasing form."

"Do you always argue both sides of a topic?"

"Whenever possible. Do you have a taste for the gothic?"

"As in novels?" she asked, surprised.

"In any way. Wyvern's seat, Crag Wyvern, is an imitation of a medieval keep, including arrow slits and a dungeon."

"That sounds most uncomfortable."

"David finds it so."

David. His name is David.

"Does a visit to such a house appeal?" he asked.

"Definitely not."

"It's become quite an attraction for travelers who venture to such a remote spot, especially ladies devoted to gothic novels."

Remote, she noted.

"Remote seems more horrid than a mock castle," she said.

"Venturesome travel doesn't appeal?

"Not at all."

"Yet you don't strike me as timid."

She flashed him a look. "I'm not, but my ventures are of a different sort."

She was expecting him to ask what she meant, which would allow her to talk about trade, but instead he glanced around. "The siege forces gather. Will you be captured, or shall I find you a sensible gentleman?"

"It's not sensible to woo me?" When he didn't respond to that, she said, "I'll take a suitor, or everyone will wonder why I'm here."

"Which raises the question, why are you here?"

He was far too sharp beneath that easygoing manner. "For amusement only."

"Poor suitors," he said and moved away.

Lucy eyed the approaching hopefuls, feeling a twinge of guilt. She'd promised nothing, but she truly did wish there were a way of signaling that she did not have marriage in mind.

She realized she was again waiting for Wyvern to approach. Because of the park, but also because of something in his eyes during the previous dance. But see, he was ready to dance with a pretty, dark-haired young woman. Something about her dress and manner suggested she was married. Idiotic to be relieved by that.

He and his partner were joined by Sir Stephen and Lady Ball, other people she knew quite well. Sir Stephen had worked with Lucy's father on reforms to apprenticeship law and the Balls had dined at Nailer Street twice. So here was another opportunity to approach. She managed to resist, but it was becoming increasingly hard. If he wouldn't come to her, she wanted to go to him. . . .

Madness! She accepted Launceston as partner, taking comfort from it being another longways dance that would give her some moments with him. When they turned together wasn't there a meaningful expression in his eyes? Didn't his hand linger on hers for a moment, as if he was reluctant to let her move on?

Surely he must ask her for the supper dance. But he didn't. She chose Northcliff again, so dependable and so very dull.

She sat to supper with some of his friends and their partners, but they were all as dull as he, whereas Wyvern was at a merry table in Lucy's sight. The Balls were there, as well as Mr. Delaney and an auburn-haired woman who must be his wife.

The other couples at her table were married, and she noticed how in every case the wife seemed a shadow of her husband. She deferred to him, agreed with him, smiled proudly at his every word.

This was precisely why she could not marry. Once she was a wife, men would look to her husband for approval of her every action. Indeed, he would have the right to overrule her decisions, even if he knew nothing about business. She would be unable to make contracts without his approval, and the whole world would see it as her holy duty to devote herself to home and children and to cease meddling in men's affairs.

Damnation. Her unhappiness at her thoughts underlined the extent of the temptation. She would resist!

In the end, however, she couldn't. As supper drew to a close, she kept her attention on her own table, but plotted how to approach Wyvern's. The Balls provided the excuse. When she rose to put her plan into action, however, she found Wyvern had already left.

"You seem abstracted, Miss Potter," Northcliff said, chiding slightly. "Are you quite well?"

"I'm sorry. A slight headache."

"I believe we can find some fresh air on the rear terrace," he said, extending an arm.

She needed to find Wyvern, but couldn't say so, especially as her urgency was mad. It was as if she feared he would disappear forever.

She didn't see him as they returned to the ballroom, nor as they walked out onto the terrace. There was indeed fresh air, but very little space, for the terrace was shallow and many others had the same idea.

Not Wyvern, however.

"How pretty the garden is," she said, for she had to say something. Unlike Aunt Mary's house this ducal residence had a garden and it was lit by colored lanterns on posts and in trees. A few people had found their way down there, perhaps with a tryst in mind.

Was Wyvern strolling the half-lit paths with some lady? Was he was committing himself to some other well-dowered catch? He'd been partnered in the supper dance with a plump woman Lucy didn't know. She'd sensed nothing special between them, but now she couldn't bear the thought. Madness, she knew, but being aware of insanity didn't seem to help.

There he was! Off to one side, shadowed by a tree, but illuminated along one side by an amber-glassed lamp.

Alone?

She watched for a moment to be sure, but yes, he was alone.

She remembered his remark about being outside a fairy circle. Despite his gloss of confidence and his apparent ease with the great, was he miserably out of place? Something about him suggested sadness, and she was powerless against that pull.

She needed to get rid of Northcliff, so she claimed a need of the ladies' room. He escorted her part of the way but then had to let her go. Once out of sight she took another direction and asked a passing servant, "How do I get out into the garden?"

The footman looked a little taken aback. Was it not open to guests? Others were there. Even if it had been forbidden, Lucy would invade, so she insisted with a look.

"Downstairs and to the back, ma'am, then through the morning room."

Uncomfortably aware of possibly intruding into private areas, she followed a quiet corridor. Then a waft of fresh air guided her into a small room which had long doors open to the garden.

She was slightly out of breath, and paused to compose herself before going forward. That hesitation gave a small, frantic voice an opportunity to protest, to scream at her to go back, not to follow the perilous calling. However, her need was irresistible, as if she were parched and cool water flowed ahead.

She walked through the doorway and down three shallow steps onto a path. Somewhere, indeed, a fountain did play, and chamber music floated out from the house. Perfumed plants scented the night air. The couples out here were strolling along paths, but Wyvern had been off to one side. Her white gown must be catching the light from the house, so she slipped into the shadows as she made her way toward the amber lamp beneath which he'd been standing. Her slippers made no sound on the grass.

A hunter stalking prey.

She paused, half behind a large shrub, heart pounding. This was the moment to retreat.

The last chance.

Chapter 13

David was accustomed to danger in the dark, and quickly became aware of someone approaching surreptitiously. A glance showed a pale gown and precious pearls. Not just danger, peril.

He'd come out here to gather the resolution to continue to avoid her, Susan be damned. He was supposed to learn more about her, was he? To coolheadedly assess if she had a flexible enough conscience to be a safe bride. Safe! During the first dance, when she'd been partnered with Nicholas, he'd wanted to snatch her and dance with her himself. By the second he'd wanted to claim her, then and there.

By the third he'd needed to pull her into his arms and hold her against all comers, perhaps even against her will. He could understand now how men in olden times had seized women by force. How irresistible it had been, despite the costs.

Paris and Helen.

Hades and Persephone.

Damnation, that's who she resembled tonight— Persephone, daughter of Spring, carried off into the harsh underworld by love-crazed Hades.

She stepped into the light. "Alone, Lord Wyvern?"

"No longer, it would seem." The amber light was doing strange things to her white gown. "A golden goddess in truth."

She was looking at him with a direct, thoughtful expression that emphasized all the ways she was wonderful and all the ways that she would be an impossible wife for him.

"When we spoke in Winsom's," she said, "and in the park, you seemed one man."

"And now I'm two?"

"And now you're a different one. One who avoids me, even dislikes me?"

"Then is it wise to be out here in the dark with me?"

Perhaps that gave her pause. "If I scream, many will come running."

He stepped forward, covering her mouth with one hand and overpowering her with his other arm, pulling her beyond the illumination of the lamp.

"And now?" he asked, blood pounding in his head at the madness of this, and at the feel of her, the scent of her. At her wide eyes.

Startled, but not afraid.

She was excited!

He let her go. Stepped away from the brink. "You see how false your sense of security was."

One gloved hand rose to hold her pearls, as if for protection, but she nodded. "I appreciate the lesson. I haven't been manhandled before and you did it so well. But if you raped me, you'd suffer for it. Unless," she added thoughtfully, "you killed me afterward. What a wonder that would be for the ton to feast on."

She was extraordinary, and not a little mad herself.

"You'd still be raped," he pointed out.

"And you'd hang."

"An earl hanged for rape? I doubt it. You should return to the house."

She let go of her pearls and flipped open a lace fan,

which sent a puff of light perfume into the air. "But there are so many shadows, Lord Wyvern, which could conceal dangers. You should escort me."

"What the devil do you want, Miss Potter?"

That fan waved slowly, untroubled by coarse language.

"Protection," she said.

"I'll follow at a distance."

"Protection from my suitors."

"Then choose one of them."

"None appeal, and I don't intend to wed. I came to Mayfair to enjoy myself, not to find a husband, and the fortune hunters are spoiling my pleasure."

"I'm a fortune hunter."

"But you've demonstrated that I don't appeal. You see?"

Like a blind man in a fog, but her light, direct manner and perhaps that waving perfumed fan was tangling his mind.

"Demonstrated how?"

"You haven't sought my hand for a dance."

"Perhaps I dangled distance like bait, hoping you'd come to me. Like this."

The fan paused. "And here I am. What now?"

He had no answer for that.

"I have a proposal."

"Miss Potter! I'm overwhelmed, but I fear we would not suit."

"Not that," she said with a soft chuckle. "You are seeking a rich bride, my lord. I'm extremely well-dowered and assumed to be seeking a title. If you pay attentions and I smile on them, it will be seen as a fait accompli. Most of the other fortune hunters will think the case hopeless and leave me in peace."

"What do I gain by this? I am, as you said, seeking a rich bride."

"The opportunity to win me?"

"You don't intend to wed."

"Yet."

"When?"

"I don't know."

"Why the delay?" He was completely fascinated.

"Marriage is so confining for a woman and I have money enough to live well."

"A solitary life appeals?"

"I could have a female companion. More than one."

"No desire for children?"

"Children are a consideration," she admitted. "If I do marry in order to have children, a substantial portion of my dowry will be put in a trust, to be used by my husband only with my trustee's consent. That is, with my consent."

"Have you told your suitors that?"

"Negotiations haven't reached this far with any of them."

"Are we negotiating?"

"For your loverlike attentions, Lord Wyvern, with the slim possibility of a reward."

"Which I don't want, remember."

"Why?" she asked, apparently honest in her curiosity.

He couldn't be honest in return. How could he tell her she was too dangerous to him? Desperation drove him to step closer, so close that she had to tilt her head to continue to meet his eyes. He needed to rattle her, or perhaps he simply needed to kiss her, beyond all civility or sense.

He cradled her face and lowered his lips to hers. Such soft lips, passive but giving no sign of protest, then parting just a little. Then kissing him back, enthusiastically.

He instantly stepped away, trying to conceal that it was retreat. A rout, even. Virago couldn't describe such lovely sweetness, but there had to be some term for the peril she presented.

Her eyes were bright now.

Who hunted whom?

"Why are you so sure you don't want to marry me?" she asked.

"I remember too many stories of goddesses who pursued mortal men for sport. They don't end well for the men."

She chuckled and he wasn't surprised. He was being ridiculous. He was also ensnared. He should be fighting to be free, but instead he couldn't resist her strange proposal.

It would allow him to keep his promise to Susan, but that was specious. He wanted to agree because it would give him an excuse to spend precious time in her company. He might yet discover that the impossible was possible. That more kisses were possible. A lifetime of them and all other delights. But if not, he would have a sip of the precious bowl to remember.

"Very well," he said, "but on one condition."

"Yes?"

"You pay me with a kiss a day."

She made a humming noise that was hard to interpret. "And why would I agree to that?"

"Because it's my price."

Her thoughtful look could be very steady indeed.

"You wouldn't prefer a guinea a day?"

"No."

"Ten?"

"No."

"A hundred?"

He should. "No."

"One kiss a day, then. Lips on lips. No more than that unless I agree."

"Do you always forge such a detailed contract?"

"I'm my father's daughter, Lord Wyvern, trained by him all my life."

"Good God. Why, then, the pretense of idiocy?"

"I was coming here as a Cit and as a reminder of a great scandal. I'd no mind to be even more of an oddity by showing that I had a brain."

"Clever women aren't so rare as that."

"Most young unmarried ladies disguise it."

"All is deception inside the fairy circle."

"I believe we've struck an honest deal," she said. "Are we agreed on our terms?"

He felt spun like a top, but he couldn't resist. "Agreed. I will be your favored escort and you will pay me with a kiss a day."

"For a week only," she said.

"Too short to have effect. Three weeks."

"A fortnight. You will need to return to pursuit of well-dowered ladies who might accept your offer, and by then I might have done with fairy matters."

"Very well," he said, having bargained to the time he'd expected, knowing that she probably had, too. Did that count as deception? Overall, she seemed to have been honest to a fault.

"Now we should return to the house," she said. "The dancing will soon begin again and I have paid today's kiss."

"The kiss was before the agreement. I owe you nothing."

Quick as a bird, she went on tiptoe and kissed him again. "There."

"Meager payment, Miss Potter, but very well." He extended his arm and she placed her gloved hand around it. Such a slight touch to create havoc.

She couldn't be truly opposed to marriage, but he didn't think she'd lied. If he could convince himself it was safe to marry her, would he then have to fight to persuade his goddess to the altar?

Lucy went with him, making sure to keep a light smile on her lips, but she was surprised he couldn't hear her heart or sense the sizzle that ran along her nerves. When he'd overpowered her so easily and dragged her into the shadows, she should have been appalled, but instead she'd felt a thrill close to flame. Not fear at all, but a fierce longing for him to embrace her ruthlessly, kiss her to distraction, and perhaps do more. At last she understood how foolish women allowed themselves to be ravished into ruin. Especially as she would only have been ravished into marriage. A marriage she wanted now, despite all the costs.

Sanity clamored a protest, but it couldn't dent her need for this man, always, everywhere.

It should be so simple!

He needed her money, and she had an abundance of it. Why wasn't he grabbing the prize?

When he'd seized her, he'd claimed to feel nothing, to be teaching her a lesson, but she knew that wasn't true. She'd heard his breathing, sensed his heat. When he'd kissed her she'd felt his tenderness. He'd broken the kiss and moved away, but not because he disliked it. Of that she was sure. Even now, entering the house and in sight of others, passion hummed between them.

She was tempted to turn him back, to entice him in some way, to overwhelm his self-control and be ravished into commitment here and now.

To capture the prize.

Perhaps her mother would have done that, but Lucy had enough of her father's cool head to resist such a dangerous path when there were other ways.

She'd won the means to spend time with him, to learn him better, to find the way. She had to suppress a smile at how he'd seen the daily kiss as a bargaining point when the prospect filled her with a shocking delight. It had taken all her nerve to lay a fortnight as the term when she'd longed for a month.

As they entered the house clocks struck midnight.

"Does that mean it's a new day?" she asked. "That I paid that kiss for nothing?"

"It was a nothing of a kiss," he said. "We start afresh. Twenty-four hours ahead for labor and payment."

Lamplight showed a spark in his eyes—of anger that he was being manipulated? Perhaps a little, but there was excitement there, too—the same excitement that sizzled inside her.

"So there are, my lord," Lucy said. "Twenty-four hours through dark and daylight, and all the shadowy times between."

Chapter 14

It was nearly three in the morning when Lucy entered her aunt's coach to return home, and some guests still danced at the duchess's ball. She wasn't yet accustomed to such late nights, so she yawned as she settled into her seat, but she was alive with a different kind of energy.

She and Wyvern had danced together twice and it had been noted. Some of her suitors had already abandoned the chase.

Dancing with him had been extraordinary.

She'd danced with many men of all types, but never with one she desired. It made even the most conventional contact significant, and the second dance had been a waltz. The parts of the dance that turned them together in one another's arms had been almost unbearably delicious. He'd held her just a little closer than was proper, but she hadn't minded, and she'd felt the same excitement in him as in herself.

Only imagine the marriage bed. . . .

She glanced at her aunt and cousin, alarmed that they might guess her thoughts, but they were afroth with chatter, about turbans, about necklines and ankles, about whether Lady Harroving really might marry the scandalous Dick Cranbrook, and whether Lord Darien was as mad as his brother.

Lucy slid back into her thoughts. She was not entirely

ignorant about marital matters. There had been girlish whispers and speculations, and sometimes a glimpse of servants in a corner doing what they shouldn't be doing. But, in addition, her father had some Indian prints that were quite startling. She and Betty had giggled over them, wondering whether normal people such as their neighbors did such things and deciding they did not.

Now, however, it seemed not quite so unbelievable. She and Wyvern kissing, touching, moving into positions . . .

"Wyvern."

Lucy jerked out of her sinful thoughts.

"You danced twice with him, Lucinda," Aunt Mary said.

Lucy admitted that she had, hoping her blushes were given an innocent interpretation.

"What did you think of him on closer acquaintance?" Clara asked.

Closer . . .

Lucy pulled her wits together. "He's an interesting man."

"But do you *favor* him?" Aunt Mary asked.

"He's the only young earl on the marriage market."

"Lucy!" Clara exclaimed. "What of love?"

"Love can come later," Aunt Mary said, "and often it is better so. I wouldn't want Wyvern for you, Clara dear, but given Lucinda's situation, she is being very sensible."

Being a scandal-ridden Cit of coarser stock and thus less able to be choosy. But even thoughts like that couldn't darken Lucy's mood.

Her aunt could think what she liked. The lottery wheel had turned, the ax had fallen. Lucy was in love with Lord Wyvern with the same blind passion that had driven her mother into Daniel Potter's arms. She could only hope it would turn out as well.

Nighttime was fertile ground for hot memories and fevered expectations, but Lucy managed to get some sleep.

She woke late, too late for the park. With kisses in mind, she was intensely interested in Aunt Mary's plans for the day. She saw some opportunities for him to woo her, but none for them to have a private moment until the evening when the Caldrosses were to attend a poetry reading at Drury Lane.

He would find a way to keep their bargain, and especially to make her pay her debt. She was sure of that.

As was usual now, she settled to her "poetry" while Clara and her aunt went over future invitations. For the first time, however, she found it difficult to write. The thoughts and emotions that jostled in her head were too powerful to be put into mere words, and some too wicked by far.

She recorded the superficial events of the St. Raven ball and a few foibles of the ton—but then she saw a way to meet in the afternoon. She still wanted to visit the exhibition of household inventions at Beech's Tavern.

She rang the bell, praying Hannah would come. She did. Probably the maids knew that Clara was with her mother.

"Hannah, can you get a letter to Lord Wyvern for me?"

Hannah looked alarmed. "You don't want to be doing that, miss."

"Doing what? I simply want him to escort me somewhere."

"You'd be better avoiding him, miss. They say his father was raving mad."

Lucy had forgotten that, and his behavior last night came to mind. Not insane, however, except with the particular insanity of love. She wondered if the previous earl might have been driven mad by his beloved fleeing into the arms of another.

"There, see," Hannah said, seeing her hesitation.

"Nonsense. There's nothing deranged about the present earl, and you must do as I say."

"If you insist, miss. And if his place isn't too far."

With frustration, Lucy realized she had no idea of Wyvern's direction. He was staying with Lord and Lady Amleigh, but where was their house? She thought it had been mentioned when her aunt had read about his arrival, but at that time she'd not thought such a detail important. She could ask, but her instincts demanded secrecy, especially from her aunt and cousin, who had no discretion at all.

"Never mind, Hannah. I've thought better of it."

"Thank the Lord for that, miss!" Hannah lowered her voice. "They say belowstairs, miss, that he's a smuggler."

"What nonsense! His mother took up with a smuggler after she left her husband, the earl."

"Such goings-on. I never heard the like back home."

"True enough. Don't gossip about what we've just discussed or I'll send you back there."

"Not sure I'd mind, miss. Things are different here. But you can trust me."

When Hannah had left, Lucy considered those words. Things certainly were different here, and she was out of her place. Could she live her life inside the fairy circle, even for love?

But he's not part of Mayfair or the ton.

He was David, the simple country gentleman who flew a kite, who bought books about agricultural improvement, who spoke with her as an equal.

Yet Lord Wyvern existed.

Who is the real man?

Her journal sometimes helped her clarify her thoughts, so she sharpened her pencil and sat to write.

The Peasant Earl?
He's not a peasant.
The estate manager turned earl?
That's the truth, but it

Doesn't feel like truth.
Could the estate manager cow
A lord and a well-born gentleman
So effectively?
Born a scandalous bastard,
Employed as a servant.
How can he be the man he is?
He is a mystery.
Too mysterious to be safe.

Lucy looked at the words, knowing they were true, knowing she should break the contract and keep her distance. Her behavior last night had been so foolhardy! It had been exciting, but precisely because it had been dangerous. Because he was dangerous. To her sanity, but in other, poorly understood ways.

When Clara came in to say they must change for their morning calls it was a relief. The mindless social round was just what she needed to quiet her wildly spinning mind.

When she didn't encounter him anywhere she made herself be glad, and when they set off for Drury Lane that evening she hoped he wouldn't be there. When her hopes were fulfilled, she sank into gloom, but no one would notice. The whole evening was devoted to an epic poem based on the story of Job.

She'd have much rather endured more Sebastian Rossiter, though love poetry wouldn't suit her mood, either. All very well for her to intend to avoid the Earl of Wyvern and all his mysteries and danger, but the wretched man had no right to avoid her!

Tomorrow, Wednesday, would be Almack's, and she finally had admittance to the select ball. He'd better be there to do his duty.

She entered Almack's fretting. Would the patronesses have raised the portcullis for him? He was an earl, but with a tainted background from both parents. She needed Wyvern to be here, not least so she could tell him what she thought of him for breaking their contract.

She needed to berate him, but she also needed his attention. Their two dances at the Duchess of St. Raven's ball hadn't entirely turned the trick, especially with no further evidence of commitment. She was still being pestered by Outram, Launceston, and a few others. She excused herself to speak to Lady Vandeimen.

Maria had Miss Florence at her side, who was cheerfully dealing with a number of suitors of her own.

"I hope you're enjoying Almack's, Lucy," Maria said.

There was no point to pretense here, for Maria knew her well. "I've enjoyed other assemblies more."

Maria's lips twitched. "It's a marvel, isn't it, how something can be made desirable simply by limiting access? As you say, it's nothing out of the ordinary, and one meets the same people as at other events."

"Minus the cads and wretches."

"A title can cover a host of sins."

"Is the Earl of Wyvern admitted?"

It slipped out. She hadn't meant to show her interest.

"He's not a cad or wretch."

"No, of course not," Lucy said, mortified. "Only titled and something of a scandal. Not himself, of course . . ."

She was becoming Silly Lucinda in truth. No wonder Maria was looking at her strangely.

"I believe he's passed muster," Maria said.

"Of course he has. I only wondered because of his odd background."

"If odd backgrounds barred people from Almack's, it would be very thin of company. Ah, there he is."

Lucy turned and saw him entering with a couple who must be his brother-in-law and sister, for the resemblance to the lady was marked. Her foolish heart performed a few completely impossible acrobatics, and a few more when he came straight to her, bringing his companions.

He made the introductions and Lucy sensed that she was being discreetly inspected. What had he told his family? She should have added secrecy to their agreement.

"You are an example of noble forbearance, Lord Amleigh," she said. "Everyone admires your gracious surrender of an earldom."

He was dark haired and gray eyed, and the word "steady" came to mind.

"It was a tussle," Amleigh said drily, "but in the end matters were arranged as they should be. May I lead you out for the first dance, Miss Potter?"

"Alas, my lord, I'm promised." She sent Wyvern a look.

"Indeed," Wyvern said. "You are mine."

He was all danger and mystery, but Lucy was no longer sane. Almack's was magical at last, and she would enjoy her first dance in happy anticipation of a kiss.

How?

Where?

When?

In the end it was quite easy. After their dance he strolled with her down a corridor toward the refreshment rooms, where there were very few people at that moment.

She went straight on the attack. "You have been very neglectful of your duties."

"Clearly we should inform one another of our plans. I didn't expect you to be a devotee of gloomy poetry."

"I think you should have been more ingenious."

"And I that you should have made yourself available to be served."

"I was at the poetry."

"And I was at the Duchess of Morbury's, which was much more amusing."

"I'm not paying you to be amused."

"Thus far, you're not paying me at all, despite being the proud possessor of thirty thousand pounds."

She fixed him with a look. "It's more than that, in fact. Good investments."

"Your father is a clever man."

"I'll have you know that I manage my money for myself."

He stopped to stare. "Do you, by gad?"

"For all your fanciful imagination, you seem to have difficulty in accepting unusual truths. I'm my father's daughter, remember, trained by him, but also with many of his abilities and talents. Do not be deceived by my appearance."

"Believe me, I haven't been since our first meeting."

His tone annoyed her. "But you disapprove of my having a brain and expertise? Or perhaps cling to the hope that you're mistaken?"

"Most men are afraid of clever women."

"That's absurd," she said. "Men rule the world."

"Beth Arden says that's because we daren't allow women any scope for their powers. We cage the lion."

"Lioness," she corrected. "You mean the Marchioness of Arden?"

"She's a follower of Mary Wollstonecraft. Rights of Woman and all that. I don't know if she believes women should be able to speak in Parliament, but she definitely wants women to be able to vote."

"And why not? Especially women of property."

"It would be the beginning of the end. Men would lose dominion over the earth."

"Nonsense." But it came out breathily, for he'd detoured into a small anteroom.

He drew her behind the door, where they couldn't be seen by anyone passing and raised an expectant brow.

"Someone could come in," she said, suddenly nervous.

"Adds a little spice. But even if someone did, a simple kiss, lips on lips, would be naughty, not scandalous. Of course, if you wish to make more of it . . ."

"Seeking to taunt me into compromising myself? Perhaps you do want to marry my money after all."

"Perhaps I enjoy the spice of danger."

Alas, so do I.

She raised her gloved hand and drew his head down, going on tiptoe so she could press her lips to his. More than a peck this time, but not much more.

So tempting to linger, but she was not so foolish as that.

She settled back to earth and fussed with her gown, hoping to conceal how devastating that meager kiss had been. Not only on her. When she looked up there was fire behind his eyes.

She unfurled her fan and waved it, but turned so as to cool him. "Spicy enough?"

"Not within a mile, but if we were to do more, we might have to become betrothed. That would deter your suitors completely, but . . ."

". . . be far too high a price to pay." They were dancing around danger.

He took the fan and turned it to cool her. "You could always jilt me when it suited you."

"But a gentleman cannot do that. You would be trapped," she said.

"Are you saying you'd hold me to it?"

"I might hesitate to add more notoriety to my name. I'd think you would feel the same."

He closed the fan and gave it back. "I was born the bastard son of a wanton and a tavern keeper, and my claim to the earldom is dubious in many people's eyes. How much more notorious could I be?"

She wanted to take him in her arms and hold him.

Before she could give in to temptation, he said, "But I do still have my honor. Given that, we should return to company."

He extended his arm, and she curled her hand around it possessively. Day by day, moment by moment, he was more and more hers, but he wasn't a man to be captured by trickery or force.

As they left the room she asked, "Where are you living?"

"You plan to sneak into my bedroom?"

"I thought to send you a letter."

"Five Millicent Row. It may not be wise to put your desires on paper."

"That rather depends on the desires," she said. "I want to visit an exhibition of household inventions."

"You plan to trade in them?"

She couldn't tell if there was a sting in that. "Perhaps. Machinery and technology are the way of the future, in industry and agriculture."

"Perhaps I'm a Luddite."

"Then know your enemy. You could send a note to Lanchester Street inviting me to visit the exhibition with you."

"You want a lot for your pay, don't you?"

"It was merely a suggestion. I do, however, expect to dance at least one more set with you tonight."

"Don't worry, you mercenary wench, you'll get what you kissed for."

Lucy decided not to challenge the taunt. She had one example of what could happen when she challenged the Earl of Wyvern, and though it had been delicious, it wouldn't be wise to push him too far.

Not yet, at least.

And certainly not here.

Thirteen days still remained, and tomorrow should include more time with him during the day.

Thirteen days and thirteen kisses, with her determining what sort of kisses they would be.

All in all, a perfect contract, as long as he did his part.

"Where do we go tonight?" Lucy asked the next day as she sat in the drawing room with her needlework, waiting for Wyvern's invitation to arrive.

"Lady Galloway's ball," Aunt Mary said. "For her daughter, Lady Iphigenia."

Lucy bit her lips on laughter, but when she caught Clara's eye they both gave way.

"What on earth is the matter?" Aunt Mary demanded.

Clara managed, "Only the name, Mama."

"It's a very pretty name."

"Yes, but in *The Peasant Earl*, don't you remember? He married Iphigenia!"

"What has that to do with anything? Oh, you refer to Lord Wyvern. It won't come to that. She doesn't bring enough money, and her father would never allow it. Such a tawdry background."

Lucy wanted to protest, particularly as her aunt had recommended him as a suitable husband for herself. But then, she, too, had a tawdry background, in that sense.

The general attitude raised a worrying concern.

Miss Ponting had claimed she'd never marry Wyvern.

Aunt Mary hadn't wanted him for Clara.

Lady Galloway would never consider him for her daughter.

For the first time Lucy wondered if her father might try to forbid the match. He wanted her to marry a lord, but that might not include a disreputable one. He didn't have the legal right to prevent the marriage, but what would she do if he opposed it?

Immediately, thoughts of Gretna Green danced in her mind. No need to emulate her mother that far. She was legally free to marry whom she wished, but she couldn't lightly dismiss her father's opposition. She'd hate to be estranged from him as her mother had been from her father.

No fear of that. She'd be returning to her "rightful world," and why should her father object to a muddled parentage when he didn't know the name of his father or mother? All the same, he might not be rational. . . .

The footman came in with a letter for Miss Potter.

Lucy took it eagerly, but she instantly recognized Betty's handwriting. It had been sent by messenger, not posted.

Some emergency?

My dearest Lucy,

Such wonderful news! Father is home! He arrived last night without warning, having outsped the letter he dispatched upon landing in Portsmouth. As all the plans are made, we have set the wedding for Saturday, but I will change the date if you cannot come, my dearest friend. If you can come, can you possibly come immediately? I hesitate to call you away from your dizzy delights, but I would dearly love to have you with me in these last few days. Reply posthaste! The messenger will wait.

Your excited and blissfully happy friend,
Betty.

"Bad news, dear?" Aunt Mary asked.

Tragic! Lucy was delighted for Betty, but this wrenched her away from Wyvern. Could she take him with her? Impossible.

"Just startling," she said and explained.

"Of course you must go, dear. I'm pleased to see a little romance in your heart. You are not at all like your mother."

"Forgive me, Aunt, but I thought you disapproved of mother's actions."

"Of her marriage, certainly, but not of her warm heart. There is something not quite womanly about a cool heart, my dear, especially in one so young."

Lucy went off to write the reply, fuming. First her father, now her aunt, both implying she was a cold fish. She was tempted to be caught in mad passion with Wyvern simply to show them!

She sent off the message and summoned Hannah to pack, but tears threatened. It hardly seemed bearable to be away for days, and she couldn't even write to tell him she was leaving, not when nothing was settled between them.

If his invitation arrived before she left, she could reply. If not, he'd hear soon enough, but that didn't seem adequate. It didn't take long to pack what was needed, and by then Aunt Mary's carriage was ready to carry her home.

There'd been no letter from Wyvern.

As the carriage rolled through Mayfair Lucy looked out, hoping to see him in the street. The beau monde was beginning to emerge for their day, and if she saw him, she could stop the carriage and give him the news.

As the carriage passed through Temple Bar into the City, she gave up hope of that.

He would hear the news, but now she wished she'd taken the bold step and written to him.

Chapter 15

She soon recognized the different rhythm. The sounds were different, and the bustle had a more purposeful nature. She'd left the fairy circle, and perhaps escaped some bedazzlement, for she began to have doubts.

This was her world, completely lost to her if she married a nobleman, especially one whose principal home was so far away. It was one hundred and seventy miles to Wyvern's seat on the Devon coast—she'd sneaked into the library to look it up. At very best speed and with hardly any breaks, the coach journey would take more than a day. Once there, she'd probably rarely return here.

She'd found Crag Wyvern on a map, situated in a thinly populated part of the coast, near two very small villages, one called Church Wyvern, the other Dragon's Cove. The very names seemed ominous.

Both lay far from cities of even moderate size. Axminster, of carpet fame, was only about ten miles, but the roads between looked uncertain. Remote didn't apply only to distance, but to the ease of getting there. It was three hundred miles from London to Scotland, but a coach could travel all the way on the Great North Road, which tolls kept in good repair.

"Is something the matter, miss?" Hannah asked.

"Just the sight of familiar places," Lucy said, blinking to clear her eyes.

If she'd come to her senses, she should be thankful, not grieving.

"Lovely to be home, isn't it?" Hannah said.

"Yes," Lucy said, but they were rolling past Winsom's and she sighed for might-have-beens. If he had been a simple country gentleman, perhaps he might have been willing to move here. She was sure her father would give him a place in the business.

Perhaps she wouldn't return to Aunt Mary's. There was no point to it anymore, and certainly no pleasure. Better to endure the preparations for her father's wedding and return to her plans. Surely if she put it to her father the right way, he would arrange for her to have a place in the business, if even in the background.

Yes, that was it. Not as his heir, but as a kind of partner.

Even so, it was a strain to put on a smile when the carriage stopped in front of her home. She went toward the door, realizing only at the last moment that she hadn't taken a key. She used the knocker for the first time she could remember.

The door was opened by Charlotte Johnson.

"Lucy? Is something the matter?"

Was it Lucy's imagination, or did Mrs. Johnson take a moment to step back and allow admittance?

"Did you not hear?" Lucy asked as she entered, taking off her gloves. "Betty Hanway's father is home and she's to wed in two days."

"Yes, of course. I simply didn't expect you back so soon." Charlotte looked at the luggage the footman was carrying in. "Put it there. Our own man will take it up."

Our own man.

Lucy thanked the footman with a coin and sent him and the carriage back to Aunt Mary's, temper already fraying.

"You're very welcome, of course," Charlotte said. "Your father will be delighted."

Lucy managed some sort of smile. "I'll go straight over to see how I can help."

"I'm sure her family . . ."

Lucy ignored that and left the house.

There probably hadn't been anything amiss about Mrs. Johnson's words or manner, but to welcome her! The woman was already ruling the roost.

She had a true smile in place by the time she entered Betty's house. Her friend raced down the stairs for a wild hug. "Lucy! Now everything's perfect!"

"My goodness, you're in danger of bursting into flame!"

Betty laughed. "I feel like that. So sudden. So exciting. So wonderful!"

Betty's portly father came into the hall. "No sooner am I home than my only daughter hastens to flee it." But he was beaming at them both. "Will I wish you a similar happiness soon, Lucy?"

Lucy smiled, for she was truly delighted to see him home safe. "It's possible, sir, but I've committed myself to no lord as yet."

"And I selfishly hope you don't. I'd wish to see you remain in our orbit, my dear. I'm away to my counting house to see what chaos my absence has achieved. I've a wedding to pay for."

Betty kissed his cheek, then linked arms to take Lucy up to her bedroom, where they'd always talked. "I'm so pleased to see you. I was afraid you'd be able to come only for the wedding day. I've missed you so."

Even so, Betty's mind was full of wedding preparations and the delights to come. Lucy happily relaxed into that, putting all troublesome thoughts aside.

She accompanied her friend to the shops for some last-minute items, then in the afternoon dined with the Hanways, finding the old-fashioned mealtime odd after dining in the evening. The talk was all of the wedding and Lucy couldn't help noting the changes it would bring. Betty's bedroom was to become a boudoir for her mother. Did Charlotte Johnson already have plans for her own bedroom?

As evening settled she had to return home. She used the knocker again, but this time the footman opened it.

Her father came out of the library, smiling. "Welcome home, Lucy. I've missed you."

Lucy went into his open arms, loving to be back, but heartsore as well. At this moment, everything about her home seemed the same, but it wasn't. She even felt it would be an intrusion to go into the library behind him. He drew her in there, however, and they sat in their usual chairs, one on either side of the empty hearth.

Did Charlotte sit in this chair at times?

Her mother's portrait was unshrouded. She'd wanted that, but had it been at Charlotte's prompting?

"Now, pet, tell me all your tonnish adventures."

He'd called her "pet" from the cradle.

Only now did it grate.

She cheerfully related balls, the theater, and Almack's, then couldn't resist a mention of Wyvern.

"A few people did murmur about mother and scandal, but then the infamous Earl of Wyvern arrived and quite turned everyone's heads."

"Wyvern? Ah, the one with the very dubious claim to the title."

"I'm surprised you've followed ton gossip, Papa."

"I keep an eye on all significant events, pet, and it's often hard to know what's significant until too late. Such a furor caught my attention. What sort of man is he? Young, I gather."

Lucy hadn't expected to have to discuss Wyvern at length.

"Young, but not callow." She took a moment to consider and then told him about the duel.

"That was well done of him," her father declared. "What wretches to risk your reputation so."

"They were both apologetic in their own way, Papa."

"If anything else like that happens, I'll have something to say."

"Please don't interfere."

"Not watch over my daughter's reputation?"

"I mean, I'm sure nothing like that will happen again."

"So he ripped a stripe off two noblemen, did he? I wonder how he came by a commanding air?"

"Couldn't it simply be his nature?" Lucy asked, wishing she hadn't exposed Wyvern to her father's keen scrutiny. "You came from lowly beginnings, but command your life."

"Fair enough, fair enough, but I'd have thought he'd be a fish out of water among the ton."

"So did I, but he seems to have a wide acquaintance, some of the highest rank."

"Born a bastard and thought to be son of a tavern keeper?" Her father had come alert.

"His mother was a lady, and his sister's a viscountess. Doubtless she provides the entrée."

"Odd, though, very odd."

"How?" she said with a laugh, trying to tease him out of his hawkish mood. Like this, her father could be dangerous to whatever prey was in his eye. "Do you think he's bribed lords and dukes to be amiable?"

"I don't like pieces that don't fit, pet. You'd do well to keep away from him."

Lucy crushed down the urge to argue. He was right, though not for the reasons he had in mind.

"It won't be hard, Papa. He's paying court to a Miss Florence." As soon as it was out she was shocked to be telling her father a lie. That didn't stop her adding, "She's the niece of Maria Celestin's first husband. You remember her? She's Lady Vandeimen now."

"Aye, I remember. Celestin was a sleazy specimen, despite his gloss, and now she's married a young rake. The woman's a fool."

"He's a very tasty rake."

Her father laughed. "Then perhaps not so foolish, as long as he doesn't ruin her. Celestin's niece, eh? Dowered by him?"

"I assume so."

"Could be a sensible match. She'll have a handsome dowry, but she's as dubious as Wyvern. Rumor says she's Celestin's daughter by a married Belgian cousin. But even if she's all she should be, she's from foreign merchant stock. Yes, a good match."

Lucy couldn't bear any more of that.

"And your match, Father? How go the wedding preparations?"

"Well enough," he said, relaxing into a smile. "Charlotte's fixing up the nursery and schoolroom areas to be just as they should be for Ann and Jane, and making some other small alterations."

Lucy reminded herself that it would be unreasonable to object.

"Will you go on a honeymoon?"

"For a short while only. To Canterbury. I suggested Brighton, but Charlotte thinks it too hurly-burly and would like to visit the cathedral. Charlotte's sister will come to care for the girls, but Charlotte doesn't want to be away from them for long."

Once they'd conversed so easily, sometimes late into the night, covering a world of subjects. Now silence threatened.

"How's trade?" Lucy tried. "Does the economy improve? I've lost track of such matters at Aunt Mary's."

"Which is as it should be. Slow improvement, pet, slow, but there's money to be made, especially now there's a proper crackdown on smuggling."

That reminded her of Wyvern's challenge about the price she paid for tea, brandy, and silk.

"Have we ever used Freetrade goods, Papa?"

He shrugged. "Your mother bought her tea cheaply, thinking she got a good price because she bought from friends of mine. I didn't like to disabuse her."

"Is it the same with the silks and lace?"

"If they're foreign made, more than likely, pet. I don't dig too deep into other men's business. Don't make that face. You enjoy the prices and sharing them with your friends."

"But I didn't know," Lucy protested.

"And now you'll pay more?"

"Yes. What of your brandy?"

"It's the way of the world and I've no mind to put any more money than necessary into the government pot to pay for another of the Regent's follies."

"But if you want smuggling stopped, you must stop buying smuggled goods! Without a market, the trade will shrivel."

He shook his head. "I expected the west end to turn your head, pet, but not in a reforming direction. Be at ease. Charlotte's a woman of firm principles, and once I explain the likely source of cheap goods she'll shun them. Could make things difficult now and then, but we'll adapt, as married couples must."

Difficulties?

Because her father's dealings weren't entirely above-board?

Lucy had never seen any sign of that, but she'd never looked.

Perhaps a rapid rise in wealth couldn't be achieved entirely on the right side of the law. Again, her world was being turned upside down.

"Is it spoken of in the Mayfair drawing rooms, then?" he asked. "The Freetrade and the price of silk?"

"That we should all buy British silk to support the industry, certainly. The Regent makes much of that, which is well done of him. Nothing about smuggling, though. Nothing of importance at all. No, that's not true. Slavery was mentioned at one gathering, with support given to Mr. Wilberforce's attempts to outlaw it everywhere. At another, there was discussion about climbing boys and alternative ways to clean chimneys."

"Brushes are much improved and can do the job."

"We use brushes here. Perhaps I can organize a demonstration."

"Don't stick your head up yet, pet. Wait until you're married and 'my lady.' Have your eye on anyone?"

Was she imagining it, or was he keen to hear her say yes?

"Alas, no," she said lightly. "I won't settle for just anyone."

"You're too much your mother's daughter for that. But the season won't go on forever. Will you stay with your aunt afterward? Perhaps go to Brighton or some similar place?"

"Do you want me to?" she challenged.

"I want you to enjoy yourself, pet." She was sure that was true, but also that he hoped she'd be away longer.

Forever?

She managed a smile. "I'm sure you and Charlotte would like the house to yourselves for a while, and I'd like to see Brighton. And the sea."

"You've never seen the sea?" he asked in surprise.

"Not unless the tidal stretch of the Thames counts."

"I suppose when we went traveling it was inland."

"And not too far and not too long, business being demanding."

"A good plan, Brighton," her father said and rose. "I'm engaged at a meeting at the Nutmeg. You won't mind me leaving you alone?"

She rose to kiss his cheek. "When have I ever?"

He left and it felt a more meaningful separation than his spending a few hours elsewhere.

The Nutmeg Inn was a favorite haunt of those merchants with interest in the spice trade. She'd never been there, and probably would not be allowed in, being a woman. There were many other such places, some with express interdicts against women.

That hadn't mattered when her father took her thoughts and concerns to such meetings and returned to talk over all that happened. But could a true partnership exist on that basis, and would her father cooperate? From their recent discussion it seemed more likely that he'd push her out again to "her rightful place." He was so sure he knew what was best for her.

She stood in fury, hands clenched, wanting to smash something. Things weren't to blame, however. People were. The world was.

Wasn't it possible to change the world?

The crepe had been removed from her mother's portrait, and something else. She scanned the room, trying to decide what was missing. The Indian statue. The goddess Lakshmi. It was supposed to bring good fortune and wealth to the house.

There'd been nothing lewd about it. It had shown an Indian lady in a lovely gown and headdress, holding a horn of plenty in one hand, pouring gold coins into a pot with another, and flowers in the other two. Perhaps it was the four arms that were intolerable to Charlotte, but more likely she thought it pagan.

There was something else.

Ah, a new china potpourri jar. A slightly different scent.

And hadn't there been a change in the hall?

She walked out and looked around. The statuette of the naked discus thrower had been replaced by a vase,

and a painting of a shepherd with his shepherdess had
gone. Were even two simpering country lovers too sug-
gestive for Charlotte?

Who would soon be Mrs. Potter and rule here.

Lucy went up to her bedroom, which was blessedly
untouched, thinking about the shepherd and his shepherdess, and the Peasant Earl and Iphigenia.

Tonight was Lady Iphigenia's ball. Would Wyvern be
there? Would he dance with her?

How much was her dowry?

Impossible to summon a carriage and race over there
to intervene, and foolish in all regards. After wasting
time looking west toward Mayfair, Lucy went early to
bed.

She expected to enjoy a night in the comfortable privacy of her familiar bed, but she lay sleepless. When the
clocks struck midnight, she realized Lady Iphigenia's
ball would still be frolicking along. When it struck one,
she knew everyone would be leaving supper to return to
the dance.

She forced her mind away from that, but then it
latched onto her father's words about the Freetrade.
She'd always believed him honest, but he saw nothing
amiss with using smuggled goods. He'd always driven a
hard bargain, and perhaps not always looked closely at
the origins of cheap goods.

She'd never come across anything she'd think of as
illegal, but her involvement had been in his prosperous
days. He'd probably done any number of shady things
when starting out, perhaps especially after his marriage.

She could imagine how that would have spurred his
ambition. He'd have wanted to prove to his highborn
bride that he was worthy. He'd have needed to give her
a life close to the one she'd abandoned for love of him.
He'd succeeded, more or less. Her mother had settled
into the City with ease and made friends. But had she

shown a preference for the company of Maria Celestin, the merchant's wife who was from the same background as she? Had she concealed a hurt from being cut off by her father?

Lucy's father had always been her rock, even when he'd failed to understand her ambitions. She'd always felt entirely sure of his love and support. If she were to elope with someone he disapproved of, he'd never cut her out of his life.

But he *was* cutting her out of his life in another way. He was turning toward his new wife and putting her first. Was it in the Bible or the wedding service that a man was commanded to forsake all others and cleave to his wife?

Whichever, Lucy had never expected to be forsaken.

She was alarmed to find herself crying, not in a burst, but in a miserable leak of eyes and runny nose and with a deep ache in her chest. Betty had always said she felt better after a good cry, but Lucy didn't find that it worked that way at all.

Chapter 16

David didn't hear that Lucinda Potter had left her aunt's house until he arrived at Lady Galloway's ball. Lord Northcliff approached him.

"The lovely Aphrodite has left these environs, Wyvern. Not your doing, is it?"

David stared at the man. "What do you mean by that?"

Northcliff's jaw set. "You singled her out. Now she flees. Damned sweet little thing."

The deuce, was he to end up tangled in a duel himself?

"First I knew about it," he said, "and I assure you I've done nothing to offend." Remembering his part, he added, "Quite the contrary, in fact. Miss Potter seemed to enjoy my company."

Northcliff took the hint. "Ah. I see. Apologies."

He stalked away and David crossed the room to his sister. "What's happened with Miss Potter?"

"Happened?" Susan asked. "Nothing."

"According to Northcliff, she's run off somewhere."

"What? What did you do?"

"Nothing! Nothing she didn't want, at least."

"David . . ."

"Nothing bad, either. Look, find out, please? If someone's hurt her . . ."

She touched his clenched fist. "Gently, dear. You can't thrash anyone yet. I'll see if the Caldrosses are here."

A minute later, Eleanor Delaney appeared at his side. "I'm sent on guard duty until Susan returns."

"What a wild man you must all think me."

"You're reasonably civilized, but you've had to learn to be less so at times. And love is not temperate."

"I don't have to love a woman to want to avenge any insult to her. One of her swarming suitors might have crossed the line. At Almack's she had no intention of leaving."

"Hard to imagine a means of insult between then and now unless she's given to wandering the night streets, or some wretch invaded her bedroom at dark of night."

David gave her a smile for that absurdity, but Lucy was given to visiting the park. He'd been there this morning and regretted that she had not. But had she been interrupted en route, assaulted, even?

Then why not come to me?

Idiotic.

She'd run home to her father.

Damnation. Who was the offender? He'd tear him apart.

Susan returned, smiling. Was that a real smile or simulation?

"She's returned to the City, yes," she said, "but not in alarm."

Some of the tension eased. "In misery? Why?"

She shook her head. "Not that, either. I didn't find the Caldrosses, but they'd left a trail of gossip. One of Miss Potter's friends is to marry in days and she's returned to assist and attend."

"She'd have known about it. She'd have said."

He saw Susan and Eleanor share a look, but was beyond caring.

Susan said, "If you find one of the Caldrosses, I'm sure

they'll share the details, but there seems to be no cause for alarm."

David wasn't satisfied. There were kisses to consider. She wouldn't lightly forego those. Or was she fleeing her debt? All his instincts said no, but perhaps he'd frightened her with that risky kiss at Almack's and she'd realized how easily she could be compromised. After all, she didn't want to marry.

He set off to find Clara Fytch and ask her to dance. She was silly but not stupid, and as they strolled toward the dance floor she said, "I'm delighted to be Lucinda's substitute, my lord. No, I don't mind! Not at all. This should focus the minds of the gentlemen I am interested in." She giggled. "That sounded very discourteous, but you know what I mean."

"Yes," David said, smiling back. If Lucinda was in trouble, then her cheerful cousin had all the sensitivity of a brick. "I gather Miss Potter has returned home for a wedding?"

"And a marvelously romantic one! At least, the bride and groom seem quite boring, but they've had to wait for her father's return from distant lands. He's home and they'll marry with all speed. Alas, I doubt my father would ever travel far."

"Then if you want romance, why not travel yourself?" When she looked blankly at him, he teased, "An elopement, perhaps?"

Her eyes went wide. "Lord Wyvern!"

The deuce. Had she thought he'd proposed that they elope?

"Scotland is so far," she said, and he had no idea what she was thinking. "Oh, look, Stevenhope is leading out Lady Iphigenia. The king's daughter is beyond your reach." She accompanied those words with a teasing smile, which was as bewildering as anything before.

David gave thanks for the beginning of the dance. Lord save him from such a tangled knot of a mind. How wonderful that Lucinda Potter's mind was straight and clear, and that her reason for returning to the City was without alarm.

He hoped she was already missing his attentions and their kisses. Come to think of it, by the time she returned she could have run up quite a debt of them.

Lucy welcomed the wedding eve, because it was such a whirl that private thoughts were impossible. In the morning she was summoned for yet another last-minute shopping expedition. In the afternoon Betty's closest friends gathered for tea.

Taxed or untaxed, Lucy wondered, as Betty blended tea from different canisters in a beautiful inlaid tea box her father had given her as a wedding gift.

Lucy enjoyed the opportunity to catch up with everyone's news. There were two friends she hadn't seen for months because they'd married last year and had new responsibilities. One of them, Amanda York, had moved out of the City to Islington for greenery and cleaner air.

"I look toward London in the worst weather and shudder," she said. "A pall of smoke. It's no wonder the nobility keep their children in the country."

"It's not so bad," defended Abigail Carpenter, who still lived in the City and had a baby son.

"Will you live in the City, Betty?" Amanda asked. "Or move out?"

Betty grimaced at being brought into the debate, but said, "Here to begin with, in James's father's house, of course. But I admit, in time I might prefer somewhere more rural. When there are children."

Lucy remembered her mother sometimes mentioning the advantages of a move out of the City. Her father had generally responded to her every desire, but he'd balked at that, saying he needed both his business and his family close-by.

"Tell us about your adventures, Lucy," Betty said, clearly wanting a change of subject.

So Lucy amused them with tales of tonnish oddities. Her account of Stevenhope at supper was much appreciated.

"It wasn't so amusing at the time," she protested.

"I'm sure it wasn't," said Abigail, "but definitely something to remember. After all, how many of us have poetry written about us?"

"'Thus Aphrodite is a wilting bloom,'" Amanda recited, "'to flourish soon as goddess of my drawing room.'"

Everyone fell into laughter again.

Lucy struck an attitude. "I wilt, I wilt!"

Betty pretended to wield a watering can. "Revive, Aphrodite!"

It was all wonderful fun, but it was beginning to seem more like a wake than a celebration. They were all in their early twenties, and some were already married and mothers. As such, they had new responsibilities and interests.

Perhaps in the coming years all her friends would marry and move to suburban villas, for it was the flow of progress, something she'd always supported. Now, she wished she could rebuild the walls of the City of London to hold her world together.

Some of her friends might never marry, but none by happy choice.

Jenny Bunyan's father had lost most of his money in the economic chaos after the war, and having also lost his wife to the influenza, he was intent on keeping Jenny at home to take care of him.

Rachel Islip had a walleye and something of an odd way to her, even though she was clever and good-natured.

Susannah Brown was plain, but had compounded her problems by trying to elope with a dashing officer. They'd been stopped and the man had turned out to be an unscrupulous fortune hunter who'd abandoned her entirely once the game was up. Now her reputation was tarnished.

Rachel and Susannah were reasonably well dowered and would probably find husbands, but would theirs be marriages of love or desperation? All three probably wondered why she was uncommitted, but Lucy wasn't prepared for Jenny's attack as they were leaving.

"No man to your taste, Lucy, not even in the west end?"

"Perhaps especially in the west end," Lucy said lightly, wondering at the tone.

"Or perhaps not anywhere."

Had Jenny guessed her secret ambition when so many others hadn't?

"What do you mean?"

"I mean," whispered Jenny, "that you've never encouraged a suitor. Some women prefer not to marry."

"I suppose that's true."

"Or not to marry men."

"What? You think they want to marry boys?"

Jenny's lips pinched. "I mean some wish to live as if married with women."

Lucy had heard of such things, though she wasn't clear on what was involved. "You think I . . . ?"

Jenny sniffed, nose in air. "You best know what sins you harbor in your heart, Lucy Potter, but I'm glad to see Betty safe from you!"

Lucy watched her go, jaw-dropped.

"What did she say?" asked Amanda, pulling on gloves.

Lucy couldn't repeat the words.

"Pay her no heed. She's become vinegary, poor dear. Her father treats her as little better than a servant. Give thanks that your father is marrying again."

"My father's never treated me as a servant."

"Of course not, but you're free now to set up your own establishment."

Lucy was bemused by the idea that she'd not wed in order to take care of her father. They had an excellent housekeeper. But what really surprised her was that Amanda thought her setting up home by herself was a matter of no moment.

"You think I can?" she asked.

"Lucy! You can marry whenever you snap your fingers! What else did you think I meant?"

"I have considered a home of my own. . . ."

"Heavens, no. No one would know what to make of you. You've always been a little different, dear, but I'm sure you don't want to be an *eccentric*." Amanda hugged her. "Marry and be happy. You'll find it's delightful, all in all."

Lucy made her way slowly across the road, feeling stunned by two attacks, though Amanda's hadn't been meant as such. Jenny's ridiculous suspicion could be laughed off, but Amanda was a sensible, good-natured friend. In her eyes there was no pleasant future other than marriage, and Lucy had to admit that she couldn't think of a single example to set against that. Nor could she think of a young unmarried woman who engaged in trade. Those few who did were older, and generally widows.

She certainly didn't want to be an eccentric.

Perhaps it was weak to shrink from that. Perhaps she should be willing to be like brave women of the past who'd flouted society to follow a dream, but examples like Joan of Arc came too readily to mind. No one was going to burn her at the stake, but she'd hate being sneered at as peculiar, whispered about as a scandal, and forever excluded from normal life.

When she arrived home, she found her father, but

Charlotte Johnson was there, too, smiling, welcoming. Oh so clearly they were intent on making her part of the new family.

She wanted to scream, but she took a light supper with them and managed to bear her part in the conversation. She told the Stevenhope story again, but Charlotte said, "It perhaps wasn't kind to make fun of the man, Lucy."

"He made a fool of himself, and I kept a straight face. I was the only one."

"Such a cruel world," Charlotte said.

"On the contrary, I find many people kind. Lady Ball and Lady Vandeimen have helped me feel at ease. They were both acquainted with my mother, of course."

Even as she spoke she could hear the edge, and was she even flaunting aristocratic acquaintances?

Charlotte showed no upset. "Your mother's lineage must make you more comfortable in that setting. I'm sure I could never be."

She made that sound like a virtue.

"Some of the activities are very interesting, and often informative." Lucy described concerts, exhibitions, and even a talk on bone carvings, but she felt *humored*.

She'd probably once felt as Charlotte did—that the beau monde flitted about in idle pleasures while others worked.

"Of course," she tried, "all these people will soon be back taking care of their estates."

"Or off to Brighton to play games with the Regent," her father said.

Unfortunately true.

Charlotte surprised Lucy. "I gather sea air is very healthy, and even sea-bathing, if done decently. I wouldn't wish to visit Brighton, but some other, quieter place might be beneficial, as might country air."

"I'm sure you're right, dear," Lucy's father said, and

she recognized the tone. He had no intention of doing any such thing.

Her mother had always accepted that tone, for it was rarely used, but Lucy had the feeling Charlotte would not. She had the horrible feeling that Charlotte had plans, not just for trips to the seaside, but for a move out of the City, to a leafy villa and clean air. And that Charlotte, in her own way, had a will as strong as her father's.

She retired early, leaving the couple alone.

Would they kiss, or were they too old for that sort of courtship?

Would they in time be engaged in battle over where to live and raise their children? Lucy could have told Charlotte how to win. Simply suggest that City air had played a part in her mother's death. With or without that, she suspected that Charlotte would triumph in the end.

She opened her journal, realizing that she hadn't written in it since returning home. She'd had infinite time and privacy, but she'd written nothing. Because thoughts written down became more real?

She forced herself to lay it down.

> *This is no longer my home,*
> *And may soon not be my father's home, either.*
> *Not here for me to visit if I wished.*
> *I will have no home.*

There. Set into words, like the carving on a gravestone.

> *I long to restore the past,*
> *To belong here once again,*
> *And live as I once lived,*
> *Part of this exciting City world.*
> *But perhaps I never did.*
> *Perhaps that was illusion.*

The world I knew is breaking up
Like the ice on the river after the Frost Fair.
Cracking, floating away, dissolving entirely.
Even if it still existed, would I want to remain,
Barred from true involvement by my sex?

The last word was clumsy because she'd worn her pencil lead down to nothing. She took her sharp knife and whittled away wood to expose a fresh, clean point. With it, she wrote:

I must accept the loss, and build a new life.

After a moment, she surrendered, though she wrote it gently, the pencil hardly pressing on the page.

David. His name is David.
David and the kite.
Playful, warm, tender with a child.
Remember that. It must be as much
A part of him as the earl in amber light.
Groomed, polished, dark and dangerous.
Too dangerous for an earl,
Or for an estate manager.

She paused to consider that.

Who is the real man?
Such mysteries should make me wary,
But instead they add to his wicked appeal.
They draw me to the flame.
He is a mystery I must explore
All my life long.

That was where this had been heading.
As her mother had wanted her father, so she had

wanted, from the first, the very first. Perhaps even from
that first glimpse in Winsom's. At least she hadn't fixed
on an impoverished young merchant. She was madly,
passionately in love with a handsome young earl. Impoverished, yes, but definitely a step up.

She couldn't help but smile.

A whole staircase up!

Her mother's father had disapproved, but her own
father would be delighted.

She remembered his queries about Wyvern, but she
knew he'd like him when they met, because in some ways
they were alike. They were both practical rather than
scholarly. They both had clear, sharp minds. They were
both strong in a particular way that came from having
had to carve out their fortunes.

Even their origins were similar. Both had grown up
believing themselves to be bastards. David had the edge
in knowing who his parents were, but his mother was a
wanton and the identity of his father had been confused.

Her new life would present challenges, but she enjoyed challenges. The wife of an impoverished earl would
have work to do. She had little experience of the management of a large house, but she could learn. She could
be frugal, for her parents had never indulged in foolish
extravagance.

There could be work for her to do on the estate and
she could learn that, too. There could even be business
to make prosper. Many noblemen had mines on their
lands. There were tin and copper mines in Cornwall. Did
that extend into Devon?

Fish? She knew nothing about the fish trade except
that there never seemed to be enough fresh fish to supply the needs of London. Dried and salted fish was im-
ported from abroad at a good profit. Could more be
made close to home?

Her money could be used to develop many types of

industry in the area. If there were fast-running streams, they could power mills and even factories. There were new developments in steam power, and new machinery to be run by it.

She laughed. Her father would say she was running away with an idea, as she was wont to do, but it felt wonderful. All she really wanted in life was a worthwhile purpose.

And an earl. A particular, unusual earl.

Who didn't want to marry her.

She shrugged that away. She knew what she felt, and what she sensed in him. She had only to remember their kisses.

He was hers to claim.

Betty's wedding took on new brilliance in the light of Lucy's thoughts. On her wedding day she'd shine with joy as Betty did. She'd look at her husband—at David—as Betty looked at James. She'd leave her wedding breakfast in expectation of a wondrous wedding night.

All the same, when she hugged Betty farewell, Betty said, "Tears? You?"

Lucy smiled and wiped them away. "Silliness."

"No, I feel it, too. It's an end of some things, isn't it?"

"And a beginning of everything."

"For you, too? You've found your love? A lord?"

Lucy longed to share everything with her friend, but this wasn't the time. "Not a Scottish one, I promise. When you return from your honeymoon, perhaps I'll have a tale to tell."

"I look forward to it. I want you to be as happy as I am."

"That would be a blessing," Lucy said and hugged her friend one last time.

A silly thought, but as Betty said, this marked an end to so many aspects of their lives.

That night in her bed Lucy couldn't help thinking of Betty, discovering the full mysteries of marriage. Knowing Betty and James, there would be laughter along with passion. But would they attempt the extraordinary positions in those Indian drawings?

The kite-flying man would be a lighthearted lover.

What sort of lover would the darkly masterful man be? Remembering the way he'd seized her in that garden, she shivered, but it wasn't with fear. He'd excited her in a way she'd never experienced before, but wanted to again, soon.

So would it be.

On Sunday morning, Lucy longed to rush back to Mayfair, but she was expected to attend church before leaving. When she went downstairs, ready to walk to St. Michael's, she must have shown the effects of a night spent in waking dreams.

Her father said, "I wouldn't have expected a simple wedding to wear you down, pet, when you're accustomed to ton gallivanting."

Lucy knew lies wouldn't work, so she said, "I lay awake a while, thinking about changes. Betty and I will never be the same again."

"True enough, but as young married women you'll be as close."

She might as well prepare the ground. "Not if I marry into the nobility."

"Ah, you have a man in mind?"

Lucy realized that this wasn't the moment, not when her father had suspicions.

"Perhaps, but nothing is settled."

"I hope not. Of age you might be, Lucy, but I'll have my say."

But not right of refusal, she said silently.

It was pleasant to attend service in the familiar church

where she'd been baptized, and to chat afterward with people she'd known all her life. But then she began to feel that they already saw her as part of another world. Perhaps it was her clothing. She was wearing the pink gown in which she'd moved to Aunt Mary's, and a bonnet raised eight inches with a confection of feathers and flowers. No other lady was dressed that way.

In church, Charlotte and her daughters had shared her father's pew. They were already treated as part of the Potter family, perhaps more comfortably a part of this world now than Lucy was.

So be it. She was reconciled to that.

As they turned to stroll back to the house, Lucy maneuvered to walk with the girls and their nursemaid, letting her father walk with Charlotte, as it should be.

When the carriage came to the door and she took farewell of her father, he said, "You'll be back home soon for our wedding, pet."

She agreed, but her mind was already turned toward other futures, other homes. Today was Sunday, which her aunt insisted on treating as a pious day. How was Wyvern to woo her, and how was she to pay with kisses?

She was sure he'd find a way.

Chapter 17

"How was the wedding?" Clara demanded as soon as Lucy was through the front door. "Did you cry?"

"Of course," Lucy said. "It was lovely, probably because Betty and James are so much in love. They glowed."

Clara clasped her hands. "I hope I'm like that on my wedding day!" But then she asked, "Was she not a little nervous?"

"No. Why should she be?"

Clara dragged Lucy up to their bedroom. "The wedding night!"

"Oh, that. She and James have known each other for years."

"You mean . . . ?"

Lucy laughed. "Not in the Biblical sense! Really, Clara."

Clara was red. "I'm sorry. I just thought . . . in the country, you know, some betrothed couples do, you know. Before the wedding."

"Truly? Why?"

"Because the farming life is hard for a childless couple. Generally, if there are no children, they adopt some from families with too many, but it's better to have plenty of their own. I thought it might be like that in the City. After all, your father must want a son. That's doubtless why he's marrying again."

It still hurt.

Lucy took off her bonnet. "Tell me, what news of Town?" *Speak to me of Wyvern.*

"Tittle-tattle. Nothing of importance. Except Stevenhope has offered for Lady Iphigenia and been accepted. So the poor Peasant Earl has lost his love. I teased him about it."

"Stevenhope?"

"Wyvern! He danced with me at Lady Galloway's ball, but only because he wanted to know why you weren't there."

"I'm sure that's not true."

"Of course it was! At least . . . I don't *think* he asked me to elope with him."

Lucy turned to her. "*What?*"

"I don't think so. It was such an odd thing to say."

"What did he say?"

"That it would be exciting to elope."

Pure rage sizzled through her. "You must have been mistaken."

"I wasn't! The exact words. More or less. Then I teased him about Lady Iphigenia, because Stevenhope was leading her out for the first dance, which can have significance, as you know. Do you think that's why Wyvern sort of proposed? Because I agreed to the first dance with him? But I have only a modest dowry, so I'm sure not, and there was nothing of *that* in his manner, though he was a little odd. Do you think madness can be concealed?"

I think a short time with you could derange anyone.

"So he didn't actually propose?" Lucy asked.

"No. But why else mention elopement?"

Lucy had no idea, but equilibrium had returned. There were a host of reasons Wyvern wouldn't want to marry Clara and scarcely a one that he should. She dragged talk back to a firm point.

"Stevenhope and Lady Iphigenia. Is she the type to enjoy being described as a wilting bloom?"

Clara giggled. "I fear so, because she *does* wilt. As if her bones were soft. Even her curls droop. And he's quite well-to-do, so she'll be a comfortable wilt as long as she can humor his mother."

"His mother?"

"Sour and eagle-eyed."

Lucy sat down. "I never even considered mothers. Never say she lives nearby."

"Not merely nearby—in his house! Not even in the dower house, though a mother-in-law can be formidable from there. I shall attempt to find a husband with a dead or absent mother."

"Wyvern's mother is as far away as a mother could be."

Lucy immediately regretted saying that, but Clara merely giggled. "A point in his favor!"

It was indeed. As was him needing to know why she was absent. He must have missed her. . . .

"Don't you think?"

Lucy had been far away. "About what?"

"Lord Darien! Is he a murderer like his brother?"

"Who's Lord Darien?"

Lucy listened to the latest scandal—a story gory enough to be in a novel. Lord Darien's brother had murdered an innocent young lady, and now suspicion hung over him, too, because bad blood ran in the family.

"Poor man," Lucy said.

"You have such a soft heart!" Clara protested. "Darien looks a thorough villain. He scowls and is scarred."

"That surely isn't to be counted against him. Didn't you say he'd been a soldier?"

"Oh, very well, but he certainly wouldn't be a comfortable husband."

"Is that what you want?"

"Of course. Don't you?"

"I'm not sure," Lucy said, but it was another deceit. A comfortable husband sounded like a feather bed—good for sleep, but not for the waking hours. And perhaps not for passion, either.

Wyvern would not be an entirely comfortable husband. He'd shown her that.

When would she meet him again?

She had his address now and could write to him. So tempting, but she had enough sense left not to show her hand so clearly. She'd wait for him to make the move.

She was sure he would.

The Caldrosses were so bold as to stroll in the park in the late afternoon, for Aunt Mary declared that admiration of God's work was suitable for His day. Conveniently, this meant encounters with others of the same devout purpose, charitably intent on sharing gossip. Stevenhope and Lady Iphigenia were mentioned, as was the Darien scandal, but there was a bounty of more trivial news.

Lucy was struck by the fact that she now knew most of the people mentioned, at least by name, and could understand much of the innuendo. Willy-nilly, she'd become part of this. But the principal person on her mind, Lord Wyvern, did not appear.

Devout obligation to family took them out of the house in the evening to dine with Lord Caldross's younger brother, a naval captain. Aunt Mary traveled with the manner of a Christian martyr approaching the Coliseum, and Lucy could share her feelings, for of a certainty Wyvern wouldn't be there, either.

She assumed her aunt expected tedium, but she soon understood why red-nosed Captain Fytch was landlocked with a position at the Admiralty. She certainly wouldn't trust him with a ship. He was on the go when they arrived, and rollicking drunk by the time they left.

He tried to pinch her cheek, with a look in his eye that suggested other desires. She made a startled movement that "accidentally" struck him just below his bulbous nose.

He staggered back, cursing.

Lucy gushed apologies while allowing Aunt Mary to drag her away.

To think she'd sometimes regretted her lack of close relatives. Wyvern's strange parentage and lack of family was more delightful by the moment. But where the devil was he, as suitor or as employee demanding wages owed? Sunday propriety shouldn't present an insuperable problem.

Perhaps he'd tired of the game. Was she out of sight, out of mind? Was he back in attendance on Miss Florence? Her heart wouldn't believe it, but her mind preached the inconstancy of men.

When they arrived home, Lucy expected even her aunt and cousin to have drained the well of chatter, but they were finding new words to wrap around Captain Fytch's flaws. From that they spun on to other sad cases of drunkenness.

When the clock struck ten Lucy used the excuse of poetry to escape to her room and be miserable. She went to the window to look out at the night sky, stewing over Wyvern's perfidy. Sunday presented challenges, but challenges existed to be overcome. He could easily have been in the park.

She took out her journal and sharpened her pencil to a particularly fine point.

Wyvern, she wrote, and underlined it.

The wretch. The inconstant slime.
We had a bargain!
Just because I left Mayfair for a while

Gives him no excuse for inconstancy.
I should turn my back on him.
But where then would I go?
Is . . .

She paused to glance at the window. Rain? It had seemed a clear night. The glass showed no droplets. That splattering again.

Not water.

Soil?

She went to look and down below, in the small moon-lit yard, stood Wyvern, looking up.

She raised the sash window. "What are you doing there?" she whispered.

"Collecting my debts. Come down."

He hadn't abandoned the game, but he was all silver and darkness down there.

She shook her head. "I don't know the way. There are servants down there."

"Are you truly so feeble?"

"Hush! Someone will hear."

"Then come down."

He wasn't trying to soften his voice at all!

"No. I'll pay you tomorrow."

She shut the window and turned away, but she bit her lip on delight. He'd not tired of the game and he'd not slipped into the attractions of Natalie Florence!

She remembered how he'd looked, all mysterious, masterful man, and for a moment she considered his mad invitation. Perhaps there was a way out. Perhaps the servants were all in bed. If any were still awake and in the kitchen area, wouldn't they have heard the foolhardy man?

No. She wouldn't be teased into folly like that, but she sat down at the desk to record the incident.

Dark and light. Tempting into folly.
But there. Daring. Wanting?

She seemed to have lost the ability to use sentences!
She collected herself and wrote:

This night, Lord Wyvern ventured
Into the yard at the back of the house.
He tried to persuade me to go down to him,
The outrageous man. Yet I was tempted.
Kisses are owed and I . . .

What was that? A thump above. She looked up. He
couldn't be up on the roof. Could he?

She hurried to the door and opened it to listen. Had
her aunt and cousin been alarmed? They were at the
front of the house, however, far from this back room, and
still talking. She closed the door and looked toward the
window—to see Wyvern looking in at her.

She ran over and opened it again. "What are you doing? How . . . ?"

He was holding onto a double rope. A rope that went
up above him and dangled to the ground. One booted
foot was in a loop, the other braced against the brick
wall.

"Grappling iron. I came prepared for a lady too feeble to escape her house. Move aside."

She obeyed before she thought not to and he swung
through the window. He was in country clothes again.

David.

"You can't come in here! My cousin sleeps with me."

"I hope you mean Clara and not the lad with dandy
aspirations."

"Of course I do. I can't believe you're doing this.
You're mad!"

This was the kite-flying man, however, light and bright in the candlelight.

"Comes in the blood," he said. "Does your door lock?"

"Yes, but I can't lock it. What would Clara think?"

"You care? I'm surprised at that in your father's daughter."

She sent him a fierce look and went to lock the door. "If Clara comes and wonders, I can say my muse needed complete privacy."

"Does that make sense?"

"Perfectly, which is more than your behavior does."

"How do you come to that? I'm here, am I not, alone with you in a locked room?"

He was still smiling, but the look in his eyes made her step back, so she came up against the door, heart hammering. "I owe only kisses, sir, and I set the nature of them. What's more, as you've had no opportunity to do the necessary service, I owe you nothing."

"Shabby, Miss Potter. It wasn't my fault you weren't available to be served. How went the wedding?"

"You know where I went and why?"

"Your aunt and cousin knew, and so the whole world knew."

"It went perfectly, being a rational match between two well-suited people."

"How chilly."

"Not at all. They're desperately in love." And now, she realized, on their second night in their marriage bed. She'd glanced toward the bed.

He strolled there and leaned his hips against the high mattress, his long legs stretched out.

"Get away from there!"

"The sooner you pay the debt, the sooner I'll be gone."

"I'm not kissing you there."

"The mere proximity of a bed being ruinous? I'm making it easier for you. My lounging like this eliminates some of the height difference. Come on, wench. Pay up."

Again, there was no reason to obey, but Lucy did. She crossed the carpet aware of moving like a wench, a wicked wench. He spread his legs and that didn't deter her. She came to a stop within them.

But not too close.

"True," she assessed, trying to take command of the situation. "Your lips are at a good height."

"Is 'good' quite the right word?" His eyes were bright with wicked temptation and the bed lay just behind him.

Hands behind her back, Lucy pecked at his lips four times and stepped back. "There. Now go."

"You consider that fair payment?"

"Perfectly within the terms of our agreement."

"But what about the interest?"

"Interest?" The look in his eyes sent a shiver through her, and yet, poor foolish woman that she was, a delicious one.

"Three days overdue. Back you come."

"Three days without work. You only deserve half pay. Now you owe me."

"Then I must pay."

"That's not what I meant!"

"And I thought you an honest woman."

"You thought me all deceit and deception."

"No more. Come closer, Aphrodite."

There was no reason on earth to obey the soft, sweet summons, but Lucy couldn't have resisted to save her life.

When she was back against him, closer to him, almost touching him, he put a finger beneath her chin and lowered his lips to hers. Lips to lips, in keeping with their bargain, but he lingered.

Lucy sighed and moved closer. His hands came behind her, holding her close. Closer than was decent, but no closer than she wanted to be. Heart pounding, she angled her head a little, seeking closeness of another sort. Their lips parted, tongues touched. Sweet heat softening her muscles and her will . . .

She jerked back, stepped back—his hands allowed it—and retreated.

He smiled in a triumphant way that curled her toes.

"Are all debts settled?" she demanded.

"For now. I'm sure you'll be prompt with your payments in future."

"Of a certainty!"

"And that you feel the insufficiency of those kisses as much as I do. You'd lie on this bed in my arms, goddess, if you weren't afraid of being caught."

Caught!

Lucy slammed back to full awareness of where she was. She gestured toward the window. "Go."

He folded his arms. "I think I'll wait until your cousin knocks."

"That could be an age!"

"How delightful."

Lucy marched to the door and turned the key. "There. She can walk straight in. If she finds you here, we'll be married within the week."

"Not wise to challenge a dragon. Can you be sure that capturing your dowry isn't my purpose after all?"

"Then I'd refuse to marry you!"

"What a tangle you're in." He rose, seeming to take up much of the modest room. "It might be a mercy to straighten it out. . . ."

Lucy heard her cousin's voice, bidding her aunt good night.

"Go!" she insisted, panic starting.

He just stood there.

She held his eyes for moments, but then quickly turned the key again, leaning back against the door. "Please go. Neither of us wants such a scandal."

"Don't we?" But then he said, "This time, I obey." He swung out of the window, but paused, looking back. "The park. Tomorrow."

Then he moved down and out of sight.

Clara turned the knob, then rattled the door. "Lucinda? Are you all right?"

Lucy ran to close the window, refusing to look down to be sure he was safe; then she hurried back to unlock the door.

"It was only that my muse particularly didn't want to be disturbed."

Even Clara looked a little dubious at that. "Did I hear the window close?"

"I was listening to a nightingale."

"And trying to capture it in words? Is it still singing?"

Lucy couldn't stop her cousin from opening the window to listen. She waited tensely, but clearly Clara saw nothing amiss. What had he done with the rope?

Clara also didn't hear a nightingale.

"A shame it's stopped," she said, closing the window again. "They're rare here." Then she glanced at the desk.

Lucy's journal lay open. The short lines served their purpose and also supported the notion of the nightingale and muse, but Lucy could only pray Clara wasn't sharp-eyed enough to be able to read any of the words at that distance.

She went as carelessly as she could to close the book and put it away. Clara didn't show any further suspicions and rang for their washing water.

Lucy saw a slight trace of dirty boot on the carpet. She went to stand on it, swiveling her foot to disperse it.

Tangled, he'd said.

Knotted!

But she had to bite her lips on a smile. That scandalous visit had been shocking, but a delight, delicious in every way.

And it had ended on a promise.

The park.

Tomorrow.

Chapter 18

When the window shut again, David emerged from the shadows of the house, crossed the yard, and climbed easily over a back wall that didn't even have broken glass along the top. He wound the rope around his torso, then picked up his evening cloak from where he'd left it and put it on. He continued down the lane, a gentleman on his way home.

He'd had to leave the hook, which was caught in the top of the ridge tile, but there'd be no other evidence.

With this adventure in mind, he'd assessed the house earlier and seen how easy it would be. He'd stood watch, and seen Lucinda at the window. He hadn't known she shared the room with her cousin, so matters could have been interesting.

A more cautious man wouldn't have attempted such a thing, but once he'd seen that it was possible, he hadn't been able to resist. Lucinda Potter's absence had been close to intolerable, and had driven home how hopeless it was to consider any other woman. He was as committed as his wild mother had been. It must be in the blood.

He'd wanted action, too. Town life was damned tame and physically stultifying, despite the availability of boxing, quarterstaff, and other such follies. He longed for his purposefully active life back home, and yes, even for the blood-firing danger of a smuggling run.

Invading Lucinda Potter's room, kissing Lucinda Potter, had come close.

He smiled as he made his way back to Con's house. He'd wondered how she'd respond to an invasion, and had been braced for anything from a gunshot to a scream. The gunshot had been possible, but he wasn't surprised that she hadn't screamed.

She was a goddess in all ways.

And as he'd suspected, riper than she knew. If not for fear of her cousin's arrival, he could probably have coaxed her onto the bed and kissed her into ruin.

Into marriage.

Aye, there's the rub.

His mind was a tangled mess, aware of all the problems and dangers, but ruled by his need for this one woman, who became more delightful at every meeting. He no longer thought her deceptive by nature, and she might have the free-thinking courage to be wife to a smuggling earl. He could make his Devon home tolerable to her. He'd even spend months here in London every year. As a peer, he should.

But she did not intend to wed, and he could see why. She was in clear possession of a fortune, an independent woman, and marriage would steal that, trusts be damned. It would be like a freed slave returning to the yoke.

Life was hard for a single woman, however, no matter how rich, and especially for such a passionate one. He could make her a good husband, and allow her all the freedom she wanted. Which couldn't start by tricking her into compromising herself.

She must come to him freely, and without doubt. His love for her could allow no other way.

Lucy did get some sleep, but not much. Being so madly in love was the ruin of rest. Even so, she woke early, full of anticipation.

The park!

The day was overcast. It might even rain. She cared not one whit. Soon she was out of doors and on her way, decorously accompanied by Hannah. She entered the park, seeking him, fretting that she was too early, too late, in the wrong part of Hyde Park. . . .

"Miss Potter. How delightful."

David.

He was in his country clothes. He raised his hat as he greeted her, and surely his eyes were warm.

"Do you walk here every morning, my lord?" she asked for Hannah's hearing as she turned to stroll with him along a path.

"Whenever possible. I miss open spaces and greenery."

"Look around, my lord. Open spaces and greenery in abundance."

"Surrounded by a million people."

"Hyde Park sits on the edge of London, not in the middle," she pointed out.

"Precise as always."

"You make that seem a fault."

"Not at all. I admire a clear mind. I admire much about you."

Lucy had to work not to show all her hopes and expectations then and there.

"Where shall we go so you can pay your daily debt?" he asked. "That stand of trees looks promising."

Extremely promising.

"You can sit on that bench there, Hannah, and wait. Lord Wyvern and I are going to study those trees."

No wonder Hannah gave her a look as she sat down, but it was as much of a smirk as a frown.

They strolled across the grass, and then the first shade of green leaves came over them. Green, greenwood, greenery. Terms often used for wicked behavior. A green-skirted lass was one who'd lain on the grass with a man.

"Such interesting bark," he said, stroking the textured trunk of a tree with his bare hand. She hadn't realized before that he wasn't wearing gloves. The informality seemed like a warning.

Lucy studied the tree. "Brown and gray, but mostly brown."

"This one is more gray."

She went with him to the next. Deeper into the cool, moist greenwood, but with the happy cries of children still nearby, cut with a sharp command from a nursemaid.

She traced a gloved fingertip over grayish bark. "A smoother texture."

"Beech." He took her hand and drew her on. "This is a similar color, but rougher. You can't truly appreciate it wearing this." He unfastened the mother-of-pearl button at her wrist and pulled off her glove, finger by finger. Then he pressed her naked hand on the fissured trunk. "Linden."

His hand was large and warm over hers, skin on skin. "Do you know all the trees?" she asked on a breath.

"Don't you?"

"No." She pulled her hand free and turned to face him. "But I could name you types of ships, and often what sort of goods they carry and what parts of the world they voyage to. I could assess fair value of most goods brought into the Port of London, and tell good quality from poor."

"I questioned your education?"

"You did, but also we should know the truth about each other."

"We come from different worlds, Miss Potter."

"We do. Green and brick. Cliffs and flat. Yours is plagued by dangerous mists."

"And yours by dirty fogs. Didn't people have to use candles at midday last January?"

"A rare occurrence."

"Unheard of in Devon."

"Where you have no lit streets at all!"

"Certainly not where I live. There's nothing you could call a street. You're correct. You wouldn't like it there."

The blunt statement stunned her. Why hadn't she seen where that verbal contest was going? She clung to what she had. "That doesn't affect our bargain. Are you not going to claim your kiss?"

Some expression moved across his face, but she couldn't interpret it, nor his tone when he said, "It's your debt to pay."

"Then I'll wait until you've earned it."

"I've walked in the park with you."

"In sight of children and nursemaids."

"And enticed you into this private bower."

"With no one of significance to notice."

She found the strength to turn and walk away. He stopped her with a hand on her arm. Not a grip. Only a touch. But it froze her in place.

She hoped he'd weakened, that he'd claim a kiss as boldly as he had the night before, but he remained still. And unreadable.

She surrendered. She reached to draw his head down, only realizing when her hand touched his warm skin and crisp hair that it was still gloveless. She froze like that, palm tingling, breath held, body tensing in a most extraordinary way.

In his eyes she glimpsed something. Surely a longing as powerful as hers.

She pressed her lips to his—more than a peck, but trying not to reveal too much. But then, with a sigh, she lingered, softening at the sweet intimacy and warm desire, moving closer.

He pulled her hard against him, and when her lips parted in a gasp, said against them, "Perilous Aphrodite."

"Am I?"

"Your kisses are. Be warned."

His lips crushed onto hers, compelling her to open fully to him, to capture him, to belong to him. She gripped his jacket, his hair, pressing to him even more than he pulled her into him, moving a leg, turning . . .

Wanting!

She thrust backward and he let her go, but then grasped her arms to steady her. She might well have tumbled.

Down on the grass.

A green girl in the greenwood . . .

"That was . . ." She didn't know what.

"Payment for the whole fortnight."

He wanted to escape their commitment. She could understand why, but she couldn't allow it. This was all dangerous and beyond sanity, and they came from different worlds, each disliking the other's. But she couldn't set him free.

"The nature of the kisses is mine to decide," she reminded him, as steadily as she could. "I'll be at Lady Ludlow's ball tonight. Don't fail me. I will have my eight days."

"Shouldn't you play Portia rather than Shylock?"

"Surely I'm the merchant in that play."

"Bassanio. The one whose ship was lost?"

"But which came safely into port in the end."

"You expect a happy ending from this?"

She couldn't answer, for the only honest one would be the one written on his face. *No.* They lusted, perhaps they loved, but their worlds could be too different for them to join together.

"I expect my eight days," she said, and headed for open ground and sanity, pulling her glove back on. Once she was in sunshine again, she sought something to say. Something safe.

He got there first. "As we're to endure the full eight days, shouldn't we progress to Christian names? You are Lucinda."

"Lucy. To my family and friends."

"Your aunt and cousin are family," he pointed out.

"Not in the same way."

"Poor Lucinda."

"She is. Quite paltry."

"Your wilting alter ego."

"Even Lucinda doesn't wilt."

"I'm sure she doesn't. I'm David."

"I know."

"How?"

"Your friend, Mr. Delaney, mentioned it."

"Ah."

"Do you, too, have an alter ego?" she asked. It was merely an attempt to keep the conversation going, but she saw a reaction.

"Davy," he said at last. "I'm not a lad anymore, but some of the family still use it."

A mere baby name hadn't caused the reaction. "By family, you mean your sister, Lady Amleigh?"

"No, she calls me David. I mean my aunt and uncle and some cousins." Perhaps she looked puzzled, for he added, "Uncle Nathaniel and Aunt Miriam raised Susan and me."

She noticed his tone. "You love them."

"Of course. They're good people. The sort that glue families and communities together with generosity and kind hearts. The world would fall apart without them."

"That's lovely."

"You seem surprised," he said.

"Perhaps I don't think of you as coming from a comfortable home."

"Why not?"

"I must have read too many novels. What of your mother? What does she call you?"

"If she called me anything, it was David."

"If . . . ?"

"We were never on close terms."

Lady Belle, who'd taken up with a smuggling tavern keeper, abandoning her children to relatives.

"That must have been hard."

"Abandon conventional thinking. Aunt Miriam was my mother from the moment of birth. If anything distressed my childhood, it was the fear that Lady Belle would take the whim to claim us back."

She wanted to hold him, to comfort that child. All she could do was drag the conversation into safer waters.

"And now you're the Peasant Earl. Such a shame that Lord Stevenhope has stolen sweet Iphigenia from you."

"A match made in heaven. He can struggle for a rhyme for Iphigenia, and she will enjoy being enversed in any way at all."

"And I am free of him, thank heavens."

"Perhaps as your favored suitor, I should compose verses about you."

She turned on him. "Don't you dare!"

"Unwise, unwise," he said. "I shall attempt a sonnet."

"I'll fine you a kiss for every line." Then she realized how that sounded. "Damnation."

"Lucy!" But he was laughing now.

It felt like a triumph to make him laugh.

"I've spent much time in the world of rough men. Sometimes my tongue slips."

"Delightful."

She frowned at him. "I meant that I will reduce the kisses I owe you, one for each line."

"You're a harsh woman, Lucy Potter."

"Best you know that, David. . . . What's your surname?"

He shrugged. "Wyvern, in proper usage. But I was David Kerslake for most of my life. David Somerford now, but I refused to deny Uncle Nathaniel and Aunt Miriam, so I'm Kerslake-Somerford."

"How very complicated your situation is."

"You don't know the half of it."

There was meaning in that wry comment but she sensed that pursuing it would take them into deeper waters.

By accident or purpose they'd walked away from where Hannah sat patiently waiting, representing normality and sanity—safe harbor. Lucy knew she should go there, but continued to move away. If she were to get anywhere with this man, she must untangle some of his mysteries.

That thought reminded her of the straightforward puzzle her father had pointed to. "Did your aunt and uncle not know that you were the earl's legitimate son?"

"No one did."

"Except your mother and the earl."

"So it would seem. It's not so unusual."

"For a titled father to ignore his son and heir, no matter how estranged from his wife?"

"What are you probing for? All the sordid details?"

Shields had raised, and horns blared a warning. *Very interesting.*

"My father remarked on how odd your situation is, that's all."

"So I have him poking around in my affairs, too. Does he have spies watching you?"

"Of course not," Lucy said, but she suddenly wanted to look around, to see if anyone was observing them. It was just the sort of thing her father might do if he had any suspicion that she was being foolish. She didn't see anyone suspicious now, but she'd be alert, and if she discovered such a thing, she'd put a stop to it.

"He's always kept track of events at all levels," she said. "One never knows when something will turn the world upside down. Yet vigilance," she added with a sigh, "didn't prevent my mother's death. That changed everything."

She wondered if she'd regret revealing that.

"As my life changed when I became earl."

"You'd rather it not have happened?"

She expected a quick yes or no, but he turned them back toward Hannah, pondering it.

"New states become normal in time. Like shoes. They can feel odd when new, and perhaps even pinch a little, but then we no longer notice them. There are aspects to being earl that still pinch, but others that I've come to accept. I can't imagine returning to the way things were. Which is just as well as it's impossible."

"No other heir to emerge from the woodwork?"

"Not unless there's an even weirder twist than the one that brought me here."

They walked on and she thought about his words.

"I found coming to the west end odd, but now it's become normal. When I was back in the City some aspects pinched a little. Some people get to wear comfortable shoes all their lives."

"Very few, I suspect. And some poor souls never walk in comfort at all."

They were close to Hannah now, though the sensible maid was staring at the Serpentine as if it were fascinating.

"You deserve comfort all your life," he said.

"So do you. Anyone can try for a comfortable future," she said, silently urging him to take her lead, to talk about their futures. Their future, together.

"Perhaps it's simply a matter of choosing the wise path," he said, raising her hand to kiss it. Anyone watching would see it as a courting gesture, but it seemed like farewell.

She tightened her fingers on his. "Will we meet here tomorrow?"

"I come from a land of cliffs and mists, far from your familiar territory. Are you sure you want to risk living there? Be honest."

Lucy wanted to say yes, but above all they must be honest. "I don't know. But I don't release you from our bargain."

"So be it." He bowed and walked away.

Lucy joined Hannah and they set off back to Lanchester Street.

Why hadn't she said yes? That had been close to the proposal she wanted. Why had she hesitated?

Perhaps she was afraid of such a drastic change. Perhaps a woman could love a man to desperation but still not be able to face moving to his world.

David returned to Susan's house, hoping to avoid his perceptive sister, but she must have been watching for him.

"Where have you been?"

"Do I have to account to you for all my movements?"

"David."

"Very well. I was keeping to our agreement. I had a tryst with Miss Potter in Hyde Park."

"That's wonderful!"

"Only to an extent. Can you truly imagine her in Crag Wyvern?"

"I find it hard to imagine any sane person in Crag Wyvern."

"Precisely."

"But you have to marry someone, and you should marry someone you love."

There was a question in that. "Yes, I love her, but perhaps that's why I shouldn't marry her. Should I carry Persephone off into the underworld?"

"When you talk like that, I know you're demented."

"Very well, look at it this way. I'm sure Mel wanted to

raise us as his children. He was a kind and loving man. Our mother wouldn't have ruled him on that. He gave us up so we'd have a better life. That's what love does. Can you deny it was for the best?"

"No," she said, frowning. "But . . ."

"Can you see Miss Potter in Crag Wyvern?" he asked again.

She sighed. "No. In the manor house, perhaps, but not in the Crag. What are you going to do?"

"I made a commitment to her and to you, and I'll keep to it. I can't resist a few more days with her. But unless I can truly persuade myself she can be happy in my life, I'll set her free."

"And if she doesn't want to be free?"

"I'll turn ruthless. I believe I've learned how."

Chapter 19

Lady Ludlow's ball was a crush, but to an unpleasant degree. It was packed because the house was too small and it presented no opportunity for secret trysts. Wyvern—David—was present and they danced, but Lucy longed for another private moment. She was sure if they could talk more about their situation, they could find a way.

The supper room was disastrously crowded, and Lucy found herself with Wyvern, the Amleighs, and some others out in the small garden, sitting on the grass on sheets commandeered from harried servants, enjoying a miscellany of food and drink foraged by the gentlemen.

The Balls were there, and Lucy was surprised to see Sir Stephen at ease on the ground. So, too, urbane Lord Charrington and the noble Marquess of Arden, though both their wives seemed more suited to the simple setting, even in silk and jewels. The other couples were the Delaneys, and an Irish couple, the Cavanaghs.

It was an odd collection of people and yet the talk flowed easily and they seemed old friends, and at least Lucy was seated at David's side, as if by right.

She leaned close to David. "What's the connection here?"

"Guess."

Sipping wine, she considered. "Ducal and commoner.

English and Irish. Politics and horse breeding. Laura Ball was a widow, and so was Lady Charrington, but surely Mrs. Cavanagh is too young."

"You're looking like a hawk with prey in sight," he said.

"I like to solve puzzles."

"Like your father."

"It's part of clever business."

"But sometimes better avoided."

She frowned at him. "There's a dangerous secret here?" But then she remembered that he was full of them. "Tell me a secret," she said.

"They're all members of the Company of Rogues."

The words made no sense. "I mean one of your secrets."

"What point to a secret once it's revealed?"

"You don't believe in honesty in marriage?"

"We're not married."

She was glad lamplight hid her blush. "I asked a theoretical question."

"Then, theoretically, honesty is desirable. But trust and kindness are more important."

"How can there be trust without honesty?"

"The trust to accept that the other keeps secrets for a good reason?"

What secrets did he have that must be hidden, even from a wife?

"As for the Company of Rogues . . ." he said.

The gentleman on her other side turned and answered. "Schoolboy nonsense," Lord Charrington said, "but the bonds still hold, and prove useful at times. As in arranging this alfresco alternative to the deadly crush inside."

Lucy turned to David. "You're a Rogue, too?"

"Too young, and I didn't attend Harrow as they all did. Amleigh is, however."

The men began to tell schoolboy tales, but their wives must have heard them too many times, for Lady Arden moved the discussion on to principles of education.

Lucy considered friendship. How would it be if a group of the girls she'd grown up with had formed so close a bond? Wonderful, especially if it lasted all life long, despite distance, changes, and marriage, but she only had Betty, and now that Betty was married, it would never be the same.

She'd never realized until now how much she'd lost in a year. .

Her mother had been a dear companion, and her father stimulating company. At his side she'd met a wide range of City men. She'd had Betty as a close friend, and so many other, more casual ones, all close at hand. She'd generally been so busy that finding time alone to catch up on her reading had been a challenge.

These days she exerted herself to avoid uncongenial company, and the only company she truly enjoyed was David's. But could he be considered a true friend if he kept secrets? Add to that, he made no secret of thinking she'd be miserable in his home area, and she feared he might be right!

As the group rose to return to the ball, Mrs. Delaney came over.

"Are you quite well, Miss Potter?"

Lucy supposed she had been silent for a while. "Perfectly," she said with a smile.

Mrs. Delaney smiled back, but seemed unconvinced. "I gather Maria Vandeimen is an old family friend, but we can never have too many allies. We're at Lauriston Street, number eighteen. If you need a friendly ear, or any other assistance, please visit. We're not gadabouts, even in Town."

Lucy thanked her and escaped, disturbed that her anxieties had been so apparent, and by the word "allies."

A different concept to friends, and one that implied contests, even wars.

She remembered how perceptive Mr. Delaney had seemed and decided to keep her distance from that couple.

The next morning she tried to make sense of everything in her journal, but ended up drawing hearts and flowers. An artist, now, was she? Love seemed to turn the most rational person into a pigeon brain!

She forced herself to write.

> *I love him.*
> *I believe he loves me.*
> *I'm accustomed to London.*
> *He lives in a distant place*
> *Of cliffs and mists.*
> *Can love survive*
> *Such rude transplantation?*
> *However, can a plant survive*
> *Without love?*

There she had it. Love was a tyrant. It allowed no liberty. Now, she had to make him see that.

She was desperate to meet him and talk about all this, but the next night would be Clara's ball and there were many minor tasks to be done. Aunt Mary protested at one point that Lucy shouldn't feel obliged to help, but Lucy hardly felt she could flit off and leave her aunt and cousin in such a fret. She pinned her hopes to the evening, when they were to go to the theater.

They did leave the house at one point, but only to the shops in search of some particular flowers that might suit Clara as a headdress.

When Aunt Mary suddenly decided a string of artificial pearls would do, Lucy felt that was a better idea, but they returned home without a Wyvern encounter. Just as well, really, for it was hard to imagine how even the most ingenious gentleman could have wooed her in the busy shops and streets, and to pay him there would have shocked the ton.

She must wait for the theater. They would meet there.

As soon as she entered the box, she saw him across the auditorium. His eyes met hers, unreadable at that distance, but he inclined his head. It made her think of two opponents acknowledging their upcoming battle, but she still couldn't suppress a smile before looking away.

Stevenhope was in the Galloway box, seeming completely satisfied with Lady Iphigenia. Clara was right. The girl managed to look as if she hadn't a firm bone in her slender body. That first ball seemed so long ago. Outram and Stevenhope had almost come to pistol point over her in another world. Now she was in a new world, a new magical circle, and it was one that completely absorbed her.

The play was some vaguely medieval piece, but Lucy hardly paid attention. She was waiting for the first intermission. She left the box with her relations to stroll in the corridor, but Wyvern didn't come to her. She didn't even see him.

He couldn't renege!

When she returned to her seat, he wasn't in his.

Had he left the theater?

No. He was truly in competition with her, and playing a game.

What should be her next move?

She almost didn't leave the box at the next interlude, but that would be no fun. As soon as she did, there he was, coming straight to her in the manner of an urgent suitor.

No, in the manner of one sure of possession.

A few other gentlemen had gathered around her and she was tempted to play a game in return, but she never had the chance. Wyvern walked through them as if they didn't exist and captured her lilac-gloved hand.

He raised it close to his lips, looking into her eyes, and simply said, "Miss Potter," as if his life was now complete.

Surely other suitors had done the same, but if so, it hadn't had the same effect. It was infinitely more powerful than poetry.

"Lord Wyvern," she said, which should have seemed inane, but didn't.

He tucked her hand into his arm and led her away. No one stopped them. Good heavens. He'd as good as stamped her with his mark. It was what she wanted, but it was still shocking.

"You're bold, my lord."

"I established my claim, as we agreed. I always attempt fair trade."

"As any good merchant should."

"Role reversal, Lucy? Do you intend to lord it over me?"

"I might if I could, but my sex prevents me. As it does so many things." She hadn't meant to let that slip out. "When and where do I pay you?"

"In a while. So you can't be a lord. What else does your sex bar you from?"

She suddenly wanted to give him the truth. "I dreamed of being my father's heir and successor."

"In *business*?"

"I see it shocks you, too."

"Yes. Unfair, perhaps, but it would be hard. I would rather keep you from all harsh winds."

She was startled by true tenderness in his eyes and

needed to kiss him, but though they'd walked to the end
of the corridor she saw no possible concealment.

Of course they could be outrageous and commit
themselves here in the blaze of a dozen candles.

Then he pulled back one of the curtains that hung all
along the wall. She'd thought them ornamental, but this
one covered an opening and he slipped them quickly behind, into a narrow, circular stairwell. The only light was
from below.

"Where's this?" she whispered.

"Probably for use of servants, but if we're lucky, none
will pass this way in the next little while."

There had been only a few people in the end of the
corridor, but they would have been seen. He was giving
service to a scandalous degree, but Lucy didn't care. He
was hers, and they would wed, and he would shield her
from harsh winds.

The narrow space only just allowed the two of them
to stand together, so they were close, sharing warmth
and subtle smells.

"This reminds me of Winsom's," she murmured.

"How?"

"The space is narrow and you are large. I thought you
dangerous then."

"And now I'm not?"

She met his eyes. "And now I know you are."

"You don't look afraid."

"I'm not."

She put a hand on his shoulder, perhaps to restrain
him, though she could never hold him off. Perhaps simply to touch. "How much of a kiss do I owe for such ardent attentions?"

"You dictate the nature of the kisses."

"But I want to be fair."

"I did mighty service," he murmured, almost into her ear.

Dry mouthed, she whispered, "A long kiss, then."

"If you dare. Too long, and who knows where it might end?"

"Then I will be cautious," she said, giving him a peck of a kiss, only half teasing.

She tried to squeeze past him, but mostly in a game. As she'd expected, as she'd hoped, he caught her around the waist.

"Not so fast unless you want to trigger another duel."

Even in a game, she was captured by a man who could overpower her with ease. As she remembered. Her heart thundered and she was hot, dizzy, and breathless with hunger for more.

By accident or design she was now on a higher step. At a better level for kissing.

He nipped her ear. "You should pay in full."

"You wretch!" But it was a whisper. She could indeed exclaim in a whisper.

He licked where he'd nipped, then kissed behind her lobe in a secret place. The warm, moist touch seemed more wicked than any kiss on the lips. She realized she was stretching her neck as if asking for more, and that her breasts . . . her breasts were aching. Demanding.

"We mustn't . . ." she said.

"We are." He blew into the trailing curls at her neck, making her bite her lip.

"Let me go."

"I'm not holding you."

He wasn't. She turned slowly against him, looking at him, seeking the truth. She saw it, a need as powerful as hers.

"Why?" she whispered.

"This isn't what you want?"

That isn't an answer to my question. But the heat inside her was building. She cradled his head and kissed him, pressing herself against him. Such sweet relief. Such fierce hungers.

They sealed together, hotly intimate in a way she'd never experienced before. A wicked way. A perfect way.

This, this . . .

This was the mystery she'd never quite understood, taking over her body in fire and torment. She pressed harder against him. His hand pushed up her skirt, grabbed her thigh, pulling her leg up, opening her.

Shocking her, but she stretched wider, as wide as she could, her foot pressing against the far wall. Her breasts. He'd freed a breast, was kissing there, sucking there. . . .

Oh, sweet heaven!

Then he thrust backward, hitting the wall behind, not far, not far enough, but far enough for air and sanity to return.

She stared at him, wanting to scream a protest, knowing she'd narrowly escaped the worst, but wanting, desperate for, the best.

He sucked in breaths, and simply said, groaned, "Goddess . . ."

Lucy knew if she pressed forward, tempted, offered, they could do it here, now, in a staircase. She'd never begun to imagine such a thing, but she knew it now, could envision it, in a tangle of bodies and limbs so very like those Indian drawings.

No, no, not like this.

She couldn't. Mustn't.

She assembled herself out of chaos. Lowered an aching leg until both feet were on the step. Stuffed her breast back behind bodice and stays. Wriggled to get everything in place, awareness of her swollen nipple fixed in her mind, along with hollow yearnings that could make her howl. She reached up to check her hair by feel.

He took over that task. "A good thing you don't have it in a complicated arrangement." His tone was light, his voice husky.

"And that yours is cropped," she said, touching it, though there was no need. "One of your shirt points is crumpled."

He touched her neck. "It scraped you. Damned starch. Behind the ear. I think your hair will cover it."

Lucy had closed her eyes at the sweetness of that touch, but then jumped when bells rang, summoning everyone back to their seats.

"We must go."

"If you're ready."

Would she ever be ready to leave this magical place? Was she ready to face the world when what they'd done should be branded on them?

She turned in the narrow space and made her way up the steps and then back into the world, blinking in the bright candlelight. The corridor was empty, but people had seen them go behind that curtain, and some would have noted how long they'd been there. Had they *heard* things?

She looked at him, astonished to find that he looked unmarked. Was it possible she looked the same? As they linked arms and strolled back toward her box, she could only hope so. Weak though it was, she still didn't want to be notorious.

"Another magical circle," she said.

"Or one of the circles of hell."

"Hell?"

"We did go down."

"And rose back to the light." She studied his face. "What is it, David? What's the matter?"

"I didn't mean that to happen. I still worry that I can't make you happy."

It was hard not to laugh with joy. It was as close to an offer of marriage as he could make here.

She gave him as close to an acceptance as she could. "You can. You will."

She slipped her arm from his slowly, wishing they didn't have to part, and returned to the box, trying to pretend that nothing of importance had happened.

Again the play passed unobserved as she relished the thoughts of all future delights.

Chapter 20

The next day David left the house early, not for the park, but to deal with some necessary business regarding the estate's debts. When he returned in the afternoon, Susan steered him into the drawing room and shut the door.

"What's happening?" she demanded.

"In what respect?"

"You and Miss Potter!"

"Is it any of your business?"

"Of course it is. I can't be completely happy until you are, too."

"Don't place that burden on me."

She bit her lip. "I'm sorry. I won't. But how can I not care? You used to be so carefree."

"Boyishly irresponsible."

"We certainly corrected that, all of us. Miss Potter?" she asked gently.

"I as good as committed myself to her last night."

"And she?"

"Replied in kind."

"Why is this not good news?"

"She may be mistaking her heart."

"She doesn't strike me as weak-minded."

He laughed drily. "No, she's certainly not. She dreamed of being her father's partner and heir."

"In *business*?"

"Et tu Brute? I would have expected you to be more sympathetic."

"Having fought the way things are, I know the pain more clearly." True enough. When younger she'd fought against the restrictions put upon girls and women.

"Why did she imagine such a thing?" she asked.

"I should have pieced together the clues for myself. She told me she was her father's daughter, trained by him. She negotiated a bargain with calm expertise. She was his only child and clearly he involved her. Why shouldn't she expect that to continue?"

"But then her mother died," Susan said, "and now he's to remarry."

"And can expect to have a son. She's been suddenly cast adrift and she's seeking a new harbor, but she's not fit to make a decision that will affect her whole life. Not so quickly."

"So you want to wait."

"I intend to return to Devon."

"Why, for heaven's sake?"

"So she can think clearly, and can't tempt me to take all decision away."

"As bad as that?"

"Every bit."

"If you leave, some other man might snatch her."

"If she's willingly snatched, it will be better for her. A normal gentleman with a pleasant country estate within easy traveling distance of London, her family, and friends."

"Love *matters*. You can make her happy."

"She'll come to her senses."

"Why are you being so disastrously *noble*?"

"You made me an earl, remember?"

"Oh, I wish Mel were here! He'd knock some sense into you!"

"*Sense?* Mel led a risky run because the Horde lost patience with being confined by the navy, which is why he's in Botany Bay."

"I give up!"

"Good."

"Very well, *be* stupidly noble, but when you're miserable, don't come to me for comfort!"

David watched his sister storm out, smiling wryly. She'd always been more fiery than he, and far less cautious, which is why she'd fallen into sinful passion with Con when they were both fifteen. When she'd told him last year he'd been shocked by the insanity of it, but now he could understand.

He wouldn't let Lucy fall into the same trap. Susan's madness could have been disastrous, just as their mother's would have been if not for Mel and the kindness of Uncle Nathaniel and Aunt Miriam. Luck had to run out at some point.

He went to his room to ring for a servant to pack for him, but a footman arrived first.

"A visitor for you, milord." The man presented the card.

Daniel Potter, Esq.

Had Lucy's father heard rumors and come to demand his intentions? Damnable if true, but he couldn't avoid seeing the man.

"In the reception room?"

"Yes, milord."

David went down.

Daniel Potter was not a big man, but he stood tall and had presence. Here was a man used to command in his world. His features were rough, but full of character, his hair a nondescript brown, but very well barbered. His build was slim and set off by fine, fashionable tailoring of the more subdued sort. A man to respect, but also to be wary of.

"Mr. Potter. How may I help you?"

"My lord," Potter said, with a nicely judged bow. "I've come to speak to you about my daughter."

Alas. "Please be seated," David said, taking a chair himself, adding nothing. Let the other man make the play.

"I understand that you've been favoring her with particular attentions, my lord."

"We have enjoyed each other's company a time or two, sir. She's a charming young lady."

"Not that much younger than you, my lord."

"Of age."

"As I believe I pointed out to you in response to an enquiry."

David thought of denying it, but that could only make him look foolish. "You did, sir."

"So you intend to wed her."

"Perhaps."

"Why only 'perhaps,' my lord?"

David raised a hand. "I mean no insult, sir. These matters take time."

"Yet you tried to cut them short."

"And you wisely pointed out a better way. I admire your daughter in many ways, but I'm not sure we would suit."

"Good, for I've come to tell you it won't do."

David stared, fighting an urge to blast the man with noble arrogance. Of course, he should agree with Potter's judgment, but instead fury ignited inside him. "May I ask why?"

His anger had no effect on the other man. "Selfishly, I'd not want her so far away as Devon, but I'd not put that in the way of her happiness. I don't believe you could make her happy."

"Again, may I ask why?"

"I've made enquiries."

What did he mean by that? David thought of one thing. "You object to the madness in the blood of the earls of Wyvern?"

"I see no reason to."

Ah. A nicely judged phrase. This was not a man to underestimate in any way. "You object to my muddled parentage? Permit me to point out that yours is rather more dubious."

Potter didn't like that, but he said, "It's what lies behind it, my lord, and what grows from it. Things that could prove dangerous to my daughter's comfort and happiness."

In other words, he knew, or at least guessed, that David was Captain Drake's son, and probably deeply involved with the perilous Freetrade. How the devil . . . ?

After a calculated pause, Potter rose. "I wish you well, my lord, but not with Lucy."

David rose, challenging him. "What if she wishes to marry me?"

"She'll get over it."

"May I suggest, sir, that you underestimate your daughter?"

"No you may not. I know and appreciate all her virtues."

David was suddenly aware of abandoning Lucy to a world full of people who didn't see the truth of her. "Yet you call her pet."

"What?" Potter was baffled. "Perhaps you are the Mad Earl's son after all."

"Think on what I've said, Potter. Talk to her. Listen to her. Love her."

"Damn you, sir! I love my daughter dearly, which is why I will protect her, even from her own folly, in all ways necessary. She is not for a damned smuggler."

David wanted to declare then and there that he'd have her. That Potter could go to hell. But the man was saying only what he'd told himself.

"There's no need for this heat, Potter. I leave Town today and don't expect to return soon. Your daughter is safe from me."

Potter studied him with narrowed eyes, but then nodded. "I'm glad to hear it, my lord. Good day."

When the man had left, David stood in thought, but nothing changed, nothing improved. Without him to distract her, Lucy would settle on some other man.

Northcliff. She'd shown some partiality there. He seemed a little dull for her, but he'd be a safe and doting husband.

Or Sir Harry Winter. He was a thoroughly good man, and not a fortune hunter. His estate lay in Essex, so within easy reach of her beloved City. Perhaps she would even be able to enjoy involvement in trade from there.

Even that fool Outram would be better.

He could easily have bloodied Potter's nose, but damn it all, he was right. In addition, his implied threat couldn't be ignored.

Susan came in. "Was Lucy's father really here?"

"In the flesh. He warned me off."

"*What?* How dare he?"

"Don't fly into alt again. He was in the right. Also, he knows."

"What?"

"That I'm Captain Drake."

"How?"

"I should have expected it. A man doesn't succeed like that without excellent intelligence on anything that might concern him. Lucy certainly concerns him, even though he's dense about her."

"But no one back home would let anything slip to a stranger."

"It needn't have been that way. He's a merchant, and possibly not above a bit of illegal trade, especially in his early days. A word to the right people and he'd know."

"Is he dangerous?" she asked.

He soothed her clasped hands. "There's no profit to him in exposing me and he has no need to serve me ill."

"As long as you leave his daughter alone."

"Exactly."

"The Rogues—"

"No! I'll not have the Rogues poking into my affairs, and Potter's right. Lucy shouldn't be married to a smuggler. She'll find someone better."

"We discussed this earlier."

"And almost came to blows. Don't fight the winds, Susan. I'm going home."

"What of marrying for money?"

"I'll have to do without for a while. I'll return to harness in due course."

She touched his cheek. "I'm sorry. This is all my fault."

"No. Lay the blame on mad, obsessive love. And may we all be free of it."

Chapter 21

Happy anticipation hadn't led to a restful night and Lucy had again woken too late to go to the park. That shouldn't matter, because he would come here to propose to her properly. Unless he'd gone to the City to speak to her father.

Oh, no. She should have warned him that her father had concerns. He might need some persuasion.

She wrote a note. She found she couldn't address the matter of their betrothal directly when he hadn't quite proposed, so she simply asked him to call. When she received no response, she was tempted to rush round to speak to him, but if he hadn't received her note yet, he must be out.

In any case, it would be hard to escape the fuss and flutter in Lanchester Street. She didn't remember her own debut ball causing a tenth of this bother. Lucy did her best to help, but when she made another silly mistake because of daydreams she apologized with the excuse of a headache.

"Then go and lie down," her aunt said testily.

Lucy escaped to her room, telling herself to calm down. If David had gone to her father, it wouldn't be disastrous. Her father couldn't forbid the marriage, and he'd come around. She opened her journal, but was stuck on hearts and flowers again.

In the end tiredness did overcome her, so she had a nap, and was reasonably coherent when it was time to prepare for the ball. Where he would be.

She wanted to dazzle him, and she had two evening gowns that she'd not yet worn, but this was Clara's night, so she chose the sprigged gauze again. For jewels, she wore a delicate parure of colored stones and seed pearls.

She thought Clara's lace gown a little too fussy, but otherwise, her cousin looked charming. The cream color suited her more than pure white would have. Her curls were tamed and the pearls looked perfect there. She wore a neat string of real ones around her neck.

At this point Clara seemed more composed than Lucy, or perhaps it was only that she bubbled all the time. Lucy was suddenly overwhelmed by a fondness for her cousin, who was delightfully uncomplicated and said what she meant.

She found a silver and ivory brooch in her box and offered it. "A gift for your ball."

"Lucinda, how kind! It will go well on my bodice."

"I think so." Lucy pinned it there. "And perhaps you could call me Lucy. It's what my father calls me, and I'd like that."

"Of course. Lucinda is more elegant, but Lucy suits you."

"Are you saying I'm not elegant?" Lucy teased.

Clara giggled. "Of course not. Though you're not quite. But you're beautiful. Have you chosen Wyvern, then?"

Lucy started, but then realized it was simply Clara's mind fluttering about.

"Perhaps," Lucy said, feeling herself blush. She wanted to babble all about him, but she retained enough sanity not to do so to one of the greatest chatterers in Town.

"So you'll be a countess! How exciting. Of course it will mean having to live in Devon."

"Not a fate worse than death."

Clara giggled. "And he shows no sign of madness yet."

"For heaven's sake, why should he?"

"His father was mad."

Lucy had completely forgotten that.

She remembered him saying something about it. That the earls of Wyvern had always been mad. Or had he said odd?

"Odd," she said out loud. "Or eccentric." Clara looked dubious, so Lucy added, "He shows no sign of insanity."

"True." Clara was surveying herself one last time in the mirror. "But then, neither did the king when he was Wyvern's age. Grandmother Greshingham remembered him as a young man with some admiration. Come, we should go down."

Lucy grabbed her fan and reticule and followed, glad to escape Clara's babble.

Madness, indeed.

For once Lord Caldross accompanied them, and he seemed truly fond and proud of Clara. The hired rooms were well decorated with flowers and lit with an abundance of candles. The small orchestra was already playing, waiting for the guests to arrive.

The refreshments were abundant and the arrangements for supper seemed excellent. The ladies' and gentlemen's rooms were suitable and servants already waited there. Other servants staffed a cloakroom where people could leave outer clothing and, if necessary, change their shoes. It was a fine, dry night, however, so most would come here in their dancing slippers unless they chose to walk.

Guests began to arrive, friends and family coming early to give the rooms a populated look, then others in numbers that should satisfy Aunt Mary.

Lucy had no place in the reception line so she chatted

to any number of people, aware again of having made acquaintances in the ton. She felt accepted. If there were looks, she suspected they were because she was firmly linked to the notorious catch of the season, not because she was a scandal and a Cit.

Where was he?

Maria arrived, with her husband and niece. Lucy saw Lord and Lady Charrington and the Balls. The Duke of St. Raven and his wife were announced. Aunt Mary had been thrilled by their acceptance, and that of the Ardens.

Lucy had wondered if it was something to do with the Company of Rogues, but that would mean that they were here for David, the friend of the Rogues. So where was he?

The Amleighs were announced. David's sister and her husband—but where was her brother? Lucy looked around, wondering if she'd missed his entrance, and then Lady Amleigh was coming toward her.

"I'm pleased to see you in good spirits, Miss Potter."

"Why shouldn't I be, Lady Amleigh?"

Lady Amleigh blinked. "I did think . . . but no matter. This event promises to be a success."

With foreboding, Lucy asked, "What's happened? Where's Lord Wyvern?"

"Oh, dear. I sent a note. In response to yours."

"Mine? He didn't read it?" Lady Amleigh's message had probably been mislaid in all the fuss. "What's happened to him?"

"Calm, please, my dear. I'm sorry. Nothing bad. My brother had already left. He was called urgently back to Devon."

"Back to Devon?" Lucy knew she sounded as if she'd been told he'd gone to the moon, but she felt that way.

"Sadly, yes. Some estate matter requiring his attention."

Something in Lady Amleigh's eyes put Lucy on the

defensive. She would not show how devastated she felt. "How tiresome for him. Will he return soon?"

"It's hard to tell. It is a very serious matter."

"The season will be much diminished," Lucy said, and escaped.

She kept a smile on her face, but it was painfully hard when David wasn't here and wouldn't be here. When he'd gone far, far away.

Why?

To escape her? She hated the thought, but there it was anyway. From the first he'd said he didn't intend to marry her. Last night he'd been carried away, but had those promising words been spoken from a sense of *obligation*?

She was alone again, even bereft of her suitors. Her plan had worked too well, and here she was, isolated.

"Lucy, is something the matter?"

Lucy turned to Maria. "Nothing of importance. I've been suffering from a headache all day, but I didn't want to miss my cousin's ball."

Could Maria believe words, tone, or expression?

"It will get worse as the heat and noise grows, so go home if you need to. Vandeimen will escort you."

"That's very kind of you."

"Alice would want me to take care of you. If you have need, Lucy, I'd be honored to be your confidante."

She'd hoped to be less transparent, but this was Maria, not some stranger.

"My substitute mother? I was outraged by the idea that my father's bride would be that, but I can see you in that way. I know you're too young, but you were my mother's friend."

"And she mine. My situation wasn't always easy and she alone could understand. She would have been pleased to see you here."

"Restored to her world?" Lucy asked, unable to hold back a bitter edge.

"Enjoying balls and parties as young people should. She worried that your father was shaping you too much in his mold. Oh, I'm sorry. I've upset you with this talk. I don't know how I could be so maladroit."

"No, no. It's the headache. Oh, blast it, I don't have a headache. It's all so complicated. . . ."

"And this isn't the place. Here comes Stevenhope with his Iphigenia, intent on showing you what a treasure you've let slip. Come round to talk whenever you wish."

Lucy thanked her, and then set to congratulating the happy couple with a sincerity designed to deflate Stevenhope's puffed-up pride.

Lord Vandeimen asked her for the first dance, doubtless at Maria's instigation, but Lucy was grateful. The only thing to do was soldier on through the night until she could collapse into misery. But damnation, even at home she'd have Clara bubbling with an excited review of her ball.

She danced the next with Lord Charrington. When Outram asked for the next she could hardly refuse him, but it soon became clear he'd taken Wyvern's departure as new hope. She had to reject him again.

When that dance ended she couldn't endure any more. She pleaded a headache and gained her aunt's uncertain agreement to Lord Vandeimen as escort.

"Perhaps your uncle, dear . . ."

"You all have obligations here, Aunt. Lord Vandeimen will see me safe home. It's going very well, isn't it?"

Aunt Mary smiled her relief. "Very well. I didn't really hope for such as the Ardens and St. Ravens. Clara is enjoying every moment."

Impulsively, Lucy kissed her aunt's cheek, startling both of them, then hurried off with tears in her eyes. Truly, she didn't know herself anymore.

Lord Vandeimen was a perfect escort, seeing to her comfort and not asking any questions.

As they approached the house Lucy couldn't stop herself from asking, "Do you know Lord Wyvern well, my lord?"

"Only as a friend of a friend, Miss Potter."

"I see. Mr. Delaney, I assume."

"No. He, too, is a friend of a friend. I meant Amleigh. We are neighbors and friends since the cradle. Our estates are nearby."

"How pleasant," she said.

He probably thought it banal, but she meant it. Friends, again. Childhood friends, still close as adults.

She let Hannah fuss her out of her finery and into bed and then lay there, abandoned.

David had gone to Devon. She couldn't believe anything could have arisen that required such urgency, but if it had, he should have written to her.

His silent departure violated everything he'd said, everything she'd felt, everything she'd believed. She could make no sense of it, and could only feel truly, deeply brokenhearted.

Now she understood how people could die of a broken heart.

Chapter 22

David traveled by mail coach with too much time to think, to regret, to devise reasons to leave at the next stage and speed back to London. All he wanted to do in life was make Lucy happy, and he knew how miserable she must be now, because her emotions would be the same as his.

They were made for each other. Mind, hearts, and bodies, they were perfectly matched, except for his involvement in smuggling, and that he was bound to a place she'd hate.

He snatched fitful sleep as the crowded coach rattled through the night. Susan had tried to get him to hire a chaise, but he didn't have money to waste, especially not now he'd thrown thirty thousand pounds away.

He'd take her penniless if he could be sure she'd be happy.

He left the coach at Honiton and hired a horse for the last part of the journey, enjoying the open air, trying to persuade himself that Lucy could come to love this countryside.

She might well like its best aspects, but she'd dislike the poorly maintained road, the nettles lurking in the hedgerow ready to sting, and the brambles curling out to snag an unwary rider's clothing or flesh.

Brambles would bear fruit, and even nettles could be

brewed into a powerful tonic, but she was accustomed to buying such things from a shop and to traveling there over well-maintained streets or walking along firm and cleanly swept pavements.

If she was thinking herself brokenhearted, she'd recover. In time she'd find a perfect man to love.

He rode into Church Wyvern, tired from lack of sleep and heartsore. He left the horse at the Kerslake Arms to be returned tomorrow, and turned toward the looming Crag. For once it suited his mood.

Reluctantly he changed direction. Within minutes word would reach the manor that he was home, and if he didn't go there immediately, one or all of his family would rush up to the Crag to see what was amiss.

He changed his mind again, however, and took the path that led down between the manor and Crag to Dragon's Cove. He was back here because he was Captain Drake, and everyone would understand his checking there first.

He wasn't entirely sure whether his uncle and aunt knew he was Captain Drake. Kerslake Manor stayed calm and contented by turning a blind eye to disruption and celebrating life's joys. He'd embraced that willingly for most of his life and wished he still had the choice. He was fairly sure they assumed that once he'd become earl he'd passed any smuggling responsibilities on to someone else. Again, he wished it were possible. There was no one else capable of managing the Horde in these difficult times.

He entered the George and Dragon by the back door and found Cousin Rachel sweeping the floor. "You're back at a good time, lad. There's word of a cargo adrift. They're keen to help."

He knew what that meant. A ship loaded with contraband had been prevented from delivering its cargo to the appointed landing and gone back out into the Channel, hoping for another try. It would have to be quick. A smuggling vessel couldn't hover for long without a revenue cutter or naval ship spotting it.

David wanted to veto any involvement, but the Horde had obeyed him and remained inactive for weeks. Fred's regular reports had assured him of that. If he didn't give them this opportunity, there'd be rebellion again, especially since he'd failed to bring back the money that could bring a new kind of prosperity here.

He'd planned employment for all, and a school to give the bright boys better ambitions than being one of Captain Drake's lieutenants. Instead he was returning further in debt than when he left.

"I'll hold a meeting here later," he said. "Pass the word."

Then he listened as she shared some general gossip—births, marriages, and even a death, along with a brawl that had cost a man an eye and a rumor of a love rivalry that could turn vicious. Captain Drake couldn't restore sight, but he was supposed to provide a Solomon-like judgment between Gabe Bridgelow and Caleb Mutter.

"Lisbet Oke's not worthy of either of them," he said. "She'll cause any husband heartbreak."

"She can't help being pretty."

"She can help the way she flirts. She's been teasing men since before she had breasts."

"Had a try for you, has she?"

"More than once."

Rachel pulled a face. "That's Lady Belle's fault, see. Married the earl and snared Captain Drake. Bound to stir ambitions."

"Heaven help me. If I had the powers ascribed to me, I'd send her to a nunnery."

"Didn't think we had any anymore."

"I'd found one."

She chuckled and David shared a smile. His situation

was no better, but these mundane problems soothed him.

He left the tavern and stood for a moment, watching the fishing boats out on the water and people ashore, dealing with an earlier catch, mending nets. Honest labor.

But he could read behind the smiles they sent him, and the greetings. The captain's back. There's a cargo out there. Now we'll see action and real work.

He climbed the path out of Dragon's Cove, aware of how much Lucy would hate the shingly surface that slipped beneath his boots. She'd probably hate the hill itself. Were there any significant hills in the City of London? He couldn't remember one in Mayfair.

He walked through a cloud of midges, wafting them away from his face, and then brushed past stinging nettle and spiky thistles.

It still galled him that Potter might think he'd bent to his will, but to stay in London to spite him would have been complete stupidity. The man might well be able to harm him and his people here, and he couldn't ignore that. But above all, as a loving father, he'd been right. Lucy deserved better than a gothic horror of a home, a remote area, and a husband committed to criminal activity.

His mind eased a bit as he returned to Church Wyvern, the village that sat snug in its hollow behind the cliffs. It was a gentler, warmer place. The people here took part in smuggling, but they were different from the salt-roughened fishing families of Dragon's Cove.

He took the path that circled the village toward Kerslake Manor, his home for most of his life. The path ran between well-tended gardens that were already producing food, but also past where Tom Oke was cleaning out his pigpen, putting the dung aside to rot down so it would be ready to enrich the garden later.

There was nothing wrong with a healthy country smell, except to those unused to it, and it would contribute to vegetables and fruit in time. Nothing grows without muck, they said, and it was true. The ordinary people knew that, and the nobility, too, for they all had estates that included farms. It was the merchants and bankers who lived apart from the land and didn't understand its ways, except that it could produce profit.

He opened the gate into the manor's orchards. It squeaked in the way it always had. This was a familiar place, full of memories of tree-climbing and other games, and the sweet abundance of autumn fruit.

Had Lucy ever been in an orchard? In springtime with the blossoms dense as clouds and bees frantically working them. Then later, when the blossoms drifted down to form a sweet carpet. Or in fruiting time, when a lad could pluck a ripe apple hanging near his head and offer it as temptation to a blushing lass.

He'd stolen his first kiss here, from Jenny Carter, both of them eleven and sure hell's fires would fall on them, but willing to risk it anyway. She was married now, with two babes.

In the Garden of Eden it had been Eve who'd tempted Adam, just as Lucy had tempted him in the Duchess of St. Raven's garden. What would Cressida St. Raven think to have her garden compared to Eden at the time of the Fall?

The other sins had been his doing, however. Amid trees in the park, at Almack's, in the dark theater stairwell. Hades, that theater stairwell.

He was determined to be sane, but he couldn't stop thoughts of Lucy beneath an apple tree with petals falling in her hair, petals that would be rivaled by her perfect complexion.

He turned desperately toward the mellow manor house. He could be sane there.

Lucy might not like the countryside, but she couldn't possibly dislike the archway into the kitchen garden, dripping honeysuckle, nor the lovely house, the gray stone whitewashed and threaded over with roses and wisteria.

He entered, as usual, through the kitchen door.

Annie, who'd been cook here since before he was born, cried, "Davy-lad!" without a hint of apology. Why not? She'd fed him milk and bread and honey, and swatted his behind with her big spoon if he tried to sneak some treat.

He gave her a hug and a kiss, then kissed the cheeks of the two blushing kitchen maids. "Shall I kiss you, too?" he asked Willie, the young scullery lad.

Willie pulled a face, but he was grinning, too.

Then Aunt Miriam came in. "David, my dear boy." She gave him a big hug and drew him away into the parlor. "Have you had a grand time in London?"

"It's certainly been grand, but it's not to my taste."

"Come now, dear, there have to be some pleasures there."

"Some sporting activities and some interesting bookshops."

"Bookshops! You were never bookish."

"I've much to learn." He suppressed the temptation to pour out his troubles and amused her with stories of balls and grand eccentrics. "I apologize for not bringing you a gift. I left in a hurry."

She didn't ask why, which meant she guessed something was amiss. Loving, perceptive family were the very devil.

"Having you here is a gift, love. But you'll be going back, surely?"

"The season's coming to an end."

"But what of Miss Potter? You went there to woo her." He was framing an explanation when she exclaimed, "You're sweet on her! How lovely."

"No—"

She just laughed. "Tell me about her. Is she pretty?"

Was his face an open book to her? It would seem so.

Denials would only make things worse, so he talked about Lucy, attempting to sound only mildly engaged. Knowing he failed. He could remember friends being like this, unable to stop burbling on about the object of their affections.

Object of their affections.

How tame, especially when linked to a cataclysmic disaster worthy of an epic poem. He was assuredly mad. Especially as his words and his aunt's delight made the impossible begin to seem possible again.

"It might not happen," he warned.

"Why not? What could she find lacking in you?"

"You're blind to my flaws."

She laughed. "That I'm not, but your virtues far outweigh them. Does she hesitate over your proposal?"

"We've not quite come to that point. Now she's of age, her thirty thousand pounds is her own. She asks why she should hand it over to a husband."

"How odd."

"Not really. Few women are in such a situation, but it gives them independence."

"I don't see why anyone, man or woman, would want independence if it meant a solitary life."

"There are friends."

She waved that idea away.

"In any case," he said, "she might not suit my needs. She plans to tie her money up in a trust."

That damped his aunt's enthusiasm. "Sensible of you to retreat, dear. She sounds a selfish sort of woman. She'd rule the roost."

She'd certainly demand to share the perch, but he'd gladly allow that.

Uncle Nathaniel came in then, beaming a welcome, and David had to repeat his tales of London.

His aunt introduced the subject of Lucy.

Uncle Nathaniel didn't take the same line. "Girlish stuff, Davy. Pay no heed. When she's wife and mother she'll see her husband's way is best."

David doubted that. What's more, he didn't want that, but now he saw a new problem. Lucy wouldn't like the geography here, but she might not like the society, either. The women here weren't weak, but they followed conventional ways. Fathers and husbands ruled. Even if the men often ended up doing as their womenfolk wished, the protocol was observed that the husband was lord and master of the household.

How would Lucy the bold, Lucy the keen-brained merchant's daughter, fit in with his family? Daniel Potter's daughter, trained by him to value goods and make shrewd business deals, and used to speaking her clear mind. She was more like Susan than Aunt Miriam, and Susan had never quite fit.

It was impossible and he must convince himself of that.

For the time being, he set to being good company, repeating some London stories for his cousins Henry and Amelia and receiving gossip in return. No dangerous rivalries among the gentry, but some minor scandals that amused him.

How simple most people's lives were.

As the light faded he said his farewells and made his way back to durance vile—to the Crag—without any hope of happiness there, now or in the future.

As if to underline the point, a wind had picked up and now carried rain. Salty rain, straight off the sea. The sort that shriveled tender plants.

Lucy Potter was a rose for a sheltered garden, not gorse for a blasted heath.

Chapter 23

The morning after Clara's ball, Lucy woke early. Despite a gusty wind and the hint of rain, she went to the park, dressing herself quietly and sneaking out without Hannah. She didn't truly hope David would appear there. It was more a sort of pilgrimage. Or a wake.

She sniffed, but there was no one here to question that, to be told a lie about hay fever, and there was certainly no new-mown grass to explain her stinging eyes.

She saw the girl with the kite again, still struggling to get it to fly, but this time because the wind was too strong for her, and too unpredictable.

Foolish, stubborn child.

Foolish Lucy, but she went to help, and together they caught the wind so that the kite soared magnificently. But then it tore the spindle out of their hands. Lucy raced after, but the spindle was unwinding at speed. It ran out of thread and the kite disappeared, the long string trailing behind.

She turned, thinking the girl would be in tears, but she was simply gaping. Then she grinned, showing a missing front tooth. "That was splendid! I'd like to be a kite."

So would Lucy, but in another way entirely. "Perhaps one day you'll be able to fly in a balloon car."

"Oh, yes. I've seen one. But the kite flew on the wind, not on hot air. Don't you think people should be able to fly on a kite if it was big enough?"

"They'd be swept away."

The girl looked up again, to the speck that had been her kite. "It might be worth it."

"Now see what you've done, Miss Minnie," said a fretful nursemaid, hurrying over and giving Lucy an unfriendly glance. "It's gone now, and nothing to be done about it. Good thing, too. Not ladylike at all, messing about with a kite."

The girl turned back to thank Lucy, but then allowed herself to be dragged away, saying, "Papa will get me a new one."

Good for Papa, but as Miss Minnie grew older, would her father continue to encourage her free thinking and inventiveness? Indeed, why shouldn't a big enough kite be able to carry a person into the sky? People flew under hot air balloons. Steam drove powerful engines. There were even boats that could travel under the water. Anything was possible.

For her, too?

Her mother hadn't given up at the first obstacle, or even the second. One of those obstacles might have been her father.

She set off home, following startling thoughts.

The common view was that an upstart Cit had seduced a lady, but there had been so many reasons for her father to resist marrying her mother, and he was a strong-willed man. He was a man who tried his hardest to avoid folly, and nearly always succeeded.

In that, he and David were alike.

Even the most ardent love would not have pushed her father into a ruinous path, and yet her parents had married. What, then, had her mother had to do to win her father?

Lucy paused to blow out a breath. She shouldn't even think this way, but she would. It was important.

It wouldn't have been easy for her parents to meet,

especially if Daniel Potter was trying his best to avoid folly, but they had met. It had to have been her mother who had made it happen. Her mother, only eighteen, but knowing what she wanted, and determined to get it.

What else had she done?

Lucy arrived at the question she'd been circling. Had her mother seduced her father? Afraid her outrageous thoughts might show on her face, she walked on again, briskly, as if trying to outpace them.

A little while ago she might have thought such a seduction impossible, but now she knew better. It didn't need a bed or a night, only a private space and a little time, and passion enough to overwhelm all controls.

She arrived home unsure whether her speculations were rational or the product of a deranged mind. She needed to talk to someone, but who?

Maria. She might know something of her parents' courtship, but would she tell?

She sent a message to ask if she could visit. At nearly eleven a note returned, inviting her immediately if it suited.

It did.

Maria greeted her warmly and they settled to tea.

"Now, tell me what troubles you."

Lucy stirred in a lump of sugar, trying to plan a way to approach such a delicate subject. "I'm not used to talking about myself. I've only recently realized that."

"Then don't, if you don't want to."

"I'm not sure." Lucy gave a little laugh. "After living for weeks in a storm of chatter I think I've embraced silence like a cloistered nun!"

Maria chuckled with her. "I can see how that might be. Have you enjoyed the season?"

Lucy welcomed a safe subject for now. "Some of the balls and musical events have been superb."

"I think it's because it's concentrated. In the City, and

in other towns and cities where people's lives don't differ much by season, all is spread more evenly. Here, the beau monde gathers for a month or two, cramming in as much intermingling, shopping, and business as possible before retreating with a sigh of relief to country ways."

"When you were married to Celestin, you lived mostly in London, didn't you?"

"He had a villa out beyond Chiswick, and a place in hunting country, though he rarely used it."

Lucy noted the "he." She didn't think Maria would phrase it that way about Lord Vandeimen.

"If you don't mind my asking, Maria, how did you come to marry Celestin?"

Maria gave a little moue, but there was a smile in it. "Folly, as I'm sure you guess. He came like a tiger amongst sheep. He had such vigor. He was handsome and could be charming, but I think his main appeal lay in being different. Not just by being a merchant, but by being a foreigner. We were sadly accustomed to French refugees from the Terror, but not to successful Belgians. You might not think it of me now, but then, when I was young, I thought taking the conventional path to marriage seemed intolerably dull."

Lucy responded to the subtle question in that. "I don't think I've ever felt that way. It's only that no conventional man appealed. Do you think that makes me lacking?"

"Perhaps other interests distracted you? You didn't sit at home working samplers."

"No. I wanted trade, not marriage. I wanted to follow my father into business. I wanted . . . I wanted to be his son. How stupid!"

Maria moved to sit beside her, to take her hand. "No, no. There's an excitement to business that domestic life lacks. And perhaps you wanted to be what your father wished you were?"

"Why didn't I want to be what my mother wished I was?"

"You responded to the most powerful wind? However, you were—are—what she wished. She loved you dearly."

"Love doesn't always mean approval."

"She approved of you. She was proud of you. I remember her commenting at times on your graces and your kind heart. And on your cleverness. She didn't dislike that."

"But she disliked my spending so much time with Father."

"I think perhaps she was a little jealous at times. I know that makes no sense, but most people can be sensible only part of the time. But also, she wanted you to have an ordinary life."

"Ah. Not like her."

"Not like her," Maria agreed. "She loved your father to a rare degree and never regretted her choice. I'm sure of that. But at times she implied that she wished her life had flowed down conventional channels to the same place."

"An impossibility."

"She knew that and accepted it. She wouldn't have done differently, given her time again."

"And you?" Lucy asked. "Would you do things differently?"

Maria looked away, frowning over that, then shrugged. "No. For how else could I be where I am? If I'd made a conventional marriage, I would never have married Van." She smiled at Lucy. "I am very happy to be where I am, and I hope you will be able to say the same one day."

They'd skirted unusual courtships and Lucy hadn't found a clear opening. She'd have to ask bluntly. . . .

"Would you like to visit my daughter? That means, of

course, I'm eager to show you how clever Van and I have been to produce such a miracle."

The moment had passed, perhaps because her courage had failed. How could she raise such a subject?

She went up to a nursery where a beautiful baby slept in a lacy cradle, watched over by a nurserymaid.

"I haven't had much to do with babies," Lucy said quietly. "I do want to be a mother."

"Another natural force, but not a smooth path."

"I know that giving birth is hard."

"And can be dangerous, but I didn't mean that. Children don't always make their parents happy. I grieved mine by my marriage, as did your mother. Van did the same by insisting on joining the army at sixteen. All our instincts clamor to keep them safe, but eventually we have to let them go into risk, even into folly and danger. It's so hard to imagine when they're young."

"What's the easy path, then?"

"Perhaps to be a wealthy spinster or bachelor. But does one always wish to be safe?"

They left the nursery and returned to the drawing room.

"Children require a man," Maria said as she sat again. "Preferably a husband."

"I'm not contemplating scandal," Lucy said with a laugh, settling into her seat, blocking all thought of the theater stairwell. "I had begun to think of Wyvern."

"I don't know him well. He's Susan's brother, and we're neighbors, but he's visited Hawk in the Vale only once. But he seems an excellent man."

"In what way?" Lucy asked, aware of revealing her heart.

"He's good-looking," Maria said, "which despite what people sometimes pretend, is not to be discounted. He's also amiable. That sounds weak, but I mean he does his best to be pleasant and kind, not to upset or embarrass. A surprising number of people don't. He makes light of heavy weather, I think Susan said once. Sometimes to her exasperation."

"He has a sterner side. He tore a strip off two men who were working up to a duel over me, almost as if he were accustomed to doing such things. As if he'd been an officer in the army."

"Ah," Maria said. "We all have many facets."

Lucy noted that "ah."

"Has he been in the army?" she asked.

"I don't believe so."

"You know something about him that I don't."

Maria was at her most smooth. "I can't know what you know, dear, and I suspect you know more of him than most."

Lucy would have persisted, but a maid knocked and entered to say that Miss Georgie was asking for her mother. The phrasing made Lucy smile, but she suspected Maria saw the summons as a means to escape.

She had no choice but to take her leave.

Maria walked with her to the door, saying, "Children and nature can be very demanding."

Lucy grasped her courage and blurted out her question. "My father must have seen all the hazards of the marriage. Did Mother have to push him very hard? Did she ever say?"

Another "ah." "She pushed as hard as she had to. She had no choice."

No choice. That's exactly how it felt.

But Maria added, "Be careful, Lucy. The Earl of Wyvern is not a simple man."

"I know that, I assure you."

Lucy walked back to Lanchester Street considering Maria's words. They contained a warning and she was sure it was justified but she, like her mother, had no choice. If her mother had been able to use passion to overcome her father's steely will, she should be able to overcome David's even if it proved as strong.

The only question was whether she should.

Chapter 24

$\mathbb{S}$he returned to find Clara alone in the drawing room, reading. The normality of that seemed shocking.

"Mother's still in bed," Clara said, "prostrated by her efforts."

"Her triumphant efforts," Lucy said. "I'm sorry to have left early."

"It did all go wonderfully. It's a shame, really, to do that only once. I wish I could have my own ball every year!"

"We have to allow each new wave their chance."

"Did you have a ball?"

"Of course. At assembly rooms like yours, but simpler. Most in attendance were old friends."

Lucy went to her room to take off her bonnet, gloves, and spencer. She thought of writing in her journal, but any thoughts would be too dangerous to commit to words. She did need to plan, however. One thing was clear—she'd get nowhere until she and David were together again, but he was in Devon and she was a day and a night's travel away.

She could simply go. She had some money with her and a trip to her bank would provide as much as she wished. She could hire a chaise and leave.

Yet she couldn't. There'd be an instant hue and cry. Even if she delayed detection, she'd eventually be pursued and caught before she reached Devon. The scandal would be horrendous, which wouldn't help her cause at all.

Oh, for an enormous kite to take her there within hours!

It seemed intolerable to be balked, but truly, she could see no way. Yet. Though her need felt urgent, it wasn't. Nothing terrible was going to happen if she didn't reach David in days or even weeks.

She tried to come up with a plan, but an hour devoted to the problem didn't present a solution. She and her father had sometimes talked over a tricky problem and two heads had proved better than one, but she certainly couldn't discuss this with him. He'd lock her up!

Who else? Betty was on her honeymoon, and in any case she would be horrified. Even Maria would feel duty bound to prevent her from such an act. She could talk to David. But he was the problem.

Her scrambling thoughts were getting her nowhere and she needed to rest her mind. She'd join Clara and read one of her novels. Perhaps one of the plots would inspire her. After all, Laura Montreville had gone to Canada, but through abduction.

Both *Self Control* and *Love and Horror* reminded her too much of David, however, so she chose *The Animated Skeleton*.

Clara smiled when she came in. "What book do you have today?"

"*The Animated Skeleton*."

"I haven't read that. You must tell me all about it."

"Wouldn't you prefer to read it without knowing?"

"I like to know what to expect. Surprises are so often unpleasant."

"You're right," Lucy said. "And secrets."

"Oh, secrets are more fun."

Clara returned to her own novel, and Lucy opened

hers, but her mind was now stuck on secrets. She hadn't uncovered David's secrets, and there clearly were significant things she didn't know. He'd admitted it. Maria's "ah" had confirmed it.

Why had Maria reacted that way? She'd said something about David having been in the army? Surely he hadn't. The more she thought, the more sure she became that one or more secrets might have sent him off to Devon. But what could they be? If she pressed Maria, would she tell all? Could Lady Amleigh be persuaded to? What of Mr. Delaney, who'd seemed familiar with David in some way? Lucy couldn't imagine approaching any of them about this.

She turned pages, pretending to read, but trying to imagine any secret that would prevent their marriage. The dramas and scandals surrounding him were the opposite of secret and not his fault. His seat was set in countryside that included cliffs and mists, but that wasn't a secret, either. In fact, he'd made a point of telling her.

Smugglers operated in his area and he didn't intend to do much about it, but that seemed to be the case all around the coast. It was neither secret nor shameful.

So, what?

A marriage?

Betty had talked of a novel where the wicked king had kept his mad wife in a nunnery and pretended she was dead so he could attempt to marry the heroine. . . .

"I don't like Siegfried. He's always bemoaning his fate."

Lucy dragged her mind back to the drawing room. "What?"

"*The Sicilian Curse*. Siegfried is pursuing the bandits who have captured Isabella, but he's ended up in the dungeon of Duke of Malbrocaccia and he's bemoaning."

"A hero should never moan," Lucy agreed. "But is his love for Isabella impossible?"

"Of course. She's betrothed to the King of Sicily."

That would be a surprise to the current King of Sicily, Lucy thought, but she didn't complicate the conversation with reality, especially as Clara had returned to her book.

Complicate with reality . . .

Despite peculiarities, she lived in a sane, modern world. David couldn't possibly keep a wife secret from his sister and friends, and none of them would condone such a thing. Maria certainly wouldn't.

"What sort of hero will you marry?"

Lucy suppressed a sigh. "None of them. Such an odd lot."

Clara giggled. "I mean, what sort of man will you marry?"

"A sensible one."

"How dull."

"There are worse things than dull—such as Steven-hope."

Clara giggled again. "Imagine poetry morning, noon, and night."

"Excruciating poetry."

"Oh, you must be particularly sensitive to that. I do wish you'd share a stanza or two."

"Not yet."

"You must wish for something more than sensible," Clara persisted. "How should he look?"

Tall, broad shouldered, honey brown hair . . .

"Not much taller than I," Lucy said. "And brown haired. Brown hair is trustworthy."

"You don't have a romantic soul!"

"Alas, I fear you're right. What is your ideal man?"

Clara looked into a dream world. "Quite tall. Blond hair, but not too pale a blond. Smiling eyes and a kind heart."

Pricked by jealousy, Lucy said, "That sounds like the Peasant Earl."

"Wyvern?" Clara stared at her. "I'd never marry him."

"Not even to be a countess?"

"What good would that be when he goes mad?"

"Clara, he's not going to go mad."

"How can you know? His father was merely eccentric when young."

"Eccentric," Lucy pointed out. "Like Poodle Byng with his silly dog and the man who dresses only in green."

"Perhaps, but he did create a torture chamber, complete with waxwork figures to be tormented."

"Clara! That's impossible."

"No it isn't! Town was agog during the court hearings on the title, and stories swirled."

"Stories were invented, you mean."

"Not at all." For once, Clara was annoyed. "Come to the library. We have illustrations."

Lucy desperately didn't want to, but knew she must. Here was a secret worth preserving—that he had inherited insanity.

As they entered the room, she noticed how carelessly Clara invaded the room. Clearly it wasn't a sanctum at all. Perhaps nothing in her current world was as it seemed.

Clara hunted through some portfolios and brought one to the table. "These were on sale last year and Mama bought a set." She untied the laces and opened the boards to reveal a set of prints. The first was titled, "Crag Wyvern."

David hadn't exaggerated the ominous peculiarity of his house. The rectangular stone building stood tall on a steep headland, truly not far from the cliff edge, showing only arrow slits to the world, and backed by billowing storm clouds.

"Unpleasant," Lucy said, "but many people have built odd homes. Horace Walpole at Strawberry Hill. Sir William Beckford at Fonthill Priory."

"Beckford's deranged," Clara pointed out. "He built that huge place and lives alone in it, and Fonthill at least has windows. Wyvern's place does have some, but they're inside." Clara flipped through a few sheets. "Here. A courtyard with trees and gardens."

Lucy relaxed. "And good-sized windows all around. I see a fountain as well."

"There was a detailed print of that, but Mama removed it. From the glimpse I had," Clara said in a whisper, "it showed a dragon behaving most improperly with a naked lady."

Not wise to challenge a dragon . . .

Dear heaven!

Clara was flipping through prints of medieval-style rooms that certainly looked unwelcoming. She paused on a sheet. "There! I told you so."

Lucy took one look and then shut the portfolio. The picture had indeed been of a torture chamber, including a rack, shackles on the wall, and a brazier full of implements. As Clara said, there had been figures howling in torment as the instruments were used by what might have been other waxworks, but had looked like real people.

Aunt Mary should have taken that print away, too. She should have burned it. No wonder Clara had been driven to the extreme of warning her.

"I'm sorry I doubted you. Hard to believe anyone could be so vile."

"Oh, not really," Clara said, putting away the prints, and switching mood in her usual unpredictable way. "After all, people go to see Madame Tussaud's waxworks when they're in Town, and some are quite horrid. Victims of the guillotine and such. I understand the Mad Earl had her create the figures for his dungeon." But then Clara turned to fix Lucy with an anxious look. "So you see."

"Yes, I see. Thank you."

"You have many other suitors," Clara said and returned to the drawing room.

Lucy remained, desolate, facing reality.

His house was as bleak as he'd said, and the setting every bit as harsh. That could be endurable, but his father truly had been mad, and viciously so. What's more, hadn't the earls of Wyvern been described as odd for generations?

She found a guide to the peerage and looked them up, but such a book didn't give scandals. All she learned was that none of them had been long lived and they had produced few children.

She replaced that book and sought a guide to Devon. She found one which gave gossipy details about notable places. Crag Wyvern got three pages and travelers were encouraged to make the arduous journey to the remote coastal spot to admire the stark medieval grandeur. They were warned, however, not to attempt to see inside the house, for the earl permitted entry only to select guests.

Ones who enjoyed lewd fountains and torture chambers, Lucy supposed.

The book was eight years old. Did David keep out visitors? Did he . . . ? No, she wouldn't believe that he amused guests with the rack or burning hot pincers.

There were numerous anecdotes, designed to amuse and titillate the reader. The first earl was supposed to have killed a dragon. There was a footnote explaining that a wyvern was a winged dragon with a serpent's tail. He'd designed Crag Wyvern to be proof against further dragon attacks. The dragon's hide was nailed to the wall of the great hall. There was an illustration.

His son, the second earl, had kept a fire burning on the battlements every night, all year round, to ward off marauding dragons. That had been a command in his father's will, but he had also been notorious for holding depraved parties that might have inspired the later Hell-fire Club.

The third earl had died young by riding his horse off a cliff. It had been judged an accident, but the book enjoyed reminding the reader of the insanity in the family.

David's grandmother had fallen to her death from the battlements. The disturbing detail was that her body hadn't been found for twelve hours. What a bleak life that implied.

Her son had been the Mad Earl. Perhaps the earls had merely been eccentric until she brought true insanity into the family, but David had her blood through his father, the Mad Earl.

According to the guide, the current earl was unmarried and without issue, but that had been the known situation at time of writing. David had been born by then, but thought to be the son of Miss Isabelle Kerslake and the smuggler with the odd name. Melchisadeck something.

Why had the earl ignored his legal heir? When she'd asked David, he'd turned cold. Because it was evidence of insanity in his bloodline? The father in *The Peasant Earl* had kept his existence secret because . . .

She would not bring novel fancies into this! These matters were real and could shape the rest of her life. Were the children of a madman inevitably insane?

No. Only think of the poor mad king. He had many children, and though some were eccentric, none showed signs of derangement. Princess Charlotte, his granddaughter, was completely normal.

She'd seen no trace of insanity in David or his sister. Surely if it lurked there, it had to show at times. Maria had described him as the levelheaded one of the pair. If Maria knew of mental instability in David, wouldn't she have felt obliged to warn Lucy?

Lucy put the book back onto the shelves and went up

to her bedroom. She must analyze the situation as if it were a matter of trade. There was no place for emotion in trade. Emotion led one astray. Led to bad bargains. Her decisions now would shape her life.

She would write in her journal to clarify her thoughts.

There is no reason to believe
That David is insane.
However, I have heard
Of occasional madness,
As with lunatics.

If he has fled because of
Impending derangement,
I must follow to find out.

There. The truth had emerged. She must find a way to get to Devon, but all the difficulties remained.

If I ask to go, no one will permit it.
If I leave on my own, I will be pursued.
If only there were balloons or kites
To waft me there and back in hours!
My father has pigeons, which fly with speed,
Carrying information that helps
Him triumph over competitors.
I'm tied to the ground, but if I
Could go and no one know . . .

Impossible, especially when her father's wedding was only a week away. She couldn't be absent for that.

Lucy paused, an idea stirring. It shocked her so much the pencil fell from her fingers. It couldn't be done. Of course it couldn't. But if it could . . .

She closed her book, thinking over it some more. The challenges were considerable, but she'd not been raised to quail at challenges. The biggest challenge was that she needed help.

She doubted Maria would support the deceit. Despite her unconventional marriages, she was a conventional lady. Even Betty might balk, but in any case she was on her honeymoon. Who was unconventional but trustworthy? As she'd realized, she was sadly short of friends.

The Delaneys? She hardly knew them, but Mrs. Delaney had given their address and a meaningful invitation, as if she'd expected Lucy to need help. Hardly help such as this, but she remembered how Mr. Delaney had neatly claimed her from her suitors. Despite his careless manner and unfashionable dress, he'd been master of that situation. What he set out to do would be done, no matter how outrageous.

Moreover he had seemed to know David quite well. He might know the best way to get to Crag Wyvern. Both David and the guidebook had described it as remote and implied some difficulty in traveling there.

Of course, the Delaneys might also know potent reasons why she shouldn't go. Then they could tell her. Otherwise, she was determined on her plan.

She'd not only settle the matter of his mental stability, but she'd be able to see just how horrible his home, his estate, and his area were. She'd be able to make a sane decision. If marriage was impossible, she felt she'd die of it, but she knew that despite poetry and novels, people didn't die for loss of love. She'd recover and she'd find a new path for her life. If she didn't cut through all this, however, she'd linger in misery all her days, haunted by what might have been.

Chapter 25

She sent round a note and was invited to call. When she arrived, Eleanor Delaney greeted her with a relaxed ease that implied that her being there was the most normal of circumstances. Indeed, it felt it.

The drawing room was casual in the extreme, and scattered with books, handicrafts, and children's toys. Three children were playing there, a boy and two little girls, one dark haired, one with her mother's auburn hair.

Eleanor introduced Lucy to her daughter Arabel, and to Arabel's friend Delphie and Delphie's brother Pierre. The lad bowed but returned to a book. Both girls curtsied and were eager to show off a collection of dolls. Oddly, the favorite of both, called Marriette, was made of twigs and scraps of cloth.

"Toys have significance according to circumstances, don't they?" Eleanor said. "Did you have a favorite doll?"

Lucy thought back. "I had pretty ones and I remember enjoying dressing them in different ways, but I left them behind without a qualm."

"As did I, as perhaps Arabel and Delphie will. Arabel is quite fond of a toy soldier and recently made a sword out of sticks."

"Don't you mind?"

"To what purpose? She will be what she will be."

That echoed Maria's thoughts.

"I wanted to be my father's heir." It no longer hurt to say it.

"If Nicholas were your father, you would be." Eleanor wrinkled her brow, smiling. "If you can untangle that."

"I can. My father shattered conventions to become what he is, but chooses convention for me."

"Perhaps he understands how hard it is to take unconventional roads, as he and your mother did."

As Maria had said.

"Apparently she wanted me to be a conventional lady. I thought my father wrong about that, but Maria Vandeimen implied as much."

"I suppose we all hope our children will find a smooth and easy path. You are contemplating barriers?"

Lucy eyed her. "You're perceptive."

"It doesn't take great insight, but Nicholas expected this. He's annoyingly insightful."

"I suspected as much."

"He predicted that you'd want to travel to Devon."

Lucy stared at her. "Now that *is* irritating."

"But is he right?"

"Yes. I can't swing in the wind like this anymore. I need to know the truth. There is a truth to be known?"

"Many of them," Eleanor said, not seeming uncomfortable with the question, but not answering it, either. "Isn't that always the case? Even conventional people have their secrets and surprises."

"And Wyvern is not conventional. Does he still have a torture chamber?" Lucy braced herself for the answer, suddenly aware that if he did, there was no hope.

"Heavens, no! Con started the destruction when he was earl. I gather there were offers to purchase what was left, but David had everything smashable smashed, everything meltable melted down, and anything flammable burned."

Lucy let out a breath. "Good. Good." She risked a direct question. "Is he insane? At times, at least?"

Eleanor didn't seem startled. "Are any of us sane all the time? I don't think he's fit for Bedlam."

That wasn't entirely satisfactory, but it was better than it might have been. Lucy had come here in a ferment of need and uncertainty, but Eleanor's calm manner was settling her. It made it seem that alarm was unnecessary and anything possible.

"I must go to Devon to find out for myself why David is so certain we should not wed, and I want to go now. No one will approve my going there, however, so no one can know I've gone. I have an idea of how it might be done, but I need help."

Eleanor smiled. "You are not at all as you appear, are you? I'll summon maids for the children and we can join Nicholas in the library."

When they entered the room, Eleanor said, "You were right on all counts, you irritating man. Except that Lucy needs to get to Devon now."

She outlined the situation as they sat and Nicholas Delaney listened.

"We live in Somerset, not very far from Crag Wyvern," he said, "and we've been thinking of leaving Town. We prefer the country and there's nothing to hold us here anymore."

"We came to help a Rogue," Eleanor explained, "and lingered to help Lord Darien."

"The murderous one?" Lucy asked, surprised.

"That was his brother," Nicholas said. "The current one's burdened by the scandal of his name."

"Like David," Lucy said.

"Even the Mad Earl of Wyvern didn't slaughter a young lady of the neighborhood and leave bloody tracks back to his house."

"Goodness, I remember that now! I'd forgotten the name."

"Alas, few in the beau monde did. Now that Darien is settled, we lingered for David. I had a hand in persuading him to claim the earldom. That was for Con's sake, but it created its own obligation."

"I see."

"I think you do."

"Balance is important in trade. In ideal circumstances everyone feels they did well from a transaction."

"Even though there is nearly always a winner and a loser."

Lucy shrugged, for it was true. "Do you have time to help me?"

"What do you need?"

His tone was so commonplace that Lucy hesitated to put her outrageous plan into words, but she must.

"No one is going to allow me to go to Devon on the instant in pursuit of Wyvern, so I have to go unnoticed." Neither listener seemed shocked. "My father marries in a week. There's no habit of communications between him and my aunt, Lady Caldross. When I returned to the City recently, she didn't write to him about it. If I say I want to return again to assist in the preparations for my father's wedding, it should happen the same way."

"And as no one will be expecting you," Delaney said, "no one will report that you haven't arrived. Ingenious. It could go awry."

"They won't hang me for it."

He nodded. "What do you need?"

"A carriage. Last time, my aunt sent me in hers, but that won't do. It must seem my father has sent a carriage for me."

"That can be arranged."

"I'll also need advice on how to get to Crag Wyvern.

I'll have to travel at speed, for I must be back in time for Father's wedding. I can't miss that."

"In the midst of this, you're concerned about such a conventional matter?"

"It's not only convention. I want to be at his wedding to wish him and Charlotte well."

"Then you'll have only a few days in Devon. Is that worth an arduous journey?"

"Yes." But she added, "How arduous?"

"It's nearly two hundred miles and toll roads will only take you to Honiton. After that, travel will be slower and in time it will be best on horseback. Do you ride?"

Lucy wanted to lie, but said, "No."

She thought he'd try to dissuade her at that point, but he said, "Pillion, then." He glanced at his wife and must have received some agreement. "We'll take you. Or rather, I will under cover of our departure for Somerset."

Lucy relaxed, all her stress smoothing away. "Thank you. How are we to achieve it?"

"You'll depart your aunt's house tomorrow for the City in a carriage I send. It will bring you here, and we'll be ready to depart for Somerset in a grand train of carriages containing family, servants, and baggage. At the Turnham Green stage, you and I will hire a chaise and six and hurtle onward at all possible speed."

Lucy laughed rather shakily. "It feels like an elopement." As her mother had eloped.

"If possible marry with all due decorum," Nicholas Delaney said.

"I'm not actually eloping."

"But you're going adventuring, which is just as chancy. Are you sure?"

Lucy took a moment to weigh it all again, as something that could actually happen.

"Yes. I have no choice, you see. And even if I'm

missed, I'll be hard to trace, so I might not be stopped before I've found out what I need to know."

"A lady of steady nerves and a clear head. David had you assessed right from the start."

"He did?"

He smiled. "But I won't say more on that. You and he must sort it out for yourselves."

Lucy thought of one thing. "I must pay for this. It's my enterprise."

She expected a polite objection, but he only asked, "You have enough money on hand?"

"I can get it. From my bank."

"Can you trust your banker not to mention a large withdrawal to your father?"

He might not go so far as to report to her father, but if they met, as they could well, he'd probably see no harm in mentioning it.

"I won't be balked by that."

"No need. I'll fund it."

"Thank you, but I will pay you back. I insist."

"Very well. Is there any wrinkle we've missed?"

Eleanor spoke. "You must pack as if truly returning to your father's for the wedding."

"I'd not thought of that. A pity to haul a trunk along."

"Leave it here and collect it when you return. A valise and a few changes of clothing will do for a few days. It will be very tiring to get there in a day," Eleanor warned. "I'll go more gently to Red Oaks, which could mean three days, and it's about the same distance."

"Nothing could be more tiring than fretting day and night."

"Ah, love," Eleanor said wryly. To her husband, she said, "Will you stay with Lucy or catch up with us?"

"Once delivered, it's for Lucy and David to deal with their affairs."

Lucy had the feeling that even a little time apart was

a trial to them, and yet they seemed such calm, sensible people.

"Is love enough?" she asked. "It must have been in my mother's case, but I've known hardship to turn wives sour."

"Husbands, too," Eleanor said. "Perhaps such people only had fair-weather affection, or perhaps trials can wear away at even the deepest love. In your case, you need only discover whether what you feel now can endure what you discover."

That felt ominous.

"David won't change? Won't move elsewhere?"

Nicholas answered. "Duty obliges him, but where love's concerned, nothing is impossible. However, it would be cruel to try to move him to the City."

"Yet not cruel to move me to the remote countryside?"

"It would be cruel not just to him, but to others. You'll see what I mean when you get there. And as for the cruelty to you, that is for you to decide."

"What about a chaperone, Nicholas?" Eleanor asked. "I don't mean on the journey, but at the Crag?"

"Lucy might prefer to stay at Kerslake Manor. Where David was born and raised," he explained. "His aunt and uncle are very respectable people. It's much more normal."

The opposite being abnormal.

With the plan laid out and possible, all the hazards became clear. She was going to slip away from London under a cloak of deception, travel alone with a man she hardly knew, and arrive unannounced at the door of the Earl of Wyvern's ominous keep.

Perhaps it was she who was mad.

But the madness was compelling.

"I must do this," she stated.

"Very well," Nicholas said, as if they were arranging a drive out to Chiswick. "You must arrange your departure with your aunt. Once that's settled, send word and we'll do the rest."

On the way home Lucy realized that she wasn't practiced in deceit. Small matters, yes, like poetry and nightingales, but not serious ones. She thanked the heavens she didn't have to attempt the deception with her father.

When she arrived she went straight to her aunt before she lost her nerve.

"I feel I should return home, Aunt, to assist with the preparations for my father's wedding."

She was prepared for objections, but Aunt Mary made none at all. "Very dutiful of you, dear."

On to the next hurdle. Would her aunt insist on sending her home in her town carriage? "I'll write to my father and ask him to send the carriage."

"That would be kind. I confess ours is often needed at this busy time." Then her aunt frowned. What had she perceived? "You will miss some promising entertainment, dear. Signor Berconi is to sing privately at Lady Ball's." But then Aunt Mary added, "Ah, Wyvern."

Lucy's heart thumped. How had Aunt Mary guessed? All she could manage was a feeble, "What do you mean?"

"I mean that you have fallen into rash behavior, Lucinda. The gossip I hear! It *never* serves to allow a gentleman liberties before marriage. Why should he believe that a lady will be a chaste and modest wife if she behaves otherwise unwed? He might've, in fact, leave Town to avoid further entanglements."

Lucy knew she was fiery red, but could do nothing about it. Her aunt's words might've even been true if she put the worst interpretation on David's leaving. Which she didn't.

"I will say no more, dear. A lesson learned. It is sensible of you to use such an excellent excuse to leave for a few days to let any talk die down. If you still favor the earl, he may change his mind, for you do offer much."

Thirty thousand pounds.

How irrelevant that now seemed.

"And he himself is not unsullied," her aunt added.

"You mean the insanity in the family."

Perhaps she hoped her aunt would dismiss that flaw, but she said, "That and notoriety. A true gentleman or lady Does Not Cause Talk. A pity about Stevenhope, but you have other admirers. Do not despair of finding a good husband. All in all you are a good girl and a steadying influence on Clara. At the end of the month we will move to Brighton for some weeks. If you haven't visited there, you might enjoy it."

Lucy was assailed with guilt. For the first time she wondered what would happen if her deception was uncovered. Her aunt would become the center of talk, but more than that, she would be hurt.

"You're very kind, Aunt," Lucy said, and meant it.

She left then and made herself consider the idea that Wyvern had fled Town in disgust. Had he felt, as Aunt Mary said, that a lady who tumbled into such scandalous extremes in a theater stairwell would never be a trustworthy wife?

Definitely a case of the pot calling the kettle black, but the world was never fair between men and women. The world approved of demure young ladies who kept their more disturbing talents under a bushel basket. It approved of ones like Lady Iphigenia, who seemed to lack any firm substance at all.

Days ago she would have been sure Wyvern had more sense, but now she wasn't sure of anything. She entered the bedroom knowing that if she were sane, she should do as she'd said and go home. If Wyvern wanted her, he would know where to find her.

She wasn't sane. She touched the bed, remembering

that magical nighttime visit. The stairwell had been fiery passion, but the bedroom invasion had been magical. That had been pure David, and it was David she loved.

She hitched up to sit on the bed, chasing a thought. David, Earl, and Dragon.

David delighted her.

She admired the dutiful earl.

She thrilled to the dangerous dragon.

But secrets, secrets, secrets!

She had to know all.

She went to the desk to write the note to the Delaneys and then had Hannah take it to a footman for delivery. If anyone asked, she'd say she was canceling a future engagement.

She also told Hannah to have her small trunk brought down for packing. As she waited for the maid to return she saw an unconsidered obstacle.

Hannah.

She couldn't leave her here, so she was going to have to take her. All the way to Devon? Her maid would be a chaperone, but the fastest post chaise was designed for only two.

When Hannah returned, Lucy hadn't come up with a solution. She set to the simpler task of choosing what to take.

She needed only plain clothing for this adventure, but to support the fiction she had to take an assortment. The second footman brought in the trunk and Hannah began to pack the items already chosen.

"What'll you take for the wedding, miss?"

Charlotte dressed simply, and she'd probably do the same for her wedding. Lucy had no desire to outshine the bride.

She said as much to the maid. "There's the dusky blue morning dress at home. If I add the new blue spencer, it will be fine enough. And the white straw bonnet with the extra trimming removed."

Hannah nodded, and found the spencer and the bonnet in its box.

"Won't you want something fine in case there's an evening event, miss?"

She must, for in the end she would be at home, involved in the wedding celebrations. Her tonnish clothes had made her an oddity in the past. "The sprigged muslin," she decided, "and the cerulean blue."

"The plain one, miss?"

"You know it's a favorite. As I couldn't bear to overtrim it, I haven't worn it here, but it will suit the City."

"It'll be good to be back home, miss."

Lucy smiled, but she no longer knew where home was. Nor had she come up with any way to deal with Hannah.

Chapter 26

The first part of the plan went off perfectly. A glossy town carriage arrived at the door. The trunk and boxes were loaded into the boot. Hannah entered the carriage and Lucy took a fond farewell of her aunt and cousin.

It wasn't long, however, before Hannah said, "Are we going the right way, miss? And why isn't Sam Travers driving?"

Lucy ignored the second part. "We're stopping at a friend's house first." But she soon saw there was nothing for it. "I'm not going home, Hannah. I'm going to Devon."

The maid's hand went to her chest. "Never say you're eloping!"

"Of course not. But I have need to visit Devon and my friends are going to take me there."

"It's that Lord Wyvern, isn't it? I knew he was up to no good, sneaking you off into the trees and kissing you there. I could see, never mind the tree trunks. And I heard tell you went off with him at the theater the other night. Oh, Miss Lucy, what are you up to?"

"Hush, Hannah. Nothing terrible, I promise. I'm traveling with Mr. and Mrs. Delaney and their children." Children made everything seem more respectable. "I simply need to see where Lord Wyvern lives before I can make a decision."

"But there's proper ways to do that, miss. Not sneaking away like this."

"Not without it seeming as if I'm committed. I want to make a free choice."

"Better to choose another, I say. Everyone mutters that he has bad blood."

"That's why I have to see for myself. You won't expose me, will you, Hannah?"

The maid rolled her eyes. "I should, and there's no mistake. I should tell your father right off. But I'll come with you."

"I'm afraid that's not possible. There'll be no room in the carriage."

"Then what am I to do?"

"I thought you could stay at the Delaneys' house for the next few days." Then Lucy was inspired. "Or perhaps you'd like a holiday?"

"Well, I never . . . ! Not but what I wouldn't mind visiting my sister, who's married to a Kentish man, out Erith way."

"Perfect," Lucy said with a sigh of relief. "We'll arrange your travel there and I'll let you know when I'll be back so we can arrive home with none the wiser."

"I'm not sure I'm doing the right thing, miss."

"You are. I promise."

Hannah looked skeptical about that, and no wonder. "And I doubt I'll be able to keep it to myself forever. I'm not a one for lying."

"I don't need you to lie. By the time we go to the wedding, it won't matter if people know."

"If you say so, miss, but I doubt your father will be pleased."

"He'll be too involved in his own affairs to pay much attention," Lucy said, praying that be true. "And you mustn't worry about your future. Whatever happens, I'll make sure you're taken care of."

*   *   *

Lucy was on the road by noon, bridges burned, die cast, hurtling along the toll road to Exeter at alarming speed in a light post chaise pulled by six horses.

They drove all day with only the shortest breaks to change horses and get refreshment. There was little conversation, for Nicholas was no chatterer and Lucy wasn't sure what to say. She might like to debate her situation and actions, but what was the point when she had no intention of turning back? She would definitely like to tease out secret information, but that would never work.

He'd brought books and offered her one. It was about the exploration of Australia, and she wondered if it had some special meaning. David's mother had gone to Botany Bay in pursuit of the man he'd thought his father for most of his life.

He'd claimed to have no feelings for them, but could that be true?

True or not, she couldn't settle to the book. Nor could she make plans or think logically about her situation, for love seemed to blank all reason from her mind. She was going to him. She would see him. Once they were together again the knots would untangle, the barriers would drop.

Nothing could withstand the force in her and in him.

They reached the Crown in Shaftesbury as the light was going and rain beginning. They decided not to attempt to travel through the night, but they rose with the sun at five in the morning to eat a hasty breakfast and hurtle on to Honiton. There they hired a gig to take them closer to the coast. After that would come pillion riding, which she didn't look forward to at all.

Their valises were put into the sturdy gig and Nicholas took the reins to drive them south toward the sea.

"You were right about the road," Lucy said as they swayed and jolted over the poorly maintained surface. "How far now?"

"About eight miles, so two hours or so if we're lucky."

She wished she could demand greater speed, but even insane love wasn't mad enough for that. The sturdy horse's steady pace was the only way, and even so it was a bumpy ride.

She tried to admire the countryside, but she couldn't help but notice how sparsely populated it seemed. Fields were under crops or grazed by animals, so it wasn't wild, but the villages were scattered, and the ones they passed through were small. The inhabitants watched them, as if strangers were a rarity.

It was a relief when Nicholas turned the gig into an inn yard in a small town, until he said, "We'll fare better on horseback from here."

Lucy rubbed her backside. "After the last mile or so, that might be a relief."

"This is riding country. Or boat. In fair weather, it's often easiest to go by sea from place to place along the coast."

"I've never traveled by boat unless a Thames wherry counts. I remember often wishing I were setting out on a merchantman headed for the Orient."

"And now?"

"I think adventure is greatly overrated. I'm not sure I can do this."

"Ride pillion the mile and a half to Crag Wyvern?"

"Commit to a life here. I see people, I see houses, I even see pretty gardens, but deep inside I think this is a savage wasteland."

"I've ventured to savage wastelands," he said unsympathetically, "and you are far off the mark. Come, let's progress to the dreadful end."

A hostler was leading out a horse fitted with a pillion saddle. Lucy eyed it resentfully, in part because she'd never ridden, not even pillion, but also because Nicholas was making light of her fears. It was not silly to be alarmed by the prospect of making a life in such a different place. Perhaps he'd been to Borneo, Hindustan, or the wilds of Canada, but she hadn't.

He was checking the various straps and fittings, but turned to look at her. "What has you smiling?"

"Have you ever paddled a canoe down a river in Canada?"

His brows went up, but he said, "Yes."

"Fleeing Indians?"

"With Indians, fleeing Americans. Why?"

"I'm simply appreciating how reality and fantasy sometimes mingle."

He didn't enquire further, but strapped their bags behind the pillion. The poor beast was beginning to look like a packhorse.

He mounted. "Ready?"

The hostler stood by to give her a hand up the mounting block, so she climbed up and settled in the seat. Once there, and with her right arm around Nicholas, she felt reasonably safe, but as they set off, she wished the horse didn't sway with each step.

"Don't go too fast, please."

He laughed. "Walking pace all the way. You could have ridden on your own."

She shuddered. "I don't think so. How far did you say?"

"A mile and a half or so."

Not far at all in London, but it felt like a great distance on this rough terrain. The road was no more than a cart track, and the hedges close enough to almost brush her skirts as they passed. When a trailing bramble caught her skirt for a moment, she gave thanks she'd been sensible and worn her brown traveling gown. She'd been tempted to try to arrive in finery, but she'd had sense enough to resist that madness at least.

Soon she'd arrive and discover the truth.

What if David was suffering an insane fit?

What did she do then?

She had to ask. "Are the earls of Wyvern mad?"

"The previous one was unbalanced, at the least," Nicholas said.

"I saw a picture of the torture chamber, and read of one who rode off a cliff."

"He could merely have been drunk."

"What of the countess who threw herself from the battlements?"

"Crag Wyvern could do that to a person."

"That isn't a joking matter!"

"Wait and see, Lucy. Not long now. To our left, beyond that hill, you can glimpse the sea."

It was a glimmer like polished silver that she might have missed. When the path turned, it disappeared from view.

"It looked cold."

"It frequently is, but the Channel is tamer than the Atlantic. You could have fallen in love with a Cornishman."

"You sneer at everything."

"I never sneer at love. It's too important. I simply stated a fact. Or do you feel you had control over whom you loved?"

"Did you?"

"No."

"But everything was straightforward for you."

She felt his laughter. "I wonder if it ever is."

"My friend Betty fell in love with a neighbor's son, a perfectly eligible man who will one day inherit his father's company."

"You wish you'd done the same?"

She almost said yes, but then remembered Maria's words. If she'd married in a conventional way, she wouldn't have married Lord Vandeimen, whom she clearly adored.

"There's no reason for my romance to be difficult," she said, "apart from Wyvern inconveniently living on the edge of nowhere. But I'm sure I can cope with that if I must."

"Then why are we on this journey?" he asked.

Because David fled London and did not intend to return, and she had to know why. She'd tried to dismiss insanity, and yet what else could drive him away? She knew she hadn't been mistaken about their passion or their love.

The road began to slope downward, pushing her a little closer to Nicholas. She held on more tightly, but he couldn't and wouldn't protect her from herself. Odd to think that she might, perhaps, prefer to be protected, even prevented.

During the urgent planning and the fast journey she'd not dwelt deeply on her actions, but this swaying amble down toward the sea had brought every problem to the top of her mind. Her journey would be seen as mad by most people, and shameful, too. David might be angry or even disgusted that she'd done such a thing.

He wouldn't have abandoned her without good reason.

The rough road now pointed relentlessly downward, and the sea was no comfort. It spread before her, steely gray to the horizon. She could understand why people had once thought the earth flat and that ships would sail off the edge.

Nicholas halted the horse and pointed left. "You can see Crag Wyvern over there."

The dark tower on a cliff top was exactly as uncompromising and isolated as it had seemed in that illustration, and as bleak as Wyvern had implied.

She could deal with that problem, at least. If they did marry, they could use her money to tear it down and build better.

Away from cliffs.

Away from endless horizons.

She focused instead on the spire of a church and thatched rooftops. There was a village below the cliffs, tucked down low, not exposed to the elements.

The road smoothed out to flat as they entered the blessedly normal surroundings of well-tended cottages and gardens mingled with small farms surrounded by outbuildings and yards of poultry and pigs. The quite elegant church had a leafy graveyard.

"Church Wyvern," Nicholas said. "David was born and raised here, at Kerslake Manor. That road to our left leads up to the Crag."

Lucy supposed its width warranted the word "road," but it was a track—rough, chalky, and very steep.

"We have to climb that?"

"By foot or on horseback. People who live here get used to slopes."

People who live here.

The handful of villagers out in the street were staring and a few more were gathering. Probably they didn't often see strangers here, especially fashionable ones, but she was struck by a kind of blankness on their faces. The only bright gaze was from an infant who was taking in wonders, thumb stuck firmly in mouth.

Then, like a spell breaking, a gray-haired man came out of the inn, smiling. "Mr. Delaney, zur. I'll be taking your horse?" The accent was thick but understandable.

The villagers resumed their business, but Lucy still felt their wary speculation. She looked around, hoping to see David, but of course he'd be up in his daunting keep.

She noticed that despite his professional courtesy, the innkeeper gave her a look that was sharp and, yes, guarded. What danger could a fashionable young lady pose to these people?

Smuggling.

That was it.

A hazard she hadn't considered.

Even David had admitted that many of his people were involved in the wicked trade. They probably regarded any stranger with distrust, but how ridiculous to think she might be a spy for the excise men.

All the same, smugglers were notoriously cruel to spies and traitors.

Chapter 27

David was in Magsy Lovell's cottage discussing the lace trade when young Gabby Oke ran in, his eyes bright with excitement.

"Strangers, zur! Least, one's been here afore, but there's a woman, too. In an odd hat!"

"Tourists," David said. "Nothing to fear, but I'll come."

He ducked out of the cottage and walked down the lane to turn into the main street. As soon as he did, he stopped, his heart giving a betraying leap. *Lucy*. With Nicholas.

Then alarm and anger surged. Did the woman have no sense at all? And what in Hades was Nicholas up to, bringing her here? He strode forward, ready to demand that.

But not with half the village watching, either from the street or from windows.

"Delaney," he said, mildly enough.

Nicholas met his eyes, his expression perhaps rueful but definitely unrepentant. King Rogue was meddling, damn him.

David turned to Lucy, perched on the back of the big horse, looking as worried as she should. She was in that plain brown gown she'd worn in the park, but it still blazoned London wealth, as did her soft, stylish hat pinned with a quartz brooch. She was completely out of place here.

But lovely.

And desirable.

And . . .

Everything was fixed in place like a ridiculous tab-
leau. The horse was nowhere near the mounting
block — on purpose? He had no choice but to go forward
and help her down.

"Miss Potter. What an unexpected pleasure."

He put his hands on her slender waist and lifted her
down, noting how slight she was, but only physically. Not
in any other way. Her being here was proof of that and
set his heart pounding with the need to pull her into his
arms and never let her go.

As soon as her feet were settled on the ground he let
her go and stepped away. "No maid?"

"No maid," she said, looking around. He could see
that she was attempting to look merely curious, but she
was avoiding his gaze. She was uneasy under so many
watchful eyes. It served her right, and would be useful.
Her being here was disastrous in any circumstances, but
especially with a run tomorrow night. Nicholas would
have to take her back where she'd come from.

But Nicholas had already had Matt Lovell, the innkeeper, unstrap a valise from the back of the pillion saddle, and he now turned the horse. "As Miss Potter is
safely in your hands, Wyvern, I'll leave and hope to inter-
cept Eleanor and the children at Honiton."

If David had commanded it, the whole village would
have poured out to block the road, but while some trace
of reason ruled the world, he couldn't do that. He could
only let Nicholas ride away. But there would be a reck-
oning for this.

Lucy was staring after her escort.

"Don't look so shocked," David said. "That's what
you get for enlisting Nicholas Delaney." When she
turned to face him, he asked, "Why?"

She was wary, which showed sense, but her chin went up. "Mad impulse?"

"We need no more madness here."

Her eyes widened, but she spoke firmly. "I needed to see what this place is like."

"Why?"

She blushed then, because the answer was obvious—to decide whether to marry him or not.

"I'd have thought it disastrous in trade to be blind to facts that don't suit you."

"Equally disastrous not to factor in everything," she countered, willing to fight, heaven help him.

"Emotions have no part in trade."

"That depends on the trade. My father paid more than the value for a painting that reminded him of something important in his life."

And your father will pay in blood to stop you marrying me.

He couldn't tell her that, because she'd brush her father's objections aside. She was of age. She had command of her money. She could marry whom she wished.

He couldn't tell her the root problem: that he was Captain Drake, smuggler-in-chief, and her father would use that if crossed. He didn't underestimate Daniel Potter's powers to wreak havoc here, and since returning he'd uncovered evidence of his probing.

A couple of scholars had arrived a few days back and were wandering about the area, being a bit too nosy, and even the Blackstock Gang, old enemies, had sent word of questions being asked about Dragon's Horde affairs. Lloyd seemed particularly jaunty, as if his quarry was within his sights.

David could only hope that Potter didn't have spies in the area now or word would be speeding to London that his daughter was here.

They couldn't stand here bandying words. Damnation,

from the look in some of the village women's eyes, they were coming to conclusions. He'd take her to the manor and put her in Aunt Miriam's hands. . . .

No, disastrous. Aunt Miriam would set to planning the wedding.

Right. She'd come here to see if she'd like living here. He'd show her that she wouldn't.

He picked up her valise. "Come."

"Where?" she asked.

"To Crag Wyvern, where else?"

Lucy hadn't expected a welcome, but she'd not expected enmity. In his country clothes, hatless, his shirt open necked, and his hair disordered by the breeze, he looked like David, but he was behaving like the masterful man who'd cowed Outram and Stevenhope.

Like the dragon.

She had reason to be wary of the dragon, but she truly had burned her boats. None of the people around—his people—would help her. Probably none would raise a finger if he threw her off a cliff, and they'd certainly keep the secret of it.

She tried to tell herself that Nicholas Delaney wouldn't have gone if he'd thought there was danger. But she couldn't be entirely sure even of that.

Then the chime of the church bell broke the dark spell and she got her nerve back. Church. Time. Normality. At the moment, at least, David was free of insanity. So what was the problem? She'd come here to find out the truth, and she would, even if she had to fight the dragon to do so.

Very soon she was wishing for a smoother battlefield.

The "road" was steep from the beginning. Worse, the surface was uneven and unstable, with stones that shifted beneath her half boots. They were leather and she'd thought them sturdy, but they'd been made for city streets, not this kind of terrain. She could feel some pointed chips of rock through the soles.

She wasn't used to thinking of herself as frail and she could dance the night away, but her legs weren't used to slopes like this and they were already protesting. She began to feel her heart's effort and had to stop to suck in breaths.

David turned back to look at her, expression as blank as those of his villagers.

"I'm not used to slopes," she said.

"I warned you."

"Cliffs. You said cliffs. Climbing with ropes. Not without!"

Had his lips twitched?

She seized on that. "You could at least give me a hand."

His reluctance hurt, but he did extend a hand to her—a strong, bare hand, tanned and capable of work. She wished she dare take off her leather glove before taking it, but that would be a dare too far.

His strength helped and she longed to complete the climb without further weakness, but she had to call a halt again. She used the excuse of a path going off to the right, sloping down.

"Where does that go?"

"To Dragon's Cove, the fishing village. The houses are tucked up the cleft in the cliffs, where there's shelter in a storm."

"Not stuck on top of a cliff," she pointed out.

"Not stuck on top of a cliff," he agreed.

"Was your house really built that way as a lookout for dragons?"

"So the stories say."

"Dragons are mythological beasts. They don't exist."

"So the stories say."

Grimly Lucy set off to complete the climb. Once up, she might never go down again except to leave.

When they arrived at the grassy top she paused again to let her heart rate settle. Here were new challenges to face, and one was simply space. She was surrounded by a grassy headland cropped by sheep, with Crag Wyvern looming over her and the sea filling the rest of the view. The endless sea, growling down beneath the all-too-close cliff edge.

She turned her back on it, but that only presented his monstrous home.

From a distance it had seemed ominous. From so close it overwhelmed, grim from foundations to battlements and without a trace of welcome.

As in the illustration, there were no windows, only arrow slits. But in the picture, she hadn't noticed the fanged gargoyles jutting out from the two corners she could see. More clustered around the huge arched entrance, which was sealed by massive wooden doors that were barred and studded with iron. The spiked bottom of a portcullis hung over them, looking ready to crash down and impale an invader.

It was exactly as illustrated, but no etching could convey the dreadfulness of it. It seemed invincible, but England was littered with ruined castles, smashed by cannonballs in ancient battles. Where did one find a cannon when one wanted one?

"Well?" he asked.

"It's horrible," she said as prosaically as she could. "But it could be torn down."

"A historical monument?" he asked.

"It's a folly."

"A folly is a useless whimsy. The Crag's been lived in since the day it was built."

"Then it's foolish, and not old enough to need preservation."

"Not even when it's unique?"

"I could build a Chinese pagoda on the opposite headland, which would be unique enough. Would that make it valuable?"

"It would probably be a profitable venture. It would draw multitudes of tourists by land and sea."

Surely a touch of humor had lightened his eyes.

Was he truly fond of this monstrosity? Or was he committed to it by some sort of reverence for heritage? Very well.

"There could be gardens around it," she said. "To soften the appearance."

"Not worth the trouble, given the harsh winds we get at times. And who's to care?"

"Anyone who comes here."

"Visitors come to shiver at its bleak awfulness. Come on."

As she walked with him toward the doors she remembered something. "There's a garden inside," she said.

He paused. "How do you know that?"

"I've seen pictures. Aunt Mary has a set. They were all the rage last year when your claim to the earldom was a cause célèbre."

A twitch of his features was probably annoyance, but that was better than the dragon's mask.

"In a normal world," she remarked as they walked toward the imposing doors, "the approach to an earl's door would be a drive, not a footpath."

"No one would bring a carriage up here, and I'm glad you understand that this is not a normal world."

"That's hard to escape when those doors must take ten men to open."

"Or one earl," he said, turning an iron ring in a normal-sized door set in the larger ones and opening it. "Enter if you dare," he said, gesturing.

It was said lightly, but perhaps even a dragon can joke.

The interior appeared oddly dark, and she didn't want to be trapped in darkness with him alone. "Servants?" she asked. There had to be servants.

"They have better things to do than open doors for me."

That was such a David comment that Lucy found the courage to walk into the dragon's lair.

She realized immediately that the lack of light was because she faced a carved wooden panel no more than eight feet from the door—which clicked shut behind her, trapping her in a gloomy space.

She turned to face him.

He had servants, but would they come if she screamed?

Then she saw that he liked her fear. He hoped, perhaps planned, to frighten her away!

Perhaps if she were sane, he would succeed, but not because of his house. Rather because of him. No wonder Outram and Stevenhope had slunk away. With some manly instinct they'd recognized the dragon in him.

People knew she was here, she reminded herself.

But they were all his people.

Except Nicholas Delaney.

What really did she know of him or his Company of Rogues? Perhaps he regularly brought maidens to the dragon's lair.

Stop that! It's what he wants, and for simple pride's sake he must not win that battle.

Chapter 28

When she was sure she could speak normally, she said, "I've been in castles, and doors like that open into a passageway high enough for mounted men and wide enough for carts. Here inside, the ceiling reaches only halfway up the doors. I see that the mounted men and carts are unlikely to climb the hill, but then, why the doors?"

"Insanity," he said. "Or simple folly, if you prefer. The rest matches the entrance. Let's progress to the great hall."

He opened a door in the wooden screen and she walked into the medieval hall she remembered from the prints. At least there was light here from a wall of small-paned windows and doors set with glass, like tall French windows. Beyond, she saw blessed greenery. The inner garden.

That let her study the room calmly. In a real castle in olden times the lord's household would gather in such a place for feasts and festivities. This one was cleverly made with dark rafters, plain stone walls, and heavy dark oak furniture, but it felt as if no one had ever feasted in the cold space. Anyone could see that most of the heat from that huge stone fireplace would go up the chimney. Even in summer she felt chilled.

"You spend pleasant evenings here?" she asked.

"I have other haunts."

The ceiling here was high and the top third of the walls was encrusted with steel weaponry of all kinds.

"Pistols?" she asked, considering a starburst of them. "A little anachronistic?"

"No one has ever claimed this place is sane. You note the dragon's hide?"

Something large, leathery, and probably moldy covered the wall above the fireplace.

"It should be scientifically studied," she said.

"You would destroy mysteries?"

She faced him. "Yes."

"What of this suit of armor?" he said, walking toward the one standing in a corner. "It is real."

"Armor is real, war is real."

"The skeleton is real," he said, opening the visor to reveal a grinning skull.

Lucy started, but did her best to show only mild concern. "Then shouldn't it be decently interred?"

"Not at all. It's the third earl, and his final resting place was specifically requested in his will."

"There must be a law against that."

"What of all the skeletons used by doctors in their studies? Not to mention the corpses used by anatomists. Have you visited a hospital to watch a dissection?"

"No."

"It not being a matter suitable for trade. Come into the garden of delights."

Lucy went through the doors braced for more peculiarities. She found none, but no delights, either. She'd visited lovely walled gardens, but here the walls were too close and too high. Even now, on a June afternoon, very little sun penetrated.

It was laid out neatly enough in beds intersected by crisscrossing paths, and someone had made the effort to find plants that could tolerate the lack of light. Some even bore flowers. Overall, however, it felt dark and sorrowful. The two trees seemed stunted.

There were windows in all the walls, but they looked into this unhappy place.

"This house needs to be turned inside out," she said. "Or right-side in."

"You have a magic wand?" he asked drily.

Money, she thought, but doubted even all her father's wealth could achieve that.

A fountain stood in the center of the network of paths. Aunt Mary had removed that picture from the collection because it showed a dragon behaving improperly with a lady. Lucy walked toward it because she knew she shouldn't. Even before arriving she knew it was different. No figures here, but two birds stretching upward, their long necks entwined.

"I heard it was scandalous," she said.

"Disappointed?"

"I'm not sure. Why the swans?"

"Herons," he corrected. "Why not?"

"Why anything? Does the fountain work?"

"Yes, but first water needs to be pumped up from the stream in the village to a cistern on the top floor."

"Not very practical."

He merely raised one brow. "Have you seen enough, Miss Potter, or do you wish to inspect everything?"

He spoke in a tone designed to force an unwanted guest into saying "Of course not. Really, I must go. . . ."

"How kind," Lucy said. "Let us proceed, my lord."

Their eyes clashed, but she held steady until he turned away.

He walked to another set of glass-paned doors and, shaking inside, Lucy followed. She would not quail before him. That would be to lose all.

He didn't want her here, which could destroy her, except that she felt the connection still alive between them.

He was rejecting her despite his feelings, not for lack of them. She must discover the problem and defeat it.

"There are a number of these doors," she said. "Do all the ground floor rooms have them?"

"Nearly all."

"That's a pleasant aspect to the design."

"Simply practical. Otherwise people would have to use the corridors that run behind the rooms. They exist, on every floor."

As if to prove his point a serving maid came out of one set of doors and walked across the garden. It seemed in keeping with the place that she was almost skeletally thin.

Then she saw Lucy and let out a squawk as if she'd seen a ghost. She hastily dipped a curtsy. "Zur, ma'am," then hurried on as if pursued.

"Are visitors so alarming?" Lucy asked.

"If any come, the servants usually know."

"And they're rare."

"Are you surprised? The dining room," he said as they entered a room similar to the great hall, though smaller and simpler. In fact, it felt monastic. The walls were whitewashed and the long oaken table was simply made. A dark sideboard was heavily carved. Three candelabra and some platters were made of pewter or some other dark, steely metal, rather than silver or gold. The only richness came from the red velvet on the seats and arms of eight carved wooden chairs.

"You eat here in solitary splendor?"

"There's a smaller dining room, but I mostly eat in my private rooms."

A slight emphasis told her she'd not see them.

"This may be more to your taste," he said, opening a side door and leading the way into a room that made Lucy feel as if she'd been transported to another place entirely.

Suddenly they were in a space that could be in any

fine house. The walls had white-framed panels enclosing yellow Chinese wallpaper and the ceiling was elaborately plastered. Pleasant paintings hung here and there, and a marble fireplace of moderate size might actually warm the space. The chandelier might be large enough to illuminate the room.

The furniture was modern and included a normal array of chairs, sofas, and little tables. Two large mirrors reflected what light there was, but that was little. She realized there was only one small window. The room had clearly been created by taking the corner space from the great hall.

"Why?" she asked. "Visitors being rare."

"Insanity. This was devised by the Mad Earl, perhaps simply to startle the unwary. When he had guests he would sometimes start the evening here. Well lit and with a fire burning, it can seem normal."

"Were you a guest here on a normal evening?"

"I was the estate manager, remember. But my sister worked here for a while, so I explored."

"Lady Amleigh? Employed?"

"The bastard child of a wanton and a tavern keeper."

"So the earl could be benevolent," she said, probing the layers she sensed beneath his reminder.

"Only when it suited some insane purpose."

He led the way across the fine carpet to a paneled door. When he opened it, she saw a circular staircase going up.

"There's one in every corner. Do you mind them? Some people find circular stairs uncomfortable."

Lucy remembered seeing wide stone stairs rising from the great hall, but she had no intention of backing down from the challenge. He and his house were on trial here, but she suspected that she was, too. If she married the dragon Earl of Wyvern, she couldn't be the sort to tremble at a circular staircase.

She started up the narrow stairs. The steps were uneven and worn in the middle as if from centuries of feet. Illusion, she dismissed, but then remembered that though Crag Wyvern wasn't medieval, it was nearly two hundred years old.

At first the staircase wasn't too bad, but when she turned beyond the opening below and couldn't see the escape above, panic tried to stir. It wasn't pitch-dark, but it was gloomy, and the dragon was close behind. She could imagine that she felt his breath, but she also began to remember another stairwell and a very different kind of heat. So tempting to pause, to turn—but anything that happened here in this twisted space would be vile.

Just keep climbing, Lucy.

A step at a time.

It has to come to an end.

Despite reason, she began to doubt it. When she saw the opening, she sucked in a breath as if she'd escaped some monstrous gullet.

When she emerged, however, she wasn't in a much better place.

She stood at the juncture of two long stone corridors. These must be the corridors that ran behind the rooms, between them and the outer walls. She could see doors in the one on her left, and light shot in through arrow slits on her right, but both were deserted and swords and axes hung at regular intervals along the outer walls.

She managed a light tone. "I hope these corridors are lit at night or someone might accidentally decapitate themself."

"But if a dragon attacks, you'd be prepared."

She met his eyes, but he was as blank as slate. "I'll bear that in mind."

"Be careful, Lucy."

It was the first time he'd used her name, and it was a warning.

The enclosed space pressed in on her, but her foolish

body responded to him, despite any danger. Insanity on both sides.

He turned on his heel and set off along the corridor to their right. It looked to go the full length of one side with no doors. She saw him brush aside a cobweb and was glad he was going first.

But then her brain cleared. Cobwebs meant this corridor wasn't much used. Was this truly how people got around the house, or was he playing dark games to frighten her away?

He'd find out that wouldn't work with her.

He stopped midway in a patch of light and she saw a small circular, unglazed window in the outer wall. It framed an image of the outside world that seemed almost miraculous from within this place.

The grass was vibrantly green, a sheep snow-white, the sky impossibly blue, and glimpsed in spire and roofs, the haven of Church Wyvern was snuggled down below, full of normal people.

Then she laughed to herself at that thought.

Was anyone normal here?

Even David?

He stood close behind her, still stirring both desire and fear.

This fear was different to the thrill of danger that had fired her in the Duchess of St. Raven's garden—oh, that haven of normality! Even when he'd seized her there, she'd not been afraid. Here she feared the unknown.

She made herself face him. "Why did you leave London?"

She hoped to put him off balance, to startle some admission, but he said, "To get away from you."

She couldn't doubt such a blunt truth.

"Because of what happened at the theater?"

"In part. I've said all along that I won't marry you, but I won't ruin you, either. Yet here you are."

"I'm not trying to ruin you into marrying me!"

"Aren't you?"

"No."

"Then why come?"

"To find out if I could marry you."

"Pointless, when I'm not going to offer you the opportunity. When I've satisfied your curiosity, I'll take you down to the manor, to my aunt. Tomorrow I'll see you suitably escorted on your way back to London."

Lucy found she had no recourse against such steady authority. Despite everything her heart and senses told her, he'd spoken the truth. He'd left London to escape her; he would not marry her; and he wanted her gone.

With that realization, this whole venture seemed shameful. Why had the Delaneys aided her? She remembered that she'd considered doing exactly what he'd accused her of—seducing him into commitment. Perhaps her mother had done that, but her father could never have been so calm and absolute in his rejection.

With what dignity she could gather, she said, "Very well." But then she saw a problem. "I didn't provide for that. I don't have enough money with me. How stupid!"

"I believe the earldom's coffers can stretch to a loan, and I know you're able to pay me back."

A touch of David in that threatened tears.

"Damnation, Lucy. You knew this couldn't be."

"This?"

"Us."

Something in his desperate tone lit an ember of hope. "Can you make me see why?"

"You want to live here?"

"No. Yes. It doesn't matter. That's not the problem, David. What is?"

"You want to live so far from London? So far from a city, even a town of any size. In the wilds of the country, where even the grass can make you cry?"

"No. I mean it doesn't. I don't have hay fever."

"Lies?"

"A minor one. I didn't want your sympathy."

"Why were you crying?"

"For loss of my old life and unhappiness with my new one. It seems so long ago now."

"Yes."

She studied him, her back pressed to cold stone, as his was pressed to the opposite wall. They were putting as much space between them as they could, but it wasn't enough.

"If you believed I would hate this place, why didn't you invite me to visit?"

"Perhaps I tried to save you a tedious journey."

She finally found the courage. "David, are you afflicted by your family's madness? Are you trying to protect me from that?"

She saw him inhale. "I should say yes. That would do it, wouldn't it?"

"Yes," she replied. "I'd hate it, and I'd try to help you, but I wouldn't marry you. Tell me. Please."

"There's no insanity in my family. I'm not the son of the Mad Earl of Wyvern. I don't carry that blood."

"You're not? But then . . ."

"Why am I earl? Because Amleigh didn't want to be, and Susan his beloved didn't want him to be, and I had the legal right."

"Because your mother was in truth married to the earl?"

"Exactly. But she fled him on her wedding night and was Mel Clyst's after that."

"You're his son."

"A tavern keeper and smuggler. Will that turn you off?"

"I'm the daughter of a foundling who doesn't know who his parents were." She stepped forward, closed the gap, and put her arms around him. "Nothing else could keep us apart. I love you, David. You and no other, for all time."

"Oh, you wretched woman."

He kissed her as she'd hungered to be kissed. Lucy kissed him back as fiercely, holding him to her as tightly as he held her to him, exploding with relief. To kiss, to be with him like this, to know he hungered for her as ravenously as she hungered for him. Any difficulties were dust, blowing away on a delirious wind.

When the kiss ended, when she snuggled against him, she said, "That was the truth, my love. The only truth that matters."

Against her hair he said, "There's more to this than kisses."

"I know."

He pushed her away. "Damnation, Lucy. I won't ruin you, and I can't marry you."

Now his rejection only stirred exasperation. "Can't, not won't? *Why?*"

But he was looking behind her, out of the window.

She turned. "People!"

Ridiculous to feel shocked, but she did. Two men were walking along the path toward them, toward the gargoyle-encrusted doors of Crag Wyvern. Two normal men, talking as normal people might, one in ordinary clothes, the other in a uniform.

David grabbed her wrist. "They can't know you're here. At least, Lloyd can't. Come on."

Chapter 29

He towed her back down the corridor, past the stair-well, and around the corner. He opened a door into an explosion of color and pushed her in.

"Stay here," he said and left, shutting the door.

Dazed from the kiss and the rush, Lucy turned to take in the extraordinary room. In a building that seemed made up of harsh angles, this room was circular and a painted dragon took up all the wall. She turned, following the green, orange, and gold beast from fanged head along lizardlike body to tail, which it was eating, so it all started again.

That seemed all too like the never-ending tangle of her life.

Can't, not won't, but still a rejection.

"Why?" she asked the dragon's huge black eye, but it didn't respond.

She forced herself to see the more normal aspects of the room. A flat window looked into the courtyard, but everything else on the walls was curved, including a ja-panned chest of drawers, a washstand, and an armoire. Even the door, she noted, was curved on the inside and the painting of the dragon flowed over it, almost making it disappear.

The bed, if a bed it was, was also circular and sat in the middle of the room. It lacked posts, bed-hangings, and pillows, but was covered by a counterpane in a fabric that matched the dragon's scales. It sat on a circular carpet with the same self-consuming dragon winding around the bed.

The ceiling was dragon free, but it was concave and painted to look like the sky in bright blue with a flaming comet streaking across it.

Seeking escape from the riot of color, she went to the window to look down into the garden. Its lack of vibrancy was a relief. From here she could see that the pale paths were laid out geometrically with the outer ones, forming a pentagon. The inner ones formed a star.

A maid—a short, plump one this time—came out on Lucy's left bearing a tray with a flagon and two tankards. She crossed the garden to Lucy's right, and Lucy worked out that David was receiving one man in the great hall. Only one?

The two men shouldn't know she was here to avoid scandal. *Especially Lloyd.*

Why especially him? Who was Lloyd? It was a Welsh name.

Irrelevant, but the men's arrival meant she now had an opportunity to explore on her own, to see whether the whole house was odd, or if David had showed her only the most peculiar parts. She opened the door and listened. Silence. Stone walls and floors could make sounds hard to detect, but there didn't seem to be many people here. She left the room and closed the door.

She was about to go right, in an unexplored direction, but then she heard faint voices from her left. Through stone walls and floors?

She hurried back the way they'd come, the voices becoming louder. If this was a gothic novel, there'd be a spy hole into that great hall. Crag Wyvern felt all too much like the deranged creation of a gothic novelist, so she began to hunt for one. She concentrated on the inner wall, running a hand along the rough surface. Then she paused. It wasn't stone-cold.

She tapped. It wasn't stone at all, but wood painted to imitate stone. Folly and deception all around her! She would not let such idiocy come between her and the man she loved.

She continued on and found what she was looking for. It wasn't exactly a spy hole, for it was a vertical slit, showing only a sliver of the great hall. It was a listening hole. When she turned her ear to it, she could hear the men quite clearly.

"Of course I give you permission," David was saying. No, the tone was all earl—distant courtesy and palpable boredom. "Though I consider filling in a cave a waste of the government's money."

"Not if it stops the wretches stashing goods there, my lord. There was clear evidence of use." A Welsh accent, so probably Lloyd.

The topic was smugglers and she guessed Lloyd was the uniformed one and a Preventive officer. He wanted to fill in a cave so it couldn't be used to hide contraband.

"The coast is riddled with caves," David said. "But I haven't objected."

The tone clearly said, Why are you lingering? She couldn't believe David could be so openly discourteous to a man who was doing his legal duty.

"You don't take great interest in trouncing the smugglers, my lord. But down Purbeck way a group of them treated a gentlewoman most foully because her husband objected to the use of his horses in a run."

"I heard nothing of it,"

"You've been away, my lord, and it's been kept quiet for the sake of the lady, but it happened, and now no one there will whisper a word."

"Most regrettable, but Purbeck is far beyond my authority."

"What happens there could happen here, my lord, if the wretches aren't suppressed."

"Pray, what do you suggest I do?"

"Tell me who Captain Drake is."

A silence made Lucy want to tear open the wall to see what was happening, but then David said, "The deuce, man, you're obsessed with Captain Drake! Have you considered that it might be a moveable identity?"

"Upon one's death or removal, yes, my lord. Melchisadeck Clyst was Captain Drake here for many years. We know that. Now there's a new one. We know that, too."

"Or a number of them. And is it not possible that whoever he or they may be, Captain Drake is controlling the smugglers in this area to avoid cruelty and mayhem?"

"He, or they, is still a criminal and it is my duty to put a stop to him."

"Haven't you heard of the Hydra, Lloyd?"

"Cut off one head and two appear in its place? Logic tells us that any creature must exhaust the possibility in time."

"What the devil does logic have to do with mythology?"

"We live in an age of reason, my lord, where there are no Hydras—or dragons. It's my duty to stop smuggling hereabouts and I will do so, by any means."

It sounded like a direct challenge, foolhardy man.

"I'm sure you'll do your best," David said, his voice icily cold.

Even in the silence Lucy could hear the Welshman's fuming frustration. "I will, my lord."

"As is your duty. If there's nothing more, Lloyd, I have pressing matters to attend to."

Gritted teeth lay behind Lloyd's "Good day, my lord," and anger spoke in the click of his booted feet on the stone floor, and the near slam of the door.

Lucy continued to listen, wondering if the other man they'd seen approaching was there and might speak.

Silence.

She realized that David could be coming back to her. She ran back along the corridor and into the circular room, afraid that he might realize she'd overheard.

Afraid?

Why would overhearing that conversation put her in danger? The Preventive officer was seeking the earl's help in suppressing smuggling, and clearly not for the first time. David had permitted the filling in of a cave, but otherwise been uncooperative. He'd made no secret of thinking action against smugglers a waste of time and money.

She was allowing the gothic horrors of this place to overturn her mind.

She hitched up to sit on the bed, but her mind circled the conversation like the dragon circling the room.

Then she shifted because of the journal in her pocket. She'd carried it there all the way from London but not written a word.

She took it and her pencil out.

I'm in Crag Wyvern,
And it's just as horrid as said.
But we kissed, and nothing can be dark.
David clashed with the officer
Whose duty it is to end
The Freetrade here.
As if they truly were enemies . . .

Lloyd had said the Hydra was mythological, but added that dragons were, too. A dangerously impertinent jab at a nobleman who's title was a dragon's name. Proof of his anger. She should be in sympathy with him. But not when his opponent was David.

Ah.

David is the son of Captain Drake.
Though he was raised by his
Aunt and uncle, that must count
For something.
The current Captain Drake is probably
A friend or even a relative. Of course
He won't betray him.

"What are you doing?"

She hadn't even heard the door open.

Lucy said the only thing she could. "Writing poetry."

"Is there no end to your talents?"

It wasn't friendly and might even be suspicious.

"Bad poetry," she said, turning the book so he could see the page, hoping he wasn't eagle-eyed. Then she shut it. "Don't ask me to read any to you."

He shook his head. "You are designed to tangle a man in knots."

"Not normal men. Who were your guests?"

"Guest. One man was my secretary, the other the local Preventive officer."

"Come to discuss ways to put an end to smuggling, I assume."

"You can assume what you wish."

That kiss might not have happened. Except that it fueled everything they said.

"Stop trying to pick a fight. My lord earl, will you marry me?"

"You have no sense of propriety at all."

"Sense and propriety are rarely connected. Why shouldn't women propose marriage to men? Why shouldn't they call out men or women who offend them? Why shouldn't young unmarried ladies sleep alone?"

"I have no idea," he said, staring at her.

"Why shouldn't they have short hair, or marry men ten years their junior? I mean, when older."

A laugh escaped. "I assume you're talking sense."

"You do? Why?"

"Because you always do."

"Then believe me when I say we are meant to be."

She slithered forward to get off the bed and walked toward him. "Gems of my aunt's dictates about propriety. She said that you'd fled London because we'd behaved improperly in that theater stairwell. That a gentleman would have to wonder whether such a lady would be a chaste wife."

"A gentleman would merely hope that the lady would be as improper as a wife."

"Why wouldn't she be?" Lucy asked, reaching him, putting a hand on his chest, working it up to the open vee of his shirt, to his skin.

He trapped her hand there. "Lucy . . ."

"A lady might wonder if a gentleman who left without a word would be a constant husband."

"Perhaps she should." But his voice was husky and his eyes dark. "Lucy . . ."

"Yes?" She took hold of his shirt and pulled him with her, backward toward the bed. Once there, she turned with him and pushed him so his hips were against it, as they had been that night in her room.

"A better height, as I remember." She moved closer. "Yes, it is, isn't it? Stairs, beds, all kinds of devices for a tall gentleman and a sadly short lady."

He gripped her waist. "There's nothing sad about you."

"I do hope not. Not now, not ever."

She pressed forward and came fully against him, and against the hard evidence that his blood ran as hot as hers. How could it not? There was one sure way to cut through all the knots.

Her mother's way.

Lucy put her lips to his. Instant fire pressed her closer, closer. She climbed over him so that he collapsed back on the bed, conquered, and she ravished him as best she could.

He rolled with her, crushed her under him.

Glorious weight and pulsing hunger.

Before he could hesitate, she kissed him again, pulling at his shirt to get her hands on his hot skin. His hand on her leg, under skirts and petticoats, his mouth hot on her neck, her shoulder.

He sat back and she thought she'd lost, but then he pulled at the front fastenings of her gown. Laughing, she brushed away his fumbling hands and untied laces so it fell open. Her light corset unhooked down the front and then only her simple shift covered her. She untied the lace that ran around the neckline so it hung loosely, exposing her.

His eyes never leaving her, he stripped off his own coat and waistcoat. He fell on her again, cradling her breasts, kissing, nipping, murmuring her name over and over. She lay back, arms wide, allowing him, reveling in the breathless ecstasy, laughing with it.

He laughed with her, but said, "We shouldn't. Stop me, Lucy. Have sense."

That made her laugh even more. She sat up to drag his shirt off him, to run her hands all over his magnificent chest. "What has sense to do with this?"

She pushed him down on the circular bed. "No top, no bottom. No beginning, no end. Aren't circles wonderful?"

"Ouroborus," he gasped—she'd straddled him. "Symbol of eternity."

"Perfect." She kissed him again, searingly aware of him hard, so close to where she wanted him to be. Needed him to be, as she needed air to breathe.

She rolled off the bed, tossed off her shift, and then

untied the laces so she could step out of her pantaloons
beneath. The look in his eyes was all she could want and
more and she smiled.

"Goddess," he said huskily, struggling out of his remaining clothes. One boot hit the wall. "But goddess of
what I have no idea. No scheming Greek or Roman
you." Naked, he said, "Nicholas would know."

She chuckled. "A wise man, Nicholas Delaney."

"I'm going to throttle him. Come here."

Lucy remembered the night in her bedroom, him saying, "Come here, wench." Feeling like a wench.

Now she felt like a goddess.

"Something from the East," she said, sauntering slowly
back. "From India. I've seen astonishing statues and
paintings."

"You're a ruined woman."

I hope so, she thought and crawled up onto the bed.
He was sitting back on his heels and one picture made
sense to her. She straddled him, straddled his long, thick
manhood. "There was one like this."

His eyes closed and he inhaled, but he opened them
to say, "Not quite."

He grasped her hips and moved her back. She resisted, thinking he was pushing her off, but then he adjusted himself and she felt him press exactly where she
needed him to be.

"Oh, yes," she said, letting her head fall forward onto
his chest. "Oh, yes."

Then it hurt. A burning, stretching sensation. In case
he hesitated, she pushed forward, forced forward and felt
the barrier break, felt him surge forward and fill her in a
most extraordinary way.

"Stop!" She instantly regretted it. "I mean, wait a moment. Let me. . . ." He eased back, and she panted her
words. "It's wonderful. But . . . oh, yes, wonderful. Yes."

She realized he was rubbing her close to where they

were joined and his other hand was teasing a nipple. He wasn't holding her at all. She was free.

She adjusted a little more.

Heard him catch his breath.

Smiled.

Rose up a little and then settled down again, watching him.

His hands stilled.

Oh, yes.

She continued the slight movement, looking at the wall, at the dragon's mouth consuming its tail. It seemed deeply meaningful.

Consummation.

Hunger.

Eternity.

He was part of her, familiar and complete in his heat, his smell, his intimate shape. His hands on her back. His mouth on her breast. Union.

A perfect tumult of shocking delights.

Then he gripped her hips and took command, moving her around him, sending off rockets, blanking her mind to everything except hot, heart-pounding pleasure. She thought she'd reached the pinnacle, reached her limit, even, but he drove her higher and higher into the sun.

She felt as if she'd flown on dragon wings and was slowly circling back down to earth. They rolled together to lie, entwined, sticky, sweaty, panting, replete.

"By the stars," she whispered. "I had no idea."

He shook his head against her shoulder. "Nor had I. That you could do that to me. Or I'd have made Nicholas take you away."

He didn't sound angry, but he meant it.

He still meant it!

She stroked her beloved's damp hair. "Don't regret, don't. There's no obstacle we can't overcome. Certainly not Crag Wyvern."

His hand stroked her. "That's the least of our problems, love."

She smiled at the word "love," but didn't misread it. "Then tell me what the problems are, David. We can defeat every one."

He looked at her. "Money can't solve everything."

It was as if he could read her mind. "I'm not sure about that, but perhaps one of the problems is smuggling? I listened through a gap in the wall."

"Of course you did," he said with a sigh. "Is there any possibility that you'll learn caution?"

"I can be cautious when it's called for, but discard it when appropriate. I go for what I want, David."

"As your father does."

She shrugged. "It comes from him, I suppose. But my mother, too. You'd rather I be hesitant and fearful?"

"I'd rather everything was different." He pulled her close, but said, "Believe me, Lucy, this is a truly dangerous mess."

"You think your wife will be in danger from smugglers, like the one near Purbeck? You're an earl."

"Don't chisel away at this." He rolled off the bed and looked around at the chaos of their discarded clothing. "As well everyone here is discreet. Would you like a bath?"

"A wash will do."

He was pulling on some clothing. "We can do better."

Barefoot in breeches and shirt, he gathered up his other clothes like a man putting together a barricade from bits and pieces. Then he came to her, his expression unreadable. He put a finger beneath her chin and kissed her, tenderly, but with worrying restraint.

"It would have been wiser not to do that, my love, but I can't regret it. I can only hope you don't. I'll be back soon."

Chapter 30

He left and Lucy contemplated her wicked legs, naked except for her plain cotton stockings and embroidered garters. She suspected there were reactions appropriate for this situation—perhaps Aunt Mary could have stated some—but doubted hers would fit.

She should probably be shocked at herself. Instead she was delighted that she'd overcome his reluctance and been proved right by his overwhelming desire. Proved right by his declaration of love. He'd called her his love twice, and he'd meant it.

She was sure she should be fearful of her sin being discovered, and especially of being with child. She might be if she wasn't so certain of David's love. If necessary, they would be married within days, and even if not, they'd be married soon.

She didn't want to rush, however. She wanted to savor every moment. She'd like banns to be read.

Aunt Mary Did Not Approve of banns. Well-bred people did not declare their intimate intentions before the congregation. Banns were more common in the City, however, where even well-bred people didn't see shame in saying they planned to marry.

Yes, she and David would declare by banns on three consecutive Sundays at their respective parishes their loving intention to wed. Then they would marry in all the joy Betty and James had shown, with her friends and family around.

The issue of Crag Wyvern could not be dreamed away. It was an unpleasant house and she couldn't imagine living here all her days, but something could be done. It, like smuggling, seemed a minor issue with everything else so perfect.

They'd have to wait until after her father returned from his honeymoon. Thank heavens it would be short. She knew he'd approve of David once he knew him, and he'd be cock-a-hoop to be leading his daughter down the aisle to become a countess.

She'd seek his advice about the situation here. The wealthier the earldom became, the more easily the people here could be turned from smuggling to legal work. The land could provide only so much. There'd need to be trade and industry for true wealth, and her father was a wizard at such things.

Hydras, dragons, and now wizards.

Perhaps myth and magic were true after all, for she and David were solidly at the heart of their own magical circle now. Her father would join them there. His daughter would be a countess and his first grandson would be a future earl. She supposed there was a secondary title to go to the infant heir, the dragon's son.

"My grandson, Lord Inchworm." Lucy giggled as she collected her scattered clothing.

David still had concerns, but nothing could resist the magic they'd created here.

David went to the Roman bathroom that was attached to the Saint George bedroom and turned on the taps. The big bath took a while to fill, but the metal cistern on the roof was kept full and in sunny weather the water became warm enough for comfort. In colder weather fires could be lit beneath to heat it, but he limited his indulgence in that.

He'd had the pictures on the tiled walls painted over, for they were in keeping with the old fountain figures—a dragon raping a woman. That had been part of the Mad Earl's tormented obsession with Lady Belle. The tile design in the bath remained. He'd tried having it painted over but the paint hadn't lasted.

When he could afford it he'd have it retiled.

When he could afford it.

In theory he should now be anticipating Lucy's dowry, but this wasn't going to progress well. Of course they must marry and there was nothing he wanted more, but as soon as her father heard of their intentions, he'd do anything to prevent the wedding.

Potter, more than most men, would understand the overruling power of love, so he'd know what he was up against. He'd be ruthless, and he wouldn't care how many he harmed in the process as long as his daughter was safe.

David also wanted Lucy safe, and happy, but he didn't see the way.

As water poured into the bath he tried to find the best path. When would Potter find out that Lucy had left London and come here? Even if he had alert spies, at least a day, then another day for orders to come back. That meant Potter couldn't use tomorrow night's run to do damage. His simplest action would be to have Captain Drake captured or killed. David didn't doubt that Potter was ruthless enough for that.

One way to forestall him was for them to marry by license. He disliked the thought of a hasty wedding, with all the suspicions it would arouse, but that would settle the matter. He doubted Potter would attempt to murder an unwelcome son-in-law, and if the Horde were cautious for a good while, he'd not be able to use that. Perhaps Lucy could convince him she was happy.

If she was.

She was ruled by love—and lust—at the moment, but she'd reacted to the Crag with all the horror he'd expected. She'd even struggled to reach it.

He tossed one of his aunt's herbal sachets into the water, hoping rosemary and lavender could soothe him, and went on to his bedroom next door. He took off his clothes and put on his robe, then found his winter one for Lucy. Far too long. He took out his sharp sheath knife.

Fred Chumley knocked, but walked straight in. "What did . . . ?"

"I'm about to have a bath," David said, hacking off about a foot around the bottom. "This is for the lady."

"Ah. Yes. I heard something. Came with Nicholas Delaney?"

"You're thinking that Nicholas is unlikely to have brought me a whore and might be displeased if I've debauched a lady of his acquaintance. Firstly, I don't give a rat's arse whether Nicholas is pleased or not, and secondly, he probably brought her here with this in mind, being an interfering bastard."

"Ah. Right. I'll make myself scarce then, will I?"

"An excellent idea. In fact, go down and warn my aunt that I'll be bringing a guest to her later."

Fred's mouth opened and shut, but then he said, "Right," and quietly left.

Wise man.

David hadn't realized how much fury simmered beneath the wonders and delights. He raged against Potter for daring to interfere, and that by doing so he might put many people at risk. But he was also angry at the woman he loved for insisting on having her way, for storming over all obstacles.

But that was part of why he loved her. And love her he did, enough to truly become insane, for he'd just taken her virginity. Taken didn't seem quite the right word, and she'd shown not a trace of distress, but she deserved tenderness now.

Tenderness and loving care.

It would be his honor to give her that at least, before the heavens fell.

He returned to the Ouroborus room and found her in her shift, neatly tied, thank the Lord, with the rest of her clothing stacked. She still looked deliciously wanton. Her smile was so open and bright he wanted to groan.

He wanted to do other things, but he wasn't going to, for a great many reasons.

He had to ask. "Regrets?"

She blushed but said, "None at all." She didn't add the expected, "You?"

That wouldn't be an oversight, not with Lucy. He'd made his regrets obvious, but she didn't care. She didn't care because she was sure any problems could be brushed away like . . . like an ant.

He tossed the brown robe to her. "Put that on. Your bath should be ready."

"Already?" she said. It only just touched the ground but was wide around her.

"I like baths." He should resist, but couldn't. He picked her up in his arms, explaining, "Your feet would get cold."

Lucy settled into his arms happily, not mentioning her shoes, which were on top of the stack of clothing on the bed. As they left the room, she said, "I've never been carried like this since I was a child. You're strong."

"You're light."

"But not insubstantial."

"As insubstantial as lead," he agreed, but smiled back. "I doubt you'll be horribly shocked, given your familiarity with erotic Indian pictures, but the inside of the bath is illustrated in an unpleasant manner."

"Like the fountain?" she guessed.

"How did you know about that?"

"The illustrations, remember? Aunt Mary had removed it, but not before Clara had seen it, so she told me."

"Are there any young ladies of the ton who retain their innocence?"

"Probably Lady Iphigenia. A lucky escape?"

"On the contrary. I pine for an innocent, wilting bride." He nudged open a door and carried her into an extraordinary room.

"Heavens above!" she exclaimed. "That's not a bath. That's a pool!"

He put her down on the tiled floor from which steps went down into a huge basin, which was half-full of water. He went to turn off a gargoyle-headed tap.

"A small pool. It's eight foot long and four foot wide."

As the water stilled she peered at the illustration. The dragon was definitely having improper relations with the lady, but was the lady screaming or in ecstasy? Lucy felt she might have looked similar in their recent lovemaking.

"Is that a *cold* bath?" she asked warily.

"Cold baths are said to be very invigorating."

"Do we need invigorating?"

He smiled. "Or to cool the blood. But no, it will be warm enough for comfort."

"Where does all the water come from?"

"A cistern above, warmed by the sun in good seasons, and by a stove beneath in harsher times. The one good amendment to the Crag by the Mad Earl. He was obsessed by a search for fertility and eternal life. A few years before he died, he decided daily bathing would do the trick and went to extremes. I'll leave you to enjoy it."

Lucy wasn't having that. She shed the robe. "I might drown."

"It's not even two foot deep."

She sat on a marble bench and began to undo one garter. "I'd feel safer if you stayed."

"'Safer' is not the word that comes to mind."

She couldn't help but chuckle. She felt such power, such potency. She unrolled the stocking and tossed it aside, then started in on the other. When she glanced up again, he was still and very intent. She stood and took off her shift, completely unembarrassed by nakedness. Then she went down the two steps to test the heat of the water with her toes. "Perfect."

"We try."

Smiling at his hoarse tone, she continued down, then sat in the scented water, which was just warm enough and lapped the tips of her breasts. Her nipples were still sensitive enough to take pleasure from the water. They even looked larger and pinker. Remembering the pleasure he'd brought, she glanced up at him. "Isn't it a bit late for caution, my lord earl?"

His eyes still held that darkness that warned of trouble, of trouble she did not yet understand, but she didn't relent. In the end he took off his robe and came to join her in the water, taking her into his arms.

"This is much better," she said, slithering against him into a cozy arrangement. "I'm less likely to wallow, and the possibilities are endless." She ran a wet hand over his wet body, learning the feel of muscle over bone. She traced a faint scar, jagged over his right ribs. "How did this happen?"

"Someone with a knife making trouble."

"And you intervened?"

"Someone had to."

"The earl?"

"It was before I became earl. I've not led a completely tame life, Lucy."

Of course he hadn't. And wouldn't.

"Do I need to learn nursing skills?" she asked, noticing a puckered scar on his shoulder.

"They probably wouldn't come amiss."

"I'd think this was from a pistol ball. You haven't dueled have you?"

"I've never needed to devise danger."

She frowned at him. "No broken bones from climbing cliffs?"

He laughed at that. "No more than you have from climbing stairs, love. I live a charmed life."

"I'd rather you live a safe one." She circled the scar with her finger. "Who shot at you?"

"A boatman."

"A fisherman?"

"One of the excise officer's men."

She heard a challenging note in it. He expected her to be shocked. She was, a little, but she should have expected it. "I knew it. You've dabbled in your father's trade. In Melchisadeck Clyst's. How could a hot-blooded lad resist?"

"Are you going to scold me for it?"

"If I'd been around at the time. It's not a game."

He kissed her. "I know that, love, but sometimes the need is irresistible."

Is . . . ?

He tasted her with soft kisses, seemingly simply for the pleasure of it and she almost purred, half-floating in warm water and sweetly cherished.

"This is heaven," she said, and he smiled.

"Perhaps I'll have clouds and angels painted on the ceiling here."

"Do we really want to be observed by angels?"

"Unfair, you think?" he said. "Them being unable."

"Are they?"

"You imagine much bawdy frolicking amid the heavenly clouds?"

"Never before, but now I wonder where the cherubs come from."

He hooted with laughter and she caught it from him so they rolled in the water, slipping and sliding against each other.

Her sliding hand touched his manly part and she looked through the water at it, long and thick in the nest of hair. She wanted to explore, but felt that would be wrong in some way. As if it were still private to him.

He captured her hand and brought it to his mouth. He kissed her palm, eyes on her. "Don't play with the dragon."

"Why not?"

"The lady beneath us might be a warning."

She remembered the mosaic image and matched it against her memories of ecstasy.

"I think she might be enjoying that."

"Being impaled by a dragon?"

"Her dragon."

"Hades, you could be right. The Mad Earl might want to portray Lady Belle as succumbing to pleasure under him." His hand cradled a breast, his thumb stroking the sensitive nipple. "Let's test the theory."

Lucy anticipated a pleasant impaling, but he delighted her with hands and mouth. The gentleness was new and wondrous, as was sliding her hands and legs over him, seeking, and finding, ways to delight him. Until passion overwhelmed thought and she drowned in a steamy pleasure beyond all control or observation.

When she drifted lazily, her body light in the water but cradled against his, she said, "Well?"

"Well what?"

"Pleasure or horror?"

He laughed against her hair. "I wasn't observing, but you screamed, and I hope it was pleasure."

"I screamed?"

"Quietly."

"A quiet scream. What a lot of interesting abilities I

have. It was definitely pleasure. I like this bath. Thank you, Crag Wyvern."

"But the rest remains."

He wasn't speaking only of the house.

She shifted to look at him. "What's the biggest barrier, love? What stands tall between us and infinite delight?" When he didn't answer, she said, "I think I deserve to know. We're past secrets."

Then she remembered what he'd once said, and she saw it in his eyes. That with true love should come trust that some secrets are necessary.

"I could ask for trust," he agreed, "but you're right. Secrets between us seem pointless now. But not here like this."

He raised them both to their feet and they climbed out. He took towels from a pile and gave her one. "I'll go and get your clothes."

Lucy suddenly remembered the journal. She'd put it back in one of the pair of pockets, but he might feel the shape and become curious. No secrets, he'd said, but she didn't want him to read her rambling thoughts about him.

"I'd rather put on something fresh," she said. "What happened to my valise?"

He looked enchantingly blank. "Yes, you had one. I remember—I put it down in the great hall when I showed you the skeleton. I'll get it."

"In a normal earl's household you would ring a bell and a minion would rush to serve."

"I don't think we want to alert the servants any more than we must," he said drily, "and in this earl's household we ring a bell only as a warning." He went to a chain on the wall and pulled. "You can hardly hear it from here, but that warns anyone outside."

"Warns them of what?"

"Deluge." He pulled out a plug in the bath and the

water began to drain away. "It exits via a gargoyle in a grand spout that would drench anyone below."

"And tell the world we've been bathing?"

"It's not that loud a bell, and anyone so close could well have guessed."

It made her blush, which seemed silly at this stage.

"So the Mad Earl wasn't entirely demented, then," she said.

"It would have been easier if he had been. He could be sharply cunning in his own insane way." He tenderly put her into the woolen robe, even tying the belt for her, then gathered her into his arms again.

Lucy liked it, but she said, "I hope you're not thinking of me as a child."

He laughed as he carried her out into the gloomy corridor. "Far, far from that, my wanton Indian goddess. I don't know the names of any."

"Lakshmi is one," she said as they went round a corner, passing another circular staircase. She supposed she'd become accustomed to them. "The goddess of good fortune and prosperity. My father had a statue of her given him by a nabob. She's said to protect from troubles, especially those related to money."

"Just what Crag Wyvern needs. Why 'had'?"

"When I went home for my friend's wedding it had gone from the library. I assume Charlotte doesn't approve."

"Charlotte's his new wife?"

"Not quite. They marry soon."

"But already she is the goddess of his house. Here we are."

But she was looking back at a skeleton hanging in a corner. "Another relative?"

"Not as far as I know. I'm sorry. I should have had it taken down."

"Oh, I'll grow accustomed. As long as it doesn't animate."

He shook his head as he carried her into a bedroom that was a contrast to everything she'd seen thus far. Here the furniture was modern, light, and bright in the sunlight coming in through a normal window to the outside—with a view of the sea.

Even as he was putting her down, Lucy said, "You fraud! You took me around the oddities, when this is the reality."

Chapter 31

He shook his head. "No, the oddities are real. My only real change since moving here has been this room and the next, and I shouldn't have indulged in those."

"Why not?" she asked. "This is glorious!"

"Only by contrast. I needed some normal rooms, but I did it as cheaply as possible. The furniture here is old stuff from Kerslake Manor, and the rest is simple cloth and paint."

"Is the earldom as penny-pinched as that?"

"Not quite, but back then I wasn't formally the earl so I shouldn't have spent anything at all on indulgences. Thank heavens the executor of the old earl's will saw that even as resident caretaker I deserved some improvements, because my sanity demanded it. The greatest expense was the window."

"Well worth it," Lucy said. "The inward-looking windows aren't the same." She took in the simple, old-fashioned furniture, the pale green walls, and cream-colored cotton hangings. A few paintings hung on the walls, but they were simple ones of no distinction. "What was this room like before?"

"You don't need to know. Yes, I know you think you do, but you don't."

She sent him a look that promised *one day*, but she said, "It's lovely now."

The light, bright colors were rebellion to the gloom and gray of the ground floor and corridors. As an added touch, someone had stenciled a buttercup yellow design around the walls where they met the ceiling. Another bright touch was the multicolored patchwork coverlet on the bed.

"I like this," she said, going to study it, thinking that nothing here was earl or dragon. It was all David.

"Aunt Miriam made one for each of us and included some material from clothes we outwore. That blue was from a sailor's top she made for me when I was mad for Nelson. That faded red is from some curtains in my bedroom at home."

Home. He'd used the word without thinking.

The manor house down in the valley was the home of his heart, but no longer his. They had both lost their homes, but that meant they both must make new ones. Or rather, a new one. If it had to be Crag Wyvern, so be it. This room gave her hope, especially the window to the outside world. Never had panes of glass seemed such a marvel.

It looked directly out to sea. Not long ago the endless sea had frightened her. From here it seemed a work of art. The arching sky made it blue at the moment, breeze-ripples touched by sunlight, but ever changing as cloud shadows moved over it.

"It's like a living painting," she said.

"Sometimes the picture is dark and stormy. And don't forget the mists. At times I can't even see the cliff edge."

She smiled at the way he was still trying to point out the disadvantages. She knew it wasn't because he wanted to scare her away, but that he wanted her prepared for the worst.

Then a ship sailed into the painting, adding interest.

"Merchantmen come by here?" she asked.

"Not so close. That's a naval frigate, the *Taurus*. She cruises up and down this stretch of coast."

"Surely smugglers don't operate in the daytime."

"No, so it's intimidation. Every now and then they fire a shot. A blank, of course, but a message."

A threat against people he cared for. She turned away from it, to him, so close, so dear. "Why don't the people give it up? Can't they earn a living an honest way?"

He took her hands, perhaps unconsciously. "Not so easily, but it's more than that. Yes, the Freetrade is illegal, but it's a way of life here and has been for generations. It's as much a part of who they are as harvest time, and they resent the government trying to take that away."

"They," he'd said, but she could tell he also meant "I." He'd been born and raised here and been wounded playing smuggling games. His father had been the smugglers' leader. It wasn't surprising if he still felt some sympathy for the Freetrade.

She didn't like it, she didn't like it at all. She'd work to stop the trade. But in the meantime she could only hope to keep him from taking risks for amusement.

"You said you changed two rooms?" she asked.

"A parlor next door." Hands still joined, he took her through an adjoining door.

She paused with pleasure. "You spent more money on this."

It was an exotically rich room. Paneling ran around the lower part of the walls, stained to a russet red. Each main panel had a carved and gilded center. The effect made her think of cordovan leather ornamented with gold.

The walls were painted red to match and a complex cornice was gilded. The upholstery on a sofa and three chairs was of the same rich brown, striped with gold.

"I spent more than I should," he agreed, "though perhaps not as much as you think. The paneling comes from a house not far away."

"It was demolished?"

"Made more stylish. Lopley Hall was owned by a nabob called Joseph Bross. He'd have known all about Indian goddesses. He was a grand old reprobate, and he brought home exotic tastes of all kinds."

"I see."

He grinned. "I think you do. He held splendid parties. When he died last year a grandson inherited, shuddering at such a barbarous place. When I heard he was having everything stripped out in order to make a pale modern home, I purchased this room from him. He was eager to give the Earl of Wyvern a very low price."

"So, some advantages to your rank?"

She meant it as a tease, but he replied seriously. "Outweighed by the burdens, Lucy. I have no choice. You do."

"My place is at your side. But there's more than that. We should be completely honest now. I'm a waif in the storm."

"What?" he asked with a puzzled smile.

"I'm serious. I have nowhere else to go. I can't endure much longer with Aunt Mary, and though the beau monde can be pleasant I don't feel I belong there. The City should be my home, but it's changed around me. My father's house is ruled by another. My friends are marrying and moving away. I once thought I had roots in the world of trade and could flourish there, but I've had to see the truth. It's a man's world, and my father's no longer willing to help me be accepted there. I could use my money to force my way in and even possibly prosper, though I wonder now how many men would do business with me without my father's support."

"You would succeed. You're a remarkable woman."

"You give me too much credit, love. I don't relish a life-long battle for acceptance in a hostile world."

"This isn't a hostile world? Mists, cliffs, smugglers, perilous countryside?"

"Not with you by my side."

He took her into his arms, as she hoped he would. He said, "I would delight in being your safe harbor," as she hoped he would. But then he added, "I'm not sure I can be."

It hurt, but she said, "Secrets. I remember. We were going to get dressed first."

"Yes," he agreed, letting her go, reluctantly. Because holding her was precious, or because of reluctance to tell her the whole truth? As they stood, he said, "The world might come crashing in at any moment."

"What?" She glanced at the window, at the cannon-bearing warship.

"My family. If they tire of waiting, they'll ascend to learn all about you. I'll go and get your valise."

He left and she missed him, but she also had her moment to retrieve her journal. She looked out into the corridor and found it empty, but she'd lost sense of where she'd been. The windows looked out to sea, but where was the circular room?

She gave up and headed right. Toward the end of the corridor she realized that the normal stairs from the hall rose there. She looked carefully around the corner but didn't see David, so she scampered across the open space and turned the corner.

Of course, here was the corridor that ran above the entrance. It might have been quicker to go the other way, but there was no point in reversing. She ran along the corridor, but then paused when again she heard voices.

". . . seemed newly confident." That was David.

"Because of the *Taurus*. Captain Truscott is a fire-eater and as fierce as he for the glory of capturing the whole Horde." The voice had a touch of the local accent, but he spoke almost as an equal. The secretary?

"Lloyd spoke as if he had new knowledge."

"I've sensed the same recently. It could be Saul."

"He'd not be so stupid."

"For enough money Saul Applin would be as stupid as can be. He's a weak link."

"He's a husband and father."

"He drinks and gambles away most of the money he earns, and he cracked Lovey's ribs while you were away. I told him if he did anything like that again I'd break his."

"I'd help you, but this is for later. Did you go down to the manor?"

"As ordered. They're all aflutter to meet your bride-to-be."

There was a slight question to that, but David said, "Yes, you may wish me happy." Lucy wished he sounded it. "I'm to take this up. Did you sort out that matter of Carter's cows?"

"For now. You need an estate manager."

"Later."

Footsteps. Lucy realized David could already be returning to the room. She ran on and around a corner. She found the right room, grabbed her clothing, and kept on her way, past the Saint George room and around another corner, accidentally brushing against the skeleton, causing it to rattle.

David was coming the other way.

"I didn't think my clothes should be left there," she said.

"Clear witted." He came to her and opened the door to his parlor. "But no one was likely to go there and my servants are very discreet."

"I'm sure they are," she said, going in and putting her pile of clothing on a sofa. "How many servants do you have here?"

"Six."

"That's not very many."

"I have few needs. If necessary more come up from

the village. My cousin Amelia teases me to host a summer ball."

"She has as vivid an imagination as you." When he looked blank, she said, "Fairy circles?"

He smiled. "We certainly need some here. Amelia sees what she wants to see. It's the Kerslake way. I'll leave you here and come back to see if you need help."

He locked the door to the corridor and then returned to his bedroom.

Lucy shook her head at her tangled world. His family sounded as odd as the Caldrosses, but he loved them, so she must make a good impression. She opened her valise, which contained only two other gowns. Remembering how out of place her fashionable clothing had felt in the City, she'd chosen the simplest ones.

She'd been right, too. The women of the village had been dressed in simple style, and some of the older ones had even worn gowns fitted to the natural waist.

She had a pink-sprigged muslin made in fairly plain style, and the clear blue that she'd balked at altering. She shook it out, suffering some doubts. There wasn't much creasing, but no one could miss that it was years old. It was still one of her favorites, though, and she realized a deeper appeal. It dated back to the old days. To before her mother's death, when her life had seemed fixed in a pleasant pattern.

Yes, a good start to a new and delightful pattern.

She put on clean drawers and a shift. She picked up the simple corset, but the blue really required a better one, which she'd packed.

Could she really ask David to lace up her corset? There were maids here and he said they'd be discreet, but if there was any possibility of keeping their sinful behavior to themselves, she wanted that.

She threaded the laces loosely and put it on over her head and then went to knock at the door.

He appeared, dressed as far as waistcoat, tussled and delicious. He looked at her in the same way, but said, "Stay laces?"

She turned and he set to work.

"Do this often, do you?"

"No," he said, giving the laces a tug.

"Not too tight. I like comfort."

"No need to pinch in your waist?"

"What do you think?"

"Begging for compliments now?"

"Storing them for my cronehood."

He kissed the back of her neck. "You'll be a beautiful crone. There."

She turned, smiling. "As long as we're together I'll be a happy one. Let me put on the gown and you can fasten the back."

He helped her and then fastened the short row of hooks. "I've not seen this before. I like it."

"It's years old, but one of my favorites. I couldn't bear to make it fashionable with lace and flounces, so I found I couldn't wear it."

"But it's suitable for Devonshire yokels."

She slapped his chest. "I wanted to look pretty for you, but yes, I hoped it would also fit in with a simpler life."

He dropped a butterfly kiss on her lips. "You succeed at both, my Lucy-love."

She smiled but pushed him away before they undid all their dressing. "Put on your coat. I have stockings and shoes to find. And then you have to tell me all your secrets."

He returned to the bedroom but left the door open. "I need to take you down to the manor now or they truly will be up here to see what's going on."

"They'll suspect?" Lucy asked, rolling a clean stocking up her leg. Scandalously, she didn't much care.

"Our wickedness? Probably not. They'll just be curious. I should have taken you there first."

She fixed her garter in place. "Why didn't you?"

After a moment he said, "I wanted to get rid of you. The manor might seem too welcoming, so I dragged you up here."

Wanted.

"How often careful planning goes amiss," she said lightly as she tied the other garter. "And then you settled it by carelessly showing me these rooms."

He appeared in the doorway, dressed apart from the lack of cravat. "Remember the rest."

"I do, but truly, David, what you've done here can be done all through the house."

"It will cost a lot of money."

"I have a lot of money."

"Which you intend to tie up in a trust."

She put on a half boot. "Only so it won't be squandered."

He came to kneel and tie the laces. She tried to read his expression. "Will you mind my keeping control of some?" she asked.

He picked up her other boot and eased it onto her foot. "I note that you aren't offering to remove all constraints."

His touch could melt her mind like wax, but she recognized a dangerous moment. Above all, she must be honest. "Why should I? You'll get ten thousand clear to do with as you wish. The rest I'll happily spend on us, our home, our land, and our children. But I won't see it go on gaming tables or worse, other women."

Still kneeling, he looked up at her. "You don't think highly of me."

"I adore you, but that's all the more reason to cling by my nails to sense. David, I drew up this plan of marriage with some anonymous man in mind. Now that it's you, it is different, but I see no reason to change my plan. It makes sense."

He stood in such a way that she feared she'd misjudged him disastrously. If he couldn't tolerate such a situation, would she have to surrender all? Could she, even ruled by love?

"Is your father as inflexible?" he asked.

"What in heaven has my father to do with this? If you think to get him to persuade me to give it all to you, you're mad on all counts."

"No, not that . . ."

"Are you saying you couldn't bear my keeping some control of my money?"

She waited, breath held, but he looked at her blankly. "Not at all, though my aunt and uncle disapprove."

Lucy didn't know what was going on. "You discussed me with them?"

"They seem able to read me like an open book. Come to the mirror in my room to tidy your hair."

"But . . ."

Then Lucy decided it would be better not to push too much for now. He'd said he didn't mind the financial arrangements, and he'd meant it.

Just as he'd meant it when he'd once said that he didn't intend to marry her.

"Secrets?" she said as she went into the room and applied a comb to her hair, which had turned riotous in the steamy bath. "This is such a mess."

"It's delightful. A golden halo."

"An angel now, am I?"

She saw his grin in the mirror. "No."

She hadn't wanted to bother with extra hatboxes, but that meant she had only the plain brown bonnet, which didn't go with this gown. What had she been thinking?

The thought of meeting David's family, his possibly disapproving family, improperly dressed, finally had her in a twitch.

"There's no need to fuss," he said impatiently. "Come on."

She gave up, found the large Norwich shawl she'd brought, and closed her valise. He picked it up and she set off with him, feeling a complete mess.

He took her down the normal stairs to the great hall. A well-built young man was crossing it.

"Ah, my dear, I introduce you to my secretary, Chumley."

Fred, Lucy remembered as she greeted him. She liked the look of him—steady, clever, and amiable. But then she remembered him saying he'd threatened, no promised, to break a bully's ribs, and sensed that in him.

Another dragon? Did they breed them in these parts, or was it the country way to be strong and ready for violence? That should give a sensible lady pause, but she was beyond that sort of sense.

As she and David left the house, she asked, "Is he the sort of secretary you can discuss everything with?"

"He's a friend as well, yes."

"I assume he has clerks."

"He, like me, must make do."

"He, like you, will be better off once we're married."

He gave her a look. "You steal my chance to beg for your hand and heart?"

"You mind?" she teased, and was shocked when he said, "Yes. But only that we've done things inside out. It must be the damned house," he added, looking back at the Crag.

"I don't mind any of it," she said, linking arms with him and turning him away. But when they came to the steep path down, she said, "I wish I had a rope."

"You have me, and I've never so much as slipped."

"Yes," she said happily. "I have you."

She remembered then that they never had talked about secrets, but she could wait a little longer. This moment was too pleasant to shadow in any way.

Chapter 32

They paused at the fork in the path to look out to sea again. The ship was still in sight.

"Don't they have anything better to do?" she asked.

"Alas, no. The government's reluctant to reduce the navy for fear of new trouble from France, so those based in British ports patrol the coasts like sharks."

"The navy are our national heroes, and they're trying to prevent a criminal trade. I wish you weren't so indulgent of the smugglers."

"I told you, Lucy, smuggling is like the sea. I can disapprove as much as I want, but that won't stop it coming in and out with the tides, or slamming destructively against the cliffs in a storm. I have to live with it, and if we marry, so will you."

"If?" she echoed, staring at him.

"When. The 'if' is in case you're thinking better of it."

How close they'd come to an edge. "There is no better without you. I'll do my best to understand."

"Don't pretend regular trade is any more blessed. Think what happens around the world so that goods can be brought here for our pleasure and indulgence. Natives tricked, bullied, and sometimes slaughtered. . . ."

She put a hand over his. "Don't. Don't let's fight these wars, not now at least. I understand what you're saying."

"I'm sorry, love, but it angers me that the crimes of

the common people are crushed whilst those of the rich and titled are winked at."

"Never say you're a republican?"

"A republican earl?"

"Perhaps one step up from the Peasant Earl," she replied, relieved to have moved onto lighter ground. There were serious issues to discuss, but not yet, when they still had so many minor tests to endure. He obviously thought the same way, for they came together easily for a kiss.

Crunching footsteps moved them apart.

A man came up the path from the sea, a heavy-shouldered man who moved ponderously like an ox, whose face turned surly when he saw them. He touched his forelock, however, as he passed, muttering, "M'lord."

"Saul," David said sharply.

The man turned back.

"I hear Lovey suffered an injury."

Saul. The man who'd cracked his wife's ribs and was in the habit of beating her.

"Aye, m'lord. She fell."

"You need to take more care of her." It was calmly said, but the man flinched.

"She's clumsy-like, m'lord!" the man protested, but then hastily added, "But I will take better care of her, m'lord."

David merely nodded.

The man hurried on, stumbling for a moment in his haste.

Lucy had never thought that modern peers needed to be dragons in ruling their territories, but perhaps it was so, particularly in the wilder parts of the country. She remembered that David's secretary had threatened to break that beefy man's ribs if he harmed his wife again and seemed confident of being able to do it. David had said he'd do the same, and just now silently threatened it. The man, Applin, had believed it and hurried away, afraid. Really, she shouldn't be so delighted by the idea of violent retribution, but she'd always known she wasn't a lady in the proper sense.

"What are you thinking?" he asked.

"That you're an unusual earl, but that I'm an unusual lady, so we're well matched."

Lucy enjoyed the return to the more normal village and felt cheered when a woman in a garden called out a good-day. But then she said, "Oh, dear."

"What?" he asked.

"I went up the hill in one outfit and I'm returning in another."

"Hell. You've addled my wits."

"I like that, except—will your aunt be terribly shocked?"

"Don't worry. She'll blame me, and she'll be appeased by news of our imminent wedding."

"You haven't begged for my hand and heart yet."

"You didn't give me a chance. You can't have it both ways."

"I can try," she said with a smile.

He laughed and kissed her. "I'll get a license."

"I'd prefer banns," she said. "I want to declare our love before our congregations."

"A license would be faster."

"Why haste? Bad enough that people here might guess we've anticipated the wedding. I don't want my friends and family in London to think the same thing. And remember, my father marries in a week. Rushing to the altar days before him would cause terrible talk."

It seemed he might continue to press for a license, but then he shrugged. "As you will."

"What bothers you, David? Speak to me."

"I don't want anything or anyone to come between us."

She paused to touch his cheek. "Nothing will, love.

Nothing can. We're both of age, and with my money we are of independent means." Careless of the fact that they could be seen, she drew his head down and kissed him. "I think I owe you some kisses."

"I know you wiped the slate clean not long ago."

For some reason that made her blush, which made him laugh. He took her hand and led her on.

David felt more adrift than he ever had, tangled by dizzy love and glimpses of future heaven, but weighed down by sure knowledge of disaster in the wings.

He'd promised to reveal his secrets and meant it. There'd been reason to want to get dressed before a serious discussion, and also reason to bring Lucy to the manor as soon as possible. He knew he'd grasped the excuses, however, putting off the moment, as if something could happen to make it unnecessary to disturb her happiness.

She thought he'd merely played at smuggling when a lad, and been shocked by that. She had no idea that he was now leader of the smugglers, or that her father was trying to overrule her will and threatening retribution.

He took her to the front entrance to the manor, which was rarely used, the back being more convenient from the village. A little formality seemed in order for such a moment. The entrance had a modest portico and the short drive ended in enough space for a carriage to turn, for the front of the manor faced a road of sorts, but he knew to Lucy it must seem a track.

"It's a pretty house," she said, "but not as large as I expected."

"It was a farmhouse two hundred years ago and isn't much changed since. The Kerslakes are farming stock, but then, so are the Somerfords.

"I like the flowers everywhere."

"Yes, the Crag and the manor are two different worlds."

"Something can be done," she said with blissful confidence.

Probably when he told her the whole situation, she'd have the same response.

I'm Captain Drake.

Something can be done.

Your father is determined we will not marry.

Something can be done.

No. Her father's interference was bound to upset her, so he'd keep that from her if he could.

He wanted to save her from all distress, but knew that was impossible. He could only strive to reduce the pain.

Lucy approached the door nervously, because David seemed tense. He'd said his family would be anxious to meet her, and that his aunt would demand a wedding if she realized their sin, but he hadn't said they'd approve of her.

The house didn't present a hostile front. The rose-surrounded door stood open and they simply walked into a paneled hall that smelled delightfully of lavender and potpourri. An old dog stood to amble over and greet David, who fondled its ears.

"We'll go through to the kitchen," he said.

But then a pretty, brown-haired young woman appeared from the back of the house, wearing an apron over her dress. "So there you are! We were about to go in search of you." She was smiling brightly, especially at Lucy, but her expression was full of curiosity.

"Lucy, I present my cousin, Amelia Kerslake. Amelia, this is Miss Lucy Potter."

"We guessed as much," Amelia said to Lucy, "when word spread that a lady had arrived for David."

To Lucy that sounded as if she were a parcel, but Amelia Kerslake showed no sign of coldness.

"Mama will be here in a moment," she said. "She felt the need to put off her apron and straighten her cap to greet David's bride. I suppose I should, too. Take off my apron, I mean." She began to untie the strings.

"Amy!" protested an older, plumper woman, joining them, cheeks flushed. "Don't run on so." But she, too, was beaming as she took Lucy's hands. "How lovely to meet you, my dear. I hope your journey here went smoothly. Come into the parlor and we'll have tea."

"Thank you," said Lucy, unable to stop smiling herself. "No one has thus far offered me refreshment."

"Davy!" his aunt exclaimed. "What have you been up to all this time?"

Perhaps David blushed. "A tour of the Crag."

"Which does have a kitchen."

"Aunt Miriam, Lucy Potter. Lucy, my aunt, Lady Kerslake."

"Away with you!" his aunt protested, laughing. "I'll be your aunt Miriam, too, dear."

Lucy wasn't sure if that was a statement or prediction but she shed any idea of being unwelcome.

"I wonder you dared," Amelia said to David as they all crossed to a room. She added to Lucy, "I've been telling and telling him that no woman will marry him unless he does improvements there. Isn't it horrid?"

"Horrid enough for a novel," Lucy agreed.

"Oh, do you read novels, too? I adore them. But I still wouldn't want to live in the Crag."

"Not even for love?"

"Oh, for that, of course. And you have money, so you can change it."

"Amelia," said her mother, sitting down in an upholstered chair.

"It's true."

"Go and supervise the tea," Aunt Miriam said, gesturing Lucy toward a small sofa. "Sit down, dear. I must apologize for my husband, but he's away on business. He won't be back until tomorrow."

"A good thing," David said, sitting beside Lucy, making them so obviously a couple. "Best to take you all in measured doses."

"Oh, you," said his aunt, shining with love for him.

This was a house of ease and love. Could Crag Wyvern ever approach the same?

"I like David's new rooms up at Crag Wyvern," Lucy said. "His parlor is a little like this."

"All that red wood and gold trim? Not to my taste, dear."

"Yes, the colors are different, but I see similarities."

Here the wainscoting was a mellow brown and the upper walls covered with white-and-blue wallpaper. But the ambience was much the same, which had probably been his intention, conscious or not.

Amelia returned with a tray of scones, followed by a maidservant bearing the tea tray. As Aunt Miriam brewed and poured, Amelia took charge of the scones.

"Do you eat scones and cream the Devon way in London?" she asked, taking the bottom half of a scone and spreading it with jam. She added a scoop of cream that seemed thick as butter, put the whole thing on a plate, and offered it to Lucy. "Try it."

Lucy took a bite and hummed her approval. She didn't think she'd ever tasted such a perfect scone. It was light and with just a trace of warmth to say it wasn't long from the oven. The dense cream was richly delicious and the tart raspberry jam the perfect complement.

"This is heavenly," Lucy said.

David's aunt beamed even more and described the process of making clotted cream. Lucy listened, guessing that everything here except the tea and sugar was produced locally. And the tea had probably been smuggled.

She wasn't skilled at cookery. At her mother's insistence she'd learned to manage a household, but she'd rarely actually cooked anything. Any skill could be learned, of course, but she'd rather make money through trade and hire a good cook.

As the chat continued she realized that the manor was still a farm, with fields spread around the area. It had its own dairy, making cheese, butter, and the clotted cream. There was also a brewhouse, and Lady Kerslake made fruit wines and many herbal medicines.

Lucy asked David, "Where does the Crag get its ale?"

"The tavern in the village, but the earldom owns the tavern, and the one in Dragon's Cove."

"And its dairy products?"

"From tenant farms, but in a way they're our own, too. Nearly everything hereabouts except the manor and its lands belongs to the earldom."

She nodded, beginning to get an idea of how everything worked and the extent of his responsibilities. She also reflected how different this house was to the one in Lanchester Street. Here she had an aunt and cousin of sorts and they both liked to talk, but Amelia's chatter made sense and David's Aunt Miriam seemed to have a warm word about everyone and everything. There had to be some things of which she didn't approve, but none had arisen so far. If she knew that Lucy had arrived in Church Wyvern in one outfit and entered her house in another, it wasn't mentioned.

When tea was finished, Lady Kerslake said, "Amelia love, take Lucy up to the room we've prepared for her and make sure she has everything she needs."

Lucy saw in David a reflection of her own reluctance to separate. How odd, when they'd met and separated so often. But they'd been so very together in the past few hours it did feel wrong to be apart. She wished she could leave him with a kiss, but blushed to see how others knew it.

Amelia took her upstairs and to a charming room.

"David's," Amelia said, but Lucy had already guessed.

It surely didn't hold his smell, but something lingered. In addition, he'd created his bedroom at the Crag in imitation of this. Plain white walls with ghosts of paintings, which she was sure were now up there. Simple furniture that might be new here because his old familiar pieces had been moved there. There was even a patchwork quilt on the bed.

Lucy went to this. "Are the pieces significant?"

"Possibly, but that was made by Grandma Kerslake decades ago. Do you have soap? No? I'll get you some." She was back quickly with a plainly cut piece of white soap.

"Is that, too, made here?" Lucy asked.

"Yes," Amelia said, suddenly anxious. "I'm sure you're used to better. . . ."

"Heavens, I'm sorry! I didn't mean to imply a criticism. I think it's wonderful that you make everything yourself."

"Do you? It's such a treat when we purchase something. I get a bar of French soap for Christmas every year. I suppose you're accustomed to be surrounded by shops."

"I'm afraid so. But not surrounded by such lovely countryside." Lucy almost laughed at saying that, but she had to say something of the sort, and thus far the countryside hadn't attacked her.

Amelia perched on the edge of the bed, swinging her feet. "Is it normal for a London lady to travel alone?" It was simply open curiosity.

"I was escorted by a Mr. Delaney."

Amelia grinned. "I heard. Up to something, I'm sure."

"What do you mean?"

"It's just the way he is. He's very exciting, isn't he?"

"David?"

"Nicholas! If he weren't married, I might set my cap at him."

Lucy opened her valise and took out items to put in drawers. "He's good-looking, I suppose, but I've never really thought of him that way."

"That's love for you, isn't it? I'm so pleased David's found a woman who loves him. I worried about his fortune hunting."

"You knew about that?"

"Oh, everyone here knows about everything. Never think to keep a secret."

"Even about smuggling?" Lucy asked, but then wondered if that was wise.

But Amelia answered without hesitation. "Secret from outsiders, of course, but not amongst ourselves."

After a moment's consideration Lucy asked, "Does everyone know who Captain Drake is?"

Something warned that she might have gone too far, but then Amelia said, "Of course. He couldn't have much authority otherwise, could he?"

"Authority involving life and death?"

"Even that."

"That's almost feudal."

"I suppose it is. There are aspects to life here that are from olden times, but don't let it worry you. We're generally perfectly civilized."

Lucy slid her journal beneath her spare shift in the drawer. "I overheard something up at Crag Wyvern. About some smugglers near Purbeck mistreating a woman because her husband defied them."

"Tom Merriwether's boys," Amelia said, pulling a face. "A horrible gang. I wish Lloyd—he's the riding officer—would put an end to them instead of harassing peaceable people here."

"Peaceable criminals?"

"Well, they are! For more than fifty years a Captain

Drake has ruled the Dragon's Horde here, ensuring no harm done to anyone."

"Life and death?" Lucy asked.

"Sometimes they need bringing into order . . . but David will be cross with me for talking of such things."

"If I'm to live here, I have to know."

"That's what I thought."

Lucy turned to put away the last of her clothing.

"Does it bother you?" Amelia asked.

Lucy turned. "What?"

"The Freetrade. Visitors here are odd. Some disapprove, but most think it exciting and many hint for sources of cheap brandy and such."

"I can't like the illegality, or the barbarity."

"Nothing here is barbarous, I assure you."

"I suppose I'll learn the local ways."

"It's lovely that you're so sensible, Lucy. I was worried that David would bring back a fancy London fashionable who'd turn her nose up at everything. What's it like, living in a city?"

That seemed an impossible question to answer, but Lucy did her best. Her accounts of shops and street lighting were greeted like stories of dragons and fairies.

"Have you never been to a city?" she asked at last.

"No further than Honiton or Axminster," Amelia said. "There's never been any need. But I would like to see London."

"You could return with me for a visit."

"You're going back?"

"I must. My father marries soon, and there will be arrangements to make."

"For your own wedding."

"Yes."

Lucy was realizing that David should return with her. He needed to ask formally for her father's permission. It wasn't necessary since she was of age, but he'd want to do it and her father would certainly expect it. They could attend her father's wedding together, and be together for the first reading of their banns. That would mean traveling together, and not having to be apart.

"Then I'd love to return with you," Amelia said. "What fun!"

The vision of an intimate journey shattered, but it might be better. Amelia would be a testament to propriety. "Would your parents permit it?"

"I don't see why not."

"You'll need to be careful when there."

"Is it very dangerous?" Amelia, too, looked as if she thought danger could be exciting.

"In some places, but I was thinking of the heart. You might fall in love with a London man, or a lord whose home is in Scotland."

Amelia laughed. "I'd never do that. I'll marry close to home."

Lucy remembered once saying something similar. "Love can be a complication."

Amelia studied her. "Is your loving David a complication? This must be very different to what you're used to."

"Yes and yes, but love is compensation enough."

"Love and family," Amelia agreed, standing. "There's family everywhere here, on all sides. Kerslakes, Bubbingtons—that's mother's family—and even the Clysts and their connections."

"I'm not accustomed to that."

"You'll find you like it overall. There are always the difficult ones and the dirty dishes, but family is wonderful."

When they went downstairs David came into the hall to meet them. "All settled?" he asked Lucy.

"In your old room."

She realized that room hadn't only been a boyhood sanctum, but his until last year, when he'd become the earl.

She took his hand. "We'll make a lovely and loving home, David. We will. Even a garden and roses."

He raised her hand and kissed it. "We can try. I doubt we can manage an orchard, though. Come, let me show you the one here."

No one seemed to object, so Lucy went happily with him back out through the front door and around the house.

Chapter 33

She found not just a flower garden, but also herbs and some fruits and vegetables. He led her over to a patch of raspberries. He picked some and offered them in his cupped hand.

Lucy took one and ate it, sweet and warm from the sun. "I've never tasted any as good."

He poured them into her hand and she ate them as they followed a path between plants large and small. Some she knew, but most she didn't.

"We have a garden at home, but grow few vegetables."

"Surrounded by shops and markets, what point would there be?"

"Amelia would like to come with us to London."

"Don't let her pester you."

He took her hand and led her beneath a fragrant honeysuckle arch to a deeper part of the garden. "Come and be kissed beneath a cherry tree." They went through a gate. "Not much is edible yet, but there are cherries." He reached up for a bunch.

She took them, smiling. "I like this."

"Being plied with fruit?"

"Courting. We are, aren't we? Strolling together in the gardens, nearby but out of sight, as we learn one another and learn to please one another."

"Courting. Inside out again, but yes, sweet. I remember thinking I'd like to bring you here and pick cherries for you. And see you here in springtime with blossoms in your hair."

They came together for a kiss as natural as breathing. When they parted she said, "It won't always be sunny and mild."

"No," he agreed, but puzzled.

"I was simply reminding myself not to be entirely bedazzled." She popped a cherry in her mouth and savored it. "You were going to tell me secrets, David. Let's get it over with."

"Like a trip to the dentist?"

"It feels very like, yes."

He led her to a wooden bench and they sat beneath an apple tree. The small fruits were only tiny promises, but she'd be here in autumn to taste them when they were full and ripe. Yet still she felt his doubts and even reluctance.

"If the secrets belong to others," she said, "if it would be dishonorable to share them, then don't. Even a husband and wife can sometimes keep secrets like that."

"I'd rather you know everything before you commit yourself."

"I'm committed. Nothing can change that."

"Rash woman."

Then, suddenly, she knew.

Pieces fell into place.

His sober tone now, snatches of conversations overheard, the encounter with Saul Applin.

"David, are you Captain Drake?"

He blinked once, but she saw the answer before he said, "I knew you were too clever to be safe."

"What does that mean?"

"The pressing reason I've been trying to break free of

you, Lucy Potter, is that I knew from the first that I'd never be able to fool you over anything."

"Of course not, and I should have realized sooner. That's the dragon!"

"What?"

She took his hand. "David, earl, and dragon."

"You always make sense, love, but at the moment you remind me of Clara Fytch."

"I've come to see three parts to you—David, the earl, and another part I haven't understood that I called the dragon. Now I see what it is. 'Drake' is another word for dragon, isn't it?"

"Yes, and as I've told you, the dragon is dangerous."

"To men like Saul," she said.

"And to men like Lloyd."

"You wouldn't kill him, would you?"

"No," he sighed. "Why are you smiling?"

"Because that's a relief, but also because this is the final piece of the problem. The key. I thought you were reluctant to marry me because of the madness in your blood, but that was solved. And that I wouldn't like Devon, but I know I can come to like it. Then perhaps because of the danger from smugglers. But it was because you're the smugglers' leader. Though I don't see exactly why that's an obstacle."

"Perhaps I thought you might object to being married to a criminal? I was convinced at one point that you'd report me to the magistrates. You seemed ardently against the Freetrade."

"I was. I am. It undermines law and order and damages legitimate trade. But I'd never *betray* you."

"I know that now. But, Lucy, I could get caught. Probably as earl I'd escape prosecution, but if anything went that badly wrong, I could be killed. You'd not only be a widow, but one entangled in scandal."

"You will not be killed. You will *not*. But I don't understand. Why do you have to be Captain Drake?"

"Inheritance. The bane of my life. As Mel Clyst's son, the mantle fell on me. Though he indulged my interest in smuggling and let me take part, he never wanted me deeply involved. He was pleased to see me in the gentry with an honest job. He'd trained his nephew John Clyst from a young age to take over, but in the run that went wrong Mel was taken and John was killed. There was no one else to hold the Horde together and prevent chaos."

"That was more than a year ago, though, wasn't it?"

"Nearly two years ago, but finding a substitute wasn't urgent until I took on the earldom, and since then I've been rather busy. It's no easy matter. Most smuggling masters are simple men, but that's why there's so often poor organization and wanton violence. To keep order and prosperity, Captain Drake has to have a range of qualities from administration to the ability to enforce stern discipline."

"A clerkish dragon, or a dragonish clerk."

"He must also be accepted by the Horde. Mel inherited from his father, and he treated John as a son. That's the best way. If he'd married an ordinary woman, his son or sons would have been natural heirs. But he fell in thrall to Lady Belle."

"That's a harsh way of putting it."

"Everything would be better if she'd followed a normal path. But as it turned out, I was the only one with the abilities and bloodline to take over."

"But you must be training a substitute now."

"They're not so easy to find. There are good, reliable men, but not ready for the role. I'm stuck with it for a while, Lucy, and you have to know that. It's a difficult and dangerous situation."

She squeezed his hand. "I think two dreadful inheritances very unfair."

"So do I, but I've had no choice."

"You're a hero, David Kerslake-Somerford."

"Devil a bit."

She kissed him. "My hero. And I'll be proud to be at your side."

"I shouldn't let you do it."

"Am I a child? And in all respects but love, I'm clever, levelheaded, and schooled to make shrewd bargains. Cease trying to protect me from myself."

His lips twitched. "A spiked mace."

"What does that mean?"

"That I adore you, goddess." He drew her in for a long, tender kiss. She snuggled against him, enjoying it, but wanting more. "The problem with our inside-outness is that courtship isn't quite enough anymore," she said.

"No, I am not going to ravish you beneath a cherry tree."

"No?"

"No," he said, capturing her wandering hand. "Or not yet. What am I saying?" he asked, standing and pulling her, laughing, to her feet. "Never. Not here. Aunt Miriam would turn gray on the spot."

"I'll go odds she wouldn't."

"Stop trying to corrupt me."

She went with him back toward the house, smiling. "Do you have a kite?"

"I did. It might still be around. Why?"

"I'd like to fly it with you on the headland."

"Why?"

"Do you remember helping a girl to fly a kite in the park?"

It clearly took him a moment. "Yes. I almost knocked her over."

"Or she ran into you. That might have been the moment when I realized that I loved you. I liked you in the bookshop. You annoyed me at Lady Charrington's ball.

I felt the attraction, but I was determined to resist. But then, in the park, I saw the heart and soul of you, the part I later came to see as David."

"Remember the dragon," he said, but they had to kiss. "I was lost from the first, but I fought as hard as I could."

"You didn't really want to marry a stupid woman, did you?"

"No, but I felt honor bound."

"You'd have been miserable."

"When I formed the plan, I hadn't met you. . . ."

"Davy, there you are!"

Lucy blinked out of a magical world to see a stalwart gentleman walking toward them, round face beaming. "And here's your Lucy. Welcome, cousin."

Lucy realized this was addressed to her.

"Lucy," David said in a resigned tone, "this is my cousin Henry Kerslake."

Lucy curtsied, beginning to feel overwhelmed by good cheer.

"Dinner's served," Henry said, "so come on in. I heard there was trouble with some cows over Harcombe way."

David answered and Lucy walked with them, suppressing a smile. Henry Kerslake wasn't one for polite chitchat with the ladies, it would seem.

Henry took his father's place at the head of the table and carved the joint of pork when it came. He was certainly comfortable in his place in the world, a secure heir with no need to venture elsewhere, already knowing how his life would progress. She felt a touch of the old resentment that her life hadn't rolled out in a similarly smooth way, but the future delights would compensate.

After the meal Lady Kerslake suggested a game of cards, but David took his leave. "I've neglected my responsibilities too long." He merely smiled at Lucy. "After church tomorrow I'll show you round the villages."

Church tomorrow, in this community which would be her home. A delightful prospect.

When he'd left, Lucy could have played the heroine's part and pined, but she was drawn into clearing away the meal and then to a game of cards. After a supper Henry went off to some paperwork and Aunt Miriam went to bed.

Though late, it was only just dark on a June night and Lucy felt drawn out the back door to look up at Crag Wyvern. There was enough light lingering in the sky to show it as a solid dark shape. If David was in one of his rooms with candles lit, she couldn't see that from here.

Up above, stars were astonishingly bright.

"Lovely, isn't it?"

Lucy startled at Amelia's voice. "Yes."

"It's because there's hardly any moon."

"I've rarely seen such a night sky. There are too many buildings in London, and often the air isn't clear."

"Why not?"

"Coal fires. Even in summer there are many businesses that need fires. Bakeries, chophouses, forges and foundries."

"That sounds unpleasant."

"Perhaps. This seems uncomfortably quiet."

"Quiet? I can hear Peggy Brown and her sister arguing and the Muncotts need to train their dog not to bark at nothing."

"There's always traffic in London. More in the tonnish part than in the City. The City generally sleeps for a while, but in the west end, by the time the beau monde rolls home with the dawn, the hawkers and deliverymen are out."

Quiet was something else she was going to have to get used to. For the moment, it unsettled her. Despite the occasional voices and some singing, perhaps from the tavern, she felt uncomfortably isolated. Yes, this place could keep secrets. Things could happen here and never be heard of outside. It was another closed circle, perhaps with sinister aspects. She shivered slightly, but then a clear birdsong split the still air.

"The nightingale," Amelia said. "We only have a few here. Lovely, isn't it?"

"Delightful," Lucy said, smiling over a nighttime visit to her bedroom.

If she were a braver woman, she'd climb the path to the Crag and invade his bedchamber, but she had no need of foolhardiness. All was settled now and she merely had to be patient to progress in a normal manner to her happy end.

Chapter 34

David heard the nightingale through the open window of his parlor. He was going over plans on his desk, but his mind wandered too often to Lucy in the valley below.

His beloved, his treasure, his goddess, thought she had all the pieces, but he'd neglected to provide one. The threat posed by her father. Perhaps he should have told her; perhaps he would still have to. But he couldn't help hoping that she would never have to know, that he could foil Potter in some way.

For instance, with luck, Potter wouldn't ever know she'd left, and she could return home for the wedding without problem. Perhaps when faced with her happiness and resolution, Potter would give up his opposition.

However, Lucy assumed he'd return with her to get her father's blessing, which would be oil on the fire. Heaven help them both! Better by far to return already married, but she wanted banns and a wedding with friends and family around her, and she deserved it all.

He threw down his quill and went to stare out at the moonless night. A thousand stars, and none with an answer.

Lucy was a resolute woman. Could she convince her father of their love?

Daniel Potter struck David as a man who believed his

way was always right. The kind of man who would think the more it seemed she loved, the more she was demented by it. And then he would strive all the harder to prevent the marriage.

David didn't see the way, and going round and round it wasn't helping. He forced his mind back to the matter in hand: the run of gin and snuff tomorrow night. Despite Lloyd's alertness, it could be done as long as the *Taurus* was elsewhere. Previously the navy and the excise service had kept a distance, because the navy saw itself as superior. Now that Lloyd and the captain of the *Taurus* were working together everything was more difficult. The two had to be separated.

David had offered the Blackstock Gang a percentage of the profits to set up a dummy run tomorrow night and make sure Lloyd knew. If Lloyd knew, the *Taurus* would know. Finally, this evening, the *Taurus* had taken the bait and sailed west. He'd sent men to act as lookouts for miles along the cliffs, to report if she turned back.

It was time to send the message to the Guernsey ship that all was set for tomorrow. He'd delayed because of Lucy's arrival. Her knowing he was Captain Drake didn't make things better. She wouldn't be in danger—she'd be fast asleep at two in the morning, along with all the family at the manor—but it felt wrong. That showed how wrong it would be when they were married and he had to leave their bed to continue doing this.

"Ah, hell," he muttered, and went to send Aaron out in his lugger to carry the message to the *Marianne* and set the whole thing in motion.

Daniel Potter unwound the message his pigeon keeper had brought him. Tiny writing on thin paper, but clear.

Yr dgt passed today en route to CW. FTR soon.

Lucy had somehow traveled to Devon, and there was to be a Freetrade run soon.

How the devil! His first impulse was to go to Lady Caldross's house to prove that Lucy was safely there, but that could create alarm where there clearly was none now. Thomas Forbes was one of his best men, sent to find ammunition and to report back anything of interest. Forbes had been able to take only two pigeons and keep them concealed, but he'd known this was crucial news.

Wyvern was behind this. He'd appeared to bow to force, but he'd known all along that Lucy was in his pocket, along with her dowry, and would go to him when summoned. He regretted increasing her dowry now, and giving her free control of it when she came of age. He'd been fooled by her apparent good sense, and so had Alice, for she'd been in favor of it. But they both should have remembered how infatuation could scramble a person's mind.

If they'd obtained a license, Lucy and Wyvern could already be married. If so he'd deal with that later. Now he had to act as if there was time to prevent a wedding, for that was the best hope.

FTR soon. A run soon, was there? Not surprising. Captain Drake had been away and all had been quiet. The smugglers would want action, and action would help him. In the middle of that, he could capture Lucy and bring her safely home.

He looked up at Alice's smiling face, so like their beloved daughter's. "She's addled at the moment, love, but never fear. I'll keep her safe."

He tossed the scrap of paper on the fire and left his house to call on his bride-to-be.

She met him at her door with pleased surprise. "Come in, Daniel."

Once in her simple parlor he said, "I have to go on a short business trip, my dear."

"So close to the wedding?"

"Because it's so close to the wedding. A minor business tangle, but if I don't untangle it now, it could interfere with our honeymoon, and we don't want that."

"No, of course not."

He took her hand. "I know it will be an inconvenience to you, but you have all the wedding arrangements so well in hand that I know I can rely on you."

She blushed with pleasure. "Of course you can, dear, so be on about your business and Godspeed."

He kissed her cheek. "Don't fear I'll linger overlong."

He returned to his house, giving thanks that Charlotte was a sensible woman. He packed the essentials himself, took money from his safe, left simple instructions for his clerks and managers, and departed to hire the fastest possible post chaise for Devon.

Chapter 35

Lucy awoke early to an excess of birdsong. She wouldn't have imagined that there could be an excess of song, but it was as if every bird in England had come to surround the house and compete. She shook her head, considering the fact that if the birds were chorusing the dawn, it could not be much after four in the morning. In Mayfair people would be rolling home to bed.

To her surprise, despite the hectic excitement of the past two days she'd slept well. Perhaps because of it, and from having her problems cleared away.

She sat up, arms around her knees, smiling over memories of yesterday and with pure anticipation of today. She might not manage much time alone with David, but he was to show her around the area, which would soon be her home. They would be together, perhaps all day long.

She slipped happily out of bed, but then winced as parts of her legs complained. Simply from walking up to his house! There was a challenge she'd never expected, but an easy one to defeat. She'd become a Devonshire woman in no time.

She considered her three gowns, wondering which to wear for church. It would have to be the traveling gown again. After church she'd be exploring the area, which meant rough paths, more slopes, and even wild vegetation. Remembering feeling stones through the soles of her shoes, she resolved to have some sturdy boots made as soon as possible.

Perhaps everyone else was accustomed to the birds, for when she left the room, the house seemed quiet. She'd like to go outside, so she went downstairs, where she found the front door unlocked. London houses were always locked at night, and the lower windows generally had grilles over them. Was the countryside truly so much safer?

When she stepped outside, the birds were still singing and the air was astonishingly fresh. She'd always found morning light brighter, but here it sparkled. She wasn't entirely reconciled to the lack of city conveniences, but she could understand how a more populous place might seem dirty and stale.

Was it safe to walk away from the house? The unlocked door said yes, but Lucy thought about unpredictable smugglers and circled the house to revisit the orchard.

As she passed beneath the honeysuckle arch she set to thinking about how to have an orchard and a flower garden up near the Crag. By the time she was startled by a gardener pushing a wheelbarrow, she'd dreamed time away going over past pleasures and anticipating a lifetime of them. The young man bobbed his head and gave her good morning before hurrying on his way with a barrow of what looked and smelled like manure. Not everything in a garden was sweet.

Did his appearance mean the family might be up? She was quite hungry.

She walked back to the house and followed the path round to the front. Before she got there, a back door opened and a young maid called, "Would you like to come this way, miss? It's quicker to the breakfast parlor."

Lucy entered a large, aromatic kitchen. An elderly

cook smiled. "Good morning, miss! What do you like for your breakfast, then? Sir Nathaniel likes his beef and Mister Henry his ham, but the ladies have bread and eggs. And chocolate."

"Just bread, thank you. And coffee, if that's possible."

"Course it is, dearie. Off you go."

Chuckling at having clearly been added to the family, Lucy let the young maid direct her to the breakfast parlor. She'd never pined for a large family, but now she saw how lovely it could be.

David woke to the day with foreboding. There was nothing eerie about that. He wasn't at ease about the run tonight, but the Horde had been inactive for too long and he knew many muttered that he was too cautious. Even the *Taurus* sailing by and firing blanks at them hadn't driven home how much more dangerous the trade was now. He didn't care what they thought of him, but he didn't want them taking mad risks again.

Then there was Lucy.

So much was better now she knew the truth about him, but she didn't know that her father opposed the match and might take strong measures to prevent it. Or that Potter might cut all connection if she defied him.

Devil take it. Had he held that information back for fear that she'd choose her father over him?

She'd be better off if they'd never met, but he couldn't want that. The thought of life without her was intolerable, but he truly was a bastard for letting control slip and taking away all choice.

He realized something else.

If anything happened to him before they wed and she was with child, she'd be completely ruined. Or more likely forced into a hasty marriage with whoever would take her. No, his Lucy wouldn't do that. So it would be ruin.

"You really are a bastard," he muttered at himself as he got out of bed.

Death was rare during a run, but that was because most runs went off smoothly. When one had gone awry, John Clyst had died. And if Lloyd learned of the plan and turned up, he and his men would fire. Anything could happen in the dark. If that damned ship returned, it might put balls in its guns once it was sure it had an illegal target.

License.

But even if he could persuade Lucy to marry that way, it couldn't happen before tomorrow. They could marry on a Sunday, but only between nine and noon. There was no way to get a license that quickly.

So he must keep as safe as possible.

He couldn't put command of tonight's run in anyone else's hands, so he could only do his best to keep out of any danger. He'd keep to his watching station on the cliff top, apart from the action down on the beach, which would be the target of any attack.

And he had the luxury of spending most of today with Lucy.

He washed and dressed, and then breakfasted with Fred, dealing with the essential business of the earldom. They also discussed the run. He'd not meant to involve Fred, but his weeks away had made that necessary. And now Fred wouldn't be left out entirely.

"You're not to get directly involved," David said. "You're to keep a monitoring station here, with Ada up the top to watch for distant signals, and with a few lads ready to run messages."

"You'll risk them and not me?"

"It's in their blood and they can run this area in the dark. They do it for fun sometimes"

"I'm learning the skill."

"You stay here and dispatch messengers if Lloyd is

anywhere in the area, or if the *Taurus* is spotted sailing this way."

"We're hoping no one will spot the *Marianne* coming in, so how do your watchers keep track of the *Taurus*?"

"Every one of them has young, sharp eyes, plus the *Marianne* will hoist dark sails and the navy ship will have white. Even starlight will show white sails." David rose. "I'm off to the manor to go to church with the family."

Fred smiled. "You're a lucky man."

David didn't smile back. "Pray my luck holds."

He walked down to the manor, greeted all the way by people bright-eyed at the prospect of some action at last. Profit, yes, but action, too. He felt it in himself. His sensible side lingered on danger and safety, but there was nothing like the time just before a run—except the knife-edged excitement during one.

But then he saw the woman he loved, bright and beautiful in the morning sunshine, smiling a welcome, anticipating their day, and that was finer than all. She was wearing the brown gown and dull bonnet she'd arrived in. He'd seen her in much finer clothing, but she'd never looked so beautiful. From beneath the bonnet, her hair curled loose around her face, a perfect frame for her sparkling eyes and smiling lips. She was a goddess, and he was proud as a peacock about escorting her to church and parading her around his villages, his for all to see.

Lucy knew she was showing every bit of her love and delight, but there were no secrets between them anymore, especially not that.

They linked arms as they walked with his family and their servants toward the church's summoning bell. The path took them through the manor's gardens and then down a footpath between cottage gardens, some better tended than others.

As they entered the mellow churchyard she asked, "How old is the church?"

"Only a bit over a hundred. The old one fell down. Inadequate foundations."

"I could wish someone had been as careless with Crag Wyvern."

He smiled. "There is the possibility that the sea will wash away the cliff from under it in time."

Not in time for us, Lucy thought.

Even though the church was newer than the one she attended in London, the service felt deeply traditional to her. Probably most of the congregation had roots here that went back many centuries, perhaps even to before the conquest. She'd read that there were stone quarries nearby that had been used by the Romans.

After the service, they walked out into the sunshine, and as usual people dallied, chatting. She was introduced to the doctor and his family. He hoped to attract some of the sea-bathing trade to the area. Lucy was all in favor of more business, but she silently wondered how it would blend with smuggling.

Eventually, people went off to their homes. She and David lingered and he showed her around the graves. There was the usual collection of small and large headstones from many centuries.

"Are your family buried here?" she asked. When he nodded, she realized that one day she would rest here, too. It was an odd thought, but not unpleasant.

"The Clysts are scattered around, but this is the Kerslake area."

A classic plinth had KERSLAKE carved on each side, but it was surrounded by unpretentious stones. Lucy read the names of Kerslakes going back to the fifteen hundreds. The baronetcy came in the late seventeenth century, and the names Nathaniel and Henry seemed to

alternate from then on. Many graves held families, but
one small headstone recorded only one name.

JOSEPH KERSLAKE, BORN AND DIED, FEBRUARY 1790
SON OF MELCHISADECK CLYST AND ISABELLE KERSLAKE

"I see they didn't try to hide the irregularity."

"What point? No one knew then why Mel and Belle
didn't marry, but they were treated as husband and wife.
Some people thought her wanton, but she was always
faithful to Mel. She made a poor first choice, but had the
courage to break free and claim her right to happiness."

Lucy studied him. "You admire her."

"I admire strong women. I think you might understand one another very well."

"Perhaps, but I would never neglect my children."

"We'll never know what she might have done if she
hadn't been able to give us into the manor's care. I doubt
she would have abandoned us to the parish, and if she'd
thought of it, Mel would never have allowed it. However,
I can't imagine her a loving mother. I spent time with
Mel, but if I encountered her, I might as well have been
any other village lad. I'm deeply grateful to have had
Aunt Miriam instead."

"Your Kerslake family is lovely. As you said, the sort
of good people who hold communities together." They
strolled along a path around the church, and she decided
to share an uneasy thought. No secrets, she remembered.

"I was always happy at home, but now I wonder what it
would have been like with brothers and sisters. Better? Perhaps, but I suspect my father would not have been quite so
keen to conduct much of his business from home."

"You're probably right. I remember times when the
four of us were hurtling around up to mischief with Aunt
Miriam and Uncle Nathaniel yelling at us to be quiet.

Unless the weather was atrocious, we were just shooed outside. We were all happy to explore like wild things, rolling home as the light went, scraped, bruised, muddy, and contentedly tired."

Lucy thought of the girl with the kite. She would enjoy such a life. "No school for you, either?" she asked.

"Of course. The vicar tutored us all when young; then Henry and I went off to school in Honiton. Amelia and Susan both spent a little time at a girls' school there, but neither enjoyed it, so they were allowed to return home."

"But you weren't."

"No, and I needed a good education. I'd my way to make. I refused to go to university, however, and learned land management from my uncle and others."

"Yet you bought a book on drainage."

"On new systems. There's always improvement these days, isn't there?"

"Always," she agreed. "But for the moment this is lovely. Parade me proudly around Church Wyvern as your bride-to-be, and then take me down to the village on the beach. I've never been on a beach."

"Never been on a beach?"

"You see all the wonders you have to show me?"

They retraced their way between the cottage gardens. People were working in some of them, despite it being Sunday. And why not? Surely God approved of wholesome work. They all smiled and called a greeting.

One gap-toothed man cried out a particularly cheery, "A grand day, sir! Grand!"

"Everyone seems happy," Lucy said.

"Fair weather."

A stout young woman called out a similarly cheery greeting as she sat spinning in the sun, healthy, happy children running around her. Then four lads hurtled around a corner in a game, shouting something about the excise men, almost colliding with them.

"Sorry, cap'n!" one said.

David clipped him around the head. "Be off to your homes."

The boys ran.

Lucy was startled by the blow, but then realized that the boy had called him "captain."

"You could be exposed so easily."

"That's why they have to learn. I want them to be learning other things, too. We need a school, and special help for the brightest ones. I want their world full of things other than smuggling."

"My father cares about the children, too. He sponsors many charities that house and educate orphans and show kindness while they do it."

"Being a foundling himself."

"Yes. He's particularly keen to provide opportunities for the clever ones to do as well as he has. I think you'll find you have much in common. That you'll like each other."

He halted to look at her. "You think so? Are you sure he'll approve of your marrying me?"

She couldn't say a wholehearted yes as yet. "Why not?"

"I'm the Peasant Earl, and possibly a mad one."

"If the madness worries him, we'll tell him the truth."

"Will we also tell him I'm Captain Drake?"

She had to pull a face. "Not if we can help it. But I doubt he's as pure as new snow. He might understand."

"Even if he accepts that, he'll not like my taking you so far from him."

"Stop!" she said. "This argument is pointless. We're to marry, and whatever reservations my father might have, he'll come around. He wants me to marry a title. He hopes a grandson will one day be an earl."

They were out of sight of others for the moment, so she paused for a kiss.

"Don't worry so, my love. All will be perfect."

Chapter 36

The path down to the village of Dragon's Cove wasn't as steep as the one up to the Crag, but the mild breeze that had stirred the laundry was brisk here.

Small whitewashed cottages lined the road and were tucked, as he'd said, up the stream's valley for protection from a stormy sea. None had much of a garden, but women sat outside in the sun, working and gossiping. A few men dawdled around who surely, like the boys, should have had tasks to do, even on a Sunday.

Everyone greeted them, but these people, men and women, seemed tougher, perhaps more windblown or even salted, and taciturn. Smugglers every one.

She smelled the salt along with seaweed and fish, and wasn't sure whether she liked it.

"What do you think?" he asked.

"That this is not as comfortable a place to live as the other village," she said.

"You're right, but it's their place. They wouldn't want to move."

They held hands as they walked down to the water's edge. The dry, pebbly sand slipped and slithered beneath her boots, and again the soles weren't thick enough. The walking was easier near the water where the sand was damp.

She shielded her eyes with her hand and looked out to sea. "No navy ship today."

"No, she's moved on."

She looked toward the horizon. "That's not her far out?"

"You have sharp eyes. That will be a merchant vessel heading toward Portsmouth or perhaps all the way around to London."

To the docks in London, which seemed in another world. She was bound to miss it at times, but her life would be here, at the side of the man she loved, working to better the lives of everyone hereabouts.

Lucy didn't think she'd make a good teacher, but she could oversee a school, and make sure lessons included the teaching of the skills needed for business. She'd support David in helping those able to progress to practical professions such as medicine and engineering, and to learn all the requirements of the modern world.

"I have something you'll like," he said. "I hope."

She cocked her head, smiling. "What?"

"Come."

They climbed back up the beach, surely exerting a whole new set of muscles, and went toward a low tavern. "The George and Dragon," she read. "Is everything here about dragons?"

"Why not? It adds a touch of glamour to the ordinary."

The inside was certainly ordinary, with a few barrels and simple wooden tables and benches. It was deserted, but he picked up something from a table.

"A kite!" she said.

"I remembered it was down here and came last night to find it. It's not been flown for years. Shall we try it?"

"Of course! There's a good wind."

"That's what I thought. It would be even better up

outside the Crag, but we don't want any danger of being carried off."

"We'd let go."

"Would we?" he asked, and she knew what he meant.

He carried the kite out and she saw that the design painted on the lozenge shape was again a dragon, with the kite's tail the dragon's tail. The colors were faded, however. This was a boyhood toy, and it had been left in the George and Dragon. His true father had been the tavern keeper there, and he'd spent time there, boy and youth. He loved his aunt and uncle as parents, and seemed to feel nothing for his mother, but there'd been a bond of sorts with his father.

"Do you want to do it?" he asked her. "It'll be easy in this wind."

"I take that as an insult, sir. You do it."

He grinned and moved backward, holding the kite up high. As he'd said, the winds caught it immediately and tugged it upward. He had only to let the string out carefully and it soared. In time he trapped the string to hold the kite in place.

"Come and hold it."

So she did, close to him, their hands together controlling the pull as they looked up. The underside was painted with the same dragon picture, a wyvern that tugged against their hold, wanting to soar free.

As if sharing the thought, he asked, "Release it, or pull it in?"

"So tempting to let it go, but I want it for our children. I want them to fly it here, on this beach."

Together they worked to bring it in, having to struggle against the kite's desire to fly free.

"It should be possible to use kites to fly!" she shouted as they were carried forward at one point.

"It should. They're a form of sail, aren't they?"

When they had it down, tamed and on the ground, she

was panting for breath, but laughing. "There's such amazing power in the world. Steam, water, wind. The future is going to be wondrous once we know how to use it."

"The future is going to be wondrous anyway, Lucy Potter."

She smiled into his sea blue eyes. "Yes. Yes, it is."

They could have kissed, but she was aware of watching eyes all around. Perhaps they were friendly, happy to see the captain with his lady. But all the same, she turned and started to gather up the kite.

As they carried it back to the tavern, she glanced at the cliff on her left. There were figures up there. With ropes.

"A competition?" she asked.

David looked up. "Training for one. Just lads."

The figures went down nimbly, kicking off from the cliff now and then. Once down, they went up again, almost as easily as they'd gone down, and pulled the ropes up after them. Training over? It seemed odd, but she'd learn the way of this place in time.

When they entered the tavern, a short, fat woman greeted them cheerfully. "Heard you had a lady with you, zur."

David introduced Lucy to his cousin Rachel Clyst, who then insisted on their sharing a toast in cider.

Lucy had never had cider. "It's pleasant. I think I prefer it to beer."

"Not harmless, though," he said, when she considered a second helping. "You need to be able to walk back to the manor."

Lucy thought he was joking, but as she walked out she felt a little unsteady. "My, my."

"Rachel honored you with the strong stuff."

"I am honored. This has been wonderful, hasn't it? I feel at home already. You will come back to London with me, won't you, and ask my father's blessing? Then we can be married as soon as the banns are read. Isn't that *wonderful*!"

She spread her arms and he caught her around the waist. "You, my goddess, are drunk."

"Only a little," she said, smiling at him, "and mostly drunk on love. I'd like to marry here, but I think it has to be in my parish for decency. Nothing too fussy, even though I'm sure my father would prefer pomp."

"You have it all planned out?"

"I've given it some thought," she admitted, with a smile. "In the night. Will your family travel to London for it?"

"I doubt they can get away at this time of year, but Amelia would enjoy it."

"Then we'll have a celebration back here when we return."

"After a honeymoon?"

"I hadn't thought about that. No. Or yes, but here."

"At Crag Wyvern?" he asked skeptically.

"Why not? Such wonderful rooms to explore, and we'll have changes to plan."

She looked up at the Crag, which presented its main entrance to them now. "We could knock out the front. The doors and portcullis are useless anyway, and no one would mourn the great hall. If we admit light that way, we won't need more windows in the outer walls."

"If we take away one wall, the whole place might fall down."

"Then so be it." She focused on him. "Do you mind? My father says I sometimes become overenthusiastic about a plan."

"Which he never does?"

"Never. He keeps a cool head about everything but the family. Only my mother's death pushed him to extremes. I can understand the depth of his loss even better now. The thought of losing you . . ." He seemed troubled so she added, "But we have a long and glorious future."

"Certain of that, are you?"

"Yes. In our glorious new Crag Wyvern. We need to change the name."

He grabbed her hand and pulled her onward. "Enough for now."

She would have liked to spend the whole day with him, but after an old-fashioned afternoon dinner at the manor he said he had work to do. As earl or smuggler, she wondered, but she didn't ask.

"Troubled cows," he reminded her.

"No one else can do that?"

"They may have to be killed. My authority will ease matters."

"Are you still the estate manager?"

"Will you scold me for that, too?" he asked, but he was smiling as he kissed her by the garden gate.

She smiled back, but said, "You need to shed some roles."

"I will, as soon as I can."

Lucy watched him go, then indulged in just the sort of pining that she'd thought stupid in heroines. That made her smile, because she had her happy ending already, with her peasant prince.

Lucy's father pushed close his spyglass, not with any force, but with resolution. There they were, and Wyvern was kissing Lucy shamelessly. Were they only waiting for a license to marry in that church, gleeful at thwarting him? It couldn't be today, and he'd make sure there'd be no wedding tomorrow.

He hid his glass and rose to walk the cliff in open view with Forbes. Forbes had made himself known here as a scholar. When they'd met a local man an hour ago he'd introduced his companion as an Oxford colleague, interested in seabirds. That gave an excuse for the spyglass if it was seen.

Various local people had given them cautious looks, which wasn't surprising with a smuggling run arranged for tonight. Forbes had confirmed that, so Daniel Potter had told him to send word to Lloyd. Chaos tonight would serve them well, and if Captain Drake was caught, it would be perfect.

No one seemed hostile, however. Forbes was an amiable man who put people at ease, even made them feel they were friends. It was a gift that made him ideal for this sort of job.

So they'd stroll the cliffs for a bit longer, watching birds, making notes, drawing diagrams, and passing the time. Then they'd retreat until later. Until the middle of the night, when the smugglers went into action and the village of Church Wyvern would empty of all the able-bodied men and women. He'd make his move then, and carry Lucy away, back to London, where he could keep her safe until her madness had passed.

Lucy returned to the house and sought the privacy of her room. She opened her journal, but was back to hearts and flowers. If her muse was intent on drawing, she'd put it to work. She began planning improvements to Crag Wyvern. If they could remove one wall, perhaps they could have a real garden.

She worked at it until Amelia came up to say her father had arrived home.

She found Sir Nathaniel as amiable and solid as she'd expected. How he and Lady Belle had come from the same nest, she couldn't imagine, but only think of her mother and Aunt Mary. He welcomed her into the family heartily, teasing her about David, but also teasing Henry about a Miss Gladford. Lucy remembered Henry spending quite some time with another family outside church.

Two newly wed couples living close-by. Children in time, cousins, running wild around the area. They wouldn't all live in the same house, of course, but they'd be to and fro easily. Her children would scamper the hills with ease, play on the beach, fly kites, and probably take out boats to fish or just for pleasure.

Lucy had hoped David might return in the evening, but he didn't. She couldn't go out in the garden to pine to the stars, for the sky had clouded over and there was even a spit of rain. She resigned herself to a game of speculation. Aunt Miriam, Uncle Nathaniel, and Henry lacked a fierce competitive instinct, but Amelia was rash. When she finally ended up with the highest trump she laughed with pleasure and scooped in the counters in the middle.

"You do realize," said her brother, Henry, "that you've speculated more than you've won. You made a loss."

"But I won," Amelia said cheerfully, "and that counts more than profit."

Lucy couldn't help but chuckle. "I'm only imagining what my father would say to such a sentiment."

"A hardheaded businessman, I assume," said Sir Nathaniel and Lucy detected a bit of disapproval.

She ignored it. "He's had to be, making his way up from nothing." She saw they didn't understand, so she told them his history, which changed their attitudes.

"A remarkable and hardworking man," said Aunt Miriam with approval.

"He is."

Even so, Lucy wasn't sure there would be true harmony between him and the Kerslakes. They were very different people, grown from different roots in different soils, and her father and Charlotte wouldn't want to spend time here. That was a shame, but she'd be able to visit London a few times a year, which would be enough.

When she went up to bed, a maid brought her washing water.

"Anything else you need, miss?"

Lucy thought the question particularly keen. Did the maid have a swain waiting at the garden gate, even this late?

"No, thank you."

"You sleep well, then, miss."

Lucy smiled her thanks and went to the window to dream, but, alas, the clouds had obscured the stars. She couldn't even pine toward Crag Wyvern, for her view took in only part of the garden and the stables.

She drew the curtains and prepared for bed. Soon she was snuggled down beneath the quilt made by David's grandmother, dreaming of her future.

Chapter 37

A noise woke her from sleep. In the house?
No, outside. Was it morning?

Clearly not.

A jingle then a thump.

She slipped out of bed and went to peer around the window curtain. It was still pitch-dark, still no stars—but then she saw a flicker of light that illuminated someone. The light seemed to be from a lantern, but what was the person doing?

She heard the clop of horses' hooves and the jingle again. Horses.

One or more men were taking the horses! She rose to give the alarm, but then she guessed the truth. Of course.

A moonless night.

The air of excitement.

Whispering servants.

Everyone but she had known that tonight contraband would come ashore.

She felt irritated that David hadn't told her, but she put that aside. He'd probably been trying to protect her from worry, the foolish man. Though she was worried now. He'd be Captain Drake tonight, and thus in danger.

He's done it many times before.

He'll have planned everything carefully.

He'll take no unnecessary risks.

Especially not now, she thought, with their wedding to look forward to.

It seemed wrong to watch Sir Nathaniel's horses being led away, but she knew that horses were taken as if by right to help carry the goods. The owners either dared not object or agreed willingly for payment of some of the contraband. Was Uncle Nathaniel out with the smugglers? That seemed unlikely, but perhaps Henry was. Or perhaps the manor played only a passive part.

She told herself this was all routine here, but she couldn't help worrying.

Something could go wrong, and there were cases of peers standing trial. They were tried in the House of Lords, but if convicted, the penalties were the same. She was sure there were other dangers. If the Preventive officer and his men turned up, shots would be fired and in this darkness anyone could be hit. In this darkness, people could fall off cliffs.

Those men "practicing" on ropes. They'd been preparing. Would David be climbing a rope in the dark?

She desperately wanted to dress and rush out to protect him, but what on earth could she do but be trouble?

Trust, he'd once said, and now she knew what he'd meant. She had to trust in his skill and competence even though she felt as if doing nothing could drive her mad.

No question of returning to bed. Pointless though it was, she had to sit by the window, to stare into the darkness and listen, praying not to hear gunshots.

She didn't dare light a candle. Her clock ticked so slowly, then chimed twice. Two in the morning and all's well. That would be the cry in London, and it would have reassured her to hear it here. Here she had no idea if all was well or not. She fumbled for her clothes and dressed.

If anything did go amiss, she wanted to be ready to go to him.

*   *   *

The church clock chimed two, and people began to slip out of houses, heading for their positions on cliffs or beach. David was already on the cliff top in front of Crag Wyvern. His eyes were well adjusted to the dark, but he could see little. The damned cloud stole the starlight. That concealed the *Marianne* and the gathering Horde, but it could hide danger, too. He felt blindfolded.

As always, they mostly communicated by sounds—the yips and hoots of night creatures told him when groups were in place. Occasionally a pinhole in a closed lantern would send a specific message. Thus far all was well, but those brief flashes seemed too bright in the dense dark. If Lloyd had caught wind of the truth, he'd see the signals, and even though the Horde had its own code, he'd know something was up—and where.

The *Marianne* had flashed a brief message that she was in position out at sea. He hadn't signaled for her to come in yet. His people weren't all in place and he hadn't received confirmation that the perimeter was clear, that there was no sign of Lloyd and his men nearby.

A prickling on his neck was warning of danger, but was that a real premonition or because Lucy being nearby made him nervous? She wouldn't be involved, she must be fast asleep, but her presence was disturbing his mind when it needed to be clear and focused. He could almost hear Mel growl to put it out of mind. When captaining a run, put everything else out of mind.

"Nothing from the Crag?" he murmured to the boy stationed beside him to look in that direction.

"No, cap'n," said Jack Applin, bursting with pride to be given this responsibility. He was a good lad, despite his father's recklessness.

It was time, but David hadn't been told the ropemen were ready. If anything went wrong, many of the men on the beach could escape a trap by going up the ropes.

He spoke to another boy. "Watch over to your right,

to the top of Puck's Point. Tell me as soon as you see a light."

"Aye, aye, cap'n."

Young eyes, best and keenest around, but giving them these tasks kept some of the boys out of danger. No matter what he commanded, all but the youngest, and some girls, too, came out to take part. Well, he'd done the same as a lad, and so had Susan sometimes.

He swept his spyglass across the invisible horizon, straining for a glimpse of the navy ship. The *Taurus* had sailed east and not been seen to return, but that prickling was warning of something.

Damnation.

This was no time to let love turn him into a nervous ditherer.

Lucy was by the window, straining to hear anything. It would all be happening on the beach, however, over the hill. Would the sound of a gunshot travel here?

Somewhere an owl hooted, and then there was an odd noise like a bark, but not. Perhaps a fox or badger. She knew they were nocturnal, but not what sound they made. She didn't know this world at all.

Then she saw another flicker of light out near the stables. Were the horses back already? Was that good news, or had something gone wrong?

The light near the stables began to wave wildly.

An alarm signal?

What should she do?

She leaned out, trying to see more, then started at a loud clatter below her window. It sounded as if someone had knocked over a bucket or tool.

"Help! Please!" someone called, but managing to do it quietly.

She tried to be as quiet. "Who is it? What's the matter?"

"Captain Drake," the hoarse voice called. "Need help."

David! Not David, but someone on his behalf. Was he wounded?

She turned to run out of the room, but was instantly frustrated by the dark. She fumbled her way to her door and opened it. Blessed sanity, a small lamp lit the corridor and stairwell. It didn't provide much light, but after such darkness it was enough. She ran down the stairs and toward the back of the house.

The kitchen was dark, the fire cold and no lamp lit. No servants, either. All out enjoying the exciting folly of the Freetrade. She thought of running back up again in search of the family, but the need had seemed urgent. David could be bleeding to death out there. Her heart beat fit to burst as she felt her way around the table and to the door. She opened it.

"Who's there?" she gasped. "Where are you?"

She saw the glimmer of the lantern to her left, and the man gasped, "Here . . . wounded . . ."

She stumbled toward the voice, straining to see. As she did so, an arm came around her waist and a heavy hand covered her mouth before she could scream.

"Don't struggle, Lucy. I don't want you hurt."

She knew that voice. Her father! She tried to shout at him through the hand, kicking in hope of striking him, wishing she was wearing boots and not slippers.

Finally she was able to whirl around. For a moment her mouth was free. She sucked in breath to scream, but a cloth was thrust into her mouth and she was wound in a cloth like a swaddled baby or a corpse in a shroud, helpless.

Her father. Efficient as always. She could at least growl.

"I'm sorry, pet," he said softly, touching her hair. "I'd rather have tried sense, but I know how one is when besotted. People are coming. Make haste, but carefully."

The man who'd captured her picked her up in his arms and carried her after her father, who carried a shielded lantern. Just two? Surely she could escape two.

David . . .

But David wasn't in danger. This had been a trick, and she'd fallen for it.

She heard noises from the house. Someone called from a window, "Is anyone out there?" Henry or Sir Nathaniel.

Amelia called, "What's happening out there?"

All in the house, all doubtless in their nightwear. They'd probably take silence as reassurance, and if they went out to investigate, there'd be nothing to see. A sensible heroine would have managed to leave some sign, if only a slipper, but hers were still laced on.

This couldn't be happening.

She couldn't be snatched like this without anyone knowing.

But yes, she could. Everyone around here was either involved in the smuggling or carefully paying no attention to noises. Perhaps Amelia and Henry had been awake as she had been, listening, but once silence fell they'd assume all was well.

She growled again and squirmed out of pure fury. How *dare* her father treat her this way? Like a child!

And why? He wanted her to marry a lord.

He must have discovered she'd come here, so perhaps it was simply outrage at that. Whatever his reasons, this couldn't work. He couldn't keep her trussed up forever. As soon as she was free she'd return to David and never speak to her father again.

Better by far to escape now.

Where in the village were they?

Her father was leading the way, carrying the lantern low with only one window open, so it cast little light. She tried to remember the direction she'd walked with David. When her porter had to turn sideways a little so her head and feet cleared the sides, she realized they were on the narrow path between the gardens. The maneuver brought her feet closer to her father. With relish, she drew in her legs and kicked him as hard as she could, truly wishing she wore boots.

He stumbled forward, but got his balance and turned, his face grotesque in the lantern light from below.

But his voice was gentle. "Ah, pet, that's why it had to be this way. You're my blood and bone and bound to fight. But you can't win this battle."

"Oh, yes, I can," she tried, but it came out as a mumble.

He stroked her hair again.

She wished she could spit at him.

He turned to walk on, and she made herself calm down.

His blood and bone, was she? Then she could be as steady as he. She took slow breaths and thought.

Her knife! Her journal was back in her room, but her penknife was in her pocket. She was swaddled, but not tightly, so her arms could move. She wriggled around, hoping the man thought she was struggling, and finally got her hand into her pocket. She grasped her knife and pulled it out, trying to think how best to use it.

If she remembered the village correctly, they would soon have to pass by the front doors of a row of cottages. There would be some people there. There had to be women looking after young children and also those too old for adventure. She need only let out one really strong cry for help to have hope.

She got her hands together in front and opened the knife, being careful of the sharp blade. She planned her movements and waited for her moment, when they were closest to the houses. Here, as they passed the first doorway.

Kicking her feet to distract the men, she stabbed the

blade up through the cloth, the sharp edge of the blade pointing in the direction of her chin. Then she pulled it forward. It cut cleanly through the layers of cloth. She reached up through the hole with her left hand to grab the rag that tied the cloth in her mouth and then sliced through it with the blade in her right.

She pulled out the cloth and screamed as loudly as she could. "Help! Help!" Then inspired, she added, "Captain Drake needs you!"

"Lucy!" her father bellowed, which was stupid of him.

The man carrying her seemed frozen.

"This'll do no good," her father snapped. "Come on, man. She's still mostly bound."

But people were coming out of buildings, some dressed and some in nightclothes, some with lanterns, but all with a weapon of some kind, from a skillet to a pistol.

"Don't hurt them!" she cried, not sure which side she meant. She gathered control. "Put me down," she said to the man who carried her, "and unwind me."

He obeyed, looking at her with wide eyes.

She realized she was still brandishing the knife, though what he thought she could do with a two-inch blade, she wasn't sure.

Once she was untangled she shook herself, wondering what to do now.

"What's amiss?" an old man in the crowd asked. "What's gone wrong?"

"Nothing to do with the run," she assured them. "I'm Miss Potter. . . ."

A woman said. "We know who you are, miss, and reckon your business is the cap'n's business. What do we do with these 'uns?"

Lord above. It sounded as if an order to kill would be obeyed.

"Let them go if they're willing. Well?" she asked her

father. She did her best to send the message not to make a bad situation worse.

"Damnation, but you're grand, Lucy. Foolish, but grand."

"Perhaps like my mother? She wouldn't be pleased about this."

He flinched. "She would want you out of this mess."

"Whatever the truth of that, I've made my choice, as she did."

He stepped closer and she raised the blade. They both looked at it in astonishment.

"Perhaps you are suited to be a dragon's countess, you willful chit. That being the case, call the alarm. The excise man's alerted."

"Your doing?"

"Yes."

She wanted to scream at him, but said, "Leave while you can."

She could see him itch to grab for her, despite her knife and the encircling villagers. He was not a man used to defeat. Was he armed? Was his man? Would they fight?

"Go," she said, "or I'll never speak to you again."

"Lucy . . ." When she didn't weaken, he gestured to his man and walked away. The villagers made way to let them through, then closed afterward as if protecting her.

But they looked to her for orders.

She remembered what her father had said. Oh, God.

"How do we call off the run?"

"It might be too late," an old man said.

"We have to try."

"There's a signal from the Crag for that," he said. "And from some other places. But someone else'll have to go. I can scarcely walk the street."

"I could go, Ma!"

"And I!"

"And I!"

Lucy looked in horror at the eager boys, all in night-shirts, none older than eight, surely. Because the older ones had work to do this night?

She saw a mother's hand touch one lad's hair—the one who'd been spinning—but then the woman said, "Off you go then, Thad, fast as you can to the Crag. You know the door in at the side?"

The lad nodded, beaming at the treat and ran off.

"It's so dark," Lucy protested.

"Bless you, miss—he'll be all right with that. They play in the dark round here, in case."

Training to be criminals!

Two other lads were already off, one carrying a lantern.

"They'll give the signal from Puck's Point, miss. Maybe sooner from there."

They were all looking to her for more instructions. She had no idea what to do.

Then Amelia ran up, lantern in hand. "What's happening?"

Could she keep her father's name out of this? "I can't explain now. But I got word the Preventive man knows. The run must be canceled. A boy's gone up to the Crag. Others somewhere—"

"Puck's Point, Miss Amelia," a man said.

"Good, good," Amelia said. "I wish Susan was still around. I've never done this sort of thing."

"Lloyd'll not be coming through the village way," a crook-backed man said, leaning heavily on his cane. "There'll be watchers up there. So likely down by Markem Slide to take 'em from the side."

"The next cove over," Amelia said. "Little more than a fissure, and hard going. We can't stop them, but if the run's canceled, they'll be too late to do harm."

"What can we do?" Lucy asked.

"Nothing more," Amelia said. "It should be—"

A *boom* shook the air.

"What was that?" Lucy cried.

"Ship's cannon," a man said.

Chapter 38

"Please God, no." Lucy grabbed a lantern from someone's hand and set off at a run toward Dragon's Cove.

She heard Amelia cry, "Lucy!" but she couldn't stop. She had to be there. If David was injured, she had to be there.

She realized she still had the open knife clasped in her hand and paused long enough to close it and put it back in her pocket.

Amelia caught up. "All right, but go more slowly. David doesn't need to find your corpse."

"Like Romeo and Juliet!" Lucy said with a wild laugh.

"What?" Another cannon boom. "Never mind. Come on."

When they reached the ridge where the road sloped down to Dragon's Cove they saw people coming up. Lanterns hung here and there outside houses, providing some light. Perhaps that was normal here in the night, so to darken them would be suspicious.

"Run's off," a man said, hurrying by, but in an orderly manner. "All to go home."

Amelia grabbed another. "Are the goods landed?"

"Nay. The warning came. Navy's chasing the Guernsey ship."

"Not firing at land?"

"Nay, they'd not do that."

Lucy and Amelia paused for breath, letting the orderly retreat flow past.

Lucy's sense of panic eased, but she shivered. "I'm not sure I can live through this again."

"You'll have to," Amelia said. "And mostly they're not like this. You'd hardly notice a thing, and the next day the only sign is that everyone's yawning over their work."

"Those children!"

"Having the night of their lives. It's in the blood."

"In yours, too?"

"A bit," Amelia said, "but not enough to take serious risks."

"Your family must all know."

"About smuggling? Of course."

"About David."

"It's not mentioned."

"What are they doing now?"

"They went back to bed. Better not to know."

"But you came out."

"I needed to know. But we'd better go home."

Lucy shook her head. "I can't." The flow of people was dwindling, so she wove her way through them down toward the beach.

Amelia caught up again with the lantern. "David will be up on top. That's Captain Drake's position. Observing and directing."

"So he'll be safe?"

"Of course. Come away."

There weren't many people coming up the road anymore. Those from Dragon's Cove would have slipped back into their houses. Perhaps some had gone up the ropes to escape another way. The beach ahead was impenetrable darkness. It was impossible to see where land ended and sea began.

Then the blackness ahead was broken by a bright

flame, and night shook under a tremendous boom. A moment later a crash sent bits of rock and dust showering down on the houses.

People cried out.

"They're firing at the village!" Amelia screamed. "Come on!"

Lucy paused, thinking of all the people in the houses, but they all knew and must do as best they could. She picked up her skirts and raced back up the hill.

Another thumping *boom*. No rock and dust pouring down here, thank heavens, but a mighty crack somewhere higher and tumbling rocks that went on and on. Pray God not onto someone's house. Panting, almost deafened by cannon fire and her own heart, she stumbled over the crest of the hill and stopped, sucking in breaths, listening for another shot.

"They . . . must be *mad*!" she gasped.

"There'll be hell to pay," Amelia agreed and Lucy was comforted to hear that she was out of breath, too. "But that captain's developed a grudge against us. The candle in my lantern's gone out." They were in darkness again.

"I might just sit here until dawn," Lucy said. "It can't be many hours off on a short June night."

Amelia was fumbling around. "This has a drawer beneath for a tinderbox. Now to see if I can work it in the dark. When I think about it, there's really no use to it if I can't."

"True," Lucy said and laughed. "I'm sorry, it's not funny."

"But we're alive, and perhaps nothing too terrible has happened."

Lucy held the lantern as Amelia scraped the flint and sparks flew. The tinder caught and she puffed at the precious glow. "There!" By the fragile light she grabbed the candle and lit it. The steady glow seemed shockingly warm in the darkness, and they both laughed with relief.

Amelia carefully replaced the candle in its holder and shut the lantern door.

"How precious light is," Lucy said. "We take it for granted, but without it how could we survive?"

"Even the ancients had fire."

"Given by Prometheus, who as punishment was chained to a rock by Zeus where an eagle ate his liver every day. It grew back, of course."

"That is rather horrid."

"Those ancient gods were. It was a lesson to mankind not to strive too far. It was ignored, and thus we have wonders."

"You sound uncertain."

"It might be better if wars had to be fought with sticks and stones. I'm sorry. I think I'm addled by all this."

"Come home. All's well."

"No it's not," Lucy said, but she didn't want to talk about her father yet. Ever, really, though she'd have to. How could he do such a thing?

When they came to the fork in the path, she heard cracking, crumbling noises up above. From Crag Wyvern? She had to go up to see.

She stumbled once, for Amelia and the candle were behind her, then had to stop to catch her breath. Together, they went on, and when Crag Wyvern came into view, they both halted.

In a macabre shadow play against wild lanterns, they saw a chaos of reflections and scurrying figures, but one thing was clear.

"That cannonball took out the south wall," Amelia said.

Bits were still breaking free and tumbling to crash and shatter below, but inside, the ranks of windows caught the light.

They made their way carefully closer.

"I don't hear screams," Lucy said. "Perhaps no one

was injured." But she couldn't help thinking that the dead don't scream.

"What are you two doing here?"

David's voice made Lucy jump, but he was alive! Despite his voice nearby, it took her a moment to see him, for he was dressed entirely in black, including a black cap over his hair, and his face was blackened, too. She flung herself into his arms. "Thank God you're safe!"

Amelia asked, "Is anybody hurt?"

"By God's mercy, nothing serious, but I'll have that captain court-martialed. It was only by luck that Ada had left her signaling position up there. Why aren't you both safe in bed?"

"It's a long story," Lucy said.

"There'll be many long stories from this night."

Amelia went off with the lantern to take a closer look at the damage. Lucy turned in David's arms to assess the situation. The cannonball hadn't entirely taken out the wall. Bits of the top story hung precariously over the gaping hole in the middle. As she watched, more stones fell to crash on debris below.

"I'm surprised one cannonball did so much damage," she said. "Castles withstood bombardments."

"They had thick walls. The Crag is a stone shell designed by a madman. Surprising, really, that it hasn't fallen down on its own before this."

"Yet it looked so massive. There's a meaning in that somewhere."

"Deceit and deception, but not for us."

"The inward-looking windows look out."

"Inside out at last," he said, shaking his head.

"Your lovely rooms are gone. But we can re-create something similar when it's repaired."

"Oh, no. It was ruined by a malicious naval cannonade, but I take it as a message from on high. Down it comes."

"Thank heavens. That's what I hoped you'd say."

"Believe me, I've not the slightest attachment to the place. We'll build a new home. Not grand, perhaps, but pleasant and wholesome. A better place to raise children."

"With raspberries, honeysuckle, and roses."

"Oh, you dreamer, but we'll try to find a way to have raspberries, honeysuckle, and roses thrive up here."

She squeezed him, happy despite everything, despite the shadow of her father's act.

What would David think of what her father had done? He was, as Maria had said, a moderate man, but would he be moderate about an attempt to abduct her? Not to mention that her father had alerted Lloyd to the run. Would he be enraged?

Despite what her father had done, she didn't want to be totally estranged from him forever. She wanted more than her mother had won.

"You're falling asleep," he said. "I'll take you back down to the manor. I'll need a bed there for the night. Where's Amelia?"

They found Amelia with the Crag's maids, enjoying the sight of the corridor skeleton hanging on its chain over nothing, dancing on air, as they said of a hanged man.

Lucy suddenly giggled. "*The Animated Skeleton*!"

"Oh, yes!" Amelia said and laughed with her.

David shook his head. "Wits turned. Fred? Fred!" he shouted.

His secretary hurried over. "Sir?"

"The place isn't safe. Everyone's to go down to the village. No one's to go back in for possessions. I'll make sure there's lodging down there, though heaven knows what we do next."

"Leave it in my hands, sir."

"You're a prince among men."

"I enjoy a bit of excitement."

"I'm not demolishing buildings on a regular basis for your amusement."

Chumley laughed, looking as if he truly was having the time of his life.

As they set off home, Amelia said, "Didn't you keep watch for that navy ship?"

"Of course we did, but the clouds blindfolded us. Captain Truscott must have become suspicious of the dummy run. It was lucky she was spotted and the alarm raised early enough."

"It wasn't that," Amelia said. "Lucy raised the alarm."

David looked at her. "How?"

She didn't want to say, but saw no escape. "I was warned that the Preventive officer had been alerted. Not about the ship."

"Lloyd's around? He'll be making himself scarce after that mad attack on the Crag. I'll enjoy being nobly outraged, and he'll keep his head low for quite a while."

Lucy thought she'd escaped, for now at least, but he asked, "How did you know? Who warned you?"

"My father," she admitted.

"Your father? By letter?"

"He's here."

They encountered people coming up the hill, lanterns bobbing, chattering with no attempt at secrecy, wanting to see the spectacle.

David called out, "Go home! Yes, the Crag's damaged, but you can gawk at it tomorrow. Go home and get some sleep."

He didn't add threats, but the men, women, and children turned meekly and flowed back down into the village. He had such authority here, but it carried heavy responsibility with it.

As they walked to the manor, he didn't ask about her

father. Lucy knew that was only a reprieve. Perhaps he guessed she didn't want to say more in front of Amelia.

As they approached the manor, David paused to strip off a dark outer layer, revealing ordinary country clothes beneath. He took off his cap, then used a cloth out of a pouch to wipe the black off his face.

"How is it?" he asked, turning to Lucy.

She saw he was David again, at least in appearance. She took the cloth, finding it damp, and removed a few streaks. "As if you've simply had an alarming evening. Your hair's standing on end in places."

He laughed and found a comb in a pocket to tidy it. "Better?"

"Yes."

He'd done this so many times before, and would so many times again.

"Can you really deceive your Kerslake family?" she asked.

"No, but there's a tacit agreement about these things."

When they arrived back at the manor, she saw what he meant. His uncle, aunt, and cousin greeted them at the back door, in nightwear covered by robes, looking concerned but bewildered.

"What's been happening?" Sir Nathaniel demanded, urging them into the kitchen, where the fire was lit and a kettle boiled. One of the maids was tending it. "Was that cannon fire?"

Lucy noticed that he didn't ask why she and Amelia had been out of the house.

"That navy ship fired real shot. Two hit the cliff and could have injured those below. A third took out the south wall of the Crag. The place will have to come down."

"Begad, that's an outrage," Sir Nathaniel said.

"Sit and have tea," Aunt Miriam said.

"Won't be missed," said Henry, surely stating what they all were thinking.

They did all sit and have tea, well sweetened, going over the outrageous event, but without mentioning why the navy ship had done such a thing. Without mentioning smuggling at all. Lucy supposed the horses were back in the stables, here and all around the area, and people were in their beds. All neat and tidy—except for the matter of her father's involvement.

She'd begun to think she could take the Kerslake way, and pretend he'd never been here, but those village people had seen him, had heard her cry for help. It would be the talk of the area tomorrow.

The excitement settled down and everyone went to bed, but it was only exhaustion that allowed Lucy to sleep at all.

Chapter 39

When she woke the next morning, she knew it was late by the sounds all around. Nothing like London cacophony, but the rattling of people working outside and in. A woman was singing in a light but pleasant voice, though Lucy couldn't make out the words.

She went to look out through the curtains. To her left she saw a lad carrying a bucket into the stables. To her right a man was picking vegetables as another tilled the soil nearby.

No sign of last night's mayhem at all.

Was David still here? She longed to see him, but dreaded the questions he must have. Despite nighttime fretting, she'd not come up with a way to smooth over the situation.

Her washing water waited, covered by a towel. Cool by now, but she used it anyway and dressed hastily in her blue. Her traveling gown had suffered in last night's adventures and the sprig muslin was too flimsy for today. Who knew what it might bring?

She went downstairs, and when she heard his voice she couldn't help but smile. She found him in the breakfast room with Amelia and Henry, obviously going over last night's events as they ate, but looking so very ordinary. So David.

It was his family here, his Kerslake side, that rooted him in good earth.

He smiled at her and rose to hold her chair.

As she sat down, he said, "Amelia's in favor of another Fonthill Priory."

Lucy gave Amelia a look. "Another folly on the hill?"

"It would bring visitors in their thousands, but I was teasing."

"Better to build down here," Henry said. "Lucy would prefer that, wouldn't you?"

Clearly any sane person would and David was waiting for her response. She took the safe way out. "I'm not sure."

David went to the door and called for Lucy's coffee. He sat down again, saying, "There's no space in the village for even a modest earl's seat. Even though I don't intend to hold great state, I don't want to look peculiar."

"Another mad earl," Henry said, nodding.

A maid came in with the coffeepot and a plate of fresh toast—a maid who could have been out on the beach last night, ready to bring in contraband. Lucy began to eat, wondering at the idle banter. The smugglers had almost been caught, a house had been irreparably damaged, people could have been killed, and yet the Kerslakes talked as if there'd been a minor ripple in their comfortable lives. Deceits and deceptions, and yet the Kerslake way was sweet.

Talk turned to where David was to live during the long time he would be homeless.

Henry said, "Mother's suggesting we turn the second parlor into a bedroom for you."

"I can lodge at the tavern."

"She'll not have that and you know it. Of course when Lucy returns to London your room will be available again. And when you wed, it'll do for both of you. You do have to return, Cousin Lucy?"

"My father's wedding," she said, avoiding David's eye.

"And I can go with you?" Amelia asked.

"If your parents permit."

"David, are you going?" Amelia asked.

"I think Lucy and I should discuss that, when you've finished your breakfast, that is."

Lucy realized she'd eaten only half a slice of toast but had no appetite for more. She rose, aware of the palpable curiosity as she left the room. She heard Henry ask, "What's going on?"

Amelia replied, "I don't know."

They left by the front door. Lucy knew that was to avoid the kitchen. Aunt Miriam was probably there and she'd be full of curiosity as well.

When they were away from the house he said, "What troubles you, Lucy?"

"I think we should get a license and marry here, or as soon as we arrive in London."

He stared at her, and then crushed her to him. "Oh, thank God. I thought you'd changed your mind."

"Changed . . . ?" she squeaked.

He relaxed his hold to look into her eyes. "I thought that the rough reality of my life was too much for you. That you wanted us to part."

"Never. Never! I admit I can't like you being in danger like that, but you, only you, are necessary for my sanity. I can't lose you."

"You won't." He kissed her gently, tasting her as if she were nectar, and she tasted him back, reassuring herself that he was safe, that they were safe together.

But then he said, "There's something I must tell you."

"There's more?" she asked, unable to avoid a touch of dismay.

He grimaced. "Someone did die last night. A Dragon's Cove man called Saul Applin."

"Oh. The one you warned about his wife."

"Yes. He'd also turned traitor, but money was found on him. Fred suspected, but I didn't believe any local man would be so foolish."

"How did he die?"

"Crushed beneath the fallen cliff. But he'd no reason to be right there. It looks as if he was hiding, knowing what was going to happen."

Or, Lucy thought, he'd caused the other smugglers to suspect and they'd inflicted rough justice. This was a wild place, but it was her wild place now.

"I suspect his wife might be relieved."

"And his children. They won't suffer by it. There's a fund to support the family of any man killed in action."

She nodded and smiled. "Of course there would be."

He smiled back, and she saw relief. "Now, let's plan our speedy wedding."

"You wanted banns."

"I told my father he wouldn't stop me, but he doesn't give up plans he thinks right. Better to forestall him."

"Ah, yes, you said your father alerted Lloyd. How?"

"He was here. He tried to abduct me and carry me back to London."

She expected fury, but he nodded. "I suppose he would, once he learned that you'd come here."

"You can't approve!"

"No, but I can understand. I've always doubted that I could make you happy, so I can't be surprised that he does."

"He had no right to disregard *my* wishes."

"Ah. I can be angry about that, if you wish. I told him he didn't appreciate your true nature."

"You told him? When?"

"When he came to Susan's house in London to forbid me to court you."

"He did *what*?"

He smiled. "I think you can be outraged enough for both of us. He'd found out that I'm Captain Drake and held that as a weapon. If I didn't desist, he'd inform on me. It would make the situation here more difficult and could lead to arrests. It could, if made public, lead to unpleasant scandal and speculation. But I gave in to his pressure because I thought he was right. That you couldn't be happy here."

"You're as bad as him."

"Not quite, please."

"This is not amusing!"

He took her hands. "No, I'm sorry, but I can't help but be relieved to have told you. I didn't want to keep a secret from you, but I thought you'd be hurt."

"I am, but I know his action came from another kind of overwrought love. I still think we should marry in haste. That insane love could drive him to try again, and that will only make matters worse. I still hope for peace in the family. But I have to tell you, I don't think he'd have cared if you'd have been caught, or even killed."

"Single-minded."

"You don't mind?"

"Yes, but you're right. We won't be better off for life-long enmity. We can try for the Kerslake way and hope your father will strategically forget some events. But we're not marrying in haste. We're marrying with due dignity and joy after banns have been read. I'll keep you safe."

She cradled his face and kissed him. "Thank you. I want that so much.

"Perhaps it's weak of me," she continued as they strolled on, "or the undermining effects of love, but I want to have my family, such as it is, all my life. I want our children to know his. I'm not sure how it would be if we were going to live in the next street, but once married we'll be a blessed distance away most of the time, and three miles away when in London."

"And families matter," he agreed. "But when we return, you're not staying in his house in London. We'll go to Susan's."

"I'd like that. I want to get to know her better."

Hand in hand they turned back toward the house.

"I think I like the Kerslake way," she said.

"It can be exasperating, but I've had a lifetime to come to appreciate it. My mother's behavior could have led to family strife. Instead, it was ignored and Susan and I were accepted into the manor as if Aunt Miriam had produced two more babies."

"Did they ignore the Mad Earl as well?"

"Fortunately he kept to himself up there." They both looked up at the Crag, hardly showing any damage from this angle. "If he'd rampaged about the village, raping the women—which he was arrogantly insane enough to have done—they would have had to do something."

"Perhaps they deterred him."

"No."

"I don't mean directly," Lucy said, "but you once talked of how their goodness kept society together. Perhaps the goodness was like holy water to the devil."

"You could be right. And Mel contributed. He was a criminal, yes, but the most solidly sensible man I've known and good at heart. His father created the Dragon's Horde way, but Mel perfected it. A Kerslake-Clyst conspiracy of goodness." He paused and looked at her. "I will bring smuggling to an end here, Lucy. Not immediately, but as soon as I can."

"Building a new house for the Earl of Wyvern will keep a lot of people employed. I thought of a name for it. Simply Somerford House."

"Dragon free. I like it."

"And it will be simple, won't it?"

He laughed. "You're the one more likely to complicate things with pillars and fancy plastering. It will be your money paying for it."

"We don't want to fritter away money that could be spent more usefully. A simple house, suited to its location. With views, but protection against storms. We'll need a good architect."

"I leave it entirely in your hands, beloved. And yes, you do detect profound relief about that."

They entered the house chuckling, which pleased the family, who'd obviously been hovering, worrying, but Kerslake-like, hoping for the best.

Chapter 40

They set out the next day, two days before her father's wedding. Amelia accompanied them in the chaise, making it a tight squeeze, but all in all it was a good thing. Such a long journey with David would have been wonderful in many ways, but too intense. Lucy wanted her path stable and smooth before she surrendered to the wild glory that circled them.

They arrived exhausted and unexpected at David's sister's house, but were instantly welcomed. By the afternoon, Lucy's trunk had arrived from the Delaneys' house, and Hannah from her sister's. The first thing Hannah asked was why Lucy wasn't at home.

"All will be at sixes and sevens there," Lucy said, "and I'm sure I can be no help. I'm going to visit, so turn me out well. I've been living in country fashion the past few days."

"So I see, miss! Your traveling gown looks as if you've been dragged through a thicket."

"I've missed you, Hannah. Let's get to work."

She chose the pink that she'd worn to leave her father's house weeks ago, and when she looked at herself in the mirror she again felt strange in fashionable finery. When she went down, David was in Town style and had even had his hair trimmed.

"Good afternoon, my lord," Lucy said to him, curtsying.

"Don't be impertinent, wench. Though you are up to the nines."

"Armored for the occasion."

He'd hired a stylish carriage from a livery stable to take them to the City, which seemed both familiar and strange.

"I'm both drawn to it and repelled," Lucy said. "This is the rhythm I've known all my life, and there's so much here I like. But the air smells. It didn't before. The sounds I took for granted, both here and in the west end, are a cacophony."

As they drew close to her home she said, "I can't predict how this will go. I didn't expect him to marry again, yet I should have. I never imagined he'd try to abduct me, and yet now it doesn't surprise me. Now I worry that he might react violently. . . ."

He covered her gloved hand with his. "He can't. And he's not fool enough to try. I can't claim to know him as you do, but he's not a fool."

"I take courage from that."

The carriage drew up in front of the house. Her home all her life, but no longer. David rapped with the knocker.

Nancy, the maid, answered, instantly smiling. "Welcome home, miss."

Lucy went in, immediately aware of more changes. New ornaments and paintings, rather cluttering the place. Too many flowers, but that could just be in preparation for whatever social gatherings surrounded the wedding.

Another new smell. Charlotte must favor a different furniture polish.

Nancy had gone toward the back of the house to alert her father. Lucy felt as if she shouldn't intrude anywhere, but she shook that off and took David into the library, where her mother's portrait still ruled. Didn't Charlotte find that odd?

She turned as her father entered, but let him make the first move.

"Welcome home, Lucy," he said, closing the door behind him. "Lord Wyvern."

David inclined his head, very much the earl.

"You bring no luggage?" her father asked.

"I thought it best to stay at Lord Amleigh's house. You must be very busy here."

"Not too busy for you, pet."

Lucy took a breath. "Father, please don't call me that. I am not your pet."

He colored. "I mean nothing by it."

"Do you not? Then why assume you could overwhelm my will by force?"

Anger pinched his features. "Just because you're of age doesn't mean I don't have the duty to keep you safe."

Lucy was aware of David solidly by her side, but leaving this to her. "Yes, it does," she said. "However, it's moot, for I will soon be married."

"Without my permission?"

"I don't need your permission, Father, but I would value your blessing."

"I'm supposed to bless your union with a smuggler who breaks his word?"

"What word?"

David spoke then. "I agreed that I wasn't a suitable husband for you, but that was an error of judgment, not a pledge."

"You think you're worthy of her?" her father demanded, his fists clenched.

"He is!"

"I am," David said. "Not ideal, perhaps, but does a man exist who is worthy of such a treasure? I will respect Lucy as an intelligent woman who knows her own mind and can manage her own affairs. Can you do as much?"

Her father might have growled. "She's my daughter. I want her happiness."

"Father," Lucy interrupted, "are you even aware that I once thought my happiness lay in being your business partner? In working by your side and one day taking over all your enterprises?"

He stared at her. "Why would you want that?"

"Because you trained me to it!"

He shook his head, bewildered now. "You were my only child, and I enjoyed having you with me, but never thought you'd take such a notion into your head. Your mother warned me, but I thought her foolish for once. Lucy, daughter, I'd not want you to become the sort of woman who could fight against such a harsh stream. I've always wanted your happiness," he repeated desperately.

"Then give us your blessing, Father. Someone pointed out to me recently that parents can't dictate their children's futures, and must expect sometimes to be surprised. I have new enterprises in mind and they are, all in all, feminine."

"I'm glad to hear it." But he said it sourly, still not reconciled.

"We have a new house to build, for a start. A navy ship that patrols the Devon coast turned its guns toward shore that night and fatally wounded Crag Wyvern."

"That'll be an expense."

She suddenly had an idea. "We hope to get some compensation from the government, but it will cost a great deal to have it just as it should be for us and our children. Your grandchildren."

She saw him understand her. "Is this blackmail? You'll cut yourself off if I don't do this?"

"No. My terms for us living in harmony are only that you accept my marriage with goodwill. However, shouldn't we all be willing to pay a fine when we act amiss? Why did that ship turn back toward Dragon's Cove?"

Suddenly he smiled. It was wry, but a smile. "My blood

and bone. I'm proud of you, p— Lucy. Yes, I'll pay for your new house. I want my grandchildren to be raised in something suitable."

"If you're imagining Palladian splendor, you'll be disappointed, but you'll also be saved a lot of money."

"As long as its quality built. I'll not see my money wasted." Her father looked at David. "I hope you realize you're marrying a challenging woman."

"A virago, even, and my complete delight."

Her father shook his head at that. "So, what are your wedding plans?"

"At St. Michael's," Lucy said, "as soon as the banns are read. You'll be home from your honeymoon by then."

"You'll marry from this house?"

Lucy hesitated over that, but she should, for all to be in order in the eyes of the world. "If we have an agreement."

He nodded. "We do. My marriage to your mother being so irregular, I've always wanted a decent one for you. I've only ever wanted the best for you, Daughter, but I see I might have gone amiss here and there. Let bygones be bygones?" He spread his arms.

The Kerslake way. Lucy went to him for a hug.

He said. "I do love you dearly, p—"

"You'll get used to it," she said, smiling at him. "Thank you for raising my dowry to thirty thousand pounds."

"He'd not marry you without it?" he asked, frowning.

"We might not have met without it. But then," she added, turning to David, "I'm sure fate would have brought us together one way or another, and the effect would have been the same."

"It would." He held out his hand and she went to him. It was as clear a transition as the usual one at a wedding.

"You'll have a house to furnish," her father said gruffly. "You can take anything from here that was yours or your mother's. I know your mother would like that."

"Thank you."

"And if you care to . . . would you like your mother's portrait?"

She turned to him, shocked.

"I have others. Smaller ones, but of her older, which are more precious to me. But I admit, it being there's a bit awkward. Charlotte doesn't entirely like it, but I don't care to move it. You'll need family portraits in your new home, and it's so like you."

"I'll treasure it. And her sewing table? And desk?"

"Anything you like. Now come with me to Charlotte so we can share our good news. Er . . ." She was astonished to see him truly uneasy, for the first time in her life. "No need to mention any awkwardness, I hope."

The Kerslake way. "Of course not, Father."

No good would be served by Charlotte learning about recent events, but she was amused to think that her father might be wary of Charlotte's disapproval.

They took tea with Charlotte, and all was amiable. She and Charlotte would never be close, but with luck they would all be comfortable together, and her father's new children—her half brothers and sisters—would be of an age with her own.

As they approached the carriage to return to Mayfair, Lucy said, "We could stroll around the corner first."

David understood and told the carriage driver to follow them.

When they entered the bookshop, Winsom looked up, smiling. "Miss Potter, come a-buying? Or are you ready to return your novels?"

"I forgot to bring them with me. I'm simply here for old time's sake. I'm to marry soon."

Winsom peered over his glasses. "Why, it's your gentleman, though polished up."

"My gentleman and my husband-to-be. Lord Wyvern."

"My lord," Winsom said, inclining his head but not overawed. "You have won a treasure."

"I have."

In silent accord he and Lucy went into the narrow aisle to look at books about trade and agriculture and to happily discuss which were most needed for their new life. They satisfied Winsom with a handsome purchase, and David carried a large package out to the carriage.

Her father's wedding went off smoothly, and Lucy had the opportunity to meet a number of old friends, her earl by her side. Betty and her husband were among the neighbors gathered outside the church to cheer the happy couple, and later in the day Lucy and David went to Betty's cozy rooms in the Greenlows' house to chatter about recent events.

David and James began to talk about building plans and went off to consult books, so Lucy could share her adventures.

"You ran off to Devon!" Betty exclaimed.

"It seemed inevitable at the time."

"And you already know about the marriage bed."

"Isn't it wonderful?"

"Astonishingly so. Oh, Lucy, I'm so glad you're happy, even if you'll be so far away."

"We'll write. And we will come back at times."

When David and James returned, they were on excellent terms and full of building ideas. Perhaps Greenlows of London might play a part in Somerford House.

They'd traveled to the City in Susan's carriage, but that had returned home, so they took a hackney back to Mayfair. Three miles is a long way and kisses became irresistible. Snuggled in his arms, Lucy said, "I suppose we've progressed from courtship, to betrothal, to soon to be wed. There'll be much to organize."

"Which reminds me."

David opened the window and told the driver to take

them to Bond Street. "A good thing the shops here stay open so late."

"What are we shopping for?"

"A ring, of course. The earldom has no family jewels, and I can't afford to drape you in diamonds, but I can manage a betrothal ring, especially with your father paying for our new home."

When they entered the glittering candlelit shop, she said, "You choose."

"No, you."

She shook her head. "I want to wear the ring you want me to wear."

"Is this some sort of test? The sort that in fairytales dooms a suitor's hopes?"

"I'm sure a dragon can cope," she said with a wicked smile.

He groaned but went to study the rings on display. She watched, and when he asked the shop attendant to take one ring out of the case, she went, feeling a little nervous, hoping it was something she'd like. He was perhaps anxious, too, as he showed her the ring.

"An opal and two rubies. Unusual."

"It couldn't be commonplace for you, love. The opal because it reminds me of the gown you wore to that first ball. The rubies for dragon's blood."

She smiled. "I like that. Very much."

She tried it on and it was just a little tight. The attendant sent it into the back workshop to be adjusted.

"I've been thinking about the dragon," she said.

"Yes?"

"You needn't sound so wary."

"I'm learning to be wary of your thinking."

"Then you'll worry a lot of the time. Have you considered Mr. Chumley as Captain Drake?"

"Fred? He's not even a coastal man."

"But he fits in well, doesn't he? And he must be clever to have risen from such a background. He truly enjoyed the mayhem that night, which seems a good qualification to me."

"He's learned cliff climbing well enough. Won the contest back in May."

"There, you see?"

"It could confuse things nicely. Maybe we can create a Hydra. Is Captain Drake the earl, or maybe the earl's secretary? If I hire the right kind of estate manager, maybe him, too, and I can build up Aaron Bartlett in the mix. We'll have too many heads to cope with."

"And you'd be in a better position to protect everyone."

"Reliably, unlike the Mad Earl. You think aright, Lucy Potter."

"I hope I always do," she said, as the jeweler came out himself to try the ring on her finger. "Perfect," she said, touching it, smiling.

Everyone around was smiling, which made her blush. But she kissed David quickly, making everyone smile even more.

They left the shop to walk along the busy gaslit street.

"You'll miss this," he said.

"I'll miss shops to hand, yes, but only when I need something and can't get it instantly. Patience is a virtue, they say."

"And anticipation makes the reward greater. As with our wedding night."

She smiled. "It does seem a long time to wait, so I expect a very great reward."

"And me without an Ouroborus room or a splendid bath."

"You'll just have to do your dragonish best without, Lord Wyvern, and I have complete faith in you."

That night Lucy took out her pretty pink journal and

turned the pages, glancing at lines that began with descriptions of the beau monde, and recorded her increasing absorption with Lord Wyvern, and then with David. She smiled at the way it wandered into scraps and flowers, and lastly to sketched but very practical plans for her new home.

She didn't expect to have further need of faux poetry to record her thoughts.

She considered for a while and then wrote,

> *Love and Horror. That's where this story starts.*
> *But horror flees, leaving only happy hearts.*
> *Love is a power of awe-inspiring might,*
> *But love is a blessing and my true delight.*

She smiled as she closed the book. She'd never be a true poet, but she'd ended with rhythm and rhyme, which seemed as good an omen for her future as any.

Author's Note

A Shocking Delight follows a story first told in a novel published in 2001 called *The Dragon's Bride*. That was about Con and Susan and took place nearly a year before the events in *A Shocking Delight*. At the beginning of *The Dragon's Bride*, David was just getting used to being Captain Drake; by the end he was adding the earldom to his responsibilities. Some characters grab the reader's attention and he is one. Ever since the publication of *The Dragon's Bride*, my readers have been asking for his story.

The Dragon's Bride was a finalist for the RITA Award for Best Historical and is available in print and as an e-book. The connected novella, "The Demon's Mistress" (which is about Van and Maria), was also a RITA finalist, and is available as an e-book.

The Dragon's Bride is the sixth book in a series about the Company of Rogues, which are now all available as e-books, and mostly still in print as well. There are fourteen in all, so if you like them, there's a feast. Many readers are now enjoying reading them one after the other and following the long story arc. There's a list in the front of this book and more information on my Web page at www.jobev.com/reghist.html.

It was on a research trip to the Devon coast in 2000 that my husband and I fell in love with the area and decided that if we moved back to England from Canada, we'd look for a home there. We did that in 2010, but not in the area used in this novel, but further west, on the coast beyond Exeter.

Dragon's Cove and Church Wyvern are very loosely based on the town of Beer in east Devon, very near to the border with Dorset. Beer was a major smuggling area in the eighteenth and early nineteenth centuries, and continued so, but as indicated in the book, the glory days were over. Increased enforcement and better communications as the nineteenth century progressed made smuggling more and more difficult. In the end, however, it was the lowering of taxes on many goods that undercut it. By the mid-nineteenth century the old smuggling world had ended, though as we know, smuggling itself never does. It simply changes to different locations, methods, and goods.

Even though Beer was an important smuggling location at the time of the book, I couldn't use it as a location for two reasons. One was that I was going to significantly alter reality, and I try not to do that to real places. The other was that at that exact time a real, and famous, person was in charge of smuggling in the Beer area. Jack Rattenbury is mainly famous because he left an autobiography, almost certainly written by someone else on his behalf, and first-person accounts of smuggling are rare. He's a fascinating character, but there'd be no place for him in my novel.

His autobiography is *Memoirs of a Smuggler*, and is available online. There's also plenty of other information about him on the Web. I did use him a bit for my idea of Melchisadeck Clyst.

Beer is a fascinating place to visit if you're in that part of England. The old town still runs down the steeply sloping road to the beach, and boats are pulled up onto the shore. There are also extensive quarries nearby that go back to Roman times and can be visited. There was significant boat building there in the past, and Beer luggers were very popular smuggling ships. Modern versions are still raced.

I've set many books in the fashionable parts of Regency London, but I enjoyed exploring the City of London for this book. That is a clearly defined area to this day, leading to much confusion. The huge London area is not a city. If you're ever asked if London is one of the largest cities in the world, that's a trick question. The only city there is the square mile of the old walled City of London. Greater London is a metropolitan area.

The Lord Mayor of London, of Dick Whittington fame, is a largely ceremonial post, whereas the Mayor of London—currently Boris Johnson—is a position of great responsibility and power.

That's why, particularly in the past, people talked of going to Town, or being in Town. Town also came to mean the western part of London, the fashionable part, the "west end," as it's still called. And yes, the population of "greater London" had reached a million by the Regency. I was surprised by that. It's wonderful what one finds when researching a book!

If you're new to my books, I hope you'll explore the rest of my work. There's a bit of everything! Most of my fiction is set in the Georgian and Regency periods, but I have published four medieval novels. I've also written a lot of novellas, and in some of those I've gone to the wild side. "The Dragon and the Virgin Princess" is set in a fantasy Middle Ages with, of course, dragons. "The Raven and the Rose" is in the real twelfth century, but involves the Holy Grail. "The Trouble with Heroes" is a science-fiction romance set on a colonized planet far, far away. They are all now available individually as e-books, and some are still available in their original print anthologies. You can find out more on my Web site, www.jobev.com.

On the Web site you can also sign up for my occasional newsletter, which will keep you up to date with

new and reissued books, and any other news. I also keep
in touch with readers through my Facebook author page,
so if you're on Facebook, check it out and "like" it.

You can always contact me at jo@jobev.com.

All best wishes,

Jo

The characters featured in *A Shocking Delight*
made an earlier appearance in Jo Beverley's

The Dragon's Bride

Here's a preview of how their story began. . . .

May 1816
The south coast of England

The moon flickered briefly between windblown clouds, but such a thread-fine moon did no harm. It barely lit the men creeping down the steep headland toward the beach, or the smuggling master controlling everything from above.

It lightened not at all the looming house that ruled the cliffs of this part of Devon—Crag Wyvern, the fortresslike seat of the blessedly absent Earl of Wyvern.

Absent like the riding officer charged with preventing smuggling in this area. Animal sounds—an owl, a gull, a barking fox—carried across the scrubby landscape, constantly reporting that all was clear.

At sea, a brief flash of light announced the arrival of the smuggling ship. On the rocky headland, the smuggling master—Captain Drake, as he was called—unshielded a lantern in a flashing pattern that meant "all clear."

All clear to land brandy, gin, tea, and lace. Delicacies for Englishmen who didn't care to pay extortionate taxes. Profit for smugglers, with tea sixpence a pound abroad and selling for twenty times that in England if all the taxes were paid.

In the nearby fishing village of Dragon's Cove, men pushed boats into the waves and began the urgent race to unload the vessel.

"Captain Drake" pulled out a spyglass to scan the English Channel for other lights, other vessels. Now that the war against Napoleon was over, navy ships were patrolling the coast, better equipped and manned than the customs boats had ever been. A navy cutter had intercepted the last major run, seizing the whole cargo and twenty local men, including the previous Captain Drake.

A figure slipped to sit close to him, one dressed as he was all in dark colors, a hood covering both hair and the upper face, soot muting the pallor of the rest.

Captain Drake glanced to the side. "What are you doing here?"

"You're shorthanded." The reply was as sotto voce as the question.

"We've enough. Get back up to Crag Wyvern and see to the cellars."

"No."

"Susan—"

"No, David. Maisie can handle matters from inside the house, and Diddy has the watch. I need to be out here."

Susan Kerslake meant it. This run had to succeed or heaven knew what would become of them all, so she needed to be out here with her younger brother even if there was nothing much she could do.

For generations this area had flourished, with smuggling the main enterprise under a series of strong, capable Captain Drakes, all from the Clyst family. With Mel Clyst captured, tried, and transported to Botany Bay, however, chaos threatened. Other, rougher gangs were trying to move in.

The only person in a position to be the unquestioned new Captain Drake was her brother. Though he and she went by their mother's name of Kerslake, they were Mel Clyst's children and everyone knew it. It was for David to seize control of the Dragon's Horde gang and make a profit, or this area would become a battleground.

He'd had to take on the role, and Susan had urged him to it, but she shivered with fear for him. He was her younger brother, after all, and even though he was a man of twenty-four, she couldn't help trying to protect him.

The black-sailed ship on the black ocean was barely visible, but a light flashed again, brief as a falling star, to say that the anchor had dropped. No sign of other ships out there, but the dark that protected the Freetraders could protect a navy ship as well.

She knew that Captain de Root of the *Anna Kasterlee* was an experienced smuggler. He'd worked with the Horde for more than a decade and had never made a slip. But smuggling was a chancy business. Mel Clyst's capture had shown that, so she kept every sense alert.

At last her straining eyes glimpsed the boats surging out to be loaded with packages and half-ankers of spirits. She could just detect movement on the sloping head-land, which rolled like the waves of the sea as local men flowed down to the beach to unload those small boats.

They'd haul the goods up the cliff to hiding places and packhorses. Many would carry the goods inland on their backs to secure places and to the middlemen who'd send the cargo on to Bath, London, and other cities. A week's wages for a night's work and a bit of 'baccy and tea to take home. Many would have scraped together a coin or two to invest in the profits.

To invest in Captain Drake.

Some of the goods, as always, would be hidden in the cellars of Crag Wyvern. No Preventive officer would try to search the home of the Earl of Wyvern, even if the Mad Earl was dead and his successor had not yet arrived to take charge.

His successor.

Susan was temporary housekeeper up at Crag Wyvern, but as soon as the new earl sent word of his arrival, she'd be out of there. Away from here entirely. She had no intention of meeting Con Somerford again.

The sweetest man she'd ever known, the truest friend. The person she'd hurt most cruelly.

Eleven years ago.

She'd been only fifteen, but it was no excuse. He'd been only fifteen, too, and without defenses. He'd been in the army for ten of the eleven years since, however, so she supposed he'd have defenses now.

And attacks.

She shivered in the cool night air and turned her anxieties on the scene before her. If this run was successful, she could leave.

"Come on, come on," she muttered under her breath, straining to see the first goods land on the beach. She could imagine the powerful thrust of the oarsmen racing to bring the contraband in, could almost hear the muttering excitement of the waiting men, though it was probably just the wind and sea.

She and David had watched runs before. From a height like this everything seemed so slow. She wanted to leap up and help, as if the run were a huge cart that she could push to make it go faster. Instead she stayed still and silent beside her brother, like he was, watchful for any sign of problems.

Being in command was a lonely business.

How was she going to be able to leave David to his lonely task? He didn't need her—it was disconcerting how quickly he'd taken to smuggling and leadership— but could she bear to go away, to not be here beside him on a dark night, to not know immediately if anything went wrong?

And yet, once Con sent word he was coming, she must.

Despite treasured summer days eleven years ago, and sweet pleasures. And wicked ones . . .

She realized she was sliding again under the seductive pull of might-have-beens, and fought clear to focus on the business of the moment.

At last the first of the cargo was landing; the first goods were being carried up the rough slope. It was going well. David had done it.

With a blown-out breath, she relaxed on the rocky ground, arms around her knees, permitting herself to enjoy the rough music of waves on shingle, and the other rough music of hundreds of busy men. She breathed in the wind, fresh off the English Channel, and the tense activity all around.

Heady stuff, the Freetrade, but perilous.

"Do you know where the Preventive officer is?" she asked in a quiet voice that wouldn't carry.

"Gifford?" David sent one of the nearby men off with a quiet command, and she saw some trouble on the cliff. A man fallen, probably. "There's a dummy ship offshore five miles west, and with luck he and the boatmen are watching it, ready to fish up the goods it drops into the water."

Luck. She hated to depend on luck.

"Poor man," she said.

David turned his head toward her. "He'll get to confiscate a small cargo like Perch did under Mel. It'll look good to his superiors, and he'll get his cut of the value."

Lieutenant Perch had been riding officer here for years, with an agreeable working relationship with the Dragon's Horde gang. He'd recently died from falling off a cliff—or being pushed—and now they had young, keen Lieutenant Gifford to deal with.

"Let's hope that satisfies him," Susan said.

He gave a kind of grunt. "If Gifford were a more flexible man, we could come to a permanent arrangement."

"He's honest."

"Damn nuisance. Can't you use your wiles on him? I think he's sweet on you."

"I don't have any wiles. I'm a starchy housekeeper."

"You'd have wiles in sackcloth." He reached out and took her hand, his so solid and warm in the chilly night. "Isn't it time you stopped working there, love? There'll be money aplenty after this, and we can find someone else who's friendly to the trade to be housekeeper."

She knew it bothered him for her to be a domestic servant. "Probably. But I want to find that gold."

"It'd be nice, but after this, we don't need it."

So careless, so confident. She wished she had David's comfort with whatever happened. She wished she weren't the sort to be always looking ahead, planning, worrying, trying to force fate. . . .

Oh, yes, she desperately wished that.

She was as she was, however, and David didn't seem to accept that she had a strange, unladylike need for employment. For independence.

And there was the gold. The Horde under Mel Clyst had paid the late Earl of Wyvern for protection. Since he hadn't provided it, they wanted their money back. She wanted that money back, but mainly to keep David safe. It would pay off the debts caused by the failed run and provide a buffer so he wouldn't have to take so many risks.

She frowned down at the dark sea. Things wouldn't have been so difficult if her mother hadn't set off to follow Mel to Australia, taking all the Horde's available money with her. Isabelle Kerslake. Lady Belle, as she liked to be known. A smuggler's mistress, without a scrap of shame as far as anyone could tell, and without a scrap of feeling for her two children.

Susan shook off that pointless pain and thought about the gold. She glanced behind at the solid mass of Crag

Wyvern as if that would spark a new idea about where the Mad Earl had hidden his loot. The trouble with madmen, however, was that their doings made no sense.

Automatically she scanned the upper slit windows for lights. Crag Wyvern served as a useful messaging post visible for miles, and as a viewing post where miles of coast could be scanned for other warning lights. Apart from that, however, it had no redeeming features.

The house was only two hundred years old but had been built to look like a medieval fortress, with only arrow-slit windows on the outside. Thank heavens there was an inner courtyard garden, and the rooms had proper windows that looked into that, but from the outside the place was grim.

As she turned back to the sea, the thin moon floated out from behind clouds again, silvering the boats lifting and bobbing with the waves. Then the clouds swept across the moon like a curtain, and a wash of light drizzle blew by on the wind. She hunched, grimacing, but the rain was a blessing, because it obscured the view even more. The sea and shore below her could have been deserted.

If Gifford had spotted the dummy run for what it was and was seeking the real one, he'd need the devil's own luck to find them tonight. Let it stay that way. He was a pleasant enough young man, and she didn't want to see him smashed at the bottom of a cliff.

Lord, but she wished she had no part of this.

Smuggling was in her blood, and she was used to loving these smooth runs that flowed with hot excitement through the darkest nights. But it wasn't a distant adventure anymore.

It was need now, and danger to the person she loved most in the world—

Was that a noise behind her?

She and David swiveled together to look back toward

Crag Wyvern. She knew he, too, held his breath, the better to hear a warning sound.

Nothing.

She began to relax, but then, in one high, narrow window, a candle flared into light.

"Trouble," he murmured.

She put a hand on his suddenly tense arm. "Only a stranger, the candle says. Not Gifford or the military. I'll deal with it. One squeal for danger. Two if it's clear."

That was the smuggler's call—the squeal of an animal caught in the fox's jaws or the owl's talons—and if the cry was cut off quickly, it still signaled danger.

With a squeeze to his arm for reassurance, she slid to the side carefully, slowly, so that when she straightened she wouldn't be close to Captain Drake. Then she began to climb the rough slope, soft boots gripping the treacherous ground, heart thumping, but not in a bad way.

Perhaps she was more like her brother than she cared to admit. She enjoyed being skilled and strong. She enjoyed adventure. She liked having a pistol in her belt and knowing how to use it.

As well that she had no dreams of becoming a fine lady.

Or not anymore, at least.

Once, she'd been caught up in a mad, destructive desire to marry the future Earl of Wyvern—Con Somerford, she'd thought—and had ended up naked with him on a beach. . . .

She physically shook the memory away. It was too painful to think about, especially now, when she needed a clear mind.

Heart beating faster and blood sizzling through her veins, she went up the tricky hill in a crouch, fingers to the ground to stay low. She stretched hearing and sight in search of the stranger.

Whoever the stranger was, she'd expect him to have

entered the house. Maisie might have signaled for that, too. But Susan had heard something up here on the headland, and so had David.

She slowed to give her senses greater chance to find the intruder, and then she saw him. Her straining eyes saw a cloaked figure a little darker than the dark night sky. He stood still as a statue. She could almost imagine someone had put a statue there, on the headland between the house and the cliff.

A statue with a distinct military air. Was it Lieutenant Gifford after all?

She shivered, suddenly feeling the cold, damp wind against her neck. Gifford would have soldiers with him, already spreading out along the headland. The men bringing in the cargo would be met with a round of fire, but the smugglers had their armed men, too. It would turn into a bloody battle, and if David survived, the military would be down on the area like a plague looking for someone to hang for it.

Looking for Captain Drake.

Her heart was racing with panic and she stayed there, breathing as slowly as she could, forcing herself back into control. Panic served no one.

If Gifford was here with troops, wouldn't he have acted by now? She stretched every quivering sense to detect soldiers concealed in the gorse, muskets trained toward the beach.

After long moments she found nothing.

Soldiers weren't that good at staying quiet in the night.

So who was it, and what was he planning to do?

Heartbeat still fast, but not with panic now, she eased forward, trying not to present a silhouette against the sea and sky behind her. The land flattened as she reached the top, however, making it hard to crouch, making her clumsy so some earth skittered away from beneath her feet.

She sensed rather than saw the man turn toward her. Time to show herself and pray.

She pulled off her hood and used it to wipe the soot around so it would appear to be general grubbiness. She tucked the cloth into a pocket, then stood. Eccentric to be wandering about at night in men's clothing, but a woman could be eccentric if she wanted to, especially a twenty-six-year-old spinster of shady antecedents.

She drew her pistol out of her belt and put it into the big pocket of her old-fashioned frock coat. She kept her hand on it as she walked up to the still and silent figure, and it was pointed forward, ready to fire.

She'd never shot anyone, but she hoped she could if it was necessary to save David.

"Who are you?" she said at normal volume. "What is your business here?"

She was within three feet of him, and in the deep dark she could not make out any detail except that he was a couple of inches taller than she was, which made him about six feet. He was hatless and his hair must be very short since the brisk wind created no visible movement around his head.

She had to capture a strand of her own hair with her free hand to stop it from blowing into her eyes.

She stared at him, wondering why he wasn't answering, wondering what to do next. But then he said, "I am the Earl of Wyvern, so everything here is my business." In the subsequent silence, he added, "Hello, Susan."

Her heart stopped, then raced so impossibly fast that stars danced around her vision.

Oh, Lord. Con. Here. Now.

In the middle of a run!

He'd thought smuggling exciting eleven years ago, but people changed. He'd spent most of those years as a soldier, part of the mighty fist of the king's law.

Dazed shock spiraled down to something numb, and

then she could breathe again. "How did you know it was me?"

"What other lady would be walking the clifftop at the time of a smugglers' run?"

She thought of denying it, but saw no point. "What are you going to do?"

She made herself draw the pistol, though she didn't cock it. Heaven knew she wouldn't be able to fire it. Not at Con. "It would be awkward to have to shoot you," she said as firmly as she could.

Without warning, he threw himself at her. She landed hard, winded by the fall and his weight, pistol gone, his hand covering her mouth. "No squealing."

He remembered. Did he remember everything? Did he remember lying on top of her like this in pleasure? Was his body remembering . . . ?

He'd been so charming, so easygoing, so dear, but now he was dark and dangerous, showing not a shred of concern for the lady he was squashing into hard, unforgiving earth.

"Answer me," he said.

She nodded, and he eased his hand away, but stayed over her, pressing her down.

"There's a stone digging into my back."

For a moment he didn't respond, but then he moved back and off her, grasping her wrist and pulling her to her feet before she had time to object. His hand was harder than she remembered, his strength greater. How could she remember so much from a summer fortnight eleven years ago?

How could she not? He'd been her first lover, and she his, and she'd denied every scrap of feeling when she'd sent him away.

Life was full of ironies. She'd rejected Con Somerford because he hadn't been the man she'd thought he was—the heir to the earldom. And here he was, earl, a dark nemesis probably ready to destroy everything because of what she'd done eleven years ago.

What could she do to stop him?

She remembered David's comment about feminine wiles and had to fight down wild laughter. That was one weapon that would never work on the new Earl of Wyvern.

"I heard Captain Drake was caught and transported," he said, as if nothing of importance lay between them. "Who's master smuggler now?"

"Captain Drake."

"Mel Clyst escaped?"

"The smuggling master here is always called Captain Drake."

"Ah, I didn't know that."

"How could you?" she pointed out with deliberate harshness, in direct reaction to a weakness that threatened to crumple her down onto the dark earth. "You were here for only two weeks." As coldly as possible, she added, "As an outsider."

"I got inside you, Susan."

The deliberate crudeness stole her breath.

"Where are the Preventives?" he asked.

She swallowed and managed an answer. "Decoyed up the coast a bit."

He turned to look out at the water. The sickle moon shone clear for a moment, showing a clean, strong profile and, at sea, the armada of small boats heading out for another load.

"Looks like a smooth run, then. Come back to the house with me." He turned as if his word were law.

"I'd rather not." Overriding her weakness was fear, as sharp as winter ice. Irrational fear, she hoped, but frantic.

He looked back at her. "Come back to the house with me, Susan."

He made no threat. She had no idea what he might be threatening, but a breath escaped her that was close to a sigh, and she followed him across the scrubby heathland.

After eleven years, Con Somerford was back, lord and master of all that surrounded them.

Also from *New York Times* bestselling author

JO BEVERLEY

Seduction In Silk
A Novel of the Malloren World

The honorable Peregrine Perriam is chosen to inherit his
uncle's portion of the family estate, bringing generations
of family squabbling to an end. There is, however, a catch:
he must marry Claris Mallow, a woman he has never met.
When he begrudgingly makes his proposal, the
headstrong and beautiful Claris chases him away at
gunpoint...and what begins as an onerous task becomes
a challenge Peregrine can't refuse.

"A Malloren novel is a keeper."
—Rendezvous

Available wherever books are sold or at
penguin.com

facebook.com/LoveAlwaysBooks